The Vintage

A Romance of the Greek War of Independence

E. F. Benson

The Vintage: A Romance of the Greek War of Independence

The present edition is a reproduction of previous publication of this classic work. Minor typographical errors may have been corrected without note; however, for an authentic reading experience the spelling, punctuation, and capitalization have been retained from the original text.

ISBN: 978-1-63637-366-9

THIS ROMANCE

DEALING WITH THE REGENERATION OF HER PEOPLE

IS DEDICATED BY PERMISSION

TO

HER MAJESTY

OLGA

QUEEN OF THE HELLENES

CONTENTS

PART I
THE VINEYARD

PART II
THE EVE OF THE GATHERING

PART III
THE TREADING OF THE GRAPES

PART I

THE VINEYARD

CHAPTER I

THE HOUSE OF THE ROAD TO NAUPLIA

Nauplia, huddled together on the edge of its glittering bay, and grilled beneath the hot stress of the midsummer noon, stood silent as a city of the dead. Down the middle of the main street, leading up from the quay to the square, lay a scorching ribbon of sunshine, and the narrow strips of shadow, sharp cut and blue, spoke of the South.

Along one side of the square ran the barracks of the Turkish garrison of occupation, two-storied buildings of brown stone, solid but airless, and faced with a line of arcade. These contained the three companies of men who were stationed in the town itself, less fortunate in this oven of heat than the main part of the garrison who held the airier fortress of Palamede behind, overlooking the plain from a height of five hundred feet. Down the west side stood the quarters of the officers, and opposite, the prison, full as usual to overflowing of the native Greeks, cast there for default of payment to the Turkish usurers of an interest of forty or fifty per cent. on some small loan; for these new Turkish laws of 1820 with regard to debt had made the prisons more populous than ever. A row of shops and a couple of cafés along the north struck a more domestic note.

A narrow street led out of the square eastwards, and passing the length of the town, burrowed through the wall of Venetian fortification in the manner of a tunnel. On the right the outline of the gray fortress hill, precipitously pitched towards the town in a jagged edge like forked lightning, rose steep and craggy, weathered by the wind in places to a tawny red, and peppered over with sun-dried tufts of grass. Along the base of this the road ran, cobbled unevenly in the Turkish fashion, and after passing two or three villas which stood white and segregate among their gardens of flowering pomegranate and serge-clad cypress, struck out into the plain. Vineyards and rattling maize fields bordered it on one hand; on the other, beds of rushes and clumps of king-thistles, which peopled the little swamp between it and the bay. The spring had been very rainless, and these early days of June saw the country already yellow and sere. The clumps of succulent leaves round the base of the asphodels were dried and brown; only the virile stems with their seeding sprouts remained green and vigorous.

The blinding whiteness of the forenoon gave place before one of the

1

day to a veiled but unabated heat, and sirocco began to blow up from the south. Furnace-mouthed, it raised mad little whirlwinds, which spun across the road and over the hot, reaped fields in petulant eddies, and powdered all they passed with fine white dust. Two or three hawks, in despair of spying their dinner through this palpable air, and being continually blown downwind in the attempt to poise, were following the example of the rest of the world, and seeking their craggy homes on the sides of Palamede till the tempest should be overpast. A few cicalas in a line of white poplars by the wayside alone maintained their alacrity, and clicked and whirred as if sirocco was of all airs the most invigorating. The hills of Argolis to the north were already getting dim and veiled, and losing themselves in an ague of heat.

By the roadside, a mile from the town, stood a small wine-shop, in front of which projected a rough wooden portico open to the air on three sides, and roofed with boughs of oleander, plucked leaf and flower together. A couple of rough stools and a rickety table stood in the shade in order to invite passers-by to rest, and so to drink, and the owner himself was lying on a bench under the house wall in wide-mouthed sleep. A surly-looking dog, shaggy and sturdy, guarded his slumbers in the intervals of its own, and snapped ineffectually at the flies.

Directly opposite the wine-shop stood a whitewashed house, built in a rather more pretentious style than the dwellings of most Greek peasants, and fronted by a garden, to which a row of white poplars gave a specious and private air. A veranda ran around two sides of it, floored with planks, and up the wooden pillars, by which it was supported, streamed long shoots of flowering roses. A low wooden settee, cushioned with two Greek saddle-bags, stood in the shade of the veranda, and on it were sitting two men, one of whom was dressed in the long black cassock of a priest—both silent.

Then for the first time a human note overscored the thundering of the hot wind, and a small gray cat scuffled round the corner of the veranda, pursued by a great long-limbed boy, laughing to himself. He was dressed in a white linen tunic and tight-fitting linen trousers; he had no shoes, no socks, and no hat. He almost fell over the settee before he saw the two men, and then paused, laughing and panting.

"She was after the fish," he explained, "and I was after her. She shall taste a slapping."

One of the two men looked up at the boy and smiled.

"You'll get into mischief if you run about in the heat at noonday without your cap on," he said. "Come and sit down. Where are your manners, Mitsos? Here is Father Andréa."

Mitsos knelt down, and the priest put his hand on the boy's rumpled black hair.

"God make you brave and good," he said, "and forgive all your sins!"

"Now sit down, Mitsos," said his father. "Who is going to taste a slapping?"

The boy's face, which had grown grave as he received the priest's blessing, dimpled into smiles again.

2

"Why, my cat, Psepséka," he said. "The greedy woman was going down to the cellar where I put the fish, and I went after her and caught her by the tail. She spit at me like a little she-devil. Then she scratched me, and I let go. But soon I will catch her again, and she shall pay for it all twice over, Turkish fashion. See!"

He held out a big brown hand, down which Psepséka had scored three red lines.

"What a fierce woman!" said his father. "But you're overbig to run about after little cats. You're eighteen now, Mitsos, and your uncle comes here this evening. He'll think you're a boy still."

The boy looked up from his examination of his hand.

"Uncle Nicholas?" he asked.

"Yes. Go and wash your hand, and then lay the table. Put some eggs to boil, and get out some bread and cheese, and pick some cherries."

Mitsos got up.

"Will the father eat with us?"

"Surely; and put your shoes on before you come to dinner."

And without waiting the boy was off into the house.

The priest looked up at Mitsos' father as he disappeared.

"He is full young yet," he said.

"So I think, and so perhaps Nicholas will think. Yet who knows what Nicholas thinks? But he is a good lad, and he can keep a secret. He is strong too; he walked from here to Corinth last week, and came back next day, and he grows like the aloe flower."

The priest rose and looked fiercely out over the garden.

"May the God of Justice give the Turks what they have deserved!" he cried. "May He send them bitterness to eat and death to drink! May their children be fatherless and their wives widows! They had no mercy; may they find none! The curse of a priest of God be upon them!"

Mitsos' father sat still watching him. Eleven years ago Father Andréa had been obliged to make a journey to Athens to settle about some plot of land belonging to his wife, who had lately died, and, if possible, to sell it— for under the Turkish taxes land was more often an expense than a revenue. He had taken with him his only daughter, a girl of five or six years of age, pretty even then, and with promise of wonderful beauty to come. On his way home, just outside Athens, he had been attacked by some half dozen Turks, and, after a desperate, hopeless resistance, had been left on the road more dead than alive, and his daughter had been carried off, to be trained, no doubt, to the doom of some Turkish harem. He must have lain there stunned for some hours, for when he awoke again to an aching consciousness of soul and body, the day was already reddening to its close, and the shadow of the hills of Daphne had stretched itself across the plain to where he lay. Wounded and bleeding as he was, and robbed of the money he had got for the land, he had dragged himself back to Athens, and stayed there for weeks, until his hope of ever finding his Theodora again had faded and died. For it was scant justice that was given to the Greeks by their masters, who treated them as a thoughtless man will scarce treat an animal that annoys him. Rape, cruelty, robbery was their method of rule, and for the unruly a noose.

3

Since that time one thought, and one only, possessed his brain, a thought which whispered to him all day and shouted to him in sleep—the lust for vengeance; not on one Turk alone, on those who had carried Theodora off, but on the whole of that race of devils. For eleven years he had thought and schemed and worked, at first only with nothing more than wild words and bloody thoughts, but of late in a soberer belief that his day would come; for organized schemes of throwing off the Turkish rule were on foot, and though they were still things only to be whispered, it was known that agents of the Club of Patriots were doing sure and silent work all over the country.

Father Andréa was a tall, finely made man, and, to judge from his appearance, the story that he would tell you, how he and his family were of pure Greek descent, had good warrant. He came from the southwest part of Argolis, a rough, mountainous land which the Turks had never entirely subdued. His father had died five years before, but when Andréa went home after the capture of his daughter, the old man had turned him out of the house and refused to see him again.

"A child is a gift which God has given the father," said he; "it were better for him to lose himself than lose God's gift; and now we, who are of the few who have not mixed with that devil-brood—we are fallen even as others. You have brought disgrace on me, and on our dead, and on our living, and I would sooner have seen you dead yourself than hear this from your lips!"

"They were six to one," said Andréa, "and they left me for dead. Would to God they had killed me!"

"Would to God they had killed you," said his father, "and her too."

"The fault was not mine. Will you not forgive me?"

"Yes, when the fault is wiped out by the death of Theodora."

"Of Theodora? What has she done?"

"She will grow up in shame, and mate with devils. Go!"

Five years passed before they met again. But one day Andréa's father, left lonely in his house, moved by some vague desire which he hardly understood himself, saddled his mule and went to Nauplia, whither Andréa had gone. He was very old and very feeble in body, and perhaps he felt that death could not be far from him; and to Andréa's cry of welcome and wonder—"I have come to you, my son," said the old man, "for otherwise we are both alone, and—and I am very old."

Day by day he used to sit looking up and down the road for Theodora. There was a bend in it some quarter of a mile farther up, and sometimes, when the spring days were warm to his bones, he would hobble up to the corner and sit waiting for her there, where he could command a longer stretch of country. But Theodora came not, and one evening, when he came back, he sank into a chair without strength and called Andréa to him.

"I am dying," he said, "and this is no season to waste idle words. When Theodora comes back"—he always clung to the idea that she would come back—"tell her that I waited for her every day, for I should have loved to see her again. And if you find it hard, Andréa, to forgive her, forgive her for my sake, for she was very little and the fault was not hers; nor is it

4

yours, and I was hard on you; yet if I had loved you not, I should have cared the less. But if, when the day comes, you spare your hand and do not take vengeance on the Turks to the uttermost, then may my ghost tear you limb from limb, and give you to the vultures and the jackals."

The old man rose from his chair.

"Vengeance!" he cried; "death to man, woman, and child. Smite and spare not, for you are a priest of God and they are of the devil. Smite, smite, avenge!"

He sank back in his chair again, his head fell over on to his shoulder, and his arms rattled against the woodwork. And with vengeance on his lips, and the desire of vengeance in his heart, he died.

From that day a double portion of his spirit seemed to have descended on Father Andréa. One hope and one desire ruled his life—to help in wiping out from Greece the whole race of Turks. To him innocent or guilty mattered not; they were of one accursed brood. But though the longing burned like fire within him, he kept it in, choking it as it were with fresh fuel. He was willing to wait till all was ready. For a year or two large organizations had been at work in North Greece collecting funds, and, by means of secret agents, feeding and fanning the smouldering hate against their brutal masters in the minds of the people. Soon would the net be so drawn round them that escape was impossible. And then vengeance in the name of God.

Mitsos had encouraged a small charcoal fire to heat the water, and he went to fetch the eggs. Two minutes of puckered brow were devoted to the number which he was free to boil. His father usually ate two, the priest—and he cursed his own good memory—never ate more than one, and he himself invariably ate as many as he could possibly get. He looked at the basket of eggs thoughtfully. "It is a hungry day," he said to himself, "and the hens are very strong. Perhaps father might eat three, and perhaps Father Andréa might eat two. Then I am allowed three, a tale of eight."

Mitsos drew a sigh of satisfaction at this liberal conclusion, and his eyes began to smile; his mouth followed suit, and showed a row of very white teeth.

"It is such a pity that I am always hungry," he said to himself; "but when Uncle Nicholas measures me he will see I have grown."

And putting the eight eggs into the pot, he ran off to pick the cherries.

For the last year both Constantine, Mitsos' father, and the boy had worked the little land he owned, like common laborers. Two years before a Turkish pasha, Abdul Achmet by name, in passing through the country had been struck by the Avilion climate of Nauplia, and had built a house on the shore of the bay. The land belonged to Constantine, and the Turk had promised him a fair price for it, feeling that a less scrupulous man would have taken it off-hand. At the same time he intimated that if he would not take a fair price for it, he would get no price at all. The money, of course, was still owing, and on Constantine's old vineyard stood the house, now finished. Abdul Achmet, who was Governor of Argos, took up his quarters here permanently, with his harem; for it was within easy distance of Argos, and on warm evenings the women were often seen in the garden looking over the sea-wall which separated it from the bay, a wall some ten feet high, over which creepers sprawled and flamed. Abdul himself was a fat, middle-aged Turk, slow of movement and sparing of speech. In temper of mind he was a Gallio, and his neglect to pay Constantine the money he owed him was as much due to negligence as to the usual Turkish method of dealing with Greeks, which was not to pay at all. His harem, for the years had long since quenched the ardor of his body, were given a good deal of freedom, and were allowed to wander about the garden, which was walled off from the country road, as they pleased.

Constantine had applied several times for payment, but had already given up hopes of securing any equivalent for the land seized. He was a Greek of the upper peasant class—that is to say, of the first class of the country—who lived on their own land and employed labor. Like his race, he was thrifty and industrious; but now, between the loss of his vineyard and the iniquitous increase in the last year's taxes, which promised to grow indefinitely, he found it difficult to do more than make a sparing livelihood. He and Mitsos worked all the spring with the laborers in the harvest-field, and in the autumn, when they had finished making the wine from a half-acre of vines still left them, as laborers in the neighboring vineyards.

Constantine felt the change in his position acutely. Instead of being a man with men under him, he was himself obliged to work for his bread, and, what was an added bitterness, it was by gross injustice, and through no fault of his own, that he was thus reduced. Every year the taxation became more and more heavy; only six months before he had been obliged to sell his horse, for a new tax was levied on horses, and all that remained were an acre or two of ground, a pony, his house, and his boat. But of late he seemed to have taken up a patient, uncomplaining attitude, which much puzzled the growling Greeks whom he met at the cafés. While others grumbled and cursed the Turks beneath their breath, Constantine would sit with a quiet smile on his lips, looking half amused, half indulgent. Only two nights before a neighbor had said to him, point blank:

"You have suffered more than any of us, except perhaps those who have daughters. Why do you sit there smiling? Are things so prosperous with you?"

The question was evidently prearranged, for the two or three men sitting round stopped talking and waited for him to answer.

Constantine knocked the ashes out of his chibouk before replying.

"Things are not prosperous with me," he said; "but I am a man who can hold his tongue. This I may tell you, however: Nicholas Vidalis comes here in three days."

"And then?"

"Nicholas will advise you to hold your tongues, too. He will certainly tell you that, and it may be he will tell you something besides. I will be going home. Good-night, friends."

And now, when Father Andréa was cursing the Turks in the name of God, though Constantine crossed himself at that name, he watched him with the same smile. Then he said:

6

"Father Andréa, I ask your pardon, but Nicholas does not like too much talk. He says that talking never yet mended a matter. You know him—in these things he is not a man of many words, save where it serves some purpose."

The priest turned round.

"You are right and wrong," he said; "Nicholas is a man of few words; but I have made a vow that for every time the sun rises, and at every noonday and every sunset, I will curse the Turk in God's name. That vow I will keep."

Constantine shrugged his shoulders slightly.

"Well, here is Mitsos. Do not curse before the boy. Mitsos, is dinner ready?"

Mitsos wrinkled up his forehead till his eyebrows nearly disappeared under his curly hair.

"Yes, it is ready; but for me, I can find one shoe only."

"Well, look for the other."

"I have looked for it," said the boy, "but it is not, and I ache for emptiness."

He raised his eyes appealingly to his father, but Constantine was firm.

"You must find it first," he said. "Come, Father, let us go in."

Father Andréa followed him, leaving Mitsos half-shod and disconsolate.

CHAPTER II

THE COMING OF NICHOLAS VIDALIS

An hour later, Mitsos, having found his shoe and eaten his dinner in decency, was curled up in the shady corner of the veranda fast asleep. He had been out fishing most of the night before, and as the harvest was over there was no work on hand except to water the vines when the sun was off the vineyard, which would not be before four. He slept, as his father said, like a dog—that is to say, he curled himself up and fell into a light sleep, from which any noise would arouse him—as soon as he shut his eyes.

He was an enormous boy, of the Greek country type, close on the edge of manhood, with black, curly hair coming down onto his shoulders, straight, black eyebrows, long, black eyelashes, and black eyes. His nose was short and square-tipped, his mouth the fine, scornful mouth of his race, quick to reflect the most passing shades of emotion. His hands and face were of that inimitable color for which sun, wind, and rain are the sole cosmetic—a particularly soft, clear brown, shading off a little round the

7

eyes and under the hair. As he slept, with his head thrown back, there showed on his neck the sharp line where the tanning ended and the whiter skin began. He had that out-door appearance which is the inheritance of those whose fathers and grandfathers have lived wholesomely in the open air from sunrise to sunset all their lives, and who have followed the same course of life themselves. He had kicked off his shoes again, and his hands were clasped behind his head, and what would at once characterize him to any one who was acquainted with the Greek peasant race was that both hands and feet were clean.

He slept for a couple of hours, and was awakened by the pale, dust-ridden sunshine creeping round the corner of the veranda and falling on his head. At first he rolled over again with his face to the wall, but in a few moments, realizing the uselessness of temporizing, he got up and stretched himself lazily and luxuriously, with a cavernous yawn. Then he went round to the stone fountain which stood at the back of the house and plunged his head into the bright cool water to finish the process of awakening, and, seeing that the tall shade of the poplar had stretched its length across the vineyard, took up his spade and went off to his work.

The stream, which passed through their garden and out into the bay below, ran for some half-mile along a little raised aqueduct, banked up with earth to keep it to its course. It passed between small vineyard plots on each side, so that the water could be turned into them for irrigation, and Mitsos went out of the garden gate straight into their vineyard, which lay just above.

Each of the vines stood in its several little artificial hollow dug in the ground, and he first cleared the water-channels in the vineyard of all accumulated rubbish and soil, so that, when he let the stream in, it might flow to all the trees. Having done this, he went back to the aqueduct and removed a spadeful of earth from the bank, which he placed in the bed of the stream itself, stamping it down to keep it firm, so that the whole of the water was diverted into the vineyard. Standing, as he did, a few feet above the surface of the vines, he could see when the water had reached them all, and then, hooking out his temporary dam from the bed of the stream, he replaced it, so as to again send the water back into its channel; then, jumping down, he hoed away round the roots of the vines, so that the water might sink well in close to them, for there had been no rain for weeks, and they must be thoroughly watered.

The sun was off the land, but it was still very hot, for the sirocco had increased in violence and was sweeping over the fields like the blast from the pit. On the windward side of the trees the dark rich green of the vine-leaves was powdered over with the fine white dust driven up from the bare, harvested fields. Mitsos stopped now and then to wipe the sweat off his forehead, but otherwise he worked hard and continuously, singing to himself the peasant song of the vine-diggers.

His work was nearly over when he saw his father coming towards him. The latter stood for a moment on the edge of the bank, looking at what the boy had been doing.

"Poor little Mitsos," he said, "you have had to work alone to-day! I was obliged to go into Nauplia. You have watered the vines very well. You have finished, have you not?"

"There are three more vines here," said Mitsos, "which are yet to be dug. But it won't take long."

His father stepped down into the vineyard.

"You can go and rest," he said. "I'll finish those."

Mitsos threw down his spade.

"Oh, it is hotter than hell!" he said. "Uncle Nicholas will be roasted coming across the plain."

"He will want a bath," said Constantine. "Do you remember his making a bath last year out of those spare planks? I suppose it holds water still?"

"I wish it didn't hold so much," said Mitsos; "it holds six cans."

Constantine laughed.

"And Mitsos' back will ache, eh?"

"I hope not; but it is a great affair to carry six cans of water from the fountain."

Constantine worked on for half an hour or so, while Mitsos looked on.

"There, that is finished," he said, at last. "You won't go fishing to-night, will you? The wind is too strong."

"It may go down at sunset," said Mitsos; "but there are enough fish for to-night and to-morrow night, unless this hot weather turns them. But I put them in the cellar in water, and I expect they will keep."

They walked back together, but as soon as they got onto the road they saw that three mules were standing opposite the house. Constantine quickened his pace.

"Nicholas must have come," he said. "He was ever quicker than a man could expect. Come, Mitsos."

The veranda was full of boxes and rugs, and the two went through into the house. A man was sitting on a low chair by the window. As they came in he got up.

"Well, Constantine," he said, "how is all with you? I have just come. And Mitsos, little Mitsos is growing still. I will give you a hundred piastres when you are as tall as your father. It is the devil's own day, Constantine, and I am full inside and out of this gritty wind. Man is not a hen that he should sit all day in the dust. May I have a bath at once? Mitsos, we made a bath together. The mule men will help you to fill it."

He laid his hand on Mitsos' shoulder.

"You look fitter than a mountain hawk," he said. "Get me plenty of water, and give me ten minutes of scouring, and then we will talk together while I dress."

Mitsos left the room, and Constantine turned to his brother-in-law. "Well?" he asked.

"He is a fine boy," said Nicholas; "I must see if he can be trusted."

"A Turk would trust him," said his father, eagerly.

"Ha! we shall not require that. But in the face of fear?"

Constantine laughed.

"He does not know what fear is."

9

"Then he has that to learn," said Nicholas, "for the bravest men learn that best. No one can be brave until he has known the cold fear clutching at the stomach. However, we shall see."

Nicholas was dressed like Constantine, in Albanian costume, with a woollen cloak thrown over one shoulder, a red embroidered jacket, cut very low and open, showing the shirt, a long fustanella and white leggings, tied with tasselled ends. He was tall and spare, and his face seemed the face of a man of forty who had lived very hard, or of a man of fifty who had lived very carefully. In reality he was nearly sixty. He was clean shaven and very pale in complexion, as one who had never lived an out-door life; but you might have been led to reject such a conclusion, if you remarked the wonderful clearness and freshness of his skin. His eyes looked out from deep under a broad bar which crossed his forehead from temple to temple; they were large and dark gray in color, and gathered additional depth from his thick black eyebrows. His nose was finely chiselled, tending to aquiline, with thin, curved nostrils, which seemed never still, but expanded and contracted with the movement of the nostrils of some well-bred horse snuffing some disquieting thing. His mouth was ascetically thin-lipped, but firm and clean cut. His hair, still thick and growing low on his forehead and long behind, was barely touched with gray above the temples. His head was set very straight and upright on a rather long neck, supported on two well-drilled shoulders. In height he could not have been less than six feet three, and his slightness of make made him appear almost gigantic.

"I have travelled from Corinth to-day," he continued, "and there is much to tell you. At last the Club of Patriots have put the Morea entirely into my hands. I have leave to use the funds as I think fit, and it is I who shall say the word for the vintage of the Turks to begin. Are there men here whom you can trust, or are they all mule-folk and chatterers?"

"The main are mule-folk," said Constantine.

"The mule-folk can be useful," remarked Nicholas; "but the man who travels with a mule to show the way goes a short journey. They follow where they are led, but some one has to lead. But is there not a priest here—Father Andréa, I think—with a trumpet for a voice? I should like to see him. As far as I remember, he talked too much, yet you would not call him a chatterer."

"He curses the Turk in the name of God three times a day," said Constantine. "It is a vow."

"And little harm will the Turk suffer from that. Better that he should learn to bless them, or best to keep a still tongue. Well, little Mitsos, is the bath ready? You will excuse me, Constantine, but I am an uneasy man when I am dirty. Come to my room in ten minutes, Mitsos, and tell me of yourself."

"There is little to tell," said Mitsos.

"We will hope, then, that it is all good. By the way, Constantine, I have brought some wine with me. Mitsos will drop it into the fountain, for it must be tepid. Tepid wine saps a man's self-respect, and if a man, or a boy either, doesn't respect himself, Mitsos, nobody will ever respect him."

Mitsos followed him out of the room with his eyes, and then turned to his father.

10

"My hands are so dirty from that vine-digging," he whispered. "Do you think Uncle Nicholas saw?"

"He sees everything," said his father. "Wash, then, before you go up to his room."

Mitsos adored his uncle Nicholas with a unique devotion, for Nicholas was a finer make of man than any he had ever seen. He had been to foreign countries, a feat only attainable by sailing for weeks in big ships. He had been able to talk to some French sailors who had once been wrecked, within Mitsos' memory, on the coast near, and understand what they said, though no one in the place, not even the mayor, could do that; indeed the latter, before Nicholas had interpreted, roundly asserted that they spoke as sparrows speak. Then Uncle Nicholas was constantly going on mysterious journeys and turning up again when he was least expected, but always welcome; and he had a wonderfully low, soft voice, as unlike as possible to the discordant throats of the country folk; and he had long, muscular hands and pink nails. Also he could shoot wild pigeon when they were flying, whereas the utmost that the mayor's son, who was the acknowledged Nimrod of the neighborhood, could do, was to shoot them if they were walking about. Even then he could only hit them for certain if there were several of them together and he got very close. Also Uncle Nicholas was omniscient: he knew the names of all birds and plants; he could imitate a horse's neigh so well that a grazing beast would leave its fodder and come to his voice; and once when Mitsos was laid up with the fever he had picked some common-looking leaves from the hedge and boiled them in water, and given him the water to drink, the effect of which was that next morning he awoke quite well. Above all, Nicholas told the most enchanting stories about what he had seen at the ends of the earth.

So Mitsos washed his hands and went up to Nicholas's room, finding him already bathed and half dressed. His dusty clothes lay on the floor, and he pointed to them as Mitsos came in.

"I shall be here four days at the least," he said, "and I want these washed before I go away. The most important thing in the world is to be clean, Mitsos."

"Father Andréa says—" began the boy.

"Well, what does Father Andréa say?"

"He says that to love God and hate the devil—I think he means the Turk—is the most important thing."

"Well, Father Andréa is right. But you must remember that I am right too. Sit you in the window, Mitsos, and talk to me. What have you been doing since I was here?"

"Looking after the vines," said Mitsos, "since the reaping was over. And I go fishing very often, almost every night."

"Then to-morrow we will go together; to-night I have much to say to your father."

"Will you really come with me?" asked the boy. "And will you tell me some more stories?"

"Yes, I have a new set of stories, which you shall hear—I want to know what you will think of them. How old are you?"

11

"Eighteen, nineteen in November; and my mustache is coming."

Nicholas turned the boy's face round to the light.

"Yes, an owner's eye might detect something. Why do you want a mustache?"

"Because men have mustaches."

"And you want to be a man," said Nicholas; "but a man makes his mustache, not his mustache the man. But before we go down I have one thing to say to you, a thing you must never forget: if a Turk ever asks you if you know aught about me, where I am, or where I may be going, you must always say you know nothing. Say you have not set eyes on me for more than a year. Do you understand? That must be your answer and no other."

"I understand, just that I have not seen you for a year, and know nothing about you."

"Yes. Whatever happens, do you think you can always answer that and no more? I may as well tell you that if you answer more than that, if, when you are questioned—I do not say you will ever be questioned, but you may be—you tell them where I am, or whether I am expected here, or anything of the kind, you will perhaps be killing me as surely as if you shot me this moment with my own gun. Do you promise?"

"Of course, I promise," said Mitsos, with crisp, boyish petulance.

"And should they threaten to kill you if you do not tell them?"

"Why do you ask me?" he said. "I have made the promise."

Nicholas laid his hand on the boy's shoulder, and with a flashing eye—"And, by God, I believe you are one to keep it!" he said.

The sirocco blew itself out during the night, and a light north wind had taken its place when day dawned. A smell extraordinarily clean was in the air, and the whole sky was brisk with the sparkling air of the south. Northwards from Nauplia the sharp mountainous outlines of the Argive hills were cut out clear against the pale cobalt of the heavens, glowing pink in the sunrise, and all their glens and hollows were brimmed with bluest shadow. To the west, a furlong away, the waters of the bay gleamed with a transparent, aqueous tint; you would have said that two skies had been melted together to make the sea. Beyond, the hills over which the Turkish road to Tripoli wound like a climbing, yellow snake, lay still in darkness. The lower slopes were covered with pines; above, the bare, gray stone climbed up, shoulder by shoulder, to meet the sky. By degrees, as the sun rose higher, the light struck first the tops, and flowed caressingly down from peak to spur, and spur to slope, till it reached the lower rounded hills at the base, and then flashed across the bay and the plain of Argos. There it caught first the tawny fortress walls of the citadel which kept guard over the town, then the town itself which clustered round its base, until suddenly from Constantine's house the sun swung over the rim of the hills to the northeast, and the whole plain leaped from shadow into light.

There had been a heavy dew during the night, and the close-reaped cornfields were a loom of gossamer webs, hanging pearly and iridescent between the stubble-stalks, and in the vineyards the upper surface of the broad, strong leaves was wet and shining, as if with a fresh coat of indescribable green. In that first moment of light and heat all the odors of flowering plants, grafted on the wholesome smell of moist earth, which had

12

been hanging as if asleep close to the ground all night, rose and dispersed themselves in the air. A breath of wind shook the web of sweet smell out of the mimosa trees that grew at the gate of Constantine's garden, and sent it spreading and shifting like the gossamers in the fields on to the veranda, and in at the open windows. The border of wild thyme by the porch trembled like a row of fine steel springs as the wind passed over it, and gave out its offering of incense to the morning. A sparrow lit on a spray of rose and flew off again, scattering dew-drops and petals. The world smiled, breathed deep, and awoke.

During the morning Mitsos was chiefly employed in making coffee, for many of the leading Greeks, to whom the secret of the imminent uprising was known, came from Nauplia to see Nicholas, and to each must be offered a cup of Turkish coffee. Nicholas sat in the veranda with his narghilé, which he smoked without intermission, and he appeared to be giving instructions to his visitors. Among the first to come was Father Andréa, whom he treated with great respect. When he rose to go, Nicholas accompanied him as far as the back gate, which led into a field path towards his house, and Mitsos, who was washing cups at the fountain screened behind bushes, heard them go by talking.

As they parted he heard Nicholas say, "Above all, be silent. We shall want you to talk later, and to talk then with the full voice. At present a word overheard might ruin everything, and the devil himself scarcely knows when he is being overheard. Even now Mitsos, whom you never noticed, but whom I noticed, knows all I say to you. Mitsos, come here."

Mitsos came, cup in hand, flushed and angry.

"You are not fair to me, Uncle Nicholas," he said. "I was not listening. I could not help hearing."

"No, little one, I am not blaming you," said Nicholas; "I only wanted Father Andréa to see. That is an instance to hand, father; please let there not be more. And here is my offering to the Christ and to my patron saint for having brought me here safely."

Nicholas was punctual to his promise to Mitsos, and soon after sunset they went off together to where the boat was lying. Mitsos carried a couple of big pewter ladles, a bag full of resin, a wicker creel for the fish, and two spears, while Nicholas walked on a little ahead with the net wound round his shoulders. They were to begin the evening's work with the spears, and later when the moon was up to sail across the far side of the bay, where they would use the sweep-net in the shallow water, where the bottom was sandy and shelving. But the nearer shore of the bay was rocky, descending rapidly into deep water, and was no place for netting. Nicholas, however, got into the boat in order to arrange the net and dispose the lead in what he considered a more satisfactory manner, leaving the boy to do the spearing alone.

Mitsos took off his linen trousers, fastening his shirt round his waist with a leather belt. He then slung the creel and the bag round his neck, and putting a half handful of resin into the ladle, set light to it, took the spear in his right hand, and rolling up his sleeves to the shoulder, stepped into the sea. He held the flare close to the surface, so that its light showed clearly on the bottom of the shallow water, a luminous lure for the fish. The spear he held ready to bring down if he saw anything.

It was a scene which Rembrandt would have painted with the hand of love. The moon was not yet risen, but in the clear starlight the edges of the serrated hills were sharply etched against the sky, and the water of the bay, just curdled by the wind, lay vast and sombre across to the farther shore. The light from the resin-flare vaguely showed the lines of the boat in which Nicholas was preparing the net, but all was dim except Mitsos' figure and a few feet of glittering, flame-scribbled water round him. The highest light was cast on his brown down-bent face and on his left arm bared to the shoulder, which stood out as clear-cut as a cameo against the darkness behind, and as he moved, the water, which lapped about his knees, was stirred into fire-crested ripples. The sea was slightly phosphorescent, and his trail was palely luminous like the Milky Way. Now and again, with a sudden splendid motion, down went the poised spear with a splashing cluck into the sea, and he would draw it up again, sometimes with a red mullet, sometimes with a thin brill flapping and struggling on the point. More rarely he missed his aim, and looked up at Nicholas smiling and showing his white teeth.

At the end of half an hour the latter had finished his fresh leading of the net, and as a stiffer breeze had awoke, ruffling the surface of the water and making it difficult to see the fish distinctly, they started to sail across the bay. Mitsos waded out to the boat, trousers and shoes in hand, set the big brown sail, and giving a vigorous shove or two with the oar sent the boat round so that it caught the wind. In a moment it heeled over without stirring, and then the whisper of its moving came sibilantly from the forefoot, and gathering speed it glided on across the dark water.

Nicholas had taken the rudder, and Mitsos sat down beside him.

"Eight mullet and a dozen other fish," he said. "That is no bad catch for half an hour. Put her head for under that point, Uncle Nicholas. Do you see it? There is a house with a light burning a little above it."

"I see. It will take nearly an hour with this wind. Well, what is it?"

"Will you tell me some of the new stories, Uncle Nicholas?"

"No, we will keep the stories for when we go home. It will take us twice as long to get back against this wind. They are long stories."

For nearly an hour they sailed on in comparative silence; the wind had freshened, and from over the hills towards Tripoli there came blinking flashes of summer lightning. The lamp in the house above the point to which they were steering had been put out, but in the half-darkness of the summer night the promontory itself was clearly visible. Towards the east the hills were blocked out with a strange intensity of blackness, for the moon was on the point of rising behind them, and the deep velvet blue of the zenith had turned to dove-color.

"Now for our fishing, Mitsos," said Nicholas, as they drew near to the shore. "Can we run the boat in behind the promontory?"

"Yes, there is four feet of water right up to the land. Just there the shore is steep. I will take in the sail."

"There is no need. As soon as we pass the corner it will be dead calm."

14

Nicholas put the helm hard to port as soon as they were opposite the little point; next moment the sail flapped like a wounded bird against the mast, and they ran up to the rocks. Mitsos jumped out and tied the boat up.

They lifted the net on shore, and made their way round the wooded headland to the little bays which they were to fish. Here the shore was sandy and shelving, and sprinkled with clumps of succulent seaweed which grew up from the rocks below, a favorite feeding ground, as Mitsos knew, for mullet and sole. Nicholas had put on Constantine's long fishing-boots, reaching up to his hips, before he left the boat, Mitsos, as before, merely taking off his shoes and trousers.

The net was some twenty-five yards long, and Mitsos, taking one end into his hand, stepped into the water at right angles to the shore. He waded out till the net was taut between them, and then Nicholas followed. As soon as the latter was some ten yards from land they both moved shorewards up the little bay, which lay in front of them, getting gradually nearer to each other as they approached the beach, till when they were within five or six yards of the land they were walking together, the net trailing in a great bagging oval behind them. The resistance of the water, the dragging of the lead along the bottom, and, it was to be hoped, the spoils enclosed made no small weight, and it was a quarter of an hour or so before they got it in. The moon had risen, and it was easy to see the silvery glitter of the fish as they lay fluttering in the dark meshes of the net. The flat, brown soles, however, required a more careful search, and the sound of their flapping, rather than the eye, led to their discovery.

They fished for an hour or two with only moderate success, until Mitsos proposed they should try a little farther down the coast, where shoals of a certain fish, as small as the whitebait, and as sweet, grazed the watery pastures. Here the depth was somewhat greater, and before going in Mitsos divested himself of his shirt, leaving it on the rocks, and went in completely naked. Nicholas, who had put himself entirely under his directions, waited in the shallower water near the shore till the boy had waded out to where the water covered him to the waist; then, as before, they moved in converging lines towards the shore.

They had approached to within about twenty yards of the beach, and within about five yards of each other, when Mitsos stopped and pointed back. The upper edge of the net, fitted at intervals with corks to keep it floating, was visible on the bright surface of the sea, trailing in an irregular oval. But inside this oval the moonlit water was strangely agitated and unquiet, quivering like a jarred metal-plate, and from moment to moment a little silvery speck would glitter on it.

"Look," he said to Nicholas, "the little fish are there. We must be as quick as we can. Sometimes if the shoal begins jumping they will all jump out."

And bending forward to get his whole weight into the work, he pushed forward towards the land.

The moonlight fell full on his body, dripping and glistening from the waist downwards with the salt water, and threw the straining muscles

15

which line the spine, and those chords behind the shoulder-blade which painters love, into strong light and shadow, as he pulled against the weight of the dragging net. Already the water came only to his knees, and the catch was imminent, when suddenly from the net there came a rustle and a splash like myriad little pebbles being thrown into the sea, and he turned round just in time to see the whole shoal, which glistened like a silver sheet, rise and drop into the water outside.

"The little Turks," he said, angrily, "they are all gone."

"Better to pull the net in and look," said Nicholas; "a part only may have leaped."

Mitsos shook his head.

"When they go like that it is all of them," he said.

Mitsos was quite right. There was a stray fish or two still in the net, but so few that they were hardly worth picking out.

"That will do for to-night, won't it?" he said. "We have fished all the best places."

Nicholas assenting, he lay down and rolled over in the warm, dry sand once or twice, and then standing up brushed the wet stuff off his body. Then spreading the net out on the rocks higher up on the beach, Mitsos went off to fetch his shirt. Nicholas employed himself in picking up a few stray fish, and put them into the creel. Then rolling up the net they walked back to the boat.

CHAPTER III

THE STORY OF A BRIGAND

The wind, which had taken them straight across the bay, still blew freshening from the same quarter, and was dead against them. They would have to make two long tacks to get home—the first, right across to the island in the middle of the bay; the second, back again to the head of it; and as soon as they were well off on the outward tack, Mitsos went to the stern of the boat and sat down by Nicholas.

"It is time for the stories, is it not?" he said.

"Yes, we will have the stories now."

Nicholas paused a moment.

"Mitsos," he said, "I am going to tell you about a part of my life of which I have never spoken to you before, for, until now, I have only told you boys' stories to amuse a boy. But now I am going to tell you a story for a man. This all happened before you were born, twenty years ago, when I was a brigand."

Mitsos stared.

16

"A brigand, Uncle Nicholas? You?"

"Brigand, outlaw, klepht, whatever you like to call it. A man with a price set on his head—it is there now for you to take if you like—a man without any home but the mountains. Yet one may do worse than live in the mountains, Mitsos, and drink to the 'good bullet,' praying one might be killed rather than fall alive into the hands of the Turk. The first part of my story is like many other stories I have told you before; it is the second part, when I tell you why I was a brigand, that will be new to you—a story, as I have said, not for a boy, but for a man.

"I used to live then at Dimitzana, in Arcadia, and I became a brigand on the night that my wife died. Why and how that happened comes later. Well, there I was living in the mountains round Arcadia, sheltering and hiding for the most part of the day in the woods, but keeping near some mountain path, so that if a Turk or two or three came by I could—how shall I say it?—do business with them. For a month or two I was a-hunting alone, and then I was joined by other men from Dimitzana, who also had become outlaws. With them I went hunting on rather a larger scale—we used to take Turks and get ransoms for them. But never did we take or molest a Greek or lay hands on any woman, Greek or Turk. For the most part we were very fortunate, and all the time we lost but few men, and of those the heads of none fell into the hands of the Turks, for if one was wounded beyond healing we all went and kissed him and said good-bye; and then one cut his head off and buried it, so that the Turks should not dishonor him."

Nicholas paused a moment, and then laughed gently to himself.

"Never in my life shall I forget when we took Mohammed Bey—a fat-belly man, Mitsos, and a devil, with a paunch for two men and a woman's skin. To see him tied on his mule, crying out to Allah and Mohammed to rescue him and his dinner from the infidels, as if Mohammed had nothing better to do than look after such swine! I told him that he would only spend a day or two with us in the mountains until his friends ransomed him, adding that we would do our best to make him comfortable. But he wept tears of pure oil and said that Mohammed would avenge him, which, as yet, the Prophet has omitted to do. But there is one drawback to that sort of life, little Mitsos—one cannot keep clean. Sometimes, if one is travelling or being pursued, one has to go a whole day, or more, without water to drink, much less to wash in. Once, I remember, we had been all day without water, and could not find any when we stopped for the night; but there was a heavy dew, and, though it was a cold night, we all sat without our shirts for an hour, laying them on the ground until they were wet with dew, and then wrung them out into our mouths. Ah, horrible! horrible!"

Nicholas spat over the side of the boat at the thought, and then went on.

"For the most part we lived up in the mountains to the north of Arcadia, but somehow or other when summer came we all began to head southward again. We never spoke to each other of where we were going, for we all knew. And one evening, just before sunset, we were on the brow of a big wooded hill above Dimitzana and looked at our homes again.

17

Homesickness and want of water—these were the two things which made me suffer, and I would drink the wringings of a shirt sooner than be sick for home.

"All next day we stopped there, sitting on that spur of wooded hill looking at home as if our eyes would start from our heads. Now one of us and then another would roll over, burying his face in his hands, and the rest of us would pretend not to notice. I cannot say for certain what the others did when they buried their faces like that; for myself I can only say that I sobbed—for some had wives there, and some children. And it hurts a man to sob unless he is a Turk, for Turks sob if the coffee is not to their taste.

"That evening I could not bear it any longer, and I said to the others, 'I must go down and see my house again.' They tried to stop me, for it is a foolish thing for an outlaw to go home when there is a price on his head; but I would not listen to them.

"And I went down to the village and walked up the street, past the fountain and past the church. I met many Greeks whom I knew, but I made signs to them that they should not recognize me. Luckily for me the garrison of Turks had been changed, and though I passed several soldiers in the street, they stared at me, being a stranger, but did not know who I was.

"Then I went up past the big plane-tree and saw my house. The windows were all broken and the door was down, for that, too, had the Turks done in their malicious anger at not finding me there. And on the door-step my father was sitting. He was very old, eighty or near it, and he was playing with a doll that had belonged to my daughter."

Nicholas paused a moment.

"Mitsos," he went on, "you do not know what it is to feel keen, passionate joy and sorrow mixed together like that, ludicrously. It is not right that a man should have to bear such a thing, for when I saw my father sitting there nursing the doll I could not have contained myself, not if ten companies of angels had been withstanding me or twenty of devils; and I ran up to him and sat down by him, and kissed him, and said, 'Father, don't you know me?' But he did not say anything. He only looked at me in a puzzled sort of way, and went on nursing his doll.

"It is odd that one remembers these little things, but the stupid face of the doll, somehow, I remember better than I remember the face of my father.

"I stopped in the village for an hour, perhaps more, and I swore an oath which I have never yet forgotten and which I will never forget. In the church we have a shrine to the blessed Jesus and another to His mother, and one to St. George, and to each of them I lit tapers and prayed to them that they would help me to accomplish my oath. They have helped me and they will help me, and you, Mitsos, can help me, too."

The boy looked up.

"What was your oath, Uncle Nicholas," he said, "and how can I help you?"

He laid his hand on Nicholas's knee, and Nicholas felt it trembling. The story was going home.

18

"I will tell you," he said; "but, first, I must tell you how it was I became an outlaw. This was the way of it:

"You never knew my wife: she died before you were born. She was the most beautiful and the best-loved of women. That you will not understand. You do not know yet what a woman is to a man, and your cousin Helen, to whom the doll belonged, would have been as beautiful as her mother. A fortnight before I became an outlaw there came a new officer to command the garrison at Dimitzana. He was a pleasant-seeming man, and to me, being the mayor of the village, he paid much attention. He would sit with us all in the garden after dinner. Sometimes I asked him to take his dinner with us; sometimes he asked me to dine with him. But Catharine always disliked him; often she was barely civil to him. He had been in the place nearly a fortnight when I had to go away for a night, or perhaps two, to Andritsaena for the election of the mayor, for I had some little property there, and therefore a vote in the matter. I left about midday, but I had not gone more than four hours from the town when I met a man from Andritsaena, who told me that the election would be an affair of form only, as one of the two candidates had resigned. So I turned my horse round and went home.

"It was dark before I got to the village, and I noticed that there was no light in my house. However, I supposed that Catharine was spending the evening with some friend, and I suspected nothing. But it got later and ever later and she did not come, so at last I went out and called at all the houses where she was likely to be. She was not at any of them, and no one had seen her. Then unwillingly, and with a heart grown somehow suddenly cold, I determined to go to the officer's quarters and ask if he had seen her. There was a light burning in one of the upper windows, but the door was locked.

"It was when I found that the door was locked that I drew my pistol from my belt and loaded it, and then I waited a moment. In that moment I heard the sound of a woman sobbing and crying from inside the house, and the next minute I had burst the door open. The room inside was dark, but a staircase led up from it through the floor of the room above, and I made two jumps of it. Helen—she was only seven years old—ran across the room, perhaps knowing my step, crying 'Father, father!' and as my head appeared the officer fired. He missed me, and shot Helen dead.

"Before he could fire again I fired at him. He fell with a rattling, broken sound across the floor, and never spoke nor moved. Catharine was there, and she came slowly across the room to me.

"'Ah, you have come,' she said; 'you are too late.'

"I sat down on the bed, and my throat was as dry as a sirocco wind, and laid the double-barrelled pistol, still smoking, by me. Neither of us, I am sure, gave one thought to the man who was lying there, perhaps hardly to Helen, for dishonor is worse than death; and for me I could say no word, but sat there like a thing broken.

"'You are too late,' she repeated; 'and for me this is the only way.'

"And before I could stop her she had taken up the pistol and shot herself through the head.

19

"The shots had aroused the soldiers, and two or three burst in up the stairs. With the officer's pistol, for I had no time to reload mine, I killed the first, and he went bumping down the stairs, knocking one man over. Then I opened the window and dropped. It was not more than ten feet from the ground, and I had only a few feet to fall."

He paused a moment and stood up, letting go of the rudder and raising his hands.

"God, to whom vengeance belongs," he cried, "and blessed Mother of Jesus, and holy Nicholas, my patron, help me to keep my vow."

He stood there for a moment in silence.

"And my vow—" he said to Mitsos.

"Your vow—your vow!" cried Mitsos. "The foul devils—your vow is to root out the Turk, and to-morrow I, too, will light tapers to the holy saints and make the vow you made. Christ Jesus, the devils! And you must show me how to keep it."

"Amen to that," said Nicholas. "Enough for to-night, we will speak of it no more."

He sat down again and took the rudder, and for five minutes or so there was silence, broken only by the steady hiss of the water round the boat, and then Mitsos, still in silence and trembling with a strange excitement, put about on the second tack. Nicholas did not speak, but sat with wide eyes staring into the darkness, seemingly unconscious of the boy.

This second tack brought them up close under the sea-wall of Abdul Achmet, and the white house gleamed brightly in the moonlight. Then, as Mitsos was putting about again on the tack which would take them home, Nicholas looked up at it and spoke for the first time.

"That is a new house, is it not?" he said.

"Yes, it is the house of that pig Achmet," said Mitsos.

"Why is he a pig above all other Turks?"

"Because he took our vineyard away and said he would pay a fair price for it. Not a piastre has he paid. Look, there are a couple of women on the terrace."

Two women of the house were leaning over the wall. Just as they went about Nicholas saw a man, probably one of the eunuchs, come up out of the shadow, and as he got up to them he struck the nearer one on the face. The woman cried out and said to him, "What is that for?"

Nicholas started and looked eagerly towards them. "Did you hear, Mitsos?" he said, "she spoke in Greek."

"One of those women?" said Mitsos. "And why not?"

"How do you suppose she knows Greek?"

"Yes, it is strange. We shall not get home in this tack."

CHAPTER IV

THE MIDNIGHT ORDEAL

For the next two days Nicholas devoted himself to the education of Mitsos. He took the boy out shooting with him and taught him how to stand as still as a rock or a tree, how to take advantage of the slightest cover in approaching game, and how, if there was no cover, to wriggle snake-wise along the ground so that the coarse tall grass and heather concealed him. There were plenty of mountain hares and roe-deer on the hills outside Nauplia towards Epidaurus, and they had two days' excellent shooting.

They were walking home together after sunset on the second day, and slung over the pony's back were two roe-deer, one of which Mitsos had shot himself, and several hares which Nicholas, with a skill that appeared almost superhuman to the boy, had killed running. The pony was tired and hung back on the bridle, and Mitsos, with the rope over his shoulder, was pulling more than leading it.

"And if," Nicholas was saying to him, "if you can approach a roe-deer as you approached that one to-day, Mitsos, without being seen, you can also approach a man in the same way, for in things like these the most stupid of beasts is man. And it is very important when you are hunting man, or being hunted by him, which is quite as exciting and much less pleasant, that you should be able to approach him, or pass by him unseen. After two days I shall be going away, but I shall leave this gun behind for you."

"For me, Uncle Nicholas?" said Mitsos, scarcely believing his ears.

"Yes, but it shall be no toy-thing to you. For the present you must go out every day shooting, but you must take the sport as a matter concerning your life or death, instead of the life and death of a piece of meat. Stalk every roe as if it were a man whose purpose is to kill you, and if ever it sees you before you get a shot you must cry shame on yourself for having wasted your time and my gift to you. But go fishing, too, and treat that seriously. Do not go mooning in the boat just to amuse yourself, or only for the catching of fish. Before you start settle how you are to make your course, in two tacks it may be, or three, and do so. Practise taking advantage of a wind which blows no stronger than a man whistling."

"I can sail a boat against any one in Nauplia," said Mitsos, proudly.

"And Nauplia is a very small place, little Mitsos. For instance, we ought to have got back from our fishing in two tacks, not three. And study the winds—know what wind to expect in the morning, and know exactly when the land breeze springs up. Go outside the harbor, too; know the shapes of the capes and inlets of the gulf outside as you know the shape of your own hand."

"But how can I shoot and fish, and also look after the vines and get work in other vineyards in the autumn?"

21

"That will be otherwise seen to. Obey your father absolutely. I have spoken to him. Also, you stop at home too much in the evenings. Go and sit at the cafés in the town and play cards and draughts after dinner, yet not only for the sake of playing. Keep your ears always open, and remember all you hear said about these Turks. When I come back you must be able to tell me, if I ask you, who are good Greeks, who would risk something for the sake of their wives and children, and who are the mules, who care for nothing but to drink their sour wine and live pig-lives. Above all, remember that you haven't seen me for a year—for two, if you like."

Mitsos laughed.

"Let it not be a year before you come again, uncle."

"It may be more; I cannot tell. You are full young, but—but—well, we shall see when I come back. Here we are on the plain again. Give me that lazy brute's bridle. Are you tired, little one?"

"Hungry, chiefly."

"And I also. But, luckily, it is a small thing whether one is hungry or not. You will learn some day what it is to be dead beat—so hungry that you cannot eat, so tired that you cannot sleep. And when that day comes, for come it will, God send you a friend to be by your side, or at least a drain of brandy; but never drink brandy unless you feel you will be better for it. Well, that is counsel enough for now. If you remember it all, and act by it, it will be a fine man we shall make of the little one."

Nicholas went to see the mayor of Nauplia the next day, and told Mitsos he had to put on his best clothes and come with him. His best clothes were, of course, Albanian, consisting of a frilled shirt, an embroidered jacket, fustanella, gaiters, and red shoes with tassels. To say that he abhorred best clothes as coverings for the skin would be a weak way of stating the twitching discomfort they produced in him; but somehow, when Nicholas was there, it seemed to him natural to wish to look smart, and he found himself regretting that his fustanella had not been very freshly washed, and that it was getting ingloriously short for his long legs.

The mayor received Nicholas with great respect, and ordered his wife to bring in coffee and spirits for them. He looked at Mitsos with interest as he came in, and, as Mitsos thought, nodded to Nicholas as if there was some understanding between them.

When coffee had come and the woman had left the room, Nicholas drew his chair up closer, and beckoned Mitsos to come to him.

"This is the young wolf," he said. "He is learning to prowl for himself."

"So that he may prowl for others?" said Demetri.

"Exactly. Now, friend, I go to-morrow, and while I am away I want you to be as quiet as a hunting cat. I have done all I wanted to do here, and it is for you to keep very quiet till we are ready. There has been much harm done in Athens by men who cannot hold their tongues. As you know, the patriots there are collecting money and men, but they are so proud of their subscriptions, which are very large, that they simply behave like cocks at sunrise on the house-roofs. Here let there be no talking. When the time

22

comes Father Andréa will speak; he will put the simmering-pot on the fire. I would give five years of my life to be able to talk as he can talk."

"The next five years?" asked Demetri.

Nicholas smiled.

"Well, no, not the next five years. I would not give them up for fifty thousand years of heaven, I think. Have you any corn?"

"Black corn for the Turk?"

"Surely."

Demetri glanced at Mitsos, and raised his eyebrows. "Even now the mills are grinding," he said.

"Let there be no famine."

Mitsos, of course, understood no word of this, and his uncle did not think fit to enlighten him.

"You will hear more about the black corn," he said to him. "It makes good bread. At present forget that you have heard of it at all. Have you got these men for me?" he asked, turning again to Demetri.

"Yes; do you want them to-day?"

"No. Mitsos will go with me as far as Nemea, and they had better join me there to-morrow night. Turkish dress will be safer."

He rose, leaving the brandy untasted.

"Will you not drink?" asked Demetri.

"No, thanks. I never drink spirits."

Nicholas left next day after sunset, for a half-moon would be rising by ten of the night, and during the day the plain was no better than a grilling-rack. Already also it was safer for Greeks to travel by night, for it was known or suspected among the Turks that some movement of no friendly sort was on foot among them, and it had several times happened before now that an attack had been made upon countrymen, who were waylaid and stopped in solitary mountain paths by bands of Turkish soldiers. They were questioned about the suspected designs of their nation, on which subject they for the most part were entirely ignorant, as the plans of their leaders were at present but sparingly known, and the interview often ended with a shot or a dangling body. But through the incredible indolence and laziness of the Turks, while they feared and suspected what was going on, they contented themselves with stopping and questioning travellers whom they chanced on, and made no increase in the local garrisons, and kept no watch upon the roads at night. Nicholas, of course, knew this, and when, as now, he was making a long journey into a disaffected part of the country, where his presence would at once have aroused suspicion—and indeed, as he had told Mitsos, there had been a price put on his head twenty years ago—he travelled by night, reaching the village where he was to stay before daybreak, and not moving again till after dark.

Accordingly he and Mitsos set off after sunset across the plain towards Corinth. The main road led through Argos, which they avoided, keeping well to the right of the river bed. Their horses were fresh, and stepped out at an amble, which covered the ground nearly as quickly as a trot. By ten o'clock the moon was swung high in a bare heaven, and they saw in front of them a blot of huddled houses in the white light, the village of Phyctia. Again they made a detour to the right, in order to avoid it, for a garrison of Turks was stationed there, turning off half a mile before its outlying farms began, so as not even to run the risk of awakening the dogs. Their way lay close under the walls of the ancient Mycenæ, where it was reported that an antique treasure of curious gold had lately been found, and as they were in plenty of time to reach Nemea by midnight, Nicholas halted here for a few minutes, and he and Mitsos looked wonderingly at the great walls of the citadel.

"They say the kings of Greece are buried here, little Mitsos," said he; "and perhaps your beard will scarce be grown before there are kings of Greece once more."

Beyond Mycenæ they followed a mountain path leading through the woods, which joined a few miles farther up the main road from Corinth to Argos, and as it was now late, and the ways were quiet, Nicholas saw no reason for not taking this road as soon as they struck it, and they wound their way up along the steep narrow path towards it.

The moon had cleared the top of Mount Elias behind them—the moon of midsummer southern nights—and shone with a great light as clear as running water, and turning everything to ebony and gleaming cream-colored ivory. Mitsos was riding first, more than half asleep, and letting his pony pick its own way among the big stones and bowlders which strewed the rough path, when suddenly it shied violently, nearly unseating him, and wheeled sheer round. He woke with a start and grasped at the rope bridle, which he had tied to the wooden pommel on the saddle-board, to check it. Nicholas's pony had shied too, but he was the first to head it round again, and Mitsos, who had been carried past him, dismounted and led his pony, trembling and restive, up to the other. Nicholas had dismounted too, and was standing at the point where the bridle-path led into the main road when Mitsos came up.

"What did they shy at?" Mitsos began, when suddenly he saw that which stopped the words on his tongue.

From a tree at the juncture of the paths, in the full, white blaze of the moonlight, hung the figure of a man. His arms were dropped limply by his side, and his feet dangled some two feet from the ground. On his shoulder was a deep gash, speaking of a struggle before he was secured, and blood in black clots was sprinkled on the front of his white linen tunic. Above the strangling line which went round his neck the muscles were thick and swollen and the glands of the throat congested into monstrous lumps.

But Nicholas only stopped the space of a deep-drawn breath, and then, throwing his bridle to Mitsos, drew his knife and cut the rope. The two horses shied so violently as Nicholas staggered forward with his murdered burden that Mitsos, unable to hold them both, let go of his own and clung with both hands to the bridle of Nicholas's horse, while his own animal clattered off down the path homeward. Then soothing its terror from the other, he led it past into the main road, where he tied it up to a tree some twenty yards on, and himself returned to where Nicholas was kneeling over the body.

24

He looked up and spoke with a deadly calm. "We are too late," he said; "he is quite dead."

And suddenly, after the hot-blooded, warm-hearted nature of his race, this strong man, who had lived half his life with blood and death and murder to be the companions of his days and nights, burst into tears.

Mitsos was awed and silent.

"Do you know him, Uncle Nicholas?" he asked, at length.

"No, I do not know him, but he is one of my unhappy race, whom this brood of devils oppresses and treats as it would not treat a dog. Mitsos," he said, with a gesture of fire, "swear that you will never forget this! Look here, look here!" he cried. "Look how they have made of him an offence to the light; look how they killed him by a disgraceful death, and why? For no reason but because he was a Greek. Look at his face; force yourself to look at it. The lips are purple; the eyes, as dead as grapes, start from his head. He was killed like a dog. If they catch you alone in such a place they will do the same to you, to you whose only offence is, as this poor burden's has been, that you are Greek. Look at his neck, swollen in his death struggle. Do you know how the accursed men killed Katzantones and his brother? They beat them to death with wooden hammers, sparing the head only, so that they might live the longer. Katzantones was ill and weak, and cried out with the pain; but Yorgi, as he lay on the ground, with arms and legs and ankles and hands broken, and lying out of semblance of a man, only laughed, and told them they could not kill a fly with such puny blows."

The boy suddenly turned away.

"Enough, enough!" he said. "I do not wish to look. It is too horrible. Why do you make it more frightful to me?"

Nicholas did not seem to hear what he said, and went on, in a sort of savage frenzy.

"Look, look, I tell you!" he cried, "and then swear in the name of God, remembering also what I told you of my wife and child, that you will have no pity on the race that has done this—on neither man, woman, nor child; not even on the poor, weak women, for they are the mothers of monsters who do these things. This is the work of the men they bear—this and outrage and infamous lust, and the sins of the cities which God destroyed."

He was silent a moment, and then spoke more calmly.

"So swear, Mitsos, in the name of God!"

And Mitsos, with quivering lips of horror, but suddenly steeled, looked at the dead thing and swore.

"And now," said Nicholas, "take hold of the feet, and we will give it what burial we can. Stay, wait a moment." He tore off a piece of the man's tunic, and, dipping his finger in the blood that still was wet on the shoulder, wrote in Turkish the word "Revenge," and fastened it to the end of the rope which still dangled from the tree. Then he and Mitsos took the body some yards distant into the copse that lined the road, and tearing up brushwood gave it covering. On this they laid stones until it was completely concealed and defended against the preying creatures of the mountain.

Then Nicholas bared his head.

"God forgive him all his sins," he said, "and impute the double of them to his murderers. Ah, God," he cried, and his voice rose to a yell, "grant me that I may kill and kill and kill; and their souls I leave to Thee, most Just and most Terrible!"

They went to where Nicholas's horse was tied up, and he, hearing the other had bolted, made Mitsos mount his, as he would have to walk back, and himself went on foot. It was in silence that they climbed the pass, but in another hour they came to the junction of the two roads from Nemea and Corinth, and Nicholas told his nephew to go no farther.

"It is safer that I should go alone here," he said; "and it is already late, and you will have to walk. Waste no time about getting back to the plain; the nights are short."

He paused for a moment, looking affectionately at the boy.

"Thus are you baptized in blood," he said, then paused, and he moistened his lips. "A great deal may depend on you, little one," he went on. "I have watched you growing up, and you are growing up as I would have you grow. Distrust everything and everybody except, perhaps, your father and myself, and be afraid of nothing, while you suspect everything. At the same time I want you, and many will want you; so take care."

He put his hands on his shoulders.

"I shall be back in a year or six months, or perhaps to-morrow, or perhaps never. That does not concern you. Your father and I will always tell you what to do. And now good-bye."

He kissed him on the cheek, mounted his horse, and rode off, never looking behind. Mitsos stopped still for a moment looking after him, and then turned to go home.

Five minutes more brought Nicholas to the edge of the village where the three men whom Demetri had sent were waiting for him. One of them was a Greek servant, who held Nicholas's horse while he dismounted and changed his Albanian costume for a Turkish dress; the others were leaders of local movements against the Turks, and were going with him to Corinth. Like Nicholas himself, they all spoke Turkish.

Nicholas dressed himself quickly, but then stopped for a moment irresolute. Then—

"Take the horse on," he said to the servant. "I will go on foot awhile."

Mitsos meantime was walking quickly along the road back towards Argos. He would scarcely acknowledge to himself how very much he disliked the thought of taking that bridle-path through the woods, for the recollection he retained of that end of rope dangling from the tree, with the fragment of tunic fluttering in the breeze, and that heap of white stones glimmering among the bushes, was too vivid for his liking. Even his pony would have been companionable; but his pony, as he hoped, was near home by this time.

Once or twice he thought he heard movements and whispered rustlings in the bushes, which made his heart beat rather quicker than its wont. Ordinarily he would not have noticed such things, but the scene at the crossroad still twanged some string of horror within him.

However, the road must be trod, and keeping his eyes steadily averted—for like his race he held ghosts in accredited horror—he marched with a show of courage past the spot, and began making his way down the rough bridle-path.

Thin skeins of clouds had risen from the sea, and the moon was travelling swiftly through them, casting only a diffused and aqueous light; but the path, with the glimmering white stones of its cobbling, showed clearly enough, and there was no fear of his missing his way. But about a couple of hundred yards down the path he heard a noise which made his heart spring suddenly into his throat and stay there poised for a moment, giving a little cracking sound at each beat. The sound needed not interpretation; two men, if not three, were running down the main road he had just left. Instantly he had left the path, and striking into the bushes at the side moved quickly up the hill again, hoping to turn them off the scent. But as they came nearer he stopped, still crouching in the bushes, and though he was, as he knew, very indifferently concealed, he dared not go farther among the trees for fear that the sound of his steps crackling among the dry brushwood should lead them to him, and, remembering Nicholas's lessons in the art of keeping still, he waited. His pursuers, if pursuers they were, seemed to go the more slowly as they turned into the path he had just left, and soon he caught sight of them through the tree trunks. There were two of them, and he saw they were Turks. As they came nearer he could hear them speaking together in low tones, and then one ran off down the path, in order, so he supposed, to see whether he was still on ahead.

Mitsos drew a long breath; there was only one to be reckoned with now, and stealing out of the bush where he had been crouching, he moved as quietly as he could farther into cover. But a twig cracking with a sharp report under his foot revealed his hiding, and the man who had waited in the path shouted out to the other. The next moment they were in pursuit.

As he pushed through the trees that seemed to stretch out fingers to clutch him, Mitsos felt in his belt for the knife he always carried with him, but to his wondering dismay found it had gone. Never in his life could he remember being without it; but this was no season to waste time, and knowing that his only chance lay in running he plunged along through the bushes in order to get back to the path and match his speed against theirs. But his pursuers were close behind him, and in jumping, or trying to jump, a small thicket which closed his path, he caught his foot and fell.

Then came cold fear with a clutch. Before he had time to recover himself they had seized him. Once he let out with his right hand at the face of one of the men, who just avoided the blow, and then both wrists were seized. They whipped a cord round his legs, tied his hands behind his back, and carried him off straight to the tree from which the end of the rope and its ghastly legend were still hanging.

A third Turk was sitting there on the ground in the shadow smoking, and as the others came up he said a word to them in Turkish which Mitsos did not understand. Then one of his captors turned to him, and speaking in Greek, "Tell us where Nicholas Vidalis is," he said, "and we will let you go."

Silence.

27

"We know who you are. You are Mitsos Codones, the son of Constantine, from Nauplia, and he is your uncle."

Mitsos looked up.

"That is so. But I have not seen him for a year—more than a year," he said.

One of the men laughed.

"Tell us where he is," he said, "and we will let you go, and this for your information, for you were seen with him yesterday in Nauplia," and he held out a handful of piastres.

This time Mitsos laughed, though laughing was not in his thoughts, and the sound was strange to his own ears.

"That is a lie," he said; "he has not been at Nauplia for a year. As for your piastres, if you think I am telling you a lie, do you suppose that I should speak differently for the sake of them? Be damned to your piastres," and he laughed again.

"I will give you one minute," said the other, "and then you will hang from that tree if you do not tell us. One of your countrymen, I see, has cut the rope, but there will be enough for a tall boy like you."

They strolled away towards where the third man was sitting, leaving him there bound.

"Perhaps the end of the rope might help him to speak," said one. But the third man shook his head.

What Mitsos thought of during these few seconds he never clearly knew, and as far as he wished for anything, he wished them to be quick. He noticed that the edge of the moon was free of the clouds again, and it would soon be lighter. He felt a breeze come up from the east, which fluttered the rag of tunic hanging from the rope, and once a small bird, clucking and frightened, flew out of a thicket near. Then the two men came up and pulled him under the tree. The end of the piece of tunic flapped against his forehead.

They untied the rope, and the one made a noose in it, while the other turned back the collar of his coat. Then the rope was passed round his throat and tightened till he felt the knot behind, just where the hair grows short on the neck.

"One more chance," said the man. "Will you tell us?"

Mitsos had shut his eyes, and he clinched his teeth to help himself not to speak. For a moment they all waited, quite still.

"Then up with him," said the man.

He waited for the choking tension of the rope, still silent, still with clinched teeth and eyelids. But instead of that he felt two hands on his shoulders, and fingers at the knot behind, and he opened his eyes. The third man, who had been silent, was standing in front of him.

"Mitsos," he said, "my great little Mitsos."

For a moment the world spun dizzily round him, and he half fell, half staggered against Nicholas.

"You!" he said.

"Yes, I. Mitsos, will you forgive me? I ought to have been certain of you, and indeed in my heart I was; but I wanted to test you to the full, to put the fear of death before you, for it was needful that I should give

28

convincing proof to others. My poor boy, don't tremble so; it was necessary, believe me. By the Virgin, Mitsos, if you had hit one hundredth part of a second sooner one of these men would have gone home with no nose and fewer teeth. You hit straight from the shoulder, with your weight in your fist. And that double you made up the hill was splendid. Mitsos, speak to me!"

But the boy, pale and trembling, had sunk down on the ground with bent head, and said nothing.

"Here, spirits," said Nicholas, and he made Mitsos drink.

He sat down by him, and with almost womanly tenderness was stroking his hair.

"You were as firm as a rock," he said, "when you stood there, and I saw the muscle of your jaw clinch."

Mitsos, to whom spirit was a new thing, recovered himself quickly with a little choking.

"I wasn't frightened at the moment," he said; "I was only frightened before, when I knew I was caught."

Then, as his boyish spirits began to reassert themselves, "Did I—did I behave all right, Uncle Nicholas?"

"I wish to see no better behavior. It is even as your father told me, that you were fit for the keeping of secrets."

Mitsos flushed with pleasure.

"Then I don't mind if it has made you think that, though, by the Virgin, my stomach was cold. But if I had had my knife there would have been blood let. I cannot think how I lost it."

Nicholas laughed.

"Here it is," he said. "It was even I who took it away from you while you were dozing as you rode. I thought it might be dangerous in your barbarous young hands."

Mitsos put it back in his belt.

"I am ready now. I shall start off again."

Nicholas rose, too.

"I will come with you as far as the plain, and then my road is forward. The piastres were a poor trick, eh?"

"Very poor indeed, I thought," said Mitsos, grinning.

The uncle and nephew walked on together, and the other two men strolled more slowly after them. Nicholas could have shouted aloud for joy. He had found what he had sought with such fastidiousness—some one whom he could trust unreservedly, and over whom he had influence. To do him justice, the cruelty of what he had done made his stomach turn against himself; but he was associated with men who rightly mistrusted everybody, except on convincing proof of their trustworthiness. Mitsos had stood the severest test that could be devised without flinching. He was one of ten thousand.

At the end of the woods they parted. Mitsos' nerve had come back to him, and the knowledge that he had won Nicholas's trust, combined with the fascination the man exercised over him, quite overscored any grudge he might have felt, for Nicholas's last words to him were words to be remembered.

29

"And now, good-bye," he said. "You have behaved in a way I scarce dared to hope you could, though I think I believed you would. You have been through a man's test, the test of a strong, faithful man. Others will soon know of it, and know you to be trustworthy to the uttermost. Greece shall be revenged, and you shall be among the foremost of her avengers."

So Nicholas went his way northward and Mitsos towards home, and just as the earliest streak of dawn lit the sky he reached his father's house. The truant pony was standing by the way-side cropping the dew-drenched grass.

CHAPTER V

MITSOS PICKS CHERRIES FOR MARIA

At Nauplia the summer passed quietly, though from other parts of the country came fresh tales of intolerable taxation, cruelty, and outrage, hideous beyond belief. But this Argive district was exceptionally lucky in having for its governor a man who saw that it was possible to overstep the mark even in dealing with these infidel dogs; partly, also, Nicholas's visit, his injunctions to the leading Greeks to keep quiet, and his hints that they would not need to keep quiet long produced a certain effect; as also did an exhortation delivered by Father Andréa, in which he spoke of the blessings of peace with a ferocious tranquillity which left no loop-hole for misconstruction.

July and August were a tale of scorched and burning days, but the vines were doing well, and the heat only served to ripen them the sooner. In some years, when the summer months had been cold and unseasonable, the grapes would not swell to full ripeness till the latter days of October, and thus there was the danger of the first autumn storms wrecking the maturing crop. But this year, thanks to the heat, there was no doubt that they would be ripe for gathering by the third week in September, and, humanly speaking, a fine grape harvest was assured.

A certain change had come over Mitsos since the events of the night recorded in the last chapter. He suddenly seemed to have awoke to a sense of his budding manhood, and his cat, much to that sedately minded creature's satisfaction, was allowed to shape her soft-padded basking life as she pleased. He used to go out in the dewiness of dawn, while it was still scarce light, to try for a shot at the hares which came down from the hills at night to feed in the vineyards, and at evening again he would lie in wait near a spring below Mount Elias to shoot the roe when they came to water. But during the day there was no mark for his gun, for the game went high away among the hills to avoid the broiling heat of the plains, or stayed in cover of the pine woods upon the mountain-sides, where the growth was too thick for shooting, and where some cracking twig would ever advertise a footstep, however stealthy.

But the sudden and violent winds of the summer months had set in, and sailing gave him day-long occupation. He made it his business to know the birth-hour of the land-breeze, the length of the dead calm that follows, and the hour when the sea-breeze again winnows the windless heaven; to read the signs of the thread-like streamers in the upper air, which mean a strong breeze; the vibration on the sea's horizon, like the trembling of a steel spring, which means heat and calm, and the soft-feathered clouds, with dim, blurred outlines that tell of moisture in the air, which will fall the hour after sunset in fine, warm, needle-pointed rain. His boat might often be seen scudding across the bay and into the water of the gulf outside, skirting round the promontories, running up into the creeks and inlets until, as Nicholas had told him he should do, he got to know the shape of the land as he knew the shape of his own head. Above all, he would practise beating out to sea in the teeth of the sea-breeze, running out to a given point in as few tacks as possible, and then, when the sea-breeze died away, he would put into some inlet, fish for a little, and sleep curled up in the bottom of the boat, awake with the awakening of the land breeze, and run back again, close hauled, past Nauplia, and up to the side of the bay, where he beached his boat. In these long hours alone on the sea he would sit in the stern, when the boat was steady on some two-mile tack, thinking intently of the new life for which he was preparing himself. Though Nicholas's stories, and the tales of oppression and outrage with which all mouths were full, made personal to him the longing for vengeance on that bestial breed, it was Nicholas himself who was the inspirer, and his indignation was scarce more than an image in a mirror of Nicholas. His uncle had long been acquiring that domination a man can have for a boy, and the main desire and resolve of his mind was to obey Nicholas, whatever order he might lay on him, and this resolve to obey was rapidly becoming an instinct over-mastering and unique. His father, far from making objections to his spending his time in sailing and shooting, encouraged him thereto, for Nicholas had bade him hire labor whenever he wanted a lad in Mitsos' place, saying that the club at Athens had authorized him to make payments for such things. Mitsos, in fact, had definitely entered into the service of his country, and it was only right that his father should be compensated for the loss of a hand.

But during these months there was little or no farm-work to be done. Early in July Constantine had put up a little reed-built shed to overlook his vineyard, and there he spent most of the day scaring away the birds that came to eat the grapes, and playing with his string of polished beads, which he passed to and fro between his hands, every now and then stopping to sling a pebble at a bird he saw settling in the vines. The sparrows were the greatest enemies, for they would fly over in flocks of eighty or a hundred and settle in different parts of the vineyard, and when he cleared one quarter and turned to clear another, the first covey would be back and renewing their depredations on the grapes. He had an almost exaggerated repugnance in taking the funds of the club unless it was

31

absolutely necessary to hire an extra hand, and until the last week before the harvest he managed alone; but then—for the grapes were tight-skinned and juicy, and a single bird holding on to a bunch with its claws and feeding indiscriminately from this grape and that would spoil the hundredfold of what it ate—he hired a boy from Nauplia, and erected another shed some fifty yards off. There they would sit from sunrise to sunset, and at sunset Mitsos returned brown and fresh, with a song from the sea, with his black hair drying back into its crisp curls after his evening bathe, and an enormous appetite. He and Constantine sat together till about nine, and then Mitsos would go off to the cafés, following Nicholas's instructions, and play cards or draughts, ever pricking an attentive ear when comments on the Turks were on the board. Nicholas's directions, however, that there should be no talking of the great matter, was being obeyed too implicitly for Mitsos to pick up much; but he acquired great skill at the game of draughts, even being able to play three games at a time.

One evening, just before the vintage began, he returned earlier than usual with a frown on his face. His father was sitting on the veranda, not expecting him yet.

"Have you heard," said Mitsos, "what these Turks have in hand about the vintage?"

"About the vintage? No."

"Instead of paying one-tenth to the tax-collector, we are to pay one-seventh; and instead of paying in grapes, we pay in wine."

"One-seventh? It is impossible!"

"It is true."

"Where did you hear it?"

"In the last hour at the café in the square. They are all clacking and swearing right and left, and the soldiers are patrolling the streets."

Constantine got up.

"I must go, then," he said. "This is just what Nicholas did not want to happen. Have there been blows between the soldiers and the Greeks?"

"Yanko knocked a Turkish soldier down with such a bang for calling him a dog that the man will never have front teeth again. They took him and clapped him in prison."

"The fat lout shall eat stick from me when he comes out. I suppose, as usual, he was neither drunk nor sober," said Constantine. "As if knocking a soldier down took away the tax. Is Father Andréa there?"

"I passed him just now on the road," said Mitsos, "going to the town."

Constantine got up.

"Stop here, Mitsos," he said; "I will catch Father Andréa up, and make him tell them to be quiet. He can do what he pleases with that tongue of his."

"But mayn't I come?" said Mitsos, scenting an entrancing row.

"And get your black head broken? No, that will keep for a worthier cause."

Constantine hurried off and caught Father Andréa up before he entered the town.

32

"Father," he said, "you can stop this, for they will listen to you. Remember what Nicholas said."

Father Andréa nodded.

"I heard there were loud talk and blows in the town, and I am on the road for that reason. Nicholas is right. We must pay the extra tax, and for every pint of wine we pay we will exact a gallon of blood. Ah, God, how I have fasted and prayed one prayer—to wash my hands in the blood of the Turks."

"Softly," said Constantine, "here is the guard."

The guard at the gate was unwilling at first to let them pass, but Andréa, without a moment's hesitation, said that he was a priest going to visit a dying man who wished to make a confession, with Constantine as witness, and they were admitted.

"God will forgive me that lie," he said, as they passed on. "It is for His cause that I lied."

Since Mitsos' departure the disturbance had increased. There were some forty or fifty Greeks collected in the centre of the square, and Turkish soldiers were coming out one by one from the barracks and mingling with the crowd. The Greeks, according to their custom, all carried knives, but were otherwise unarmed; the Turks had guns and pistols. There was a low, angry murmur going up from the people, which boded mischief. Just as they came up Father Andréa turned to Constantine.

"Stop outside the crowd," he said, "do not mix yourself up in this. They will not touch me, for I am a priest."

Then elbowing his way among the people, he shouted: "A priest—a priest of God! Let me pass."

The Greeks in the crowd parted, making way for him as he pushed through, conspicuous by his great height, though here and there a Turkish soldier tried to stop him. But Andréa demanded to be let into the middle of them with such authority that they too fell back, and he continued to elbow his way on. He was already well among the people when two voices detached themselves, as it were, from the angry, low murmur, shrilling up apart in loud, violent altercation, and the next moment a Greek just in front of him rushed forward and stabbed a Turk in the arm. The soldier raised his pistol and fired, and the man turned over on his face, with a grunt and one stretching convulsion, dead. There was a moment's silence, and then the murmur grew shriller and louder, and the crowd pressed forward. Andréa held up his hand.

"I am Father Andréa," he shouted, "whom you know. In God's name listen to me a moment. Silence there, all of you."

For a moment again there was a lull at his raised voice, and Andréa took advantage of it.

"The curse of all the saints of God be upon the Greek who next uses his knife," he cried. "Who is the officer in command?"

A young Turkish officer standing close to him turned round.

"I am in command," he said, "and I command you to go, unless you would be seized with the other ringleaders."

"I shall not go; my place is here."

"For the last time, go."

33

"I offer myself as hostage for the good conduct of the Greeks," said Andréa, quietly. "Blood has been shed. I am here that there may be no more. Let me speak to them and then take me, and if there is more disturbance kill me."

"Very good," said the officer. "I have heard of you. But stop the riot first, if you can. I desire bloodshed no more than you."

The group had now collected round them, still waiting irresolutely, in the way a crowd does on any one who seems to have authority. Father Andréa turned to them.

"You foolish children," he cried, "what are you doing? The Sultan has added a tax, it is true, but will it profit you to be killed like dogs? You have knives, and you can cut a finger nail with knives, and these others have guns. This poor dead thing learned that, and he has paid for his lesson. Is it better for him that he has wounded another man now that he has gone to appear before God? And those of you who are not shot will be taken and hanged. I am here unarmed, as it befits a priest to be. I am a hostage for you. If there is further riot you yourselves will be shot down like dogs, or as you shoot the little foxes among the grapes and leave them for the crows to eat; I shall be hanged, for I go hostage for you; and the tax will be no less than before. So now to your homes."

The crowd listened silently—for in those days to behave with aught but respect to a priest was sacrilege—and one or two of the nearest put back their knives into their belts, yet stood there still irresolute.

"Come, every man to his home," said Andréa again. "Let those who have wine-shops close them, for there has been blood spilled to-night."

But they still stood there, and the murmur rose and died, and rose again like a sound carried on a gusty wind, until Andréa, pushing forward, laid his hand on the shoulder of one of the ringleaders.

"Christos," he said, "there is your home, and your wife waits for you. Go home, man, lest you are carried in feet first."

The man, directly and individually addressed by a stronger, turned and went, and the others began to melt away till there were only left in the square the Turkish soldiers and Andréa. Then he spoke to the officer again:

"I am at your disposal," he said, "until you are satisfied that things are quiet again."

The officer stood for a moment without replying. Then, "I wish to treat you with all courtesy," he said, "and you have saved me a great deal of trouble to-night. But perhaps it will be better if you stop in my quarters for an hour or two, though I think we shall have no more of this. With your permission I will give you in custody."

And with the fine manners of his race, which the Greeks for the most part could not understand and so distrusted, he beckoned to two soldiers, who led him off to the officer's quarters.

The Turkish captain remained in the square an hour longer, but the disturbance seemed to be quite over, and he followed Father Andréa.

"You will smoke or drink?" he said, laying his sword on the table.

"I neither smoke nor drink," answered Andréa.

The officer sat down, looking at him from his dark, lustreless eyes.

"It is natural you should hate us," he said, "and but for you there

34

would have been a serious disturbance, and not Greek blood alone would have been shed. I am anxious to know why you stopped the riot."

Father Andréa smiled.

"For the reason I gave to the rioters. Is not that sufficient?"

"Quite sufficient; it only occurred to me there might be a further reason, a further-reaching reason, so to speak. I will not detain you any longer. I am sure no further disturbance will take place."

Andréa rose, and for a moment the two men faced each other. They were both good types of their race: the Greek, fearless and hot-blooded; the Turk, fearless and phlegmatic.

"I will wish you good-night," said the captain; "perhaps we shall meet again. My name is Mehemet Salik. You owe nothing to me nor I to you. You stopped the riot and saved me some trouble, but it was for reasons of your own. I have detained you till I am satisfied there will be no more disturbance; so if we meet again no quarter on either side, for we shall be enemies."

"I shall neither give quarter nor ask it," said Andréa.

The vintage began the next week, and for the time Mitsos had to abandon his boat and gun for the wine-making, since he alone knew the particularities of manufacture which Constantine practised—the amount of fermentation before finally casking the wine, the measure of resin to be put in, and the right quality of it, all which were as incommunicable as the unwritten law of tea-making for an individual taste. The small vineyard close to the house, which was all that was left to them after the seizure of the bigger vineyard by the Turk, contained the best vines, which, being nearer to hand, had inevitably received the better cultivation. These again were divided into two classes, most of them being the ordinary country stock; but the other was a nobler grape from Nemea, which yielded the finest wine. They were always gathered last, and fermented in a barrel by themselves.

The evening before the grape-picking began, several girls from neighboring farms came to find labor in the gathering for a couple of days, as the harvest would not be ripe in other vineyards for a day or two yet. Constantine engaged four of them, who came early next morning, just as he and Mitsos were getting out the big two-handled panniers in which the grapes were carried to the press from the vineyard, which lay dewy and glistening under the clear dawn. Spero, the boy who had been employed for the last week in scaring birds, was also engaged for the picking, and in all they were seven. For the larger half of an hour they all picked together, until two of the big baskets were full and the treading could begin. The press, an old stone-built construction, moss-ridden and creviced outside, and coated inside with fine stucco, stood close to the house. The bottom of it sloped down towards a small wooden sluice which opened from its lower end, and which could be raised from the inside when there was sufficient must trodden to fill one of the big shallow casks in which it was fermented. Mitsos had spent the previous day in washing and scouring it with avuncular thoroughness, scrubbing the sides with powdered resin, and when Spero had wanted to assist in treading the grape instead of gathering, he looked scornful, and only said:

"We do not make wine for you to wash in. Get you back to the picking."

They poured the first two big panniers of grapes into the press just as the sun rose, stalks and all, and after turning his trousers up to the knees, and scrubbing his feet and legs in hot water, Mitsos stepped in and began the treading. The purple fruit was ripe and tight-skinned, and the red stuff soon began to splash and spurt up, staining his legs. Another basket came before he had got the first two well under, and by degrees the pickers gained on him. The day promised a scorching, and the press, which had at first stood in the shade, had been swung round into the full blaze of the sun before a couple of hours were over. About nine o'clock Constantine, who had just carried up another basket with Spero, and stayed for a moment looking at Mitsos dancing fantastically in the sun, saw that there was already stuff enough to fill a cask.

"There is food for a cask there," he said to Mitsos, "but it is not trodden enough yet. You will not keep pace without some one to help you."

Mitsos paused a moment and wiped his face with the back of his hand.

"I am broiled meat," he said. "Yes, send one of the girls. Make her wash first."

Constantine smiled.

"There speaks Nicholas," he remarked, "who is always right."

So Maria was sent to help Mitsos. She was a pretty girl, about seventeen years old, fawn eyed and olive skinned. As she stood on the edge of the press before stepping in, with her shoes off and her skirt tucked up, Mitsos found himself noticing the gentle curve of her calf muscle from the ankle to behind the knee, and how prettily one foot, pink from the hot water, broadened as she rested her weight on it for a moment. He gave her his hand to help her down into the press, and their eyes met.

"We shall do nicely now," he said.

Constantine meantime had fetched one of the casks, open at the top, and with a tap at the bottom, about six inches above the other end, from which the fermented liquid would be drawn off when it was clear, and placing it under the sluice, looked over to see if the must was sufficiently trodden. No baskets had come in for a quarter of an hour, and Mitsos and Maria between them had reduced the whole must to one consistency.

"It is ready now," he said to Mitsos; "raise the sluice."

The must had risen above the ring by which the sluice was raised at the lower end of the press, and Mitsos and Maria groped about for half a minute or so before they found it. Once they tightly grasped each other's fingers, and both exclaimed triumphantly, "I've got it."

Maria found it first; but the wood had swollen with the scouring of the day before and it was stiff, so Mitsos had to raise it himself. Then with a gurgle and a gulp the purple mass of pulp, juice, stalks, and skins poured riotously out, splashing Constantine, and foaming into the cask with a lusty noise. When it was three-quarters full Mitsos closed the sluice again, for in the process of fermentation the must would swell to the top, and Constantine and Spero took the barrel, clucking as it was moved, off into the veranda out of the sun, and covered it with a cloth.

36

They all rested for an hour at mid-day, and ate their dinner in the shade of the poplar by the spring. The others had brought their food with them, with the exception of Maria, who said she was not hungry and did not care to eat. But Mitsos, pausing for a moment in his own meal, saw her sitting close to him looking rather tired and fagged from the morning's work, and fetched her some bread and some fresh cheese, cool and sweet from the cellar, and Maria's want of appetite vanished before these things. After dinner they all lay down and dozed for that hour of fiercest heat, when, as the poet of the South says, "even the cicala is still," some in the veranda, some in the shade of the poplars. Mitsos was the first to wake, and he, under a stern sense of duty, aroused himself and the others. Maria had disposed herself under a farther tree, where she lay with her hands clasped behind her head, and her mouth half open and set with the rim of her white teeth. She had drawn up one leg, and her short skirt showed it bare to above the knee. Mitsos stood looking at her a moment, thinking how pretty were her long eyelashes and slightly parted mouth, and wondering why it had never occurred to him before that she was pretty, when she woke and saw him standing in front of her. She sat up quickly and drew her skirt down over her leg, and a faint tinge of red showed under her skin.

"Is it time to go on?" she said; "and I am nothing but a bag of sleep."

"I will help you up," said Mitsos, putting out his hand.

But she stretched herself, smiling, and got up without his assistance.

Then the work went on till nearly sunset; a second cask and a third were filled, which were taken away to the veranda, where they were put on trestles and covered like the first; and, as there would not be time to fill a fourth before sunset, they stopped work for the day.

Mitsos and Constantine ate their supper together, but afterwards Mitsos said he would not go to the café to-night, he was sleepy, and to-morrow would be as to-day. The two sat there in silence for the most part, the father smoking and playing with his beads, and Mitsos lying full length on the floor of the veranda intermittently eating a cherry from the remains of their supper.

About nine he got up and stretched himself.

"I am for bed," he said. "How pretty Maria is. I wonder why I never noticed before that girls were pretty."

Constantine smiled.

"We all notice it sooner or later," he said. "I noticed it when I was about as old as you."

"Did you? What did you do then?"

"God granted me to marry the one I thought the prettiest."

"My mother? It is little I remember of her. But I am not going to marry Maria. Yet she is even very pretty."

The second day was devoted to picking the remainder of the ordinary grapes, which Mitsos and Maria trod, as on the day before, and Mitsos feeling a desire—to which he had hitherto been a stranger—to look well in a girl's eyes, told her stories about the shooting, and his own prowess therein—for all the world like a young cock-bird in spring and the mating-time strutting before his lady. The girls were not required for the third day's picking, and in the evening Constantine paid them their two days' wage. Mitsos walked back with Maria through the garden, and together they washed their feet of the must at the spring. A little further on they came to the cherry-tree, and here he told her to hold out her apron while he picked a little supper for her, again taking pride to swing himself with an unnecessary display of gymnastics from one bough to another, while Maria looked on from below with up-turned eyes bidding him be careful, and saying, as was indeed true, that there were plenty of cherries on the lower boughs, and his exertions were needless. Something in his conduct seemed to amuse her, for as they said good-night at the gate she broke out into a laugh, and, with the air of a great, fine lady to a pretty boy, "Good-night, little Mitsos," she said; "and will you come to my wedding?"

Mitsos, in spite of his determination of the night before, felt a perceptible shock.

"Your wedding? Whom are you going to marry?"

"Yanko. At least, so I think. He has asked me, and I have not said no."

"Yanko Vlachos? That ugly brute?"

Maria laughed again.

"I don't find him ugly—at least, not to matter."

Mitsos recollected his manners.

"I beg your pardon," he said. "I like Yanko very much. He knocked a Turkish soldier down last week—such a bang on the back of his head!"

"Oh, he's a very good man," said Maria, walking off with a great, important air.

Mitsos went slowly back to the house, his strutting over.

The third day was devoted to the gathering of the finer grapes, which were fermented by themselves in a separate cask. These the two boys and Constantine picked together, until all the trees but one were stripped, but instead of throwing them in stalk and all, they picked each grape separately off the bunches and shed them into the cask, until there was a layer some fifteen inches deep. Mitsos trod these as before, while his father and Spero went on picking, and when they were sufficiently pulped he poured on to them about a quart of brandy. More grapes were then put in, trodden, and more brandy added. When the cask was three-quarters full they moved it away with the others, but covered it more closely with two layers of thick woollen blanket. The remainder of the fine grapes were sufficient to fill another half-cask.

Then there came the final act of the grape-gathering, a page of pagan ritual surviving from the time when the rout of Dionysus laughed and rioted through the vineyard. Mitsos fetched a big bowl from the house, and Constantine cut all the grapes from the remaining vine. These he placed in the bowl and left in the middle of the vineyard for the birds to eat.

For the next two days the must required no attention, though the fermentation, owing to the heat of the weather, was going on very rapidly, and by the end of the second day the thin acrid smell mingled strongly with the garden scents. Once or twice Constantine raised the cloths which covered the casks to see what progress it made, or drew a little from the tap at the bottom. But the stuff was still thick, and had not cleared sufficiently to be disturbed yet.

On the second day Mitsos went off to get fresh resin for the wine. The ordinary pine resin was generally used by Greeks for this, but Constantine always preferred the resin from the dwarf pine, which was less bitter and finer in quality. The sides of Mount Elias were plentiful with the common pine, but the dwarf pine only grew on the hills round Epidaurus, a five hours' journey. Mitsos took his gun with him on the chance of sighting and slaying game, and started off on his pony before dawn, for the way wound over low, unsheltered hills, a day-long target for the sun; but before he reached the shoulder of mountain in which was cut the old grass-grown theatre, about which the dwarf pines grew, the sun, already high, had drawn up the heavy dews of the night before, and the air was quivering with heat like a man in an ague fit. The growth of these pines was that of bushes rather than trees, some of them covering a space of ten yards square, gnarl-trunked, and sprawling along the ground. On some dozen of them he selected a place near the root and cut off a piece of bark a few inches square in order that the resin might ooze from the lips of the wounded trunk, placing below each a flat stone to catch the dripping. In a few days' time there would be sufficient resin collected for the year's wine. On several trees he found the incisions he had made in previous years, in some of which, where the flow of resin had continued after he had removed it for the wine, it had gone on dripping until a little pillar, like the slag-wax from a candle, stood up between the stone and the tree. He cut off one of these to see whether it was still good, but the damp had soaked into it, and the outside surface was covered with a gray fungus growth which rendered it useless.

He ate his dinner under shelter of the more shady trees which grew higher up the slope, and waited till the sun had lost its noonday heat, listening lazily to the bell on the neck of his pony, which was grazing on the hill-side above, dozing and wondering what the next year would bring for him. He had no idea what Nicholas would call on him to do, but he was willing to wait. The love of adventure and excitement was fermenting in him, though he was contented to go on living his usual life from day to day. Nicholas, he knew, would not fail; some day, he knew not when, the summons would come, and he would obey blindly. Then he thought of the horrible scene which Nicholas and he had looked on three months ago, when they saw that dead, misshapen thing dangling from a tree, and his blood began to boil and the desire to avenge the wrongs done to his race stirred in him.

"Spare not man, woman, or child," Nicholas had said.

He lay back on the short turf and began to think about Maria. Supposing Maria had been a Turkish woman, and Nicholas had put a knife into his hand while he was looking at her mid-day sleep beneath the poplars, and told him to kill her, would he have been able? Could he have struck anything so soft and pretty? Fancy that heavy lout, Yanko, marrying Maria; he was all fat, and sat drinking all day at the wine-shop, yet he was never drunk, like a proper man, and he was seldom sober. Then Mitsos for the first time in his life became analytical, though his vocabulary boasted no such word. Why was it that since the day he stood in front of Maria as she lay asleep he had regarded women somehow with different eyes? What was it to him whether Yanko or another had her? Hitherto he had thought of women in the obvious, work-a-day light in which they are presented to a Greek boy, as beasts of burden, hewers of wood and drawers of water, inferior beings who waited on the men, and when alone chattered shrilly and volubly to each other like jays, or a bushful of silly, jabbering sparrows—creatures altogether unfit for the companionship of men. But since that moment he or they had changed; there was something wonderful about them which men did not share, something demanding protection, even tenderness, affording food for vague, disquieting thought. He had not understood at all, not having known his mother, why Nicholas had spoken as he had of his wife, except in so far that she was a possession of which the Turks had robbed him. But Mitsos could think of nothing the loss of which would make him devote his life to the extermination of the race that had robbed him of it. Even if the Turks took away his gun he realized that he would not wish to destroy the whole race for that. The brutal hanging of a man was a different matter; a man was a man, and a woman—Well, that woman was Nicholas's wife. Suppose the Turks killed Maria, would that be worse than if they killed, say, Nicholas? Well, not worse, not nearly so bad in fact, but, somehow, different.

Thus knocked Mitsos at the door of the habitation called love, and waited for its sesame.

CHAPTER VI

THE SONG FROM THE DARKNESS

When Constantine looked at one of the casks of fermenting wine on the fourth day, he saw that the crust of skins, stalks, and stones had risen to within six inches of the top, like coffee on the boil, and was thickly covered with a pink, sour-smelling froth. The fermentation was at its height, and it was time to mix up the crust with the fluid again to excite it even further. In one cask, into which the ripest fruit from the more sun-baked corner of the vineyard had been put, this crust had risen even higher, and threatened to overflow. The ordinary custom in Greece at this time was for a naked man to get into the cask and stir it up again, a remnant, no doubt, of some now insignificant superstition; but Constantine, though he still put the grapes of one vine in a bowl for the birds to eat, did not think it necessary to make this further concession, but only stirred up the frothing mass with an instrument like a wooden pavier. The crust was already growing thick and compacted, and it was ten

40

minutes' work to get it thoroughly mixed up again with the fluid in each case, and from the seething, bubbling surface there rose thickly the sour fumes of the decomposing matter, heavily laden with carbonic-acid gas. One cask leaked slightly round the tap at the bottom and was dripping on the floor. A little red stream had trickled down to the edge of the veranda, and he noticed that it was full of small bubbles, like water that had stood in the sun, showing that the fermentation was not yet over. He caulked this up with a lump of resin, and then moved all the casks out of the shade for an hour or two, so that the heat might hasten the second fermentation, which naturally was slower and less violent than the first. The cask and a half of fine wine, however, he did not touch; there it was better that the fermentation should go on slowly and naturally.

That evening Mitsos went out fishing, as the work of wine-making was over for the present. In four or five days he would have to go over to Epidaurus to get the resin from the pine-trees, but just now there was nothing more to be done. Later on the vines would have to be cut back, but Constantine preferred delaying this till the leaves fell and the sap had sunk back again into the roots and main stem.

Though the day was one of early autumn, and in most years the serenity of summer would continue into the middle or end of October, the top of the hills above the farther side of the gulf had been shrouded all day in thick storm-boding clouds, and as sunset drew near these spread eastward, making a sullen sky. The sun, as it dropped behind them, illumined their edges, turning them to a dark translucent amber, and the afterglow, which spread slowly across the heavens, cast a strange lurid light through the half opaque floor of cloud. The night would soon fall dark, perhaps with storm. It was very hot, and the land breeze was but a languid air, and blew as if weary with its travel over the broiling plain, but there was quite enough of it, with Mitsos' economical methods, to send the boat along at a good pace. He sailed almost before it out seaward for two miles or so, meaning to fish from the island, but then changed his mind, and went back on tedious tacks to the head of the bay, the water seeming to him a thick thing, and the boat going but heavily. Dark fell, dense and premature, and when an hour later he put the boat about on the last tack he had to keep two eyes open as he neared the land; but as there were no other boats abroad, he did not think it necessary to light his lantern at the bows. Against the dark sky and the dark water it would hardly have been possible to see the brown-sailed craft from more than forty yards distant, and even then, if the thin white line of broken water at the forefoot had not caught the eye, or the stealthy, subdued hiss as it cut through the sea fallen on the ear, it might have passed close and unnoticed. Then, with a curious suddenness, he saw faintly the white glimmer of the sea-wall of Abdul Achmet's house straight in front of him, and knew that in the dead darkness he had taken too starboard a course. However, by running up as close as possible to this, one tack more would certainly take him across to the fishing bay where he was bound, and sitting rudder in hand, he waited till the last possible moment before putting about. He had, however, forgotten that the wall would take the wind from him, and when he was about fifty yards off, the sail flapped once and fell dead against the mast, and the boom swung straight, the line of white water faded from under the forefoot, and the hiss of the motion was quenched. He got up for an oar, so as to pull her round again, when quite suddenly he heard the sound of a woman's voice from the terrace singing. For a moment or so he stood still, and then his ear focussed itself to the sounds. She was singing a song Mitsos knew well, a song which the vine-tenders sing as they are digging the vines in the spring of the year, and she sang in Greek:

> "Dig we deep around the vines,
> Give the sweet spring showers a home,
> Else the fairest sun that shines
> Sends no sparkle to our wines,
> Lights no lustre in the foam."

He could not see the singer; all he saw was the circle of black night, the faint lines of his boat a shade blacker against it, and just ahead the white glimmer of the wall. The voice, low and sweet, came out of the darkness like a bird flying through a desert—a living thing amid death. Mitsos stood perfectly still, strangely and bewilderingly excited. Then he took up his oar and turned the boat's head round, rowed a few strokes out, and waited again. But the voice had ceased.

He felt somehow unaccountably shy, as if he had intruded into another's privacy; but having intruded, he was determined to make his presence known. So just as the sail caught the wind again he stood up in the stern, and in his boyish voice answered the unseen singer with the second verse:

> "Dig we deep, the summer's here;
> Saw we not among the eaves
> Summer's messenger appear,
> Swallows flitting here and there,
> Through the budding almond leaves?"

The boat bent over to the wind, the white line streaked the water, and he hissed off into the night again.

He sat down, let go of the tiller, and let the boat run on by itself. He had never known that that common country song was beautiful till he had heard a voice out of the darkness sing it—a voice low, sweet, soft, which might have been the darkness itself made audible. Who was this woman? How did she, a Greek, come to be in the house of a Turk? Then with a flash of awakened memory he brought to mind the evening when he and Nicholas had sailed home after fishing; how a man came up and struck a woman who was leaning on the sea-wall; how she had cried out and said, in Greek, "What was that for?"

The flapping of the sail in the last breath of the wind roused him and he looked up; the breeze had died out, and he was floating in the middle of a shell of blackness. He had no idea where he was until he saw the lights of Nauplia, where he least expected them, on the left of the boat instead of behind him, dim, and far away. For his craft, left to itself, had of course run straight before the land-breeze out into the mouth of the gulf, and now the breeze had died out and he was miles from the land. That did not trouble him much; fishing was a minor consideration, and spending the night in the boat was paid for by a shrug of the shoulders. He wanted one thing only—to get back to the white glimmering wall, to the voice from the darkness.

A puff of hot air wandered by the boat, the sails shivered for a moment and were still again. A veiled flash of lightning gleamed through the clouds over the Tripoli hills and was reflected sombrely across the sky, and a peal of thunder droned a tardy answer. A faint rim of light, like the raising of tired eyelids, opened over the sea, and he saw the ropes of his boat stand out sharp against it. Then, suddenly, there came from the hills a sound he knew, and knew to be dangerous—the shrill scream of a mountain squall from the highlands to the west of the gulf. He sprang to the ropes and had the sail down just before it struck him, but in less than a minute the bows were driven round, and the white tops of little waves began to fleck the bay. He felt the salt spray on his face and hands, and laughed exultantly. This was what he wanted.

With a joy in the danger of the thing he hoisted the sail, struggling and pulling to be free, and in a moment he was tearing back straight to the head of the gulf, with the rudder pushed hard a-port.

At the pace he was going the boat was quite steady, cutting through the waves instead of rising to them, and now and then one was flung over the bows like a white rag. The wind screamed, the white snakes of foam flew by, and, bareheaded, Mitsos clung with both hands to his rudder, controlling the course of the boat like the rider of a restive horse, laughing to himself for some secret glee, and every now and then shouting out a verse of the vine-diggers' song. Before long the wall appeared again, and he took in his sail; the water was already rough, and was dashing up against it; but he let the boat drift on till he was within thirty yards of it. The rim of light over the sea had widened, and he could see the edge of the top of the wall quite distinctly, and, behind, the tall sombre cypresses in rows. But there was no one there.

Just then the rain began hissing into the sea like shot, and for a few minutes turning the whole surface milky white. Mitsos, frowning and peering awhile into the darkness, put up his collar, and with some difficulty proceeded to put about. The wind was blowing hard ashore, and he had to take down the sail altogether and row. Even then he seemed hardly to be making way against the maddened air, and it was a quarter of an hour's hard work to get far enough from the shore to sail again. Then he fetched a long tack towards Nauplia, and from there managed to handle the boat back opposite the shore where his house stood. The surf was breaking nastily on the rock-ridden beach, and he had to get through a narrow channel, both sides of which were shoal water, not sufficiently deep to allow the boat to pass. But he had the light from his own house and that from the café opposite to steer by, and he knew that he could run in when they were in a line. As he neared the shore he could see it was impossible to bring the boat round sharply enough, and while there was yet time he beat out again for a quarter of a mile and approached it more directly. This time he was successful, and the boat skimmed past the tumbled water on each side—and as he passed he saw sharp-toothed rocks foaming and gnashing at him—safe into the smoother water of his anchorage. Constantine was waiting up for him, and when his tall figure appeared in the doorway, he looked up with relief.

"Mitsos, you shouldn't sail on nights like these," he said; "the best seamen in the world might not be able to handle a boat in such a squall. How did you get in?"

"It's easy enough when you get the lights from the house and the café in a line," said Mitsos; "besides, I was six miles out in the bay when the squall came down."

"Six miles out? You have not been long getting back," said his father, marvelling at the lad's knowledge.

Mitsos walked to the door to close it, turning his back on Constantine.

"No, there was a fine wind to sail on," he said, and whistled the vine-diggers' song beneath his breath.

Constantine did not ask any more questions, and Mitsos went to make himself some hot coffee and get out of his wet clothes, for he was drenched from head to foot.

Two days after this the ordinary wine had cleared completely, and it was racked into fresh casks, for if it stood too long on the lees in contact with the skins and stalks it would become bitter. The crust itself Constantine removed from all the barrels and put into the still for the making of spirits. This only required one man to look after, and on the day Mitsos went to Epidaurus to get the resin he employed himself with it.

The apparatus was of the simplest. He placed all the crusts from the barrels in a big iron pot, under which he lit a slow charcoal fire; into a hole in the lid of this, which screwed on to the body, he inserted a bent iron pipe, on to which he screwed another pipe made in spirals. A big wooden tub filled with water, through the bottom of which passed a third pipe fitting at one end into the spirals which lay in the water, and communicating at the other with the glazed jar into which the spirit was to be stored, completed the apparatus. The fire drove off the alcohol from the fermented crust in a vapor, which distilled itself into spirit as it passed through the tube that lay in the cold water, and dripped out at the farther end into the jar.

He finished the day's work by soon after five, and, having business in Nauplia, set off there at once; so that Mitsos, returning a little later from Epidaurus with the resin, found him out, and, without waiting to get any food, he set off again at once down to the bay.

It was drawing near that moment when all the beauty of the day in sea, land, and sky is gathered into the ten minutes of sunset. The sun, declining to its setting, was dropping slowly above a low pass in the hills, shining with an exceeding clearness, and it was still half an hour above the horizon when Mitsos got into the boat. The land-breeze was blowing temperate and firm, and his boat dipped to it gently, and glided steadily on the outward tack. Between him and the Argive hills hung a palpable haze of thinnest blue; but the whole plain slept in a garment of gold, woven by the

44

level rays. The surface of the water, unruffled under the shadow of the land, was green and burnished like a plate of patinated bronze, and the ripple from the bows broke creamily and flowed out behind the boat in long, feather-like lines. As the sun neared its setting, the golden mist grew more intense in color, and the higher slopes of the mountains turned pink behind their veil of blue. The sky was cloudless from rim to rim, except where, low in the west, there floated a few thin skeins of vapor, visible against the incredible blue only because they were touched with red. Just as Mitsos neared the wall on his second tack the sun's edge was cut by the ragged outline of the mountain, and in ten minutes more it would have set.

She, the nameless, ineffable she—and Mitsos never questioned that this was the sweet singer—was leaning on the edge of the wall looking seawards. She saw Mitsos sitting in the stern of his boat, and guessed at once—for few boats passed so close—that it was he who had sung the second verse of the vineyard song two nights ago, and that it was his boat which passed close under the wall last night, when the other women of the harem were there with her. She had not known till she saw him that she wished to see the owner of that half-formed boyish voice, which had come so pleasantly out of the darkness; and now, when she did see him, she looked long. He, too, was looking, and her eyes made a bridge over the golden air that lay between them and brought them close together.

The boat drew nearer, and she dropped her eyes and began playing with a spray of roses that trailed along the top of the wall. She picked a couple of buds, smelled them, and then very softly she began the first verse of the vine-diggers' song.

The boat had got under shelter of the wall, and drifted windlessly near. Mitsos was still looking at her; her eyes were still cast down. She sang the first verse through, and the first two lines of the second verse, and then apparently she recollected no more, for she stopped, and from the boat Mitsos sang very softly the two lines that followed. Still, without looking up, she sang them after him; he finished the verse, and she sang the whole through.

From the bay the sun had set, but the mountains on the east glowed rosier and rosier every moment. All that Mitsos saw was a girl's slender figure wrapped in a loose white cloak, with a gold band round the waist—a hand that held two rosebuds, a face veiled up to the eyes, eyes down-dropped, and eyelashes that swept the cheek.

"There is a third verse," he said.

Then she looked up, and her eyes smiled at him, and they were as black as shadows beneath the moon.

"I will learn that another night," she said, softly, "if it be you will teach me; and this is for your teaching. Go, now; others are coming."

Half carelessly she threw into the boat the roses she had picked, and turned away.

Mitsos waited a moment longer, and then, hearing voices in the garden behind the wall, rowed quickly away. His thoughts were a song; his mind, one sweet secret frenzy, that made the heart quick and the eye bright. All the common details of life were seen and taken in by him but dimly, as sounds come dimly to a sleeper, and are but the material out of

45

which he weaves a golden vision; for the first splendor of love, hackneyed as a theme, but as an experience from generation to generation ever new, was dawning on him.

Maria was married next morning, and Mitsos went without emotion to the wedding. The bride and bridegroom appeared to him to be admirably suited to each other.

About four o'clock that afternoon the lad was just about to set off down to the shore when his father appeared.

"We'll finish with the wine this evening," he said. "Come and begin at once, Mitsos."

Mitsos paused a moment.

"I was just going sailing," he said. "Cannot it wait till to-morrow?"

"No; it had better be finished now. Besides, you can sail afterwards. Come, it won't take a couple of hours."

"Uncle Nicholas told me to sail every day," he began.

"And to obey me, Mitsos."

Mitsos stood for a moment irresolute, but soon his habit of obedience reasserted itself.

"Yes, father," he said; "I am sorry. I will come."

The casks in which the first fermentation had taken place had been thoroughly scoured with boiling water, which had quite got rid of the sour-smelling fermented stuff, and they were to rack the cleared resinated wine back into them. They filled each cask again three-quarters full, and into the remaining space they poured a portion of the fine wine, dividing it equally among all. To Mitsos the process seemed insufferably long and tedious. The sun had set before the casks were filled, and it was dark before the work was over. Never before, it seemed to him, had the taps dribbled so dispiritingly. His father now and then addressed some remark to him, which he barely answered, and after a time they both lapsed into silence. Mitsos knew that he was behaving badly, and he thought he could not help it. Perhaps she was there; perhaps—bewildering thought—she was even wondering why he did not come. How could he simulate the slightest interest in the wine of grapes when the wine of love was fermenting within him, driving him mad with those sweet, intoxicating fumes for which there is no amethyst?

At last it was over. No, he would not eat now; he would eat when he came in, and ten minutes later he was on his way. Soon the wall began to glimmer in front of him. Something, it looked only like a white shadow, was leaning on it, and as he drew nearer he heard again the voice singing low in the darkness, singing the common country song which had become so beautiful.

CHAPTER VII

THE PORT DUES OF CORINTH

Nicholas got safely across to Corinth early in the morning after he had parted from Mitsos, but was obliged to wait there two days for a caique to take him to Patras. The revolution for which the leading Greeks throughout the Peloponnese were preparing was there in the hands of the Archbishop Germanos. Like Nicholas, he too had felt the cruel appetites of the Turk, and, like Nicholas, he was willing to leave revenge unplucked until the whole scheme was ripe to the core. An agent of his had met the latter at Corinth, bidding him come, if he had a few days to spare, at once; if not, as soon as he could. But as Nicholas had left Nauplia with the idea of proceeding to Patras at once, he sent the messenger back, saying he was on his way, but that for greater security he would come by sea. That he was suspected of being concerned in intrigue against the Turk he knew, and as his plans were now already beginning to be thoroughly organized, and the club had made him their principal agent in the Morea, he wished to avoid any needless risk in passing through the garrisoned towns on the gulf.

On the second day, however, a Greek caique laden with figs was starting from Corinth, and Nicholas went on board soon after dark, and about midnight they started.

For a few hours an easterly breeze drew up from the narrow end of the gulf, but it slackened and dropped between three and four in the morning, and daylight found them becalmed, with slack sails, some eight miles out to sea, and nearly opposite Itea. To the north the top of Parnassus wore morning on its face, and stood high above them rose-flushed with dawn, while they still lay on a dark, polished plain of water as smooth as glass. On the opposite side of the gulf, but farther ahead, Cyllene and Helmos, on the north side of which last winter's snow still lay heraldically in bars and bezants, had also caught the light, which, as the sun rose higher, flowed like some luminous liquid down their slopes, wooded below with great pine forests.

Nicholas had pillowed himself on the deck, and woke when the sun had risen high enough to touch the caique. The captain and owner of the boat, who had been all night in the little close cabin below, came up as he roused himself and sat down near him.

"The wind has dropped altogether," he said; "we may be here for hours. Are you in a hurry to get on?"

Nicholas filled his pipe very carefully.

"I am never in a hurry," he said, "if I am going as quick as I can. I would make a wind if I could, but I cannot, and so I am content to wait. If swearing would do any good I would even swear, but I find it has no effect on the elements. You have a good heavy cargo."

"A good, heavy cargo?" said the man. "Yes, and we should have a dipping gunwale if those devils had not seized six crates of figs at Corinth."

47

"The Turks?" asked Nicholas.

"Who else? Port dues, they call them. Much of a port is Corinth—a heap of stones tumbled into the water, and five rickety steps."

"Harbor dues! They are a new institution, are they not?"

"A month old only," said the man; "but if I hear right they will not be very much older when they are taken off again."

"Taken off? How is that?" asked Nicholas, blandly.

"They say there will soon be a great cutting of the swines' throats. I spend my life on the sea, and for the most part my ears are empty of news; but surely you know what was being said at Corinth?—that before a year is out we Greeks shall not have these masters any longer."

One of the crew was standing near, and the captain motioned him to go farther off.

"I do not like to say this before my own men," he said; "but why should I not tell you? you will be landed at Patras, and you will go your way and I mine. Besides, for all your Turkish clothes you are no Turk, for they are a short-legged folk. I heard it at the café last night. Four Turks were talking about the arms which they say the peasants are collecting. They spoke of one Nicholas Vidalis as a leader—they expected to take him, for word had come to them that he was travelling to Corinth."

"Thus there are disappointed men," thought Nicholas. Then aloud, "Who is this Nicholas?"

"Nay, I know him not," said the man. "I am from the islands. I thought it might be you could tell me of him."

"From which island?" asked Nicholas.

"From Psara."

Nicholas lit his pipe with a lump of charcoal and inhaled a couple of long breaths, silent, but with a matter in balance.

Then, looking straight at the man, he said:

"I am Nicholas Vidalis, the man whom the Turks would dearly like to catch. But at present they catch me not, for I am a clean and God-fearing man, and I hate the Turk even as I hate the devil, for the two are one. And now there are two ways open to you—one is to give me up at Patras, the other to try to help me and others in what we are doing. For this will be no time for saying 'I have nothing to do with this; let those who will fight it out.' You will have to take one side, and you had better begin at once. See, I have trusted you with my secret, because you may be of use to me. You come from Psara, and you probably know the coast of Greece as a man knows the shape of his boots and gaiters. We have got plenty of men to fight on land, and plenty to pay them with; what we want are little ships, which, in case of need, will hang about the Turks if they try to escape from their destruction, and sting them as the mosquito stings the slow cattle in the evening."

Nicholas paused for a moment, and his face lit up with a blaze of hatred.

"For it is already evening with them," he cried, "and when the day dawns night shall have swallowed them, and they will awake no more. Do you know what is the strongest feeling that ever grips a man's heart? No, not love, nor yet fear, but revenge. And if you had suffered as I have suffered you would know what it is to be filled with one thought only—to see blood in the sunrise and blood in the setting of the sun; to feel that you have ceased to be a man and have become a sword. That is what I am, and the hand that holds me is the right hand of God. And by me He will smite and spare not. And when there are no more to smite, perhaps I shall become a man again, and live to see peace and plenty bless a free people. But of that I know nothing, and I do not greatly care. Come, now, what answer do you give me?"

Nicholas rose to his feet; the other had risen too, and they faced each other. There was something in the earnestness and intensity of this man with one idea which could not but be felt, for enthusiasm is the one fact that cannot be gainsaid, a noble disease in which contagion ever makes infection. And his companion felt it.

"Tell me more," he said, eagerly; "but wait a moment—here is the wind."

He hurried aft to give orders to the men. Far away on the polished surface of the water behind them, smooth and shining as a sealskin, a line had appeared as if the fur had been stroked the wrong way. In a couple of minutes the men were busy with the ropes, and two stood ready to slacken the sheets of the heavy square sail if the squall was violent, and one stood at the tiller, for some cross-current had turned the boat round, and it would be necessary to put about. Meantime the rough line had crept nearer, and behind it they could see the tops of little waves cut off by the wind and blown about in spray. A couple of men had put out the long sweep-oars, and were tugging hurriedly at them to get the head of the boat straight before the wind before it struck them. But they were not in time; the wind came down with a scream, the boat heeled over till the leeward gunwale touched the water, and the mast bent; then, and with a perfect precision, the sheets were slackened for a moment to let her right herself; and, braced again, she began to make way, and in a few seconds they were scudding straight down the gulf almost directly before the wind, till, with their increasing speed, it seemed to die down again. The water all round them was broken up into an infinite number of little green foam-embroidered wave troughs, through which, at the pace they were going, they moved as quietly as a skater over smooth ice.

Nicholas had a careful eye to the handling of the boat during these operations, and he saw that the little crew of six men knew their work perfectly, and that they were quick and prompt at the moment when a mishap might easily have occurred. He never let slip the smallest opportunity which might some day prove to be useful, and he knew that for anything like united action it would be necessary for the Greeks to have, if not command of their sea-coast, at any rate the power to communicate with each other. The outbreak, as he would have it, would take place first in the Peloponnesus, but, not to fail of its completeness, it would have to spread over the north. Patras and Missolonghi were within a few miles of each other by sea, but unless there was free communication by the waterway they would be powerless for mutual support. To some extent both his fear and his hope were realized.

49

Half an hour later he and Kanaris, the captain of the boat, were breakfasting together, and Nicholas was explaining to him exactly what the weakness of the movement was, and the necessity for conjunction between the sea and land forces. He wished him, he said, to continue to exercise his trade for the sake of appearances, but always to be ready at a moment's notice. When the outbreak took place it was quite certain that many of the Turks, especially those on the sea-coast, would try to escape by sea. That must not be; it was no polite or diplomatic war on which they were to embark; their aim from the first must be the annihilation of the Turks. He told him in detail how this means of escape was to be cut off, as will appear later, and as he unfolded his bloody plan Kanaris's heart burned within him, and he promised, in the name of God, to help him gather that red vintage.

About mid-day the wind went down, and they lay becalmed again; but Nicholas, who, as he had said, was never in a hurry when he was going as quick as he could, felt that his time could hardly have been better employed. Kanaris, it appeared, was of a large Psarian clan; for generations he and his had been seafaring folk, men of the wind and wave, whose help Nicholas knew to be so essential. He promised, if possible, to come to Psara himself before the year was out; but he said that his hands were very full, and he could pledge no certainty.

For three hours or so they lay on a tossing water, for the wind of the morning had roughened the narrow sea, which so quickly gets up under a squall from the mountains, and great green billows came chasing each other down from the east beneath the brilliant noonday sun, which turned them into a jubilant company of living things. The boat, lying low in the water with its heavy cargo, reeled and rolled with a jovial boisterousness, alternately lifting up sides all ashine with the sea over the crest of a wave, and burying itself again with a choking hiccough in its trough. The sun drew out from the crates of figs their odor of mellow luxuriance, which hung heavy round the boat, dispersed every now and then by a puff of wind which blew in the salt freshness of the sea.

By four o'clock, however, the wind, still favorable, sprang up again, and on they went into the sunset, the black nose of the boat pushing and burrowing through the waves, and throwing off from its sides sheets of spent foam. As the hours passed Kanaris felt ever more keenly the fascination and strength of this strange man, and after supper they sat together in the stern watching the heavens reel and roll above them, and the top of the mast striking wildly right and left across a hundred stars. Nicholas, perched on the taffrail, balancing himself with an exquisite precision to every movement of the boat, talked in his deep low voice of a thousand schemes, all blood-stirring, with the Turk for target. For no one knew better than himself the value of personal power, and the success of his proselytizing had been to a large extent, even as in the case of Mitsos, the outcome of his own individuality, which could so stir the minds of men, and fan to a flame the smouldering hatred against the Turks, and cause it to leap up in fire.

Germanos, the Metropolitan Bishop of Patras, had only just risen next morning when his messenger came back, having travelled through the night to announce Nicholas's coming, and also report the same talk in the cafés which Kanaris had heard. The bishop smiled to himself at the idea of any untoward fate laying hands on Nicholas, and told his servant to let it be widely known that Nicholas had been taken and killed.

"For," as he said, "the Turks will be delighted to believe that (and men always succeed in believing what they wish), and all Greeks to whom Nicholas is more than a name will know that this is one of those things which do not occur. I am ready for breakfast, and let a room for my poor dead friend be got ready, and also a bath in which the body may be washed."

Germanos was a splendid specimen of a Greek of unmixed blood, now nearly or quite extinct. His family came from the island Delos, still unviolated by the unspeakable race, and from generation to generation they had only married with islanders. He was rather above the middle height, and his long black cassock made him appear taller. In accordance with Greek rite, neither his hair nor beard had ever been cut, and the former flowed black and thick onto his shoulders, and his beard fell in full rippling lines down as far as his waist. Though for three or four years his life had been one long effort of organizing his countrymen against the Turks, the latter had never suspected his complicity, and he intended to take the fullest advantage of their misplaced confidence in him. Though Germanos had not trodden the world so widely as Nicholas had done, he was nevertheless a man of culture—shrewd, witty, and educated. And Nicholas too, though for the sake of the great cause he would have condemned himself cheerfully never to speak to a man of his own rank and breeding again, found it a pleasant change, after his incessant wanderings among peasants, to mix with his own kind again. His few days with Constantine at Nauplia, it is true, he had much enjoyed, for it was impossible not to be happy when that apostle of happiness, the little Mitsos, was by; and Constantine, too, was of the salt of the earth. He only arrived in the evening, just before dinner, and they sat down together as soon as he had washed.

"There is a good man to hand, I think, to-day—the captain of the boat I came by," said he. "I suggested he should come and talk with us to-morrow. I would have brought him with me, but he was busy with his fig cargo."

"My dear Nicholas, you are indefatigable. I do not believe there is a man in the world but you who would wake at dawn on the gulf and instantly set about making a proselyte. You should have been a priest. What made you see a patriot in him?"

"It was a long shot," said Nicholas. "He spoke without sympathy of the new Turkish harbor dues at Corinth, and told me my capture was imminent. I risked it on that."

The archbishop frowned.

"New harbor dues? It is time to think of harbor dues when there is a harbor."

"So he said," answered Nicholas. "Their methods have simplicity. They seized six crates of his figs."

"We are commanded," remarked Germanos, "to love all men. I hope

I love the Turk, but I am certain that I do not like him. And I desire that it will please God to remove as many as possible of his kind to the kingdom of the blest or elsewhere without delay. I say so in my prayers."

Nicholas smiled.

"That gives a double sound," said he; "you pray not for their destruction, but for their speedy salvation. Is that it?"

"To love all men is a hard saying; for, indeed, I love my nation, and I am sure that the removal of the Turks will be for their permanent good. What does the psalmist say, though he was not acquainted with the Turk, 'I will wash my footsteps in the blood of the ungodly'?"

"As far as I can learn the ungodly were expecting to wash their footsteps in my blood at Corinth," said Nicholas; "but they behaved as it is only granted to Turks to behave. They expected me twenty-four hours after I had gone away."

"How did things go at Nauplia?"

"Better than I could possibly have expected. I found the very man, or rather the boy, I wanted in my young nephew."

"The little Mitsos? How old is he?"

"Eighteen, but six feet high, and with the foot of a roe-deer on the mountains. Moreover, I can trust him to the death."

"Eighteen is too young, surely," said Germanos. "Again, you can trust many people to just short of that point, and they are the most dangerous of all to work with. I could sooner work with a man I could not trust as far as a toothache!"

In answer Nicholas told him of that midnight test, and Germanos listened with interest and horror.

"You are probably right then, and I am wrong," he said; "and a boy can move about the country without suspicion where a man could not go. But how could you do so cruel a thing? Are you flesh and blood—and a young boy like that?"

"Yes, it was horrible!" said Nicholas; "but I want none but those who are made of steel. I knew by it that he was one in a thousand. He clinched his teeth, and never a word."

"What do you propose to do with him now?"

"That is what I came to talk to you about. It is time to set to work in earnest. The Club, as you know, have given me a free hand and an open purse. Mitsos must go from village to village, especially round Sparta, and tell them to begin what I told them and to be ready. The Turks are, I am afraid, on the lookout for me, and I cannot travel, as you say, in the way he can without suspicion."

"What did you tell them to begin?" asked Germanos.

"Can you ask? Surely to grind black corn for the Turk. It must be done very quickly and quietly, and chiefly up in the villages there in Maina. You say you are collecting arms here?"

"Not here, at the monastery at Megaspelaion. Many of them have been bought from the Turks themselves. There lies a sting. The monks carry them in among the maize and reed stalks. Father Priketes was met the other day by a couple of their little Turkish soldiers, who asked why

52

they were carrying so many reeds, and he said it was to mend the roof. Reeds make a capital roof."

"Yes, the monastery roof will want many mules' loads of mending," said Nicholas. "Do you suppose they suspect anything?"

"Certainly, but they have nothing to act on; besides, I would be willing to let them search the monastery from top to bottom. Do you remember the chapel there, and the great altar?"

"Surely."

"The flag-stone under the altar has been taken up and a hole made into the crypt. The door into the crypt, which opens from the passage in the floor below, has been boarded over and whitewashed, so that it looks exactly like the rest of the passage wall. It is impossible to detect it. Mehemet Salik, the new governor in Tripoli, appointed only this month from Nauplia, was there last week and examined the whole place. He is a young man, though suspicious for his age."

"That is good," said Nicholas. "Your doing, I suppose. How many guns have you?"

"About a thousand, and twice as many swords. In another month we shall be ready. Megaspelaion makes a far better centre than Patras would, as it is so much nearer Tripoli. That is where the struggle will begin."

"Who knows?" said Nicholas. "When we are ready we will begin just where it suits us. Personally, I should prefer—" He stopped.

"Well?"

"It is this," said Nicholas. "It is no gallant and polite war we want; we do not want to make terms, or treaties, or threats. We want to strike and have done with it; to exterminate. I should prefer, if possible, striking the first blow either at Kalamata or Nauplia. Then the dogs from all round would run yelping into Tripoli, as it is their strongest place, and so at the end there would be none left."

"Exterminate is no Christian word, Nicholas. The women and the children—"

"The women and children," said Nicholas, rising and pacing up and down the room; "what are they to me? Once when I was an outlaw I spared them—yes, and spared the men, too, only sending them riding back face to the horse's tail. But did they spare my wife and my child? If there is a God in heaven I will show them the mercy they showed me!"

Germanos was silent a few moments, and waited till Nicholas had sat down again.

"Will you drink more wine?" he asked; "if not, we will sit on the balcony; it is hot to-night. I think you are right about striking the first blow somewhere in the south, so that they shall go to Tripoli. I had thought before that it would be better to strike at the centre. But your plan seems to me the wiser. Come outside, Nicholas."

Germanos's house stood just out of the town, high up on the hill, which was crowned by the castle, and from his balcony they could see the twinkling lights in the fort below like holes bored in the dark, and beyond the stretch of starlit water, and dimly on the other side of the gulf the hill above Missolonghi shouldering itself up in the faint black distance. Before long the moon rose above the castle behind them, and turned the whole

53

world to silver and ebony. Cicalas chirped in the bushes, and the fragrance of the southern night came drowsily along the wind. Every now and then a noise would rise up for a moment in the town, shrill to its highest, and die away again.

A boy brought them out coffee, made thick and sweet in the Turkish manner, and two narghilés with amber mouth-pieces, and brazen bowls for holding the coarse-cut tobacco. On each he placed a glowing charcoal ember, and handed the mouth-pieces to the two men. For a long while they sat in silence, and then Nicholas spoke:

"It will be no time for mercy—I shall go where my vow leads me, and I have vowed to spare neither man, woman, nor child. I will show them the mercy they showed me, and no other."

"God make you merciful on that day, as you hope for mercy," said Germanos. "For me, I shall not be a party to any butchering of the defenceless. There will be plenty of butchers without me. Blood must be shed; it cannot be otherwise. Fight and spare not, but when the fighting is over let the rest go out of the country, for we will not have them here. But for massacre, I will not make myself no better than a Turk!"

The two narghilés bubbled in silence again for a few minutes, and at last Germanos broke in with a laugh:

"The Turks all think you are dead," he said. "I told the boy to let it be widely known that you had been killed at Corinth. It is just as well they should believe it. Mehemet Achmet, the sleepiest man God made, was here this afternoon, and he regretted it with deep-seated enjoyment. They seemed to know all about you here!"

"But none in Patras know me by sight," said Nicholas, "and as I am dead they never will. It is possible that it may prove useful to me. What are your plans for to-morrow?"

"We will do what you like. It might be well for you to see Megaspelaion. We could get there in a day if the wind held to Vostitza. They have, as I said, a curious little crypt there, which is worth a visit."

Nicholas smiled.

"It is impossible for a man to see too much," he said, "just as it is impossible for a man to pretend to know too little. I would give a fortune, if I had one, for a face like my brother-in-law Constantine's, for it is as a mask in carnival time, behind which who knows what may be? Yet there is force in him, and Mitsos obeys him as—as he obeys me! And yet he is too large a lad to take commands easily."

"Perhaps no other influence has come in yet. To fall in love, for instance, sometimes makes a good lad less obedient than an orphan to his parents."

"The little one in love would be fine," said Nicholas. "He would send the whole world to the devil. Why, shooting is the strongest passion he has known yet, and he shoots as if all the saints were watching him."

"I hope some of them are," remarked Germanos, "and that they will especially watch him when he is inclined to send the whole world to the devil. I hope Mitsos will not think of including me."

"I will warn him when I see him next. I shall go on there, I think, in November. I must get back to Maina first and see my cousin, Petros

54

Mavromichales, who is the head of the clan, and find out if the clan are prepared to rise in a body. That man Kanaris was handy enough with his boat, but I would back Mitsos to sail against him in any weather."

"Ah! that fire-ship is a horrible idea of yours, Nicholas."

"Horrible, but necessary. We must not have supplies of arms and gunpowder coming to the Turks by sea, and there must be no escape out of the death-trap which we will snap down on them. And now let me tell you all that is in my mind, for it may be we shall not meet again till the great Vintage is ripe for the gathering."

For an hour or so Nicholas talked eagerly, unfolding his schemes, Germanos listening always attentively, sometimes dissenting, but in the main approving. He spoke of the Club of Patriots in north Greece, who had given him leave to act in their name until the time came for them to send a delegate who would act openly; for at present if it became known that the leading men of Greece, many of whom were in official positions under the Turks, were concerned in schemes of revolution, the whole project would be a pricked bubble. He sketched the rising of the peasants, in whom the strength of the war would lie; the flame that should run through the land, as through summer-dry stubble, from north to south and east to west; and it seemed in after years to Germanos that a spirit of prophecy had been on the man.

And as Nicholas went on another vision rose before the bishop's eyes: the vision of his church, the mother of their hearts, throned not only there, but in the glory of an earthly magnificence, in visible splendor the bride of her Lord. Therein to him was food for hope and aspiration, and his thoughts drifted away from war and bloodshed to that.

And when Nicholas had finished he met an eye that kindled as his own, but with thoughts that were not spoken, but partook of their sweet and secret food in silence and self-communing.

CHAPTER VIII

THE MENDING OF THE MONASTERY ROOF

Kanaris had finished his unlading the same evening, and he was ready at daybreak to take Nicholas and Germanos as far as Vostitza, a fishing village lying some four miles from the mouth of the gorge, at the top of which stands Megaspelaion. Here the archbishop and Nicholas would get mules and reach the monastery the same evening. Vostitza, with their fair wind, was not more than four hours from Patras, and on arriving there the archbishop went straight to the house of the Turkish governor, from whom he procured mules, and to whom he introduced Nicholas as his cousin; and the three talked together a while over a cup of coffee, discussed the idle rumors that were abroad concerning a movement against the Turks among the Greeks, and found cause for comfort as lovers of peace in the undoubted fact that Nicholas had been killed two days before at Corinth. He was a turbulent, hot-headed man, said the archbishop, and did not value the blessings of tranquillity. His cousin also had met him, a quarrelsome, wine-bibbing fellow, quoth Nicholas; he could have had no more appropriate end than a brawl in a wine-shop.

Thus they chatted very pleasantly and harmoniously while their mules were being made ready, and Said Aga, who was no man of the sword, being rotund and indolent in habit, was much relieved to find that Germanos scoffingly dismissed the idea of any hostile movement being on foot among the Greeks. True, there had been disturbances lately; a Turkish tax-collector had been killed at Diakopton, three miles from Vostitza. Had they not heard? The news had come yesterday!

"Alas! for this unruly people," said Germanos. "What was the manner of it?"

"I hardly know," said Said Aga. "It was the usual story, I believe. He had taken to himself a Greek woman, and the husband killed him. The man has fled, but they will catch him, and he will suffer, and then die. For me, I shrug my shoulders at these things. We Turks have certain customs, and the Prophet himself had four wives, and when we are the lords of a country we must be obeyed."

"True," said Nicholas, "quite true, and we must submit. It is not the will of God that all men should be equal."

He caught Germanos's eye for a moment.

"I am glad that you think there is nothing in these rumors," went on Said Aga. "Your countrymen would hardly be so foolish as to attempt anything of the sort. But the rumors are somewhat persistent. It was even said that the monks at Megaspelaion were collecting arms, and my colleague Mehemet Salik, a very energetic young man who was lately put in charge at Tripoli, thought best to make an inspection there. But he was quite satisfied there was no truth in it."

Germanos laughed heartily.

"That is a little too much," he said. "You may at least rest assured that we priests of God are men of peace. Our mules, they tell me, are ready. A thousand thanks, Excellency, for your kindness."

They mounted and rode up the straying village street, paved with big, uneven stones. The villagers were all out in the fields for the fruit harvest, and the rough, shaggy-haired dogs, keeping watch in the deserted house-yards, came rushing out barking and snarling with bared teeth at the sound of their mules with their tinkling bells and iron-shod feet grating over the cobbles. The mule-boys paid little attention to their noisy menaces, though now and then some dog more savage or less wisely valorous than his fellows would come within stick distance, only to be sent back with better cause for crying than before.

But in ten minutes or so they got clear of the village, and taking one of the field roads struck across the plain towards the mouth of the gorge, about four miles distant. The grapes were not yet so far advanced as at Nauplia and still hung hard, and tinged with color only on the sunward side; but the fruit harvest was going on, and under the fig-trees were spread coarse strips of matting on which the fragrant piles were laid to dry. A few late pomegranate-trees were still covered with their red wax-like blossoms, but on most the petals had fallen, and the fruit, like little green-glazed pitchers, was beginning to swell and darken towards maturity. The men were at work in the vineyards cutting channels for the water, and through the green of the fig-trees you could catch sight every now and then of the brightly-colored petticoat of some woman picking the fruit, or else her presence was only indicated, where the leaves were thicker, by the dumping of the ripe figs onto the canvas strips below. The sun was right overhead before they struck the mouth of the gorge, and the heat intense— a still, fruit-ripening heat in the heavy air of the plains. But as they approached the hills a cooler draught slid down from between the enormous crags, bearing on it the voice of the brawling torrent, which is fed by the snow of Cyllene and Helmos, and knows not drought.

Here the country was given up to olives and wheat, and occasional clumps of maize near the bed of the stream. The oleanders were still in flower, and their great clusters of pink blossom marked the course of the river. Another mile took them to the ford, on the far side of which the path began to climb through the ever-narrowing gorge. Further up they found it impossible to keep to the course of the stream, for the road had been washed away in places and not repaired, and leaving it on their right, they turned up over a steep grassy stretch of moor, sprinkled here and there with pines. Looking back they could see below them the hot luxuriant plain they had left, trembling sleepily under the blue haze of heat, and further off the shimmering waters of the gulf. As they ascended the vegetation changed: pines entirely took the place of the olives, and the grass, all brown and dead below from the summer's heat, began to be flushed with lively green, and studded with wild campanulas and little blue gentians, throbbing hotly with color. Then descending again they passed along the upper slope of the cliffs above the gorge and saw before them the deep, sheltered valley stretching up to Kalavryta, a land of streams and a garden of the Lord.

The sun was already near its setting when they joined the main road leading up to the monastery from the valley, and they struck into a train of some half-dozen mules covered and enveloped in loads of reeds, the tops of which brushed rustling along the ground behind like some court lady's dress. Two of the monks from the monastery were in charge of these, and when they saw who it was with Nicholas they stopped and kissed the archbishop's hands. As they moved forward again he said:

"I see you are carrying reeds, my sons. From where did they come, and for what purpose?"

"From Kalavryta, father," said one. "We have six mules laden with them. The monastery roof needs mending."

"That is good. Observe, Nicholas, how fine these reeds are. They seem to be a heavy load. The monastery roof, they say, wants mending."

The younger of the two monks smiled.

"A great many things want mending, father!" he said. "We are making preparations for mending them."

Nicholas, who was in front, checked his mule.

"And have you black corn," he said, "good black corn for the Turk?"

The monk shook his head.

"I do not understand," he said.

Germanos smiled back at Nicholas.

"A roof for the monastery first, Nicholas," he said; "there will be time for the good black corn when the roof is mended. And now, my son, I will ask you to go forward quickly and tell Father Priketes, with my salutations, that my cousin and I will arrive very soon. We shall stop with him for a day, or it may be two, for we wish to superintend this mending of the monastery roof, and see that it is well done for the glory of God."

Another half-hour through the gathering dusk brought them in sight of the monastery, which from the distance was indistinguishable from the face of the cliff, against which it was built. Chains of light shone from the narrow windows, row above row, some from the height of all its twelve stories, twinkling a hundred feet above them, as if from cottages perched high on the cliff, others larger and nearer from the windows of the sacristy and library. To the right stood the great gateway, about which several moving lanterns seemed to show that the news of their coming had anticipated them, and that due preparations were being made to receive the archbishop. As they got close they could see that the monks were pouring out of the arch, and taking their places in rows on each side of the terrace leading up to the gate. In front of them stood the novices, some mere boys of fourteen and fifteen, but all dressed alike, and all with long hair, that had never known the scissors, flowing onto their shoulders. In the centre of the gateway—a tall, white-bearded figure—stood Father Priketes, who helped the archbishop to dismount, and then knelt to receive his blessing. Germanos paused a moment as he entered, and said in a loud, clear voice to them all:

"The peace of God be upon this holy house and all within it, and His blessing be upon the work"—and his voice dwelt on the word—"upon the work you are doing."

Nicholas was already known to Father Priketes, but the latter looked as if he had seen a ghost when he caught sight of him.

"We heard you were dead," he said.

Nicholas smiled.

"I am delighted to know it, father," he said. "Do not destroy the idea, if you please."

They passed on to Father Priketes's rooms, where they were alone.

"I see your repairs are going on steadily," said Germanos. "We passed some laden mules on the way. Nicholas wished much to see what you were doing. He is—how shall I say it?—our overseer; we are the workmen. He will tell us when the work must be finished. Let us go at once to the chapel, my brother, and thank St. Luke, your founder, and the Blessed Virgin, that they have brought us here safe. That is the first duty of the soldiers of God."

58

Father Priketes led the way to the chapel, and pushed open the great brazen door for Germanos to enter. He knelt in turn before the great altar, the altar to the Beloved Physician, and before the black relief of the Virgin, made, as tradition says, by the hands of St. Luke himself, and said for himself and Nicholas a thanksgiving for the aid of the Saints which had brought them safely to the end of their journey. They then supped with Father Priketes, and went back to the chapel.

The place was but dimly lighted with oil lamps, and after locking the door behind them—for at present only a few of the monks had been trusted with the secret of the crypt—the father lighted a lantern and led the way up to the east end. Then after crossing himself he drew from underneath the altar a small crowbar, and creeping under with the lantern, he prized away a square paving-stone, which covered a hole large enough for a single man to creep through. Rough wooden steps had been erected from the floor of the crypt up to the level of this, and one by one they descended. The crypt was some forty feet long by twenty broad, and the light of the lantern struck from all the walls a reflection of steel. Since Germanos's last visit, they had largely added to the number of arms, and on a hasty glance Nicholas reckoned that there could not be less than fifteen hundred guns.

His eyes glistened as he moved the lantern round the walls, and he turned to Father Priketes.

"This will make a hole in the Turks bigger than the hole in your roof," he said. "You have enough, I think. They will be hungry, these reeds; grind their food for them, and do not let them feel stint of that."

"Already?" asked Father Priketes.

"Already! It is August now, and when our vineyards are green with the fresh leaves in the spring, the juice of the greater vintage shall be spilled. And there will be a mighty gathering; the wine-press will be running red, and fuller than the vats of Solomon. Where can you stow the food for all these hungry throats?"

"There is room here, is there not?"

"Surely, room and to spare; but it would not be well to keep it here. Whoever enters here must carry a light; a chance spark, and he may cry to the Virgin in vain."

Father Priketes paused a moment.

"You shall take a walk with me to-morrow and we will see. You are satisfied at present?"

"I shall never be satisfied," said Nicholas. "I should not be satisfied if I saw all the armaments of angels in array against the Turk. But it is time to think of other things. Could you raise men at once?"

"Five hundred in one minute from within these walls," said Father Priketes, "and two thousand more in the time it would take an eager man to climb up here from Kalavryta."

Nicholas looked round again, smiling as a man smiles to look on one he loves.

"This feeds my soul," he said. "And swords too, little sickles for the gathering! Look you, perhaps we shall not meet again till after our vintage has begun; but remember this: After four months from now, we cannot tell when the day of the beginning of the gathering will come, and so be ready.

59

Whatever the archbishop orders, do it, for he and I work together. And, O Father, let no man take thought for himself on that day. What matters it to whom the honor and the glory go, if once Greece is free? If you desire such things, I give to you now by bequest all the honor and riches that may come to me. Forgive me for saying this, but that is the only loophole where failure may creep into our camp, and that I fear more than ten Sultans and their armies. I say the same thing to all, and I remind myself of it daily. I have been chosen to conduct this matter, for the present, in the Morea, and I will give my life and all I possess to it; and in company with others, of whom the archbishop is one, and Petros Mavromichales, of Maina, another, I will do my best, so help me God, honestly and without a selfish mind. The moment a single dissentient voice is raised, not in the matter of councils or plan of actions, on which we will listen to all that is to be said, but of command and obedience, I only ask leave to serve in the ranks. Let us deliberate together by all means till the time comes to act, but when that time comes, and a word of command goes through the country, let there be no delay. For all will depend, so I take it, on the speed with which we act when we come to action. This is the beginning and the end of success, and all that lies between."

"But how is the word of command to come," said Father Priketes, who had secretly hoped for a little independent campaign, "if you are not with us? Must I not act on my own judgment?"

"No, a thousand times no," said Nicholas. "What I have seen here shows me that you in Megaspelaion and Patras will be no small portion of our first success. How the war will spread afterwards, God knows; but when the first grapes are cut it will be you, so I think, to garner them. This is why you must obey absolutely. Nothing will be left to your judgment. A message will come, and you will obey."

"How am I to tell who your messenger is?"

Nicholas smiled.

"Some afternoon, when you are sitting in the spring sunshine, or perhaps some night in this next winter, when you are sleeping, a monk will come to you and say, 'There is a man here, or a boy it may be, or a girl even, who wishes to see you, and we cannot understand what he means.' Then you will delay not, but go and see what it is. You will say, 'I am Father Priketes; you have a message for me?' And the message will be in this form: 'I am bidden to ask you if there is corn to be given to those who need it?' And you will say, 'Is it black corn they need, and are the needy hungry, or are they Turks?' And the messenger will say, 'Send black corn for the Turks to Kalamata or Kalavryta, or wherever it is, and let two hundred or five hundred or a thousand men carry it.' Other instructions may come as well, but always in that form. And as you obey, so may the Lord give you a place among His saints in heaven."

Father Priketes was silent for a moment.

"You are right, Nicholas," he said; "and I swear by the picture of the mother of God that I will obey in all things. Come, shall we go up again?"

They climbed up into the chapel, and went out down the vaulted stone passage to the story below, where another passage, whitewashed and boarded on both sides, led to the monks' library and Father Priketes's own rooms. Nicholas, who carried in his hand an olive-wood stick, tapped the panelling carelessly as he went along, and once stopped a moment and smiled at Germanos.

"The wall seems to be a little less thick here than at other places," he said. "Mehemet Salik, however, was too cunning to attend to such simple things."

"The Lord be praised for making so many clever men," said Germanos, piously. "To have a fool for an enemy has been the undoing of more good people than Satan himself."

They went on to Father Priketes's room where they had supped before, and Nicholas lit himself a pipe.

"That is quite true," he said. "A fool is always blundering into the weak place by accident—there is nothing so disconcerting; whereas a clever man is on the lookout for less patent weaknesses, and passes over the patent ones on purpose. And the Turk is both clever and indolent—a very happy combination."

"For us," said Priketes, who had, as Nicholas once said, a wonderful faculty for seeing that which was obvious.

"As you say, for us," said Nicholas; "and we intend to profit by it. And now, father, with your leave I will go to bed. I have seen all I came to see, and think I had better push on to-morrow. You will find, no doubt, a prudent place for your granary. It is impossible to be too prudent now, just as it will be more than possible to be too wary hereafter. When once we get into the open we keep there until all is finished."

"Where do you go now?" asked Germanos.

"Southwards," said Nicholas. "I must travel as widely as I can in Messenia, and also see my cousin Petrobey. The Maina district will be raised by him. If once the war begins, as I would have it to begin, I shall be at ease about the rest. Only the beginning must be as sudden as the thunderbolt. Ah, but there is fever in my blood for that!"

Nicholas, as his custom was, rose early next morning and went from the dark-panelled room, where he had slept, down towards the chapel. The great green bronze bell hanging in the wooden balcony outside had just begun to ring for matins, and the sound, grave and sonorous, floated out over the valley like a dream. He waited there awhile looking at the blackened Byzantine paintings which covered the roof, till the monks began trooping up the cobbled passage, and with the first of them he went inside the chapel. From the centre of the roof hung a great gilt candelabrum in the form of a crown, and from side to side of the building ran a row of silver lamps—some thirty in number—which had been burning all night, but looked red and dim in the fresh morning light. Set in the gilt altar-screen were the paintings of the Panagia and of Christ, and at the south end—more precious to the faithful than all—the wax relief of the Virgin and Child. The silver panel, behind which it is placed, had been opened, and Nicholas, with the others, made his obeisance before it. The head of the Virgin and the head of the Child are all that can be seen, and these are black with age; the rest is one mass of chased gold. The crown

61

which the Child wears is studded with rubies and emeralds grown dim; His mother's crown is less magnificent; and on the silver rail in front of it hang the offerings of those to whom, in the days of faith, its contemplation had brought healing of many diseases. Over the gate to the altar hung two stoles of red velvet, in which the priest who said the mass would robe himself. A border of gold holly leaves ran down them on each side, and down the middle they were embroidered with floreated and cusped ornaments in red and gold, in the centre of each of which was worked the figure of Christ. On the north wall, by the easternmost of the monks' stalls, hung the picture of the daughter of the Emperor Palæologus. She is dressed in a red cloak with golden eagles embroidered over it; her hair is golden auburn, and she raises a face charmingly childlike and naïve, and holds up hands of prayer to the gracious figure of the Virgin who stands beside her.

Priketes and Germanos were the last to enter, and when the short prayers were said, Nicholas went out with them, and they walked up and down the terrace awhile talking. Some of the elder monks, with their purple cassocks trimmed with fur wrapped closely round them, sat outside the iron-sheeted gate, under the fresco of Adam and Eve being driven out from Paradise, which fills the triangular space above it, watching them with eager attention, for it had become known who Nicholas was and what his errand. On their right rose the enormous mass of the monastery, crowned by an overhanging cliff of gray rock, which the smoke from the chimney had stained in places to a rich vandyke-brown, in the hollow of which, as in the hollow of a sheltering hand, the great pile of buildings stood, seeming rather to have been the core round which the rock rose than to have been built into it. In front the ground fell rapidly away into the valley, but was terraced up into little gardens, full of cypresses and poplars or figs and plane trees; under these stood many little wooden arbors, trellised over with vines, where the brethren spent their tranquil days; and a hundred riotous streams—some conducted down wooden shoots, some straying over the paths—rattled headlong to join the river below. Further down, the hill-side was covered with low-growing scrub, and on the opposite side of the valley, the village of Zachlórou hung on by teeth and nails to the climbing moor. A company of swallows cut curves and circles in the thin morning air, their black backs showing metallic, like oxidized steel in the sunlight, and a great flight of white pigeons clattered out of the rock above and settled in a cloud by the fountain. In one of these little arbors Germanos and Nicholas drank their coffee and smoked a pipe of the monastery tobacco until the latter's horse was brought round. Then, rising,

"We shall meet again," he said, "when the vintage is ripe, or, if we meet not, we shall both be laborers in the treading; you here, I perhaps in the south. So now, father, give me your blessing, for I must go on my way."

CHAPTER IX

THE SINGER FROM THE DARKNESS

November went out with a fortnight of cold showers and biting winds, and the woodcock came down in hundreds to the plain of Nauplia. Often when the curtain of cloud which veiled Mount Elias day by day was rent raggedly in two by some blast in the upper air, the higher slope of the mountain, it could be seen, was sprinkled with snow. Then the peak would again wrap itself in folds of tattered vapors as a beggar throws his torn cloak over his shoulder, and perhaps would not peer through the mists again for a couple of days. Down in the plain scudding showers swept across from north to south and east to west, and the earth, still thirsty from the long drought of the summer, drank them in feverishly as a sick man drains the glass by his bedside and turns to sleep again.

Mitsos had many round oaths for this horrible weather, but like a wise lad cursed and had done with it. The bay and the sweet possibilities of the bay were only in the range of thought, but the woodcock were more accessible, and with something of the air of a martyr he would pass a long day on the uplands towards Epidaurus, and come back, after the fall of dark, with a leash of woodcock, and an appetite which bordered on the grotesque, singing and contented. But later in the evening he would be twitched by an eager restlessness, and make many journeys to the door to see if the weather had cleared, or showed signs of clearing, only to be met by a buffeting clap of windy rain in the face, which made him close it again quickly, for where was the use, he argued, of lying rolling and rocking off the white wall if he was to be alone there? Once or twice during this fortnight he had sailed by it, but his wages were only a wetting. Constantine was somewhat puzzled and perplexed at Mitsos' behavior about this time, but he took it all with his habitual serenity of tolerance, and likened him in his own mind to a colt who is just beginning to find out that he is a horse, and, knowing his own strength and learning his needs, whinnies and kicks up his heels. He knew that it would be useless to try to extract unvolunteered information out of Mitsos, and he guessed more nearly to the truth than he knew, that Mitsos' somewhat spasmodic moods were merely the natural results of his budding manhood, and were as inexplicable to him as they were to his father. Meantime, though they had neither heard nor seen anything more of Nicholas, Constantine felt that Mitsos was growing in the way he would have him grow, and was increasing in self-reliance and surefootedness of mind just as he was increasing in bodily strength and stature.

But Mitsos was exercising more self-control than his father gave him credit for. That acquaintance with Suleima, the Greek girl in the harem of the Turk, begun so strangely, had ripened no less strangely. He had sat below the wall night after night and talked to her from his boat, rocking gently in the swell, or standing still and steady in the calm water, till with a

63

sign she motioned him away, seeing some other woman of the harem or one of the servants come out into the garden.

Then Suleima had made a confidante of one of the elder women, who, seeing Mitsos' handsome, laughing face, had given her sympathy, and, what was better, a practical exhibition of it, and had promised to watch in the garden so that they might talk without fear of interruption; stipulating, however, through Suleima as interpreter, half laughing, yet half in earnest, that Mitsos should give her a kiss for every time she watched for them. Suleima had felt herself flushing as she interpreted this into Greek, but Mitsos' tone reassured her as he answered,

"She might as well do it for nothing. Oh, don't translate that, but say we are very much obliged. Pay-day is long in the house of a Turk."

Then there came an evening, only just before the weather had broken, when Mitsos took down to the boat a little rope ladder. Suleima had told him that he was to come there late, not before midnight, and she would have gone to her room early, saying she was not well. Then, if possible, she would come out to him, and they would go for a sail together.

It was an evening to be remembered—to be lived over again in memory. Her reluctance and eagerness to come; the terrorizing risk of discovery, which none the less was a whetstone to her enjoyment; her delight at getting out, though only for an hour or two; her half-frightened, childish exclamations of dismay as Mitsos put about, when the water began to curl back from the forefoot of the boat as they went hissing out to sea before the wind; her face looking as if it was made of ebony and ivory beneath the moonlight, with its thin, black eyebrows, and long, black eyelashes; her sense of innocent wickedness, as in response to Mitsos' entreaties she unveiled it altogether; her curious, fantastic story of how she was carried off years ago by a Turk, and had forgotten all about her home, except that her father was a tall man with a long, black dress; her pretty, hesitating pronunciation of Greek; her bewildering treatment of himself as if he was a boy, as he was, and she a person of mature experience, as she was not, being a year younger than he; the view which she took of this moonlight sail as just a childish freak, heavily paid for if discovered, and to be repeated if not, while to him it was the opening of heaven. Then, as he still remained serious, looking at her with wide eyes of shy adoration, she too became just a little serious as they turned homewards, and said that she liked him very much, and that old Abdul Achmet was a fat pig. Then in answer to him—Oh, no, she was quite content where she was, except when Abdul was in a bad temper or the eunuch beat her. There was plenty to eat, nothing to do, and they were all much less strictly looked after than in other harems, for Abdul was old and only cared for one of them. For herself she was a favorite servant of his chief wife, and not really in the harem. It was not very exciting, but if Mitsos would come again now and then and take her for sails she would be quite happy. Finally, it was useless for him to come except when it was fine, for the harem was always locked up in wet weather, and she would not be able to get into the garden. Also, she hated rain like a cat.

Then intervened the fortnight when the climate of Nauplia, which for the most part is that of the valley of Avilion, gave way to the angry moods of a child—to screaming, sobbing, and steady weeping. The surface of the bay was churned up by the rain and streaked with foam by the wind, and the big poplar-tree, under which Maria had slept, shook itself free of its summer foliage and stood forth in naked, gnarled appeal to the elements. For a fortnight the deluge continued, but on the night of the 1st of December, Mitsos, waking at that strange moment when the earth turns in her sleep, and cattle and horses stand up and graze for a moment before lying down again, saw with half an eye the shadow of the bar of his window cast sharply onto the floor of his bedroom by the slip of the crescent moon, which rode high in a starry sky, and when he woke again it was to see a heaven of unsullied blue washed clean by the rain.

Half the day he spent dreaming and dozing in the veranda, for he meant to be out on the bay that night, and after his mid-day dinner he went down to overhaul the boat, taking with him his fishing-net and a bag of resin. He had wrapped up in the centre of the net the pillow from his bed, for Suleima had said that the net on which she sat before smelled fishy. But after supper that night he found himself beset by a strange perplexity, the like of which he had never felt. His fustanella was old and darned; it was hardly suitable. It did very well before, but somehow now— and the moon would be larger to-night. The perplexity gained on him, and eventually he took out and put on his new clothes, only worn on festa days, which were thoroughly unsuitable for rough fishing by night. He brushed his hair with extreme care, and wished it was sleek and smooth like Yanko's, instead of growing in crisp, strong curls, put his red cap rakishly on the side of his head, and laced up his brown cloth leggings to the very top. All this was done with the greatest precision and seriousness, and he went down-stairs on tiptoe for fear of wakening his father, who was already abed, and had left injunctions with him to lock the door and take the key with him if he was likely to be late.

It was about half-past ten when he set off, and the moon had risen. It took him an hour or more to reach the dim, white wall, for the breeze was yet but light and variable. As he neared it he began to feel his heart pulsing in his throat, as it had done one night before when he passed the scene of the hanging by the wayside, but somehow differently, and he peered out anxiously into the darkness to see if there was any one there. Something white glimmered on the wall, down went his sail, and a few minutes later the nose of his boat grated against the stone-work.

She gave a little chuckling laugh.

"I thought you would come," she said, "on the first night of stars. They are all in bed. I listened at Mohammed's door; he was Mohammed no more—only a grunt and a snore."

Mitsos said nothing, but threw the ladder and rope on the wall and sprang up himself.

"Yes, I have come," he said. "Ah, how I have been cursing this rain— may the saints forgive me!—but I cared not, and cursed."

Suleima looked at him a moment.

"Why, how smart you are!" she said. "Is it the Greek use that a man goes fishing in his best clothes? Oh, my clean fustanella!" she cried, looking sideways on him.

Mitsos smiled. The best clothes had been a good thought, in spite of a momentary confusion.

"Hush!" he whispered, "we will talk in the boat. I will hold the ladder. There, it is quite steady."

The girl stepped lightly down the rungs, and Mitsos, directing her to sit still, threw the ladder and rope back and let himself down onto the side of the boat.

"Where shall we go to-night?" he asked.

The girl laughed gently—the echo, as it were, of a laugh.

"Oh, out, out to sea," she said; "right away from this horrible place. Where shall I sit?"

Mitsos took the pillow out of the net and put it for her at the stern of the boat.

"See," he said. "I remembered that you said the net smelled fishy, and I have brought you my pillow to sit on. There—is there a more comfortable seat in all Greece?"

She sat down, and the boy busied himself with the boat for a few minutes. He had to row out a dozen strokes or so until they got from under the lee of the wall, and the wind, catching the sail, slowly bulged it out taut; the boat dipped and bowed a moment and then began to move quickly forward towards the mouth of the bay. He stood a few seconds irresolute until Suleima spoke.

"Well, have you finished?" she asked.

"Yes. We shall run straight before the wind as far as you like."

She pointed with her hand to the seat beside her.

"Come and sit by me," she said.

There was silence between them for several minutes—she with a smile hiding in the depths of her dark eyes; he, serious and tongue-tied. The air was full of the freshness of the night and of the sea, but across that there came to him some faint odor from her—a warm smell of a live thing, too delicate to describe. Then she drew from her pocket a small box and opened it.

"See what I have brought you," she said—"Rahat-la-koom. How do you call it in Greece? Sweets, anyhow. Do you like sweets?"

She took a lump of the sticky, fragrant stuff out of the box and offered it to Mitsos as a child offers sweets to another child.

"Do you like it?" she asked again. "Abdul gave me the stuff last night. I was afraid when he gave it to me, but he did not stop. As I told you, I am not of the harem."

Mitsos flushed. Suleima spoke with the naïveté of a child, and yet somehow it made him ashamed to think that even he was sitting alone with her, and furious at the thought that that fat Turk, whom he had seen at Nauplia only a few days before, should dare to give her sweets.

"How silent you are, Mitsos!" she went on. "Tell me what you have been doing all this time. For me, I have done nothing—nothing—nothing. I have never been so dull."

Mitsos looked up suddenly.

"Are you less dull now?" he said. "Do you care to come out like this with me?"

"Surely, or else I should not come. I think I have even missed you, which is odd, for I never missed any one before. I care for none of those in the house, and some I hate."

Mitsos took her hand in his.

"Promise you will never hate me," he said.

Suleima laughed.

"That is a big thing to promise," she said, "for 'never' is the greatest of all words, greater even than 'always'; but I don't feel as if I should ever hate you. I liked you since the first, even before I had ever seen you, when you sang that song out of the darkness. It was very rash and foolish of you, for Abdul would make nothing of having a sailor-boy shot. Supposing I had been—well, some one else—I should have told Abdul, and thus there would have been no more songs for Mitsos."

"But because it was you, you did not?" asked Mitsos, awkwardly. "Yet if it had not been you, I should not have sung to you."

The girl's hand still rested in his, but suddenly she disengaged it.

"You are talking nonsense," she said, quickly, yet finding nonsense somehow delightful; "of course, if you had not sung to me you would not have sung to me. By the way, Zuleika—"

She stopped suddenly.

"Who is Zuleika?" said Mitsos; "and what of her?"

"Oh, nothing. Zuleika is the woman who watched to see that no one came while we talked. She's quite old, you know, though not as old as Abdul. Well, why shouldn't I tell you? Zuleika is getting impatient for her payment. She watched four times, she said, but I am sure it was only three. Won't you pay her?"

Mitsos got up and stood in front of her.

"Zuleika, what is Zuleika to me?" he said again.

The girl stared at him for a moment. "Are you angry, Mitsos? Why should you be angry? But—but—"

Mitsos turned away impatiently.

"Why are you angry?" repeated the girl. "Is it because of what Zuleika said? I told you because I thought it would please you. Most men, I think, would like to hear that sort of thing. Zuleika says you are the handsomest boy she ever saw, and she is pretty herself—at least I suppose she is pretty."

Mitsos had the most admirable temper, and though it had been touched in a quarter where he could not have anticipated attack, he regained it in a moment.

"Never mind Zuleika," he said, sitting down again; "go on talking to me. I like to hear you talk, and give me your hand again. Put it in mine; it is so soft and white. I never saw a hand like yours!"

Suleima laughed.

"There you are, then. Oh, Mitsos, don't squeeze it so; you hurt me! What shall I talk about? I have nothing to talk about. Nothing ever happened to me. Zuleika—"

"Don't talk about Zuleika!" said Mitsos, between his teeth.

"Well, you told me to talk. I don't want to talk about Zuleika. Oh, Mitsos, look how far we are out! There is Nauplia behind us. We must go back!"

"No, not yet."

"But we must! It will take us an hour or more to get back! Please let us go back, Mitsos?"

Mitsos sat still a moment.

"Tell me you don't want to go back," he said, in a whisper.

"Of course I don't; why should I tell you that? I should like to be thus with you always, you alone, and no other."

Mitsos sprang up.

"I'll put about," he said.

There were two or three moments of confusion, as the heavy sail flapped and shook. The wind had veered a point towards the east, and they could get back in a couple of tacks. Mitsos stood up till the boat had settled down on the homeward journey, and then, with the tiller in one hand, he sat down again by Suleima's side.

"It will be fine weather now," he said, "and will you come out with me again? You tell me you like it."

Suleima nestled a little closer to him. "Yes, I like it," she said, "but we must not go too often. But if you care to, you can come to the wall in fine weather always, and I will tell you whether it is possible. And, Mitsos, next time we go out bring your spear and resin, and let me see you fish. I should like to see you do that. Do you catch many?"

"The devil fly away with the fish!" said Mitsos. "I would sooner talk to you."

"How funny! I would sooner you fished; and, you see, we can talk, too. Will you let me help?"

Mitsos took up one of her hands again.

"It would be a heavy net you could draw in!" he said. "You have never felt the tug of a shoal."

"A whole shoal?" asked Suleima. "How many fish go to the shoal?"

Mitsos laughed. "Fifty for each of your fingers," he said, "and a hundred to spare. Sometimes they all swim together against the net, and though they are very little, many of them are strong, and pull like a horse. I cut my finger to the bone once against the net-rope. Look, here is the mark."

He held up his great brown hand, and Suleima traced with her little finger a white scar running up to the second joint of his forefinger.

"How horrid!" she said, concernedly, still drawing her finger up and down his. "Did it bleed much?"

"Half a bucketful. I must put the boat on the other tack. Take care; the sail will come across again."

The air struck cold as they went more into the wind, and Suleima wrapped her black bernouse more closely round her and nestled under shelter of the lad.

"You are cold?" he asked, suddenly.

68

"No, Mitsos, not if you sit like that. But isn't it ice to you? Have another piece of Rahat-la-koom?"

Mitsos grinned, showing his white teeth. "That will keep out the cold finely," he said. "Give it me yourself!"

They were rapidly approaching the wall, and in ten minutes more Mitsos stood up and took in the sail. The speed slackened, and, standing at the bows, he leaned forward, and, thrusting out with the pole, he brought the boat alongside. Then, springing up again, with the rope in his hand, he told Suleima to throw him up the end of the ladder. This he held down with his foot on the far side of the wall while she climbed up, pleasantly feeling the muscles of his leg strain as she stepped onto the rope.

The ground on the inside was a foot or two below the top of the wall, and, standing on the top a moment before stepping down, she suddenly bent her head down to him, and, brushing back his curls with her hand, kissed him lightly on the forehead.

"Good-night, little Mitsos," she whispered.

Then all in a flash her face flushed. "Mitsos," she said, quickly, and with a curious shyness, "promise me you will never kiss Zuleika; she is an old witch!" and without waiting for his reply she ran across to the dark house.

Mitsos sat perfectly still, tingling and alert, and he felt the blood throb and beat in his temples. He half started from his place to run after her, and half raised his voice to call, but remembered in time that he was close to the Turk's house. Something which let the two sit together like children was dead, but something had taken its place, and his heart sang to him.

He dropped down again into the boat, and for half an hour more he sat there without stirring, hearing the ripples tap against the side, and seeing them break in dim phosphorescent gleams of light. Then, with wonder on his lips and a smile in his eyes, he went silently home through the still night.

It was the night of the 1st of January, 1821, and Mitsos and Suleima were again sailing across the bay; this time, however, not out to sea, but to the shelving bays underneath the Tripoli hills, the scene of the fishing with Nicholas. It was the first time the two had been able to go out together since the night last recorded, for on that occasion Suleima had been caught by the eunuch coming in from the garden. Luckily for them both, Mitsos had not been seen, and her excuse was that she had a headache and could not sleep, so had sat in the garden for a while. Nothing more could be got out of her, and Zuleika, for one reason or another, had been loyal enough to preserve silence. But Suleima got beaten, and she judged it more prudent not to have any more headaches for a time. But as the fate that watches over wooings would have it, one night a fortnight afterwards the eunuch was found drunk, a particularly heinous crime, and, to one of his religion, blasphemous; and he was, therefore, dismissed. Suleima was sedulous to note the habits of his successor, and observed with much approval that he went to bed early and slept soundly, and at length she ventured to resume her excursions. She had more leisure than usual after her detection, for she was solitary behind lock and key; she had no sweets to eat, and her thoughts were ever with Mitsos. She, who had hardly seen a man, and had certainly never in the last ten years spoken to one except to the black, thick-lipped eunuch and Abdul Achmet, whose small, sensual eyes looked at her like a mole's about his fat, pendulous cheeks, could hardly believe that they and Mitsos, with his sun-browned, boyish face and fit, slender limbs, were creatures of the same race. From the first time that she had seen him only dimly as he sat in his boat, swaying regularly and gracefully to its motion, and heard him singing the old song which she remembered from her childhood, she had thought how charming it would be to live on his pattern, as free as the spring swallows, wholesomely and cleanly in the open air. Surely he had caught something, indefinable perhaps, but none the less certain, from wind and sun—a something which reminded her of a clear, light summer morning, when it was so pleasant to come out of the close, perfumed house, to have a breath of a more airy fragrance thrown at her by the sea-breeze, and feel with a cool shock a few dew-drops from the great climbing rose about the door shaken onto the bare flesh by the wind; for, unlike the Turks, she came of an outdoor race, and the inherited instinct had not been altogether eradicated by her hot-house, enclosed life.

Then by degrees this feeling had grown less general, but more personal. It was doubly delightful to be able to talk confidentially and naturally, as one child talks to another, to some one of her own age. She liked talking to Zuleika, but she preferred talking to Mitsos; it was a pleasure to make him laugh and show the milkiness of his white teeth, and she could always make him laugh. Zuleika had hideous teeth; one was all black and discolored, and for whole days together she would sit, a sloppy, dishevelled object, by the fire, saying it ached. She felt quite sure that Mitsos' teeth never ached, and for herself she did not know what aching meant. Again, when Abdul Achmet laughed, his cheeks wrinkled up till his eyes were nearly closed, and two queerest little dimples were dug one on each side of his mouth. What would happen, she had thought once, if she made him laugh and then held his eyes open so that they could not shut? She would have liked to try.

Then Mitsos—she felt it in her bones—evidently liked her very much, in quite a different way from which any one had liked her before. Zuleika liked her in a tepid, intermittent manner; but when her tooth ached she ignored her altogether, and had once slapped her in the face for a too obtrusive sympathy. And when Abdul came and took her chin between his fingers and turned up her face to his, and told her that she was getting very pretty, she turned cold all over. It reminded her of the way he had pointed at one of the turkeys in the yard and said it was becoming beautifully fat. Again, it had been quite unaccountably delightful to sit close to Mitsos and shelter under him from the wind, to be close to him and know him near. Finally, when they parted that night, and she had brushed back the curls from his forehead and kissed him, her feeling had been more unaccountable still. She had done it unthinkingly, but the moment it was done a whole mill-race of thoughts went bubbling unbidden

70

through her head. She wanted to do it again, she wanted him to take her in his arms and press her close to him—she would not mind if it hurt. She hated Zuleika. She understood in a moment why, if Mitsos knew the least part of what she felt, he should have been angry when she told him what Zuleika said, and the next words had come out of her mouth outstripping, so it seemed, her thought. Then she had felt suddenly shy and frightened; she longed to stop where she was, for surely Mitsos understood what was so intimate to her. And so, being a woman, she instantly ran away, and never looked behind.

To-night she had sat by the wall for half an hour before he came, and the thought that perhaps he would not come had brought into her eyes silent, childish tears. He must come; she could not do without him. For herself she would have sat on the wall every night for months to go out with him; surely he could not be tired in a week or two of coming and not finding her there. But with the rising of the moon she had seen a sail far away that got nearer, and at last the boat grated gently against the wall.

"Is it you, Mitsos?" she whispered, and for answer the rope was flung up to her, and her young, black-eyed lover sprang to her side. She descended the ladder silently and stood in the stern; while he joined her, and with a vigorous push they were floating again alone in the centre of the vast, dim immensity. He set the sail and came and stood in front of her.

"Suleima," he whispered, "last time you kissed me. Will you let me kiss you?"

"Yes, Mitsos," she said, with a great, shy, bold joy in her heart, and put her face up, and he would have kissed her lightly on the forehead as she had kissed him. But suddenly that was impossible; they were no longer children, but lovers, and the next moment his arms were flung round her neck, her mouth pressed close to his, and each kiss left them hungrier for the next.

The wind was straight behind them, and they sat where they had sat before, and talked in low voices as if in fear of the jealousy of the stars and the night. Mitsos had got his fishing-spear and bag of resin on board, and after a while, at Suleima's suggestion, they went straight before the wind to the bay, where Mitsos said he could catch fish if she cared to see him. Half an hour's sail brought them across, and, grounding the boat by a bush of blackthorn that grew thick on the top of the rocks on the edge of the tideless sea, he took Suleima in his arms and waded through the shallow water to the head of the bay where he would fish, to save her the tramp through the undergrowth, which was thick and soaked with the night dews. She was but a feather's weight in his strong arms, her head lay on his shoulder, and she threw one arm round his neck for greater security. He made her a nest under a clump of rushes that grew on the edge of the dry sand, and then went back for his fishing things. To carry Suleima to land, he had only the shallowest water at the edge of the sea to walk through, and he had just turned up the bottom of his trousers; but where he was going to fish it would be deeper, and, as usual, he slipped them off, buckling his shirt, which reached to his knees, round his waist. He then lit his flare, and, stepping off into the deeper water, which was half-thigh deep, he went slowly along, peering cautiously at the bright circle of light cast by the resin.

Fish were plentiful, and Suleima, from her nest near, clapped her hands and laughed delightedly when Mitsos speared one larger than usual, and held it up flapping and wriggling to show her. She got so excited in his proceedings that she left her seat, and walked along the edge of the sand parallel with him, observing with the keenest interest what he did. Then, when she got tired of watching, Mitsos declared he was tired of fishing, and waded to shore with a creel full of fish.

Suleima had brought with her some Turkish tobacco, which she had taken from the house, and gave it to Mitsos to smoke. The other women of the harem all smoked, she said; for herself she had tried it once, but thought it horrid to the taste. But Mitsos might smoke it—yes, she would even light his pipe for him; and with a little pout of disgust she lit it at the flare and handed it to him, and he smoked it while they looked the fish over.

It was a night for the great lovers of romance to be abroad in; the air was of a wonderful briskness, making the pulse go quick, yet gentle and soft; the moon had set behind the hills to the west, and they sat close together beneath the wonderful twilight of stars, in a little sheltered nook beneath a great clump of tall, singing rushes. On the ground, in front, lay the resin flare, already burning low; but as Mitsos would fish no more that night he did not replenish it. Lower and lower it burned, but now and then it would shoot up with a sudden leap of flame, revealing each to the other, and Suleima would smile at Mitsos; but before she could see his mouth smile in answer, the flame would die down again into a flickering spot on the glowing, bubbling ash. But in the darkness she knew he smiled back at her; a whispered word would pass from one to the other, and the last flicker of flame showed a lover to the sight of each. Then drawing closer in the darkness, as if by some law which was moving each equally, their lips met again in the kiss that seemed to have never ceased between them. And the wind sang gently in the rushes, while before them spread the broad waters of the bay, just curdled over by the breeze; above, the austere stars burned down on them; behind, rose the empty-wooded hills, where once the soft armies of Dionysus revelled in love and wine, rising into the peaks above Tripoli.

The wind dropped for a moment, the rushes were silent, and in the lull Mitsos heard a mule bell behind them no great way off. He sat up and peered across the vine-grown strip of plain which lay between them and the mountain, but the skeins of night mist hung opaque and pearly gray above it.

In a few minutes, however, the sound got sensibly nearer, and the two rose and moved a score of yards farther down the beach, for a footpath round the head of the bay to Nauplia led across the top of it. Then across the sound of the bell they could hear the pattering footsteps of the mule, and in a few minutes more it and its rider emerged from the path which lay through the vineyards onto the open ground at the head of the beach. Just then the rider checked his beast, dismounted, and tied some grass round

72

the tongue of the bell in order to muffle it, and struck a light with a flint and steel which he caught in tinder, and blew it gently till it sufficed to light his short chibouk. His face was towards them, and in the glow of the kindled tobacco it stood out vividly from the dark. It was Nicholas.

He mounted again and rode on, but Mitsos sat still, breathing hard and vacantly, and seeing only Nicholas's face standing out like a ghost in the darkness. Suleima touched him gently on the arm.

"Who was it?" she said. "He did not see us."

"It was my uncle," said Mitsos, in a dry voice. "No, he did not see us."

Then his self-control gave way, and he flung himself back on the ground.

"I am afraid," he said—"I do not know what is going to happen. He has come for me. I know it."

"For you?" asked Suleima. "What do you mean?"

"I shall have to go," said Mitsos. "Holy Virgin, but I cannot. I know nothing about what he wants me to do. I only know that I may—that I shall have to go away; that I shall have to leave you and perhaps never see you again. Oh," he cried, "I cannot, I cannot!"

Suleima was frightened.

"Mitsos, do not talk like that," she said, half sobbing; "do not be so unkind."

Mitsos recovered himself and felt ashamed.

"Oh, dearest of all and littlest," he said, soothingly, "I am a stupid brute to frighten you. Everything will be all right—I will come back—it is sure that I will come back. Only I promised him to do what he told me, and help him in something—it does not matter what—and I expect he has come to tell me he wants my help."

"Will not you tell me what it is?" asked Suleima, willing to be comforted.

"No, I promised I would keep it secret. But this I may tell you. You know they say—never repeat this—that the Greeks are going to rise against the Turks and turn them out. There may be fighting and bloodshed. But you hate the Turks as much as I do, darling, so you will be as glad as I if this comes true. Perhaps it might even happen that Abdul's house may be attacked, but you are quite safe if you will only do one thing. If ever it is attacked do not be afraid, but call out in Greek that you are a Greek and no Turk. And, oh, Suleima, pray to the Virgin and the Blessed Child that that day may come soon, for it will be thus and then that we shall be able to go together always."

"Is it about that you are going away?" said Suleima, with a sudden intuition.

Mitsos longed to tell her, but his promise to Nicholas kept him dumb. Then, as he had to answer, he lied boldly and unreservedly.

"It has nothing whatever to do with it," he said. "But oh, Suleima, forgive me for so frightening you—I did not mean what I said. And will you come to the wall again as often as you can? I may have to go away—indeed, I am afraid that is sure, but I do not know for how long. The first night I am back I shall come again to the wall, the dear white wall where we first met."

Suleima felt quite comforted. She was sure that nothing could go really wrong as long as Mitsos drew breath, and she bent down his head and kissed him.

"Yes, Mitsos, I will come to the wall whenever I can, hoping only that you may be there, because, you know, I care for you more than all the rest of the world. And now carry me back to the boat, strong-armed one. It is time I went back."

Mitsos stooped and lifted her up. As his hands were full, he hung the creel round his neck, and Suleima carried the extinguished flare. His heart was a dead weight within him, for he felt certain why Nicholas had come; but he was apparently his old cheery self, and Suleima forgot about the rather disquieting moments just after Nicholas had passed. What he should do he could not form the least idea; at present it seemed to him impossible that he should go away and leave her. He felt willing to throw to the winds all he had promised Nicholas. Nicholas had told him that he should be one of the foremost of his country's avengers. He shrugged his shoulders, for just now the desire for vengeance on Turks was less than the memory of a dream. Were there not plenty of others to avenge Greece? Why should he give up all that was dearest to him, this dear burden that was his, and go out on an undesired adventure?

But as long as Suleima was with him he stifled all these thoughts, while the boat skimmed seawards on the outward tack. They put about opposite the island and ran straight for the wall. The wind had freshened, and to Mitsos the boat seemed to be going terribly fast, for he grudged each moment. But he had quite lulled Suleima's disquietude, if not his own, and she lay with her head on his shoulder, half asleep, looking up now and then into his wide-open eyes, and pressing her arm more closely round his neck. He had to rouse her when he must get up to take in the sail, and she smiled at him sleepily like a child just wakened.

Then he fixed the ladder, and she climbed up, clung to him for a moment without words, for there was no need of speech between them, and went quickly and silently across the garden.

It was after two when Mitsos landed opposite his house, and he saw with some surprise that there were lights still burning. He opened the door, and, bending his head to pass under the low jamb, entered. Constantine and Nicholas were sitting there, Constantine silent, Nicholas talking eagerly, and Mitsos observed that he held his pipe unlit in his hand. His uncle sprang up when he came in.

"Ah, he is here! Mitsos, the time has come. You must go at once."

Mitsos looked at him a moment steadily and silently—their eyes were on a level—and then he turned aside and put down the fishing-creel in the corner. His decision, though the result of years, was the deed of only a moment.

Then he faced Nicholas again.

"I am ready," he said; "tell me what I have to do."

PART II

THE EVE OF THE GATHERING

CHAPTER I

MITSOS MEETS HIS COUSINS

Since August Nicholas had been travelling about the Peloponnesus, being received everywhere with a sober, secret welcome as one of the accredited leaders of the revolution. The Turks, through whose Kismet the truth of the ever-increasing rumors had begun to break, had long held him in indolent suspicion, but had taken no steps to counteract the report of his death, for they hoped—if Turks can be said to hope—somewhat ingeniously, but wholly mistakenly, that such news would prove to be a cooling draught to this ill-defined fever of revolution. The Greeks, however, as Germanos had said, knew "that Nicholas was not the sort of man who died," and Turkish ingenuity went strangely wide of its aim. In fact, it enabled Nicholas to move about more freely, and to take a liberal advantage of the fact that he was supposed to be beyond the reach of war and rumor of war. Indeed, in October, finding himself back at Corinth, where he had business with one of his fellow-workers, he had filled an idle afternoon with carving a little wooden cross on which he painted his name, and below, with a two-handled meaning, the text, "The trumpet shall sound, and the dead shall be raised." He was to leave Corinth that night, and after the dark had fallen he and his host went to the Greek cemetery and planted this eloquent little monument over a newly made grave. When it was discovered it caused a certain amount of intelligent amusement among the Greeks; but the Turks seemed to miss the point of the joke. Not even they would have dared to disturb a Greek cemetery, for the dead had in their eyes a sacredness which the living altogether lacked; and it remained there for a year, when subsequent events saw it planted over the most honored grave in Greece.

December and the first half of January Nicholas had spent in the country of his kin, south of Sparta, and it was from there he had fled in haste to Nauplia, for his presence in Maina, which was notably patriotic, had become too insistent to be disregarded, and the Turkish governor of Tripoli, Mehemet Salik, had demanded of the Greek bey of that district, Petros Mavromichales, usually known as Petrobey, that he should be given up on the old charge of brigandage. Petrobey, like Germanos, was of high rank, and the Turks seemed to have had no suspicion that he himself was a leader of the revolution; but, as a matter of fact, he and Nicholas, who was

75

staying with him at the time, read the letter together and consulted what should be done.

Nicholas was disposed to shrug at it altogether, or merely to send back an answer that he was officially declared to be dead and buried—witness the grave and its monument; but Petrobey thought otherwise. His own usefulness to the cause was immensely increased by the fact that he at present stood outside suspicion, and he advised Nicholas to retire where they were not likely to look for him, while he himself would prosecute a vigorous and indubitably unsuccessful search elsewhere, as an evidence of his own unimpeachable fidelity. Had not Nicholas got a brother-in-law—his own cousin—at Nauplia? Nauplia was an excellent hiding-place, for it was under the very nose of the Turkish governor, and people always looked everywhere else first. But it would be necessary to have some extremely trustworthy person who could communicate between them; and Nicholas had spoken to him of his nephew. This nephew lived at Nauplia, did he not? How very convenient! Nicholas should go to Nauplia and send his nephew back to Maina, where he could be very useful.

With this, Petrobey wrote an exceedingly polite letter to Mehemet Salik, saying that his house was Mehemet's house, and that he himself was honored by the commands of the deputy of the Shadow of God. Nicholas, it was true, as he had learned by inquiry, had been seen lately in Maina, or so gossip would have it; but as they had been told that he was dead not long ago at Corinth, there might be some confusion on this point. However, the bearers of the letter to the deputy of the Serene Presence would be his witnesses that he had sent out twenty men to scour the country-side, and no doubt the hound of hell, if still alive, would be found. He should in this case be sent with spitting to Tripoli.

Petrobey was the head of the numerous and powerful clan of the Mavromichales, the thews and sinews of the revolution. He himself, though a Greek, was governor of the district of Maina, and had been appointed to this post by the Sultan, for the attempt to put the government of Maina, or rather of the Mavromichales, into the hands of a Turkish official, had not proved a success, the last three Turkish governors not having been permitted by the clan to hold office for more than a month. His brothers and cousins were mayors and land-owners of the villages for miles around, and, like Nicholas's family, with whom they were connected twenty times in marriage, it was their pride that they had kept their blood clean and not mated with devils, and the wrong done to Nicholas's wife they took for a wrong done to themselves, demanding, so they swore, "a red and hot apology." So when, in the presence of the five soldiers who had brought Mehemet's letter, Petrobey sent for his brother-in-law Demetri, and told him that that bastard cousin of the clan, Nicholas Vidalis, was being sought for by the deputy of the Shadow of God who cast his serene effulgence over Tripoli, Demetri was suitably astounded, and the Turkish soldiers were much impressed. They had the further satisfaction an hour later of seeing twenty mounted men set off southwards in search of Nicholas, following well-authenticated information; and later in the afternoon they themselves took horse on their return journey to Tripoli, having drunk a little more than was good for them at Petrobey's expense,

76

the bearers of that reply the sentiments and wording of which were an edification.

Nicholas and he supped together, and it was arranged that Nicholas should start that night from Panitza, so as to reach Gythium before morning.

"I regret," said Petrobey, "my dear cousin, that I cannot speed you on your way myself, and can send none of our clan with you; but perhaps it would be outstepping the bounds of prudence if I went myself, and, as you know, the Mavromichales of this immediate district have gone to look for you southwards. They will no doubt be back from their quest before midnight; but I should advise your setting out before then."

Nicholas laughed.

"I shall do very well, my cousin," he said. "I shall reach Nauplia in two days or three, and send Mitsos back at once. He is absolutely and entirely trustworthy. I think I told you of the test."

"You did. He should be very useful to us; for it is time, I think, that the mills were set grinding, and a boy like that can go freely to and fro without suspicion. Your health, dear cousin; I will break my custom and drink wine with you. I drink to you and to vengeance."

The men clinked glasses, emptied them, and filled them again.

"I do not easily forget," said Nicholas, "and the Turk shall not easily forget me. The corn will grow high this summer, for the fields will be rich. Your health, dear cousin, and the memory of one whom we forget not!"

They sat in silence for a space, for Petrobey knew that Nicholas spoke of his wife, and having finished their meal they drank their coffee, and Nicholas's horse was brought round. The two men walked to the end of the village together, the lad leading the horse behind, and there they stopped a moment.

"I may not see you again," said Nicholas, "till the feast is ready. And on that day, my cousin, you and I will fall to with good appetite. I wish you a good appetite for that feast." And after the manner of relations and friends they kissed each other, and Nicholas mounted and rode off.

Eight days after his departure Mitsos arrived, having passed without impediment through Tripoli and Sparta. Following Nicholas's directions, he had kept his ears very wide open at Tripoli in his lodging at a Greek inn, and he had heard things which he thought might be of interest. First and foremost the letter which Petrobey had written to the deputy of the Shadow of God had been received, and was supposed to have given satisfaction, for Mitsos had fallen in with one of the Turkish soldiers who had taken it, who reported that the matter was to be left entirely in Petrobey's hands, which seemed a mark of confidence in his fidelity. Also, the meeting of primates and bishops at Tripoli, which usually took place at the beginning of April, was summoned for the beginning of March. Lastly, Mehemet Salik was fortifying with feverish haste the walls of the city.

Mitsos had spent the second night at Sparta; the third at Marathonisi, a town on the coast; and the noon of the fourth day saw him climbing the steep hill into Panitza. His horse was tired with the four days' journey, and a couple of miles below the village he got off and walked behind it, cracking his whip every now and then, partly to encourage it, and partly because he could crack a whip louder than mortal man. Petrobey, who was outside the big café at the entrance to the village, saw the tired horse and the extremely vigorous-looking young giant walking by its side as they passed, and, after a few moments' inspection, said to a young man who was sitting with him:

"That is he, no doubt. Nicholas seems to have chosen well."

The two got up and followed the boy till he, seeing them, stopped and asked for Petros Mavromichales's house.

"And what do you want with Petrobey?" asked that gentleman.

Mitsos surveyed him with easy indifference, raising his eyebrows slightly at the question.

"See, friend," he said, "I have my business, and you, for all I know, have yours. If you will tell me where is his house, good; if not, I will ask some one else."

Petrobey laughed.

"You are Mitsos, no doubt," he said. "Welcome, cousin, for Nicholas's sake and your own."

"I really am very sorry," said the boy; "but how should I know? I have come from Nauplia. Uncle Nicholas arrived safely."

"That is good, and you have arrived safely, which is also good. This is my son Yanni, Mitsos, and your cousin. Yanni, take your cousin's horse and then join us."

Mitsos hesitated a moment before giving the bridle to Yanni.

"Thank you very much," he said; "but I can put the horse up myself if you will show me where. My father told me always to put it up myself. They laughed at me at the inn at Tripoli for doing so."

"Indeed," said Petrobey, glancing at the boy's shoulders; "I would never laugh at you, Mitsos. What did you do?"

"I knocked one of them down," said Mitsos, genially, "and thus there was no more laughter."

"The horse will be all right here," said Petrobey, smiling. "Give Yanni the bridle, lad."

Mitsos obeyed, and they went into the house, where dinner was being got ready. Dinner was a daily crisis in the house of Petrobey, and, leaving the two boys in the veranda, he went round to the kitchen for fear that the cook, who, he said, was a man to whom God had not granted a palate, should be too harsh on the sucking-pig which they were to eat.

"Can you conceive," he said, on his return, spreading out his hands with a gesture of eloquent despair, "the fool stuffed the last one I ate with garlic! Sucking-pig stuffed with garlic! A man without a palate, little Mitsos!"

Yanni burst out laughing at this, and Petrobey turned to him with good humor shining in his great rosy face, which he tried most unsuccessfully to school into severity.

"Yanni, too," he went on, "that lumpy son of mine, does not know quail from woodcock, and lights his pipe before he has finished his wine. Come, boys, dinner first; we will talk afterwards. Bring the mastic, son of a locust," he bawled into the kitchen.

During dinner Petrobey hardly spoke, because speech spoils food.

He ate sparingly and slowly, dwelling on each mouthful as on a mathematical problem. His face grew anxious as the time for sucking-pig approached, and his deep-gray eyes bore an expression of profound thought as he laid down his knife and fork, after putting the first piece of crackling into his mouth. Then his face cleared again, and he drank a little water briskly, for, except rarely, he did not touch wine.

"Hardly crisp enough," he said, curling his long gray mustache up from his lips. "Hardly crisp enough, but creditable. What say you, Mitsos?"

The latter exhibited a phenomenal appetite after his journey from Marathonisi, and Yanni looked on in admiration, which eventually expressed itself Homerically:

"You are a good man," he said, "because you eat well."

After dinner they sat out in the sun under the shelter of the southern veranda, and here Mitsos learned what he had to do.

"Your uncle Nicholas," said Petrobey, "has told me that I can trust you completely; and I have many things to tell you, any of which, if you chose to give information to the Turk, would see me, and many others besides, strung to the gallows."

Yanni, who was lying on a straw mat near Mitsos, refilled his pipe and grinned.

"Me among them, Mitsos," he said, glancing up at his big cousin. "You will please to remember that."

But Mitsos did not answer, and only looked gravely at Petrobey.

"We shall no longer be cursed by these devils," continued he, "for the Turks will vanish out of our land like snow in summer. What you and Yanni have to do is to go through a certain district, calling at certain villages, and speaking to certain men. This first journey, on which you will set out to-morrow, will take you a fortnight or so—ah, but the victuals will be poor, little ones, but perhaps you don't mind that—and then you will come back here. And remember, Mitsos, that you will be doing what none of us could do; for two boys, dressed as peasants dress, driving a couple of seedy mules laden with oranges, can pass where Nicholas and I could not. On this first journey Yanni will go with you, for he knows the country, but after that there will probably be other work for him to do, and also for you—plenty. You will go to the houses of these men and ask this question, 'Are you grinding corn?' and they will answer, 'Corn for the hungry, or corn for the Turk?' And you will say, 'Black corn for the Turk. If you have not begun grinding, begin, and grind quickly.'"

Mitsos was listening breathlessly.

"What does it all mean?" he asked.

Petrobey smiled, and unslinging his powder-flask from his belt, shook out a little into his hand, and tossed it into the air.

"Pouf!" he said; "black corn for the Turk."

Mitsos' eyes flashed.

"I understand," he said; "black corn, and good for Turks."

"For the first journey that will be all," went on Petrobey. "Yanni will be with you, and it will be simple enough. After that you may have to go here, there, anywhere. You will certainly have to go to Nauplia, where you

79

will find Nicholas; and Yanni will, I am afraid, have to go to Tripoli for a little while."

"The black devil take Tripoli," muttered Yanni.

"And why does Yanni go to Tripoli?" asked Mitsos.

"Perhaps he will not, but if he goes it will be as a hostage for my good conduct. But there is no need to be so round-eyed, Mitsos; we are not going to have him murdered. I shall not behave badly till he is safe again. Dear me, yes, I wish I could go instead. Mehemet Salik has a cook of a thousand. But—who knows?—idle words may reach the Turks at Tripoli, and if so I shall send Yanni as a hostage. But about this journey you must be as quick and quiet as you can. Never answer any questions about Nicholas or me or yourselves—you cannot be too careful. Never sleep in a village when you have given a message. Sleep mostly by day out in the woods and travel at night, though you must be careful to arrive at the village where you give these messages by day in the manner of ordinary peasants. Finally, be ready to run, if running is possible; if not, to fight. Which would you prefer?"

Mitsos kicked out a leg tentatively.

"I have no marked choice," he said; "perhaps I would rather fight."

"I hope no need will come. Try to avoid any suspicion. I don't think you need provoke any. But if you do, remember that you must try to run away first. The point is that you should do your business quietly."

Yanni turned round and looked at Mitsos.

"You would prefer fighting, would you not, cousin?" he said. "But I don't see how there will be either fighting or running to do, father. We only go to friends, give our message, and pass on."

Petrobey got up.

"That is what I hope," he said, "but you cannot tell. Some of those whom we thought our friends may be treacherous. And now I have to see Demetri, and you boys can stop here, or you can take Mitsos to see some of his cousins, Yanni. We will talk again this evening."

Petrobey whistled to the great sheep-dog, wolfish and savage, who got up, and with all his hackles raised made a second examination of Mitsos' legs, growling gently to himself. The boy sat quite still under this somewhat trying inspection, and the dog after a few moments laid his head on his knee and looked him in the face. Mitsos lifted his hand very gently and stroked the brute's ears, while Petrobey watched them.

"There, go along," said Mitsos, after a few moments, and the stately dog turned and walked across to Petrobey.

"That is curious," said the latter. "Osman is not usually friendly. I suppose he saw you were not afraid of him."

Mitsos looked up smiling.

"I was horribly afraid," he said, "but I tried not to show it. Big dogs are fools; they never understand."

"You will find that men are even greater fools; they always mistake bluff for bravery," said Petrobey, walking off.

Yanni got up from where he was lying and sat himself in his father's chair. He was a big-made young Greek, rather above the average height,

80

with a look of extreme fitness about him. His movements were all sharp and nimble, like the movements of some young animal, and he rolled himself a compact and uniform plug of tobacco for his chibouk with a few passes of his quick fingers. His hands, like his father's, were long and finely made, and Mitsos watched him admiringly nip off the loose ends of the tobacco.

"How quickly you did that," he said. "Will you fill my pipe, too? I am so glad we are going together, cousin."

"I, too. It is good to hunt in couples. It is a halving of the cold and the tiredness, and a doubling of all that is pleasant. This is Turkish tobacco, Mitsos, and it is better than ours. Father never smokes. So when a Turk sends him a present of tobacco it is good for me. Have you ever smoked the Turkish?"

Mitsos started, and a flush spread under the brown of his cheek.

"Yes, the other day only. I found it very good. Tell me more of the journey."

"Old clothes, even very old clothes," said Yanni, "like poor peasants," and his Mavromichales's nose went in the air. "Old mules, and very slow-going; but a pistol each, new pistols with two mouths that speak like the lightning. Father gives us one each. On the mules a load of stupid oranges and a couple of blankets each. Come to the other side of the house, cousin; we can see our first day's journey from there."

Panitza stood high on the scrub-covered slope leading up to the pine forests and the naked crags of Taygetus. Sixteen miles to the north rose the spearhead of the range, Mount Elias, sheathed in snow for a couple of thousand feet down, and cut against the intense blue of the sky with the keenness and edge of steel. From Panitza their path lay for five or six miles along the upward slope, and where it struck the ridge they could see the huddled roofs of a village, which Yanni said was Kalyvia, where they delivered their first message. From there the track crossed a pass and went down the other side towards the sea. It was rough, cold going on the heights, and it would be a full day's journey to get down to Platsa, where they would sleep. After that they would travel chiefly by night, and sleep when and where they could, avoiding as far as possible all villages but those where they were charged with messages. "Oh, it will be very good," said Yanni. Mitsos' thoughts went aching back to the bay of Nauplia; but he agreed. Besides, he would go to Nauplia again soon.

It had been an immense relief to him that he was not going alone, though in that moment when Nicholas had told him that the time was come he had made his self-surrender absolute, and would have taken upon him any outrageous task which might have been imposed. But the four days of travelling alone from Nauplia had been like a sick man's dream. He had set off at daybreak, and taking the same path by which Nicholas had come the evening before, he reached in an hour the little bay where he had fished, and sat down under the clump of rushes where they had sat together, looking at the well-known places with the eyes of a dog that comes back to a deserted house which has once been home. In the sand he could see the footprints made by his own bare feet as he came up from the water, and close beside them the print of Suleima's little pointed shoes.

They had overlooked two or three small fish, which were lying still fresh and clean after the cool night, where they had emptied the creel to count their spoils, and by them was the dottle of the pipe he had smoked. And at the sight of these little things the child within him cried out against his fate. Nothing in the world seemed of appreciable account except the need of Suleima. Yet it was no less impossible to go back: even as he said to himself that he would return, he knew that Nicholas's gray, questioning eyes were unfaceable. He was hedged in by impossibilities on every side. And then because there was something more than the child within him, some stuff out of which real men are made, he got up, and mounting again went on his way. All that day and the next days his heart-sickness rode him like a night-hag, and it was but a heavy-souled lad who trudged so bravely into Panitza cracking his whip. But to be among people again, and men who received him cousin-fashion—for in those days the tie of blood was a warm reality—had an extraordinary sweetness for him, for he felt lonely and sick for home; above all, to find that for the present he would be with Yanni, a boy of his own age, who took for granted that they were going to have the best of hours together, and only knew one side of things, and that the cheerful side, was surpassingly pleasant. Again, because he was beginning to be a man, the confidence placed in him made him feel self-reliant, and because he was still a boy the unknown adventurous days in front of him were very tonic to the spirit. And so it was, that when they set out early next morning, Petrobey, looking after them, said to Demetri that Nicholas was a very wise man; and Mitsos whacked his mule gayly over the rump, and whistled the "Song of the Vine-diggers" with more than cheerfulness of lip, and took the road with an open heart.

CHAPTER II

MITSOS AND YANNI FIND A HORSE

It was a morning to make the blood go blithely. There had been a slight frost during the night, and the rough grass in the ditches was stiff and sprinkled with the powdered cold, and the air was brisk in the nostrils. To the right the ground fell away sheerly to the outlying hills bordering the plain, which lay unrolled beneath them like a colored map, with extraordinary clearness, in counties of yellow-green, where the corn was already springing, alternating with territories of good red earth, showing where the leafless vineyards stood. Beyond again lay the dim, dark blue of the sea, and across that, more guessed at than seen, the stencilled shapes of the hills beyond the gulf. Their path, a cobbled Turkish road, ascended steadily, skirting about the edges of the deep ravines, and making detours round the acuter slopes which rose above them to the top of the mountain ridge; and the mules ambled slowly along with their panniers of oranges on either side, while Mitsos and Yanni walked behind, dressed in their roughest peasant clothes, talking of the thousand things of which boys talk. It took them nearly three hours to reach the foot of the last slope on which the village stood, and here they halted for half an hour to eat and drink, in order that they might pass straight through without waiting after giving the message.

Yanni, who knew the village, soon recognized the house to which they were going, which stood somewhat apart from the others, and had a low outlying building a stone's-throw below it.

"That is the house," he said, "and that shed near is the mill. There is a big stream coming down from the mountains there which turns the wheel."

"They should grind quickly, then. Shall we go on?"

The house in question they found was entered from a yard, the door of which was closed, and their knocking only seemed to rouse a dog inside to the top pitch of fury. But at last a woman came out on the wooden balcony overlooking the street, and asked them what they wanted.

"We want Yorgi Gregoriou," shouted Yanni. "Ah, do you not remember me?"

The woman took up a piece of wood and threw it, as a man throws with force and precision, at the dog inside. The barking broke off short in a staccato howl, and Mitsos guessed that she had hit.

"Yanni Mavromichales, is it not?" asked the woman.

"Surely."

She disappeared into the house, and in a moment her step was heard across the yard. As soon as the door was opened the dog flew out like a cork from a bottle, only to find himself between the devil and the deep sea—his mistress, an authentic terror, standing on one side, and Mitsos' whip flirting out at him like the tongue of a snake on the other. So he scuffled away to a safe distance and barked himself out of all shape.

"Come in, Yanni," said Gregoriou's wife. "What brings you here?"

"A message from Petrobey to Gregoriou."

The woman's eye travelled slowly up to Mitsos' face, as if she could only take him in by sections.

"And the giant?" she asked. "Is he from a fair?"

Yanni shouted with laughter.

"No; it is my cousin. But we are in a hurry, as we go far to-day. Where shall we find Gregoriou?"

"He is at the mill. You will find him there, and then come back and drink a glass of wine."

The stream that worked the mill was confined within a masonry-laid bed for a hundred yards above the house, to narrow its course and concentrate its energy. From the end of the yard ran out a tall, stout-built wall; along the top of this the water was conducted to a wooden shoot, below which was the mill-wheel. The mill seemed to be in full working order, for an ear-filling booming came from within, shaking the rickety door on its hinges. The two tried the latch, but found it locked, and it was not till Yanni had shouted his name that it was cautiously opened.

"Yanni Mavromichales?" queried a voice from inside.

"No other."

"What do you want?"

"This only. Are you grinding corn?"

There was a pause, but the door was still held ajar only.

"Corn for the hungry, or corn for the Turk?" asked the voice.

"Black corn for the Turk."

The door was opened and a little wizened man appeared on the threshold. He had a white beard, cut close and pointed, and a pair of heavy eyebrows. His face was a map of minute wrinkles, as the sea is covered with ripples under the land-breeze, and two suspicious eyes peered narrowly out from under their overhanging brows. Mitsos was standing close to the door, and this grotesque little apparition, as he opened it, gave a shrill squeal of dismay, and would have shut it again had not Yanni prevented him.

"Who is that?" asked the little man, pointing to Mitsos.

"My cousin," said Yanni, "who comes with me on the business of the corn. Oh, all our necks are in one noose. Do not be afraid."

The little old man seemed strangely reassured at this brutality of frankness, and setting the door wide—"Come in, both of you," he said, shortly.

Inside the noise of the mill was almost deafening, but Gregoriou pinned the wheel, the two stones stopped grinding, and only the water splashed hissing down the channel.

"Black corn, did you say; black corn for the Turk?" said the little old man, peering into Yanni's face, with blinking eyes, like a noonday owl. "I grind corn all day, for there will be many hungry mouths. Look you, I am no fighting man; I leave that to those who are taller than the pillars in the church, like this cousin of yours; but where would the fighting be without such as I? But, lad, don't give hint of this to the woman-folk, else I shall have the clan of them a-screaming round me like the east gale in the mountains."

He rubbed his hands together and broke out into a screeching cackle of a laugh, which showed a row of discolored, irregular teeth.

"Look here," he said, opening a bin behind the door, "is not this good, strong corn? I have ground it all myself. None but I have ground it."

His face took an expression of diabolical cunning.

"They have promised to buy it of me, all at a sound price," he said; "but it is not that so much that makes my heart go singing—it is that I want it to do its work well, and give the Turk an indigestion of lead. This is good business for me. I will be a rich man, and I shall have brought death to many devils."

He slipped back to the lever that brought the wheel under the stream, and as the stones began to turn again, from their lips there dribbled out a black powder, which he scooped up in a wooden ladle and emptied into a cask. Then, seeing that the door was still open, he gave another shrill animal cry of fright and sprang to lock it. "Charcoal!" he

84

shouted to them across the rumbling din of the stone, "charcoal ground fine, for so it is the more nourishing. And here are the sulphur and saltpetre. To-night I shall mix them carefully—oh, so carefully—and I shall be glutted with the thought that there will be a red death for every stroke in the mixing."

And then he got him back to the stones and fed them tenderly with fresh lumps of charcoal, as one would feed a sick dog.

Mitsos and Yanni were in a hurry to take the road again, and so they left him absorbed in the grinding, and heard the key grate in the lock as soon as they got outside.

From Kalyvia their road topped the watershed of the mountain, and thereafter descended in leaps and strides, almost due west, down to the plain which skirts the bay of Kalamata. They got to Platsa, where they were to sleep that night, an hour before dark, and for the sake of appearances drove their mules to the market-place, and made a display of selling their cargo of oranges. The khan where they put up consisted of two rooms, one occupied by the owner and his family, the other being the café of the village. They sat up smoking and talking till it emptied, and then made themselves beds of their blankets and saddle-bags. The village was inclined to inquisitiveness, but Mitsos told them that they had come from Sparta with oranges and were going home to Tsimova—a possible, and even a plausible, explanation of their presence; and with that the village must be content.

They descended next day onto the coast and into the warm fresh air of the Greek lowlands in winter, and Mitsos called the hierarchy of Heaven to witness that only the shrewdest pinch of cold would drive him again into foul khans while there were trees to sleep under and good grass beds for the limbs. If rooms untenanted by the grosser vermin were supposed to be beyond the reach of orange-sellers, he would have no room at all, but only God's out-door inn.

Mid-day brought them to Prastion, and to the delivery of the second message. They had no trouble in finding the recipient, for he was the mayor of the village, and was known to be in his vineyard hoeing vines. Yanni waited with the mules in the street, while Mitsos went to seek him. He looked up as the lad came striding towards him across the hollowed vine-beds.

"You are Zaravenos?" asked he.

Zaravenos assented slowly and suspiciously, as if he would sooner have been some one else.

"Are you grinding corn?"

The man put down his mattock and looked round suddenly to see that there was no one within hearing.

"Yes, yes," he said, quickly. "But of what corn do you speak—corn for the hungry, or corn for the Turk?"

"Black corn for the Turk."

"Praise the Virgin. But is the time come? Tell me who sent you; was it Nicholas, whom I know well?"

Mitsos thought of Petrobey's injunctions.

"Nicholas? Who is Nicholas?" he said. "But this I have to tell you: if you have not begun, begin, and grind quickly. That is all."

The man looked at him again.

"Surely you are Mitsos," he said. "Nicholas told me about a mountain of a Mitsos, whom perhaps he would send to us. Why do you not tell me? I have no better friend than Nicholas. He was here a month ago. Where is he now? Is he safe?"

But Mitsos shook his head.

"I do not know whom you mean," he said, though his heartstrings thrummed within him.

For six days the two went on travelling in a northerly direction, sometimes keeping close to the coast, sometimes visiting strange, gaunt little villages perched high on the flanks of Taygetus. They travelled for the most part at night, trying if possible to come by daybreak within a mile or two of the village whither they were bound. They would then turn off into some wood, or, if they were close to the coast, down onto the beach, and, after tethering and feeding their mules, would breakfast and sleep till about mid-day, when they entered the village, delivered their message, and passed on. Sometimes it would be received eagerly and with shining eyes, and the news would spread at once that the time for which they were waiting had come. Sometimes, if there were Turks about, it would be taken and answered with guardedness and caution, and once the man to whom they had been sent shook his head and said he knew nought of the matter. This was beyond doubt an occasion when running away was necessary, and little time was lost in running.

They reached Kalamata on the seventh day—little did Mitsos think how or when he would see it again—and after spending two nights there (for they had been instructed not only to give messages to three leading Greeks, but also to inquire of the strength of the Turkish garrison, and see to the truth of the report which had reached Petrobey that the fortifications there, as well as at Tripoli, were being repaired), took a boat down the coast to the port of Tsimova, whence their road lay southward through Maina, and then eastward back to Panitza, and it was in this district that red-handed adventure met them.

They had now been twelve days from home, and Yanni remarked discontentedly that there were only four more to come. He had never spent more enchanting days than these in the company of Mitsos, with whom in a healthy, boyish manner he had fallen completely in love. Mitsos never lost his temper, and maintained an immense, great serenity under the most disquieting conditions; as, for instance, when they lost one of the mules during their morning's sleep the day before, when they were up on the spurs of Taygetus, and had to hunt it high and low in a blinding snow blizzard, and came back to find that the other mule had made use of his solitude in rolling himself in some thorn bushes while they were away, converting their blankets into one prickly fricassee. The splendid cousin had gazed at them ruefully a moment, and "I would I were a tortoise" was his only comment.

Mitsos had fully responded to the frankness of his cousin's adoration, and had confided to him his interrupted love-story, which

86

raised him in Yanni's eyes to hero rank. Besides, he was big and strong and entirely magnificent.

Mitsos had just awakened Yanni on this particular morning, reminding him that it was after mid-day and they had a long tramp ahead of them that afternoon. Nymphia, the next village to which they had a message, lay below them on the plain, a mile or two distant. But Yanni refused to go before he had eaten somewhat, and as remonstrance was vain, they fished out bread and meat from the saddle-bags and made a meal. They were sitting thus some thirty yards from the path, which lay through the heart of an upland pine forest, when they heard the going of four-footed steps, and Yanni got up to see if either of their mules had slipped its tether and was preparing to give them another hunt. But it proved only to be a Turkish soldier riding down in the direction of the village to which they were bound. He asked the bush-bowered Yanni what was his business there, and Yanni, who had a wholesome dislike of all Turks, very rudely replied, "Breakfasting, pig," went back to Mitsos, and thought no more of the matter.

The soldier rode quickly on through the village and turned into a house that lay some half-mile below. He found no one there, and tying his horse up went down across a couple of fields to a low, huddled building, beside which stood a mill-wall. He knocked at the door and was admitted at once.

"Krinos," he said to the man who opened it, "I passed a boy on the road through the wood, whom I am sure I saw yesterday at Kyta, and two days ago at Akia, only before there were two of them. It is worth while waiting to see if he comes with a message to you."

"But if there are two of them," said Krinos (for God had made a coward), "there are only two of us."

"Nonsense; admit one only; and this is a boy, and we are men. Besides, there is no time to send to the village, and whom should we find there? They are all Greek of the Greeks. And the boy may be here in a few minutes. Remember, he is not to be killed yet. He has to speak first."

"If it is a Mavromichales he will never speak," said Krinos.

"That is yet to be seen. I will stand behind the door, seize him as he enters, and if there are two of them, lock the door behind the first."

Now from Pigadia, where the boys had delivered the message to a man who said he knew nought of the matter, they had been quite right to go on their way as quickly as they could. The Turks had set spies all over the country, since the rumors of an approaching outbreak had reached them, who were instructed to affect sympathy and co-operation with the revolutionists, and give information at headquarters of all they could learn. The day after Mitsos and Yanni had left Pigadia, still going northward towards Kalamata, this spy had had occasion to make a journey southward. At Tsimova he had inquired whether the boys had been seen, and hearing they had not, for they were then at Kalamata, gave information to the Turkish magistrate, and went on his way. At Nymphia he visited Krinos, who was also in Turkish pay, and told him to extract any information he could if they came his way. From there he had taken ship and gone on to Gythium, which was out of the boys' route.

The magistrate at Tsimova, with characteristic Turkish indolence, holding a clew in one hand, would scarcely trouble to move the other in pursuit. He just let the soldiers of the place know that there would be some small reward given to any of them who apprehended either of the boys; and one of them, the same who had seen Yanni on the wooded path, being anxious that no other should bite at his cherry, had obtained leave of absence and went a-hunting alone. He had seen Yanni on the previous days at Kyta and Akia, and thought it worth while to follow him on to Nymphia, where, as he knew, there was a Greek whom his countrymen supposed to be a revolutionist, but who was really in Turkish pay.

So the soldier hid behind the door, and Krinos went on grinding powder, which he intended to sell eventually—not to the Greeks, but to the Turks. The trap was neatly laid, and smelled of success.

Krinos's mill was of an old-fashioned type, consisting not of two stones, but of one, which was hung with its axle horizontal to the floor, in size and shape resembling a stone-roller, and underneath it ran the long tray in which the corn or charcoal was ground. The tray could be withdrawn for the emptying and filling, and he had just slid it out, as the charcoal was already sufficiently powdered, when the interruption for which he and the soldier had been waiting came. Krinos had not time to put it back, and the stone remained revolving about eight inches from the ground.

Yanni and Mitsos had gone cheerily down the hill-side ten minutes after the Turk into the village, where Yanni met a slightly intoxicated cousin, who grinned, and queried "Black corn?"

Yanni looked so important and mysterious at this that Mitsos burst out laughing, and they all three stood in the road and laughed together for no reason, except that one was drunk and two were of a merry mind. Yanni went so far as to explain that they were in a hurry, but no more; and, having inquired where Krinos lived, they passed through the village and out towards the house.

Just below Krinos's house the ground sloped sharply away, so that from the door only the roof of his mill could be seen. This prevented Krinos, who was peering out of the mill-door to learn whether there were two of them, from seeing either till they should pass the house and begin to descend towards the mill. Mitsos tapped at the house door, then knocked, and then shouted; but there was no answer. Yanni followed, and in the court-yard saw a horse tied up. Mitsos had given up the attempt to make any one hear, and he said to Yanni:

"He's not in. What are we to do?"

Yanni scratched his head thoughtfully.

"There's another building farther down which looks like a mill," he said; "we will go there. But wait a minute, cousin; there is a thought in my head."

"Out with it, then."

"Have you in your mind how that when we were breakfasting we heard a horse on the path, and I went to see if it was either of our mules? You remember it turned out to be a Turkish soldier; and this is the horse, or my mother did not bear me."

88

Mitsos' eye brightened.

"Let us think a moment," he said. "What do you make of it?"

Yanni put his head on one side, like an intelligent but puzzled collie dog.

"It is a nice horse," he said, vaguely, "and that is why I noticed it. It would be rather amusing if—hush, I can hear the mill going! Krinos must be there, and—and I shouldn't at all wonder if the Turk was there also!"

Mitsos smiled serenely.

"It is a little trap," he said; "very pretty. What shall we do? What a devil Krinos must be."

"It isn't certain," said Yanni; "but we'll make sure. This is the way. The Turk saw only me, therefore I will go down there alone. I wonder if there are any windows this side. Wait a minute while I see."

He stole out to the edge of the hill, and reconnoitred from behind a bush.

Krinos was standing at the door, and even as Yanni looked, a head wearing a red soldier's fez popped out and back again, and he crept back with suppressed excitement in his eyes.

"They are both there," he said; "two of them and two of us. Oh, Mitsos, this is very good! You see, we must go to deliver our message, otherwise we should be doing better to run away now; but there is the message to deliver, and that is the first order. This is what I will do: Tie up your mule here, and get behind that bush. Then I will walk down to the mill with my mule, and I expect when Krinos sees me he will go back into the mill and wait; if he does, run down ever so quickly and quietly—there are no windows this side—and hide behind the corner of the house. Then will I come and knock at the door, and I expect that when I give the message Krinos will let me in, and if you hear me shout, in with you. There will be no running away."

"It won't go," said Mitsos; "there will be two of them. They may kill you before I can get in."

"O best and biggest of fools!" whispered Yanni, excitedly; "this is no time for talk. They will not want to kill me, for what would that profit them? They will wish to take me to the Turks—and be damned to all Turks!"

"You are right; come on."

Mitsos crept to his post behind the bush, after tethering his mule well out of sight, and Yanni went unconcernedly down the hill-side. As he had expected, as soon as Krinos saw him he strolled back into the mill and shut the door. Yanni waited a moment, and beckoned to Mitsos, who strode noiselessly down and stood behind the corner of the wall, while Yanni came slowly on, reached the mill, and tapped at the door. A voice from inside answered him.

"Who is that?" it asked.

"It matters not," said Yanni. "Are you grinding corn?"

"Corn for the hungry, or corn for the Turk?"

"Black corn for the Turk."

The door was thrown open and Yanni entered. The moment after it was flung to again, and a half-muffled shout came from inside. Mitsos sprang out and threw himself against the door, and went reeling in.

Yanni was struggling in the grasp of two men, the Greek and the Turk, and Mitsos, without losing a moment, flung himself onto Krinos, who was nearest him, and dragged him off with a throttling grip. Krinos dropped his hold on Yanni and turned round to grapple with his new assailant, whom, to his dismay, he saw towering half a head above him. At that moment all Mitsos' cheerfulness and good spirits were transformed into a white anger at the treachery of the man, and, tightening his hold, he wrestled for his life. His extra four inches were counterbalanced by Krinos's extra ten years of hardened bone and knitted muscle, and for the first few seconds they toppled wildly about, and either might have won the fall. But then Mitsos' height began to tell; he heard, with a fierce joy, the cracking of some bone in its joint, and knew it came not from him.

Then, for a moment, he felt his adversary's right arm slacken, and knew that his hand was fumbling at his belt, whether for a knife or pistol he could not tell. His own pistol was in his belt, but tumbling, as he had, headlong into the middle of the fight, he had forgotten to take it out. But there was no doubt what that fumbling at the belt meant, and, throwing all his force into one effort, he lifted his opponent off his feet and threw him. Krinos's left hand, with which, alone, he was holding Mitsos, lost its grasp, and the man went head over heels backward, and Mitsos, by the force of his own throw, fell forward half across him. Just in front of them the millstone was turning with a slow relentlessness, and for a moment Mitsos thought his own head was going to strike it; but he fell free. Not so the other; there was a moment's cessation of the noise; then came a hoarse cry of agony, a horrid crack, and the stone began to turn again. Krinos's head had fallen right beneath it, and it was cracked as a nut may be cracked in a hinge.

There was no time for exultation. Mitsos picked himself up and gained his feet just as Yanni and the Turk, who were still struggling together, fell—the Turk uppermost. Mitsos saw him reach his hand to the butt of his pistol and draw it, keeping his knee on Yanni while he cocked it with the other hand. But in a moment he had done the same, and the two reports were almost simultaneous. Just above Yanni's head there appeared on the wooden floor a raking furrow, as if some wild beast's claw had struck and torn it; but the Turk fell back, shot through the head.

The smoke cleared away, and Mitsos pulled Yanni from under the soldier; he lay quite still, and the edge of his black curls was singed and burned. Mitsos propped him up against the wall, and ran to get water from the millstream outside. When he came back Yanni's eyes were open, and he was looking about in a dazed, confused way. Mitsos poured a draught of it down his throat and sluiced his head, whereat Yanni looked up and smiled at him.

"Did I not say it would be very good?" he murmured. "Oh, Mitsos, the black devils!"

He sat up and looked round, then pointed at the dead body of the Turk.

"I think I was stunned by the fall," he continued. "I remember falling and hitting my head an awful bang. So you shot him. Where is the other?"

He staggered to his feet and looked round at the millstone; it was streaked and clotted with something dark and oily, and its edges dripped with the same. Krinos's fingers, though he had been dead two minutes at the least, still opened and shut, like seaweed under the suck of a ground-swell, and the nails scratched impotently on the rough-splintered floor.

"We fell—he fell there," said Mitsos. "Come outside, Yanni. It is not good to stop here. Here, let me put my arm round you; you are unsteady yet."

Mitsos looked anxiously round as they got out, but no one was in sight. Yanni's mule had strayed into the field; and, after depositing his cousin against the wall, Mitsos went after it, and, muffling its bell with grass, led it round to the back of the mill, where Yanni was sitting. The latter was quickly recovering, but he felt his head ruefully.

"An awful bang!" he said. "Did he fire at me? My hair is burned."

"Yes," said Mitsos, "and I at him. Fancy a soldier so bad a shot; but he was made silly at the sight of my pistol, I think. If he hadn't been a fool of a man he would have first fired at me; for, indeed, he had you safe. But I suppose there was no time to think."

"That was well for me," said Yanni.

Mitsos spat thoughtfully.

"Yanni," he said, "we must think very hard what we are to do next. If Uncle Nicholas was only here! No one seems to have heard the shots, and we must get away as quickly as we can. Are we just to leave things as they are and go? Oh, do think, Yanni, and think quickly! My head is just one buzzing."

"The black devils!" snarled Yanni. "Treacherous, black devils!"

"Oh, never mind them," cried Mitsos; "they are in hell. What are we to do?"

Yanni's eye brightened.

"This will we do," he said. "There is much powder here. Blow up the whole place. If we leave it as it is they will find those dead things. Yes, Mitsos, that is the way."

Yanni got up.

"Come inside," he said, "and see if there is plenty of powder."

The two went back and stopped the mill-wheel, for it was a blood-curdling thing to see its shredded burden carried round and round. Mitsos dragged the headless wreck away and laid it by the Turk in the centre of the room, while Yanni searched for the powder.

"Look," he said, at last, "here is a whole barrel. That will do our work. I know how to make a train. I have done it at home to blow up rocks. We must waste no time. Go back to the house, Mitsos, and bring your mule—oh yes—and the Turk's horse, too; it will not do to leave that, and take the lot into the woods above the path, lower down there. Then come back here. I shall be ready. I will make a train that will give us about three minutes."

Mitsos ran up to the house, as Yanni suggested, and led the two animals down. He stopped at the mill to tie Yanni's mule to his own, and

91

then struck straight off the path into the trees, and tethered them all some three hundred yards off where the trees grew thick. Then he went back to Yanni.

Yanni had laid a train from the centre of the room, where the bodies were, out under the door, making it of moist powder wrapped in thick paper. He had waited for Mitsos to lift the barrel, for he was still weak and unsteady, and they bored a hole through it, so that the dry powder ran out into the end of the train, and then closed the lid tight to increase the force of the explosion. Mitsos put the barrel in the centre of the room, laid the two bodies on it, and placed over it all the loose articles he could find.

"I will fire it," said he, "because it will be best to run, and you can't run just now. Come out, Yanni, and I will show you where the horses are. Look; do you see that big white trunk at the edge of the wood? Walk there and keep straight on; you will find them two hundred yards inside. Now go."

Mitsos waited till Yanni had disappeared, and then, locking the door and pushing the key underneath it, fired the end of the train and ran as hard as his legs would move after Yanni. He found him with the beasts, having taken from the Turk's horse the trappings and saddle, which bore the star and crescent, and thrown them into a thick bush. A few moments afterwards a great quiver and roar came to them from the direction of the village, and they knew that the powder had done its work.

Mitsos made Yanni mount the Turk's horse, and they hurried off through the trees, meaning to make a long detour and come down upon the next village from the far side.

CHAPTER III

MITSOS HAS THE HYSTERICS

For a space they went on in silence; it was as much as Yanni could do to grip his horse, for he still felt nauseous and giddy reelings in his head, and Mitsos trotted behind, with an incessant stick for the mules to make them keep up the pace. They were of the sedater sort, that hitherto had strolled through life, and they did not take kindly to a higher rate of going. But at the end of some half an hour Yanni reined in.

"Let's go slow a bit," he said, "for we are out of the range of risks. We are in our own country again; no one saw us go to the mill except my cousin Christos, and they might pull his tongue out before he spoke. Besides, there is nothing to say. The mill blew up. The matter is finished."

Mitsos assented, and threw himself down on the ground panting and blown, for the pace had been stiff. However, a few minutes' rest and a drink from the wooden wine-flask set his blood to a slower time, and he opened his mouth, and, to Yanni's intense astonishment, began to swear. He was in a white-hot rage, and he cursed Krinos in the name of every saint in heaven and every devil in hell, and labelled him with each several vile and muddy epithet he knew, and of these the Greek tongue boasts an inimitable profusion.

Yanni was still looking on in surprise when Mitsos' mood veered, and he began to laugh, rocking himself to and fro.

"Did you hear his head crack?" he jerked out. "It cracked like a green nut in September. No, it was more like a pomegranate under the heel. Is my head as messy inside as that, think you, Yanni? He thought his powder would make him a rich man, and the powder has made chicken-food of him. Oh, Yanni, what shall I do? I shall laugh till the Judgment Day."

Yanni's experience had not included an exhibition of hysterics, but he judged that they were not healthy things, and must be stopped if possible.

"Mitsos," he said, angrily, "don't make a fool of yourself. Stop laughing at once. Stop laughing!" he shouted.

Mitsos stared at him a moment like a chidden child; the fit ended as suddenly as it had begun, and he sat still a minute or two, idly plucking the fragrant shoots of thyme, or tossing them in the air.

"It has been a great day, Yanni," he said. "This sort of adventure is like wine to me. I think it must have made me drunk. And now I have cursed that devil I feel better. But I was so angry all the way here that I thought I should have burst. I wonder what made me laugh just now. Uncle Nicholas told me once that men sometimes went crazed the first time they killed any one. He told me that I should probably be blooded before I came home again. My eyes! it was so funny," and he began laughing again.

"Oh, Mitsos, dear Mitsos, for God's sake don't laugh. It's horrible to hear you," said Yanni, with a sudden panic fear that Mitsos was indeed possessed.

Mitsos made a great effort and checked himself.

"That's right," said Yanni, soothing him as he would soothe a child. "Drink some more wine, and then stop quiet a while. Go to sleep if you like."

Mitsos drank some wine, shifted to an easier position, and putting his head on Yanni's knee, who was leaning against a tree-trunk just above him, stretched out his great length, and in a couple of minutes was fast asleep. Yanni was not very comfortable, but he sat as still as a stone for fear of waking Mitsos. How odd it was, he thought to himself, that this great cousin of his should have behaved so queerly. He had been so perfectly cool and collected while there was anything to be done, but as soon as the need for doing anything was over he was just a baby. During his struggle with the Turk he remembered seeing Mitsos' face as he threw Krinos, and that mask of fury seemed to bear no resemblance to the cheerful cousin; he was like a wild beast. If anything had been wanting to put the final touch on Yanni's conviction that Mitsos was the king of men, it was that uprising of the wild beast within him.

93

The sun had come out as they sat there and shone full onto Mitsos' face, and Yanni, as gently as a woman, pushed his cap over his eyes that it should not waken him, and with infinite craft filled his pipe and managed to get a light from his flint and steel. He felt almost jealous of this girl whom Mitsos loved. It was not fit that he should go a-mooning after womankind, who were—so Yanni thought—an altogether inferior breed. It was Mitsos' business to fight, and do the work of fifty men. How splendid he had been one night at Kalamata, when they sat in the café after supper! The keeper of the house had tried to make Mitsos drunk, for the sport of seeing so long a pair of legs in mutiny, and had promised him that if he could drink two okes of wine he should not pay for them. This had suited Mitsos excellently, for he was as thirsty as Sahara. He had drunk them in less than half an hour, and, to show that he was as sober as a woman, he had played draughts afterwards with one of the Greeks there, and beat him easily in the first two games. Then his misguided little opponent had tried to cheat, and Mitsos rising up, a tower of wrath, had dealt the other so shrewd a blow over the head with the draught-board that he was fain to play no more, for other reasons than that the draughts had rolled to all corners of the café. Several men looking at the game had seen him cheat, and applauded most cordially Mitsos' method of correction. They then asked him to drink more wine, but Mitsos thanked them and refused, saying he was thirsty no longer. However, they stopped on, smoking and talking, as there was to be no journey the next day, and Mitsos had sung the "Song of the Vine-diggers" as Yanni had never heard it sung before, for his heart and voice were in harmony. Decidedly there was no one in the world like him.

The inimitable cousin stirred in his sleep, woke, and stretched himself.

"Oh, little Yanni," he said, "what a brute I am! Have you been sitting here all the time with my head on you? Why didn't you knock it off? But the sun is getting low, and we must be on the road. How's the head?"

"Oh, it's all right," said Yanni; "a bruise like a walnut, but it doesn't ache any more. You ride, Mitsos. I can walk perfectly."

Mitsos wrinkled up his nose.

"Indeed! Get on the horse."

And he broke out again with:

"Dig we deep around the vines."

They struck straight down the hill, guessing that they had gone beyond the village where they meant to sleep, threading their way slowly through the aromatic-smelling pines, and going softly on the fallen needles. A gentle wind from the south whispered in the boughs overhead, and Mitsos, purged by his sleep from the unwonted trouble of his nerves, whistled and sang as they went along. The sun was near its setting when they got out of the wood, but they found their guess had been correct, and soon struck the road leading into the village from the north. This village, Kalovryssi, was a stronghold of the Mavromichales, and Yanni knew that they would have a great welcome when they appeared. At the same time, there was a small depot of Turkish soldiers there, and it had been worth while to take the precaution of making a detour and entering from the north.

This Turkish garrison of Kalovryssi had a strangely comfortless life of it, for the scornful clan, secure in their remote position, made it quite clear that they were not to be interfered with in any way. If the government thought fit to keep soldiers there, well and good, they should be unmolested till the time came; but in the interval they would be wise to keep exceedingly quiet, buy their provisions at double price without a murmur, and if they ventured to meddle in any way with the Mavromichales's womankind, why the Mavromichales would see to it. Otherwise they did not interfere with the soldiers, except perhaps on festa days, when the clan got drunk in honor of the saint and demanded diversion in the evening. Then it is true they called them by shocking names, and warned them for their own sakes to keep within barracks, lest ignominious things should happen to them.

The two boys entered the village unmolested and went to the café, where they were sure to find friends, and no sooner had they got there than a great bearded man, as tall as Mitsos, came tumbling over chairs and tables and took Yanni off his horse as if he had been a child; for this clan were warm-hearted, Irish-souled folk, and the two were kept like kings that night.

The great bearded man was Petrobey's brother, and to him Yanni knew they might freely tell everything. Never in his life had that genial giant been the prey of so many conflicting emotions. He positively trembled with suspense when Yanni described how he had gone into the mill alone, and kept interrupting him to say "Go on, go on." He stared at Mitsos admiringly when he heard how that young man had won the fall with Krinos, and gave a whistle of keen appreciation and cracked his fingers when he learned that Krinos' skull had been crunched beneath the stone. He wiped his forehead nervously when Yanni told him how he had been thrown; he bit his lip when the Turk drew his pistol; and finally, when Mitsos shot the soldier through the head, he sprang off his chair, danced excitedly around the room, and embraced Mitsos with much fervor. He choked with laughter when he heard how they had decided to blow the mill up, and said "Pouf!" with loud solemnity when he was told that the explosion had taken place satisfactorily; finally, when Yanni came to Mitsos' hysterical fit in the wood his face clouded with anxiety, and he ran to the cupboard and fairly forced down his throat about half a pint of raw spirits.

"Well," he said, when the recital was over, "but this is a great day for the clan. And you, too, are of the clan," he said, turning to Mitsos, "and by the God above who made the clan, and the devil below who made the Turk, the clan is proud of you. Ah, but there will be a score of them in presently, and if the dear little Turks happen to meet any of them in the street as they go home again, I would not be surprised if we find them hanging upsidedown by the heels in the morning. You will be near two metres high, Mitsos!"

The clan, as Katsi Mavromichales had prophesied, soon learned that there was something going forward, and dropped into his house in groups of three and four to learn what it was. The recital had to be gone through again to a most appreciative audience, for Katsi took on his own broad shoulders the responsibility of making it public, and the only thing that failed to make the harmony of the evening complete was that the little soldiers had all gone home before the clan came out. The latter contemptuously supposed the soldiers were tired, for were they not little men? A few of the younger of the members had gone in a party to the barracks and tried to rouse the little men by throwing stones at the windows, but without result, and had subsequently quarrelled so violently at the café over the rival merits of the two corollaries, "The little men sleep sound" and "The little men are very deaf," that Katsi had to go out and knock their heads together, which he did with cheerful impartiality, the one against the other.

Confirmatory news of the effects of the explosion came from Nymphia next morning, and fulfilled the most sanguine hopes. The mill, so said the Greek who brought word, was blown to atoms, and as for Krinos, he was as if he had never been. A broken skull had been found some yards off, but of the rest of him no adequate remains were extant. It appeared also that there had been another man with him at the same time, for over forty teeth had been found by the enterprising youth of the village, which was more than Krinos ever had.

Katsi and a fine selection of cousins accompanied the two for a mile or so out of the village next morning to set them on their journey. There were no more messages to deliver, for they were now in the country of the clan, which was worked from Panitza by Petrobey, and Mitsos, as the slayer of the Turk and the treacherous Krinos, enjoyed the sweet sacrifices of hero-worship offered by his cousins. Two of them in particular, of about his own age, could only look at him in a state of rapt adoration, and feebly express their feelings by quarrelling as to which should lead his mule. Yanni, good lad, grudged Mitsos not one word or look of this admiration which was so showered on him; it warmed his heart to see that others like himself recognized the greatness of their splendid cousin.

On the brow of the hill above the village Katsi and the elder men stopped and went back to their work, but the younger ones escorted them as far as their mid-day halt—lithe, black-eyed young Greeks, girt about with the dogs of the clan, Morgos and Osman, Brahim and Maniati, Orloff and Machmoud, Psari and Drakon, Arapi, Cacarapi, Vlachos, Mavros, Tourkos and Tourkophágos, Maskaras and Ali, all great, stately dogs, shaggy-haired and eyed like wolves, and a contingent of smaller dogs of the most rascally kind, Pyr and Perdiki, Canella and Fundouki, who prosecuted an eternal feud with each other to keep themselves fighting fit, and allowed no man to pass along the road until a passage had been whipped through them by one or other of their masters. To Mitsos, who had lived so much alone, with only the companionship of his father, to be thrown suddenly among this crowd of boys of his own age, who welcomed him as a cousin and hailed him as a hero, was an incomparable pleasure,

96

and with Nauplia, and all that Nauplia held, getting nearer day by day, he was utterly content.

All that afternoon they travelled quietly on, keeping close to the coast, and about sunset saw Mavromati, where they were to sleep, perched high upon the hills below an eastern spur of Taygetus. The tops of the range were covered with snow, and the low sun for a few minutes turned the whole to one incredible rose. But below in the plain there was already a hint of spring in the air; the worst of the winter was passed, its armory of storms and squalls was spent, and the earth had stirred and thrown forth the early crocuses. And something of spring was in the hearts and in the eyes of the boys as they wondered, not knowing that they wondered, what the year would bring. For another more glorious spring was ready to burst forth, and that, which in Greece through a winter of bleak and storm-smitten centuries had lain battered by the volleyings of oppressive clouds, and bitten and stung with frost, had meanwhile so drunk life into all its fibres from that which would have done it to death, that already the green of its upspringing was vivid on the mountain-side, and held promise of a perfect flower, tyranny being turned into the mother of freedom, and smiting into strength.

CHAPTER IV

YANNI PAYS A VISIT TO THE TURK

Their last day's journey to Panitza was no more than a five hours' going, and by mid-day the two boys had crossed the ridge of mountain which toppled above it, and saw it nestled in a hollow below them. There, too, they found Petrobey himself, who had ridden out to meet them, both to give them news and take theirs. After they had eaten, Mitsos told their story, at which the soul of Petrobey was lifted high within him, and he was filled with an exceeding joy when he heard of the fate of Krinos.

"But all this spying and suspicion among the Turks make the next order the more necessary," he said, when Mitsos had finished. "Yanni, lad, I am very sorry, but it is Tripoli for you and Nauplia for Mitsos."

Yanni looked up at Mitsos.

"Oh, lucky one!" he said, below his breath, "see that Suleima has forgotten you not."

Then aloud:

"When shall I have to go to that kennel, father?" he said.

"You can stay here two days or three, and then you and Mitsos will go together. That Mehemet Salik has a sharp nose; but you shall be red herring to him, Yanni, and he will smell no farther afield."

Yanni wrinkled up his face with an expression of pungent disgust.

"I want no Turk smelling round me," he said. "It is the devil's business. How long must I be there, think you?"

"Not long, I hope. A month, perhaps. It will be an experience worth paying for, even for you. They will treat you royally, for they have no desire to make enemies among the clan. I want Mitsos to go with you as your servant for a day or two, so that he too may have free access to the governor's house and know where you will be in case they get more alarmed and keep you close, so that when the time comes for your escape he may easily find you."

"That will be a fine day for me," said Yanni.

"And what for me," asked Mitsos, "after I leave Yanni there?"

"You go to Nauplia with a letter from me for Nicholas, but I expect you will stay there just as long as the gull when he dips in the sea and out again. There will then be another journey for you northward to Patras to speak with Germanos. However, Nicholas will tell you all that."

Yanni sat up and pulled Mitsos' hair.

"O lazy dog," he said, "is it for this I pay you wages, that you should lie in the grass by your master"—and he felt in his pouch and found his tobacco gone—"and, by the Virgin! take his tobacco, and then not be able to fill a pipe fit for a Turk to smoke?"

"Fill it for me, Yanni," said the other, returning the tobacco, "and let go my hair before there is trouble for a little cousin of mine."

"You shall brush my clothes and sew my buttons," continued Yanni, "and lay my supper, and eat of my leavings. It is a fine thing to have a good strong servant. There's your pipe."

Mitsos reached out a huge hand, plucked Yanni's pipe from his mouth, and lit his own at it.

"There is a good clean smell abroad to-day," he said. "It is the first of spring. Just think; last year only I went out picking flowers with the little boys and girls on this day, and here am I now a man of war. It was good to sleep under the pines and wake to them whispering; was it not, Yanni? Perhaps that will come again when the kennel-work is over."

"Easter candles give I to the Mother of God," said Yanni, "for the days that are gone, and a candle more for every day we journey together, Mitsos."

"The Blessed Mother of God will have a brave lighting up one night, then," said Petrobey, "if things go well with us. There's many a tramp for you both yet. And who will be paying for the candles, little Yanni?"

The third day after, the two set out for Tripoli, Yanni trinketed out in his best clothes, as was fit for the son of a great chief, and going forward on a fine gray horse, Mitsos behind him on his own pony, in the dress of a servant, leading the baggage-mule. Four days' travelling, for they rode but short hours, being in no way very eager to get to the "kennel-work," as Mitsos called it, brought them to Tripoli, where Yanni went straight to the governor's house, leaving Mitsos outside in the square with the beasts.

The house stood on one side of the square, but to those outside showed only a bald face of wall, pierced here and there with a few iron gratings. As Mitsos waited he saw a woman's face thickly veiled peering out from one of these, and guessed rightly that here were the women's quarters. An arched gateway leading into the garden and closed by a heavy door, which had been opened to Yanni by the porter, and shut again immediately after he had entered, alone gave access to the premises. After waiting a few minutes the door was again opened, and a Turkish servant came out to help him to carry in the luggage. But the luggage was but light and Mitsos carried it all in himself, while the porter, leaning on his long stick, and resplendent in his embroidered waistcoat and red gaiters trimmed with gold, looked at him with indolent insolence, playing with the silver-chased handle of his long dagger. Behind the gate stood a small room for the porter, and on the left, as he entered, the side of the block of building he had seen from the street. A door was pierced in the middle of it, but the windows, as outside, were narrowly barred. The path was bordered on each side by a strip of gay garden-bed, and following the porter's directions he went straight on and past the corner of the main block, from the end of which ran out another narrow building right up to the bounding wall away from the street. In front of this lay a square garden planted with orange-trees and flowering shrubs, the house itself running from the square to the bounding wall at the back.

This second block of narrow buildings was two-storied, the upper story being faced by a balcony which was reached from below by an outside staircase. Four rooms opened onto this, and, still following his directions, he knocked at the first of the doors and a young Turk came out, who, seeing Mitsos with the luggage, reached down a key and proceeded to open the doors of the next two rooms. These, he said to Mitsos, were his master's rooms, and the end room was a slip of a place where he could sleep if his master wished to have him near. So Mitsos, as Yanni did not appear, unpacked his luggage and waited for him.

Yanni came up presently, accompanied by the porter, and was shown into his rooms, where Mitsos was busy arranging things. He shut the door hastily, and, waiting till the steps of the porter had creaked away down the balcony steps, broke out with an oath.

"The very devil, Mitsos," he said; "but this is no good job we are on. Here am I, and from within this kennel-place I may not stir. I sleep and am fed, and for exercise I may walk in that pocket-handkerchief of a garden and pick a flower to smell, but out of these walls I don't move."

Mitsos whistled.

"It is then good that I came," he said. "I suppose this Turk next door is your keeper. Oh, Yanni, but we shall have bitter dealings with him before you get out of this. I shall stop here to-night—there is a room I may use next this—and you inside and I outside must just examine the lie of things. I will go out now, round to the stables to see if the horses are properly cared for, and before I come back I will have gone round the outside of this place and seen what is beyond these walls. And you look about inside."

Mitsos returned in about an hour. "It wasn't good," he said, "but it might have been worse." From the square it was impossible to get into the place, except through the gate, and equally impossible to get out. To the right of the gate stood the corner house of the square, and next to it a row of houses opening out on the street leading from the square, and there was no getting in that way. On the left the long wall of the back of the house looked out blankly into another corresponding street running into the square, but farther down things were not hopeless; for the house next Mehemet's stood back from the street in the middle of its garden, and was enclosed by an eight-foot wall. "None so high," quoth Mitsos, "but that a bigger man than you could get up." Standing on the top of the wall, it would be possible to get onto the roof of the block of buildings in which they were, and from there down onto the balcony, which was covered in and supported by pillars, one of which stood in front of Yanni's door. "And where a man has come, there may two go," said Mitsos, in conclusion; "so do not look as if the marrow had left your bones; Yanni."

"It's all very good for you," said Yanni, mournfully; "but here am I cooped up like a tame hen for a month, or it may be more, in this devil-kennel place, with a garden to walk in and an orange to suck. Eh, Mitsos, but it will be a gay life for me sitting here in this scented town. A fat-bellied, slow-footed cousin will you find when you come for me. I doubt not I shall be sitting cross-legged on the floor with a narghilé, and a string of beads, and a flower in my hair."

"Oh, you'll soon get fit again on the mountains," said Mitsos, cheerfully. "I expect it will be quick going when I come to fetch you out of this."

Yanni nodded his head towards the Turk's room next door.

"Some night when you come tramping on the roof overhead," he said, "will he not wake and pluck you by the two heels as you come down onto the balcony?"

Mitsos grinned.

"There will be fine doings that night," he said. "If only you looked into the street we could arrange that you should be at the window every night, and I could whistle you a signal; but here, bad luck to it! I could whistle till my lips were in rags and you would not hear. I shall have to come in myself."

Mitsos stopped in Tripoli two days, and before he left Yanni had plucked up heart again concerning the future. However much the Turks might in their hearts distrust the scornful clan, they could not afford to bring that nest of hornets about their ears without grave reason. Yanni had but to ask for a thing and he had it; it was only not allowed him to set foot outside the house and garden. About his ultimate safety he had no shadow of doubt. Mitsos had examined the wall again, and declared confidently that he would not find the slightest difficulty in getting in, and that their exit, with the help of a bit of rope, was in the alphabet of the use of limbs. The Turk who was Yanni's keeper was the only other occupant of that part of the house, the story below being kitchens and washing-places not tenanted at night. "And for the Turk," said Yanni, "we will make gags and other arrangements." In the mean time he announced his intention of being a model of discretion and peacefulness, so that no suspicion might be aroused.

Mitsos was to start on the third day, and it was still the grayness that precedes sunrise when he came into Yanni's room equipped for going. Yanni had told Mehemet Salik that his father could not spare him longer,

100

and that he was to go home at once; whereat Mehemet had very courteously offered to put another Turkish servant at his disposal, a proposition which Yanni declined with some alacrity, as such an arrangement would mean another Turk in that block of building.

"And, O little Mitsos," said Yanni, "come for me as quick as may be. I shall be weary for a sight of you. Dear cousin, we have had good days together, and may we have more soon, for I have a great love for you."

Mitsos kissed him.

"Yes, Yanni," he said, "as soon as I can come I will, and nothing, not Suleima herself, shall make me tarry for an hour till you are out again."

"Ah! you have Suleima," said Yanni; "but for me, Mitsos, there is none like you. So, good-bye, cousin; forget me not, but come quickly."

And Mitsos swore the oath of the clan to him that neither man, woman, nor child, nor riches, nor honor, should make him tarry as soon as it was possible for him to come again, and gave him his hand on it, and then went down to saddle his pony with a blithe heavy-heartedness about him, for on one side he was leaving an excellent good comrade, but on in front there was waiting Suleima.

All day he travelled, and the moon which rose about midnight showed him the bay just beneath him, all smooth and ashine with light. He had taken a more roundabout path, so as to avoid passing through Argos at night, and another hour of quick going brought him down to the head of the sandy beach where he had fished with Suleima, and when he saw it his heart sang to him. A southerly breeze whistled among the rushes, and set tiny razor-edged ripples prattling on the pebbles, and sweet was the well-remembered freshness of the sea, and sweet, but with how exquisite a spice of bitterness, the remembrance of one night three weeks ago. Then on again down the narrow path, where blackthorn and olive brushed him as he passed, by the great white house with the sea-wall he knew well, and into the road just opposite his father's house. The dog rushed out from the veranda intent on slaughter of this midnight intruder, but at Mitsos' whispered word he jumped up fawning on his hand, and in a couple of minutes more Nicholas, who was a light sleeper, and had been awakened by the bark, unfastened the door.

"Mitsos, is it little Mitsos?" said the well-known voice.

"Yes, Uncle Nicholas," he said, "I have come back."

Mitsos slept late the next morning, and Nicholas, though he waited impatiently enough for his waking, let him have his sleep out, for though he despised the necessities of life, such as eating and drinking, he had the utmost respect for the simpler luxuries, such as the fill of sleep and washing, and it was not till after nine that Mitsos stirred and awoke with a great lazy strength lying in him. Nicholas had had the great wooden tub filled for his bath, and while he dressed made him coffee and boiled his eggs, for times had gone hard with Constantine, and he could no longer keep a servant. And as soon as Mitsos had finished breakfast he and Nicholas fell to talk.

First Mitsos described his adventure down to his parting with Yanni, and the man of few words spoke not till he had finished. Then he said—and his words were milk and honey to the boy:

101

"It could not have been better done, little Mitsos. Now for Petrobey's letter."

He read it out to Mitsos:

"Dear Cousin,—This will Mitsos bring you, and I desire no better messenger. He will tell you what he has been doing; and I could hear that story many times without being tired. Yanni, poor lad, is kennelled in Tripoli, and in this matter some precision will be needed, for now we are already being rung to the feast ['Petrobey will not stick to home-brewed words,' remarked Nicholas], and my poor lad must remain in Tripoli till the nick of the moment. Once he is safe out we will fall to, and he must not be out till the last possible moment. Oh, Nicholas, be very careful and tender for the boy. Again, the meeting of primates is summoned for early in March. Moles and owls may not see what this means. Some excuse must be found so that they go not; therefore, cousin, lay hands on that weaving brain of yours until it answers wisely ['What a riddling fellow this is!' growled the reader], and talk with Germanos through the mouth of Mitsos. A further news for you. The monks of Ithome have turned warmly to their country, so there will be no lack of hands in the south, and they from Megaspelaion had better keep to their own country, and outbreak at the same time as we at Kalamata, so shall then be the more magnificent confusion, and from the north as well as the south will the dogs run into Tripoli. Some signal will be needed, so that on the day that we rise in the south they too may make trouble in the north; some device of fiery beacons, I should say."

Here Petrobey's epistolary style broke down and he finished in good colloquial Greek:

"Oh, cousin, but a feast day is coming, and there will be a yelp and a howl from Kalamata to Patras. By God! I'd have given fifty brace of woodcock, though they are scarce this year, to see that barbarian nephew of yours throw Krinos under the millstone; and my boy Yanni has the cunning of an old grandfather. I think Mitsos can tell you all else. Come here yourself as soon as you safely may. The mother of God and your name-saint protect you!

"Petros Mavromichales.

"Tell Mitsos about the devil-ships. There will not be much time afterwards."

Nicholas thumped the letter as it lay on the table.

"Now, Mitsos," he said, "tell me all that you have to do. Yes, take a pipe and give yourself a few minutes to think."

Mitsos smoked in silence a few minutes, and then turned to Nicholas.

"This is it," he said. "First of all, I go to Patras—no, first I shall go to Megaspelaion to tell the monks that they will be wanted in the north and not the south, and arrange some signals, so that we from Taygetus or

Panitza or Kalamata can communicate with them. Then I go to Patras, bearing some message from you to Germanos, whereby he shall excuse himself from going to Tripoli with all the primates, for that is a trap to get them into the power of the Turk. Then there is some business about devil-ships which I do not understand, and at the last I have to get Yanni safely out of Tripoli. But before that I imagine you will have gone to my cousin Petrobey."

Nicholas nodded approvingly.

"You have a clear head for so large a boy," he said, "though apparently you are not so crafty as Yanni. Now what we have to do, now this moment, is to invent some excuse whereby Germanos and the primates will find means to disobey Mehemet Salik when he summons them to Tripoli. Oh, Mitsos, but it is a wise man's thoughts that we want."

Mitsos knitted his forehead.

"Can't they go there and then escape, as Yanni is to do?" he said, precipitately.

Nicholas shook his head in reproof.

"Fifty cassocked primates climbing over a town wall! Little Mitsos, you are no more than a fool."

Mitsos laughed.

"So Yanni often told me," he said. "I'm afraid it's true."

"Try and be a shade more sensible. Think of all the impossible ways of doing it, and then see what is left, for that will be the right way. Now first, they must either refuse to go point-blank or seem to be obeying. Certainly they must not refuse outright to go; so that leaves us with them seeming to obey."

"Well, they mustn't get there," said Mitsos; "so they must stop on the way."

"That is true. Why should they stop on the way? We will go slow here."

"There must be something that stops them," said Mitsos, with extreme caution.

"Yes, you are going very slow indeed, but it is a fault on the right side. Something must stop them, which even in the eyes of the Turks will seem reasonable and enable them all to disperse again, for they will all go together from Patras. Oh, why did my mother give birth to a fool?"

Mitsos suddenly got up and held his finger in the air.

"Wait a minute," he cried, "don't speak to me, Uncle Nicholas.... Ah, this is it. We will imagine there is a Turk in Tripoli friendly to Germanos. We will imagine he sends a letter of warning to Germanos. Do you see? Germanos reads the letter aloud to the fathers, and they send to Tripoli demanding assurance of their safety, and so disperse. Quick, Uncle Nicholas, write a letter from the friendly Turk in Tripoli to Germanos, which he will read the fathers on the journey."

Nicholas stared at Mitsos in sheer astonishment for a moment.

"Out of the mouth of big babes and sucklings!" he ejaculated. "Oh, Mitsos, but it is no less than a grand idea. Tell me again."

Mitsos was flushed with excitement.

"Oh, Uncle Nicholas, but it's plainer than the sun," he cried. "I go to

Patras, and before now the summons for the primates and bishops will have come. I take to Germanos your instructions that they assemble as if to go, and make a day's journey or two days' journey. Then one morning there comes to Germanos a letter from Tripoli, from a Turk to whom he has been a friend. 'Do not go,' it says, 'without an assurance of your safety, for the Turks are treacherous.' So Germanos sends back a messenger to Tripoli to ask for an assurance of safety, and meantime they all disperse again, and by the time the Turks can bring them together with an assurance of safety or what not, why the feast, as my cousin Petrobey says, will be ready."

Nicholas sat silent a moment.

"Little Mitsos," he said, at length, "but you are no fool. I was one to say so."

Mitsos laughed.

"Will it do then?"

"It is of the best," said Nicholas.

The more Nicholas thought it over, the more incomparable did Mitsos' scheme appear. It was amazingly simple, and, as far as he could see, without a flaw. It seemed to solve every difficulty, and made the whole action of the primates as planned inevitable. It would be impossible for them to go to Tripoli, and by the time the demand for safety had reached Mehemet Salik, and been granted, they would have dispersed.

The second piece of business was to let them know at the monastery that their arms and men would not be needed, as Nicholas had expected, in the south, but for a simultaneous outbreak in the north; and there was also to be arranged some code of signals that could travel in an hour or two from one end of the Peloponnesus to the other. The simplest system, that of beacon-fires, seemed to be the best, and was peculiarly well suited to a country like the Peloponnesus, where there were several ranges of mountains which overtopped the long intervening tracts of hills and valleys, and were clearly visible from one another. From Taygetus three intermediate beacons could probably carry news to the hills above Megaspelaion, and two beacons more to Patras.

There were, then, two messages to be conveyed to Megaspelaion— the first, that their arms would be required in the north, so that there was no need of their beginning to make depots of them southward, as Nicholas had suggested in his last visit there; and the second, to arrange a system of beacons with them. It was not necessary that Mitsos should give the first message himself, as Nicholas had told them to be ready to receive a messenger—man, woman, or child—who spoke of black corn for the Turk, though it must be delivered at once; but for the second it were better that he carried with him not only a letter from Nicholas, but also one from Germanos, with whom they would have to arrange the beacons between Patras and the monastery. Also, he wished Mitsos to take a message to Corinth, and go from there to Patras, where he would see Germanos, and thence return by Megaspelaion, not to Nauplia, for Nicholas would already have joined Petrobey, but back to Panitza.

Mitsos nodded.

"But who will take the first message to Megaspelaion?" he asked.

Nicholas turned to Constantine.

"Whom do we know there? Stay, did not one Yanko Vlachos, with his wife Maria, move on to monastery land a month or two ago?"

"Maria?" said Mitsos. "Maria is a very good woman. But I doubt if Vlachos is any use. He is a wine-bibbing mule."

"Where does he live?" asked Nicholas.

"At Goura, a day's journey from Nemea."

"Goura? There are plenty of good folk there. You had better go out of your way at Nemea, Mitsos, spend the night with Yanko, and arrange for the message being taken; and then go back next day to Nemea, and so to Corinth, where you will take ship. Pay him horse-hire and wage for four days, if it is wanted. I will give you letters to Priketes and Germanos. What else is there?"

"Only the business of the devil-ships, of which I know nothing; and to get Yanni out of the kennel."

"The devil-ships can wait till Panitza. When will you be ready to start?"

Mitsos thought of the white wall, and his heartstrings throbbed within him.

"I could go to-morrow," he said. "The pony will need a day to rest."

Nicholas rose from the table and walked up and down once or twice.

"I don't want Yanni to stop at the house of that Turk longer than is necessary," he said. "It was a bold move and a clever one of Petrobey's, but it may become dangerous."

Mitsos said nothing, for it was a hard moment. Had not the thought of this evening—the white wall, the dark house on the bay with Suleima—been honey in the mouth for days past, and become ineffable sweetness as the time drew nearer? Yet, on the other hand, had he not sworn to Yanni the oath of the clan—that neither man, woman, nor child should make him tarry? He desired definite assurance on one point.

"Uncle Nicholas," he said, at length, "if I went to-day would Yanni get out of Tripoli a day sooner?"

Nicholas turned round briskly.

"Why, surely," he said; "when this business is put through there is still but little more to do, but until it is all done Yanni is clapped in his kennel. The moment it is over he is out."

Mitsos sat still a moment longer.

"I will start to-day," he said. "It is only a short day's journey to Nemea. Write your letter, please, Uncle Nicholas, and then I will go."

"I don't know whether it really matters if you go to-day or to-morrow," said Nicholas, seeing that the boy for some reason wished to stop.

"No, no," broke out Mitsos. "You think it is better for me to go to-day. The sooner the business is over the sooner Yanni comes out. You said so."

Nicholas raised his eyebrows at this outburst. He did not understand it in the least.

"I will write, then, at once," he said. "It is true that the sooner Yanni comes out the better."

Mitsos stood with his back to him, looking out of the window, and two great tears rose in his eyes. He was giving up more than any one knew.

Nicholas saw that something was wrong, but as Mitsos did not care to enlighten him, it was none of his business. But he had a great affection for the lad, and as he passed he laid his hand on his shoulder.

"You are a good little Mitsos," he said. "The letters will be ready in an hour. You will have dinner here, will you not, and set out afterwards? You cannot go farther than Nemea to-night."

So after dinner Mitsos set out again, and it seemed to him as he went that the heart within him was being torn up as the weeds in a vineyard are rooted for the burning. And on this journey there was no thought that he would soon come back. He was to return, Nicholas told him, not to Nauplia, but to Panitza, where there would be work for him to do until the time came for him to get Yanni out of Tripoli. By then everything would be ready, the beacons would flare across the Peloponnesus, and simultaneously in the north and at Kalamata the outbreak would begin. The reason for this was twofold. The Greek forces were not yet sufficiently organized to conduct the siege of Tripoli, which was strongly fortified, well watered, and heavily garrisoned. Kalamata, however, was a more pregnable place, the water supply was bad inside the citadel, and the garrison not numerous. Again, it was a port, and by getting possession of the harbor, which was not defended, and separate from the citadel, they would drive those who escaped inland to Tripoli. The movements in the north, too, would have the same effect. Tripoli was the strongest fortress in the Peloponnesus, and by the autumn, when, as Nicholas hoped, the Greeks would be sufficiently organized to undertake the siege, it would be the only refuge left for the Turks who were still in the country. Then it would be that the great blow would be struck which would free the whole Peloponnesus. In the interval the plan was as far as possible to cut the country off from the rest of the world by a fleet which was being organized in the islands, and by means of the fire-ships which should destroy the Turkish vessels seeking to leave it, and prevent others from coming into the ports. For practical purposes there were only four ports—at Corinth, Patras, Nauplia, and Kalamata. The first two would be the care of the leaders of the revolution in the north; for Kalamata and Nauplia, Nicholas and Petrobey had arrangements in hand.

That night Mitsos slept at Nemea, and all next day travelled across the great inland plain where lie the lakes. Through the length and breadth of that delectable country the spirit of spring was abroad—crocuses and the early anemones burned in the thickets, and the dim purple iris cradled bees in a chalice of gold. Brimming streams crossed the path, and the sunlight lay on their pebbly beds in a diaper of amber and stencilled shadow, and Mitsos' pony at the mid-day halt ate his fill of the young, juicy grass. But in the lad's heart the spring woke no echo; he went heavily, and the glorious adventure to which he had sacrificed his new-found manhood, fully indeed and without a murmur, seemed to him a thing of little profit. And if he had known what hard days were waiting for him, and the blank agonies and bitterness through which he was to fulfil his destiny, he would, it is to be feared, have turned his pony's head round and said that an impossible thing was asked of him. But he knew nothing beyond this two-week task now set him, and to this he was committed, not only by his promise to Nicholas—and, to do him justice, his own self-respect—but by the oath of the clan, which rather than fail in he would have sooner died.

The second evening a little before sunset he saw Goura close before him, standing free and roomily on a breezy hill-side, and ringed with vineyards. Behind lay the great giants of the mountain range—Helmos cowled in snow, and Cyllene all sunset-flushed. Yanko's house proved to be at the top of the village, and there he found Maria with a face all smiles for his welcoming. Yanko was still in the fields, and Mitsos and Maria talked themselves up to date with each other till he came home.

Oh yes, he was a good husband, said Maria, and he earned a fine wage. He was as strong as a horse, and when he let the wine-shop alone he did the work of two men. "And I am strong too," said she, "and when he doesn't come home by ten in the evening it will be no rare thing for me to bring him back with a clout over the head for his foolishness. And why are you here, Mitsos?"

"Business," he said; "business for Nicholas. It is Yanko who can do it for us. I may tell you about it, Maria, for so Nicholas said. He is wanted to take a message to the monastery. Four days' horse-hire, if he wishes, will be paid, and he will be doing a good work for many."

"On business against the Turk?" asked Maria.

"Surely."

Maria shook her head doubtfully.

"Yanko is a good man," she said, "but he is a man of the belly. So long as there is food in plenty, and plenty of wine, he does not care. But he will not be long; you shall ask him. It is so good to see you again, Mitsos. Do you remember our treading the grapes together in the autumn? How you have grown since then! Your height is two of Yanko, but then Yanko is very fat."

Maria looked at him approvingly with her head on one side; she distinctly felt a little sentimental. Mitsos reminded her of Nauplia, and of the days when she was so proud of being engaged to Yanko while still only seventeen, and of having Mitsos, whom she had always thought wonderfully good-looking and pleasant, if not at her feet, at any rate interested in her. She had been more than half disposed, as far as her personal inclination had gone, to put Yanko off for a bit and try her chance with the other; but she was safe with Yanko, and he did quite well. But it both hurt her and pleased her to see Mitsos again—he was better looking than ever, and he had a wonderful way with him, an air of breeding—Maria did not analyze closely, but this is what she meant—to which the estimable Yanko was quite a stranger. And this brave adventure of his, of which he told her the main outlines; his kinship to, and rapturous adoption by, the great Mavromichales' clan, lent him a new and powerful attraction. And when Yanko's heavy step was heard outside Maria turned away with a sigh and thought he seemed earlier and fatter than usual.

Yanko, always sleek, had grown rather gross, and his red, shiny face and small, boiled-looking eyes presented a strong contrast to Mitsos' thin, bronzed cheeks and clear iris. But the husband seemed glad to see him, and agreed that Mitsos' errand had best wait till after supper.

So after supper Mitsos expounded, and Yanko shifted from one foot to the other, and seemed uncomfortable. "And," said Mitsos, in conclusion, "I can give you horse-hire for four days."

Yanko sat silent for a while, then abruptly told his wife to draw another jug of wine. Maria had a sharp tongue when her views were dissentient from his, and he would speak more easily if she were not there. Maria, who had listened to Mitsos with wide, eager eyes and a heightened color, went off quickly and returned in equal haste, anxious not to lose anything.

"It's like this," Yanko was saying. "What with this and that I've a lot of farm work on my hands, and, to tell the truth, but little wish to mix myself up in the affair; and as for four days' horse-hire, it will pay my way, but where's my profit?"

Mitsos frowned.

"You won't go?" he said, half rising; "then I mustn't wait, but find some one else."

At this Maria burst out:

"Shame, Yanko!" she said. "I have a mule-man for a husband. It is that you think of nothing but piastres, and are afraid of taking on yourself for two days such work as Mitsos spends his months in. Am I to sit here and see you drinking and eating and sleeping, and never lift a hand for the sake of any but yourself? Ah, if I was a man I would not have chosen a wife with as little spirit as my husband has."

Maria banged the wine-jug down on the table, and cast a scornful look at Yanko. Then she crossed over to Mitsos and took his glass to fill it, filling her own at the same time.

"This to you," she said, clinking her glass at his, "and to the health of all brave men."

Then with another scowl at Yanko:

"Can't you even drink to those who are made different to yourself, if they are of a finer bake?" she said; "or is there not spirit in you for that? I should have been a mile on the way by this time," she said to Mitsos, "if it had pleased the good God to make me a man and send you with such a message to me."

"You, Maria?" said Mitsos, suddenly.

"Yes, and how many days of horse-hire does Yanko think I should have asked for my pains? Nay, I should have lit candles to the Virgin in the joy of having such work given me to do, if I had had to beg my way."

Mitsos remembered Nicholas's directions.

"Will you go?" he said. "You would do it as well as any man. It is just Father Priketes you have to ask for, and give the message."

"Nonsense, Maria," said Yanko; "a woman can't do a thing like that."

Maria's indignant speeches had a touch of the high rhetorical about them, but Yanko's remark just stamped them into earnestness.

"You'll be drawing your own wine for yourself the next few days," she said, "and I shall be over the hills doing what you were afraid of. I'm blithe to go," she said to Mitsos, "and to-morrow daybreak will see me on the way."

Yanko, on the whole, was relieved; it would have been a poor thing to send Mitsos to another house in quest of a sturdier patriot than he, and Maria's offer had obviated this without entailing the journey on himself. Poor Yanko had been born of a meek and quiet spirit, and the possession of the earth in company with like-minded men would have seemed to him a sufficiently beatified prospect. He had no desire for brave and boisterous adventure, new experiences held for him no ecstasy: even in the matter of drinking, which was the chiefest pleasure of his life, he maintained a certain formula of moderation, never passing beyond the stage of a slightly fuddled head; and a wholesome fear of Maria—not acute, but steady—as a rule, drove him home while he was still perfectly capable of getting there. The rule of his life was a certain sordid mean, which has been the subject for praise in the mouth of poets, who have even gone so far as to call it golden, and is strikingly exemplified in the lives of cows and other ruminating animals. He was possessed of certain admirable qualities, a capacity for hard work and a real affection for his eminent wife being among them, but he was surely cast in no heroic mould. He had no fine, heady virtues which carry their own reward in the constant admiration they excite, but of the more inglorious excellences he had an average share.

Mitsos arrived at Corinth next night after a very long day, and found a caique starting in an hour or two for Patras. He had just time to leave Nicholas's message to the mayor of the town, get food, and bargain for a passage to Patras for himself and his pony. The wind was but light and variable through the night, but next day brought a fine singing breeze from the east, and about the time that he landed at Patras Maria saw below her from the top of a pass the roof of the monastery ashine with the evening sun from a squall of rain which had crossed the hills that afternoon.

Her little pinch-eared mule went gayly down through the sweet-smelling pine forest which clothed the upper slope below which the monastery stood, and every now and then she passed one or two of the monks engaged on their work—some burning charcoal; some cleaning out the channels which led from the snow-water stream, all milky and hurrying, after a day of sun, down to the vineyards; others, with their cassocks kilted up for going, piloting timber-laden mules down home, and all gave Maria a "Good-day" and a "Good journey."

Outside the gate a score or so of the elder men were enjoying the last hour of sunlight, sitting on the stone benches by the fountain, smoking and talking together. One of these, tall and white-bearded, let his glance rest on Maria as she rode jauntily down the path; but when, instead of passing by on the road, she turned her mule aside up the terrace in front of the gate, he got up quickly with a kindled eye and spoke to the brother next him.

"Has it come," he said, "even as Nicholas told us it might?" and he went to meet Maria.

"God bless your journey, my daughter!" he said, "and what need you of us?"

Maria glanced round a little nervously.

109

"I want to speak to Father Priketes, my father," she said.

"You speak to him."

"Have you corn, father?" she said.

A curious hush had fallen on the others, and Maria's words were audible to them all. At her question they rose to their feet and came a little nearer, and a buzzing whisper rose and died away again.

"Corn for the needy or corn for the Turk?" asked Priketes, while round there was a silence that could have been cut with a knife.

"Black corn for the Turk. Let there be no famine, and have fifteen hundred men ready to carry it when the signal comes, and that will be soon. Not far will they have to go. It will be needed here, at Kalavryta."

Maria slipped down from her mule and spoke low to Priketes.

"And oh, father, there is something more, but I cannot remember the words I was to use; but I know what it means, for Mitsos, the nephew of Nicholas, told me."

Father Priketes smiled.

"Say it then, my daughter."

"It is this: if you have guns stored in readiness southward, get them back. It will not happen just as Nicholas expected. You will want all your men and arms here."

"It is well. What will the signal be?"

"I know not; but in a few days Mitsos will come from Patras. Oh, you will know him when you see him—as tall as a pillar, and a face like a spring morning or a wind on the hill—and to see him does a body good. He knows and will tell you."

"I will expect Mitsos, then," said Priketes. "You will stay here to-night; there shall be made ready for you the great guest-room—for you are an honored guest—the room where the daughter of an emperor once lodged."

Maria hesitated.

"I could get back to some village to-night," she said. "I ought not to delay longer than I need."

"And shame our hospitality?" said Priketes. "Besides, you are a conspirator now, my daughter, and you must use the circumspection of one. What manner of return would you make at dead of night to where you slept before, with no cause to give? To-morrow you shall go back, and say how pleased your novice brother was to see you—and the lie be laid to the account of the Turk, who fill our mouths perforce with these things—and how you had honor of the monks. Give your mule to the lad, my daughter. It shall be well cared for."

So Maria had her chance, and took it. An adventure and a quest for the good of her country were offered her, and she embraced them. For the moment she rose to the rank of those who work personally for the good of countries and great communities, and then passed back into her level peasant life again. Goura, as it turned out, took no part in the deeds that were coming. Its land was land of the monastery, and the Turks never visited its sequestered valley with cruelty, oppression, or their lustful appetites. Yet the great swelling news that came to the inhabitants of that little mountain village, only as in the ears of children a sea-shell speaks of remotely breaking waves, had to Maria a reality and a nearness that it lacked to others, and her life was crowned with the knowledge that she had for a moment laid her finger harmoniously on the harp which made that glorious symphony.

Mitsos' work at Patras was easily done. Germanos was delighted with the idea of the forged letter from the Turk, and was frankly surprised to hear that the notion was born of the boy's brain. Being something of a scholar, he quoted very elegantly the kindred notion of Athene, who was wisdom, springing full-grown from the brain of Zeus, for Mitsos' idea, so he was pleased to say, was complete in itself, mature from its birth. Mitsos did not know the legend to which the primate referred, and so he merely expressed his gratification that the scheme was considered satisfactory. The affair of the beacons took more time, for Mitsos on his journey south back to Panitza would have to make arrangements for their kindling, and it was thus necessary that their situation should be accessible to villages where Nicholas was known, and where the boy could find some one to undertake to fire the beacon as soon as the next beacon south was kindled. Furthermore, though Germanos knew the country well, it would be best for Mitsos to verify the suitability of the places chosen, "for," as the archbishop said, "you might burn down all the pine-woods on Taygetus, and little should we reck of it if Taygetus did not happen to be visible from Lycaon; but we should stand here like children with toy swords till the good black corn grew damp and the hair whitened on our temples."

As at present arranged, Mitsos would be back at Panitza on the 10th of March, after which, as Nicholas had told him, there would be more work to do before he could go for Yanni at Tripoli. It was, therefore, certain—taking the shortest estimate—that the beacon signal could not possibly occur till March 20th, but that on that evening and every evening after the signalmen must be at their posts waiting for the flame to spring up on Taygetus. For the beacons between Patras and Megaspelaion there would be no difficulty; two at high points on the mountains would send the message all the way, and the only doubtful point was where to put the beacon which should be intermediate between that on Taygetus and that on Helmos, which latter could signal to one directly above the monastery. Germanos was inclined to think that a certain spur of Lycaon, lying off the path to the right, some four miles from Andritsaena, and standing directly above an old temple, which would serve Mitsos as a guiding point, would answer the purpose. If so, it could be worked from Andritsaena, and the priest there, at whose house Mitsos would find a warm welcome if he stayed for the night, would certainly undertake it.

Mitsos went off again the next day, with the solemn blessing of the archbishop in his ears and the touch of kindly hands in his, and reached Megaspelaion in two days. Here he had news of Maria's safe arrival. "And a brave lass she is," said Father Priketes. The business of the beacons was soon explained, and next morning Father Priketes himself accompanied Mitsos on his journey to the top of the pass above the monastery, in order to satisfy himself that from there both the points fixed upon—that on the spur of Helmos, and also that towards Patras—were visible.

111

Their way lay through the pine-woods where Maria had come three days before, and a hundred little streams ran bubbling down through the glens, and the thick lush grass of the spring-time was starred with primroses and sweet-smelling violets. Above that lay an upland valley, all in cultivation, and beyond a large, bleak plateau of rock, on the top of which the beacon was to burn. Another half-hour's climb saw them there, a strange, unfriendly place, with long parallel strata of gray rock, tipped by some primeval convulsion onto their side, and lying like a row of razors. In the hollows of the rocks the snow was still lying, but the place was alive with the whisper of new-born streams. A few pine-trees only were scattered over these gaunt surfaces, but in the shelter of them sprang scarlet wind-flowers and hare-bells, which shivered on their springlike stalks.

A few minutes' inspection was enough to show that the place was well chosen—to the south rose the great mass of Helmos, and they could clearly see a sugarcone rock, the proposed beacon site, standing rather apart from the main mountain, some fifteen miles to the south, just below which lay the village of Leondari, whither Mitsos was bound, and towards Patras the contorted crag above Mavromati. Here, so Priketes promised, should a well-trusted monk watch every evening from March 20th onward, and as soon as he saw the blaze on Helmos, he would light his own beacon, waiting only to see it echoed above Mavromati, and go straight back with the news to the monastery. And the Turks at Kalavryta, so said Priketes—for it was on Kalavryta that the first blow was to descend—should have cause to remember the vengeance of the sword of God which His sons should wield.

CHAPTER V

THE VISION AT BASSAE

From the village of Leondari, held in a half-circle of the foothills of Helmos, where was to be the second link in the chain of beacons, it was impossible to see Andritsaena; but the mass of Mount Lycaon stood up fine and clear behind where Andritsaena was, and a series of smaller peaks a little to the west would prove, so Mitsos hoped, to be the hills above the temple. He and his host climbed the beacon-hill and took very sedulous note of these, and next morning the lad set off at daybreak to Andritsaena, which he reached in a day and a half. The country through which he travelled, an unkind and naked tract, was not suspected by the Turks to be tinged with any disaffection to their benignant rule, and his going was made without difficulty or accident. He found welcome at the house of the

112

priest to whom Germanos had given him a letter, and after dinner the two rode off, on a fair, cloudless afternoon, to the hills above the temple, to verify its visibility from Taygetus on the south and the crag of Helmos on the north. An Englishman, whom the priest described as a "tall man covered with straps and machines," had been there a year or two before making wonderful drawings of the place, and had told them it was a temple to Apollo, and that the ancient Greek name for it was Bassae. "Yet I like not the place," said Father Zervas.

An hour or so after their departure, fleecy clouds began to spin themselves in the sky, and as they went higher they found themselves involved in the folds of a white fabric of mist, which lay as thick as a blanket over the hill-side, and through which the sun seemed to hang white and unluminous, like a china plate. This promised but ill for the profit of their ride, but Zervas said it was worth while to push on; those mists would be scattered in a moment if the wind got up; he had seen them roll away as the housewife rolls up the bed-linen. But as they got higher the mist seemed to thicken, and the sun was expunged, and when, by the priest's computation, they must be near the temple, they could scarcely see ten yards before them, and the gaunt, contorted oak-trees marched swiftly into their narrow field of vision, and out again, like ghosts in torment. Shoulder after shoulder of gray hill-side sank beneath them, dripping with the cold, thick mist, and unutterably waste, when, after moving ten minutes or more across a featureless flank of hill, gigantic shadows peered at them from in front, a great range of columns faced them, and they were there.

Mitsos' pony, tired with the four days' journey, was lagging behind, and Mitsos had got off to relieve it on the steeper part of the ascent, when suddenly there came from out of the chill, blank fog a scream like that of a lost soul. For one moment a superstitious fear clutched at the boy, and his pony, startled, went off at a nimbler pace to join the other, and Mitsos had to break into a run to keep up. Then suddenly the sun stared whitely through the mists, and in five seconds more the wind, which had screamed so shrilly, was upon them. In a moment the hill-side was covered with flying wreaths of vapor, which the wind tore smaller and smaller till there was nothing left of them; it ripped off ribbons from the skirts of the larger clouds, which it drove like herded sheep down the valleys, and as Mitsos gained the ridge where the temple stood, a brilliant sun sat in cloudless blue, looking down upon the great gray columns. At their feet in every direction new valleys, a moment before muffled in mist, were being carved out among the hill-sides, and already far to the south the plain of Kalamata, rimmed with a dim, dark sea, sparkled green through thirty miles of crisp air. Down in the valley through which they had come some conflicting current of air tilted the mist up in a tall column of whirling vapor, as if from some great stewing-pot below, and as it streamed up into the higher air it melted and dissolved away, and in five minutes the whole land—north, south, east, and west—was naked to the incomparable blue.

Mitsos gazed in wonder at the gray columns, which seemed more to

113

have grown out of the hill than to have been built by the hands of men; but the priest hurried him on.

"It is as I hoped," said he; "the wind has driven the clouds off; but they may come back. We must go quickly to the top of the hill."

The lad left his pony grazing by the columns and ran up the brow of the hill some two hundred feet above the end of the temple. Northward Helmos lifted a snowy finger into the sky, and clean as a cameo on its south-eastern face stood the cone above Leondari, as if when the hills were set upon the earth by the stir of the forces of its morning it had been placed there for their purpose. Then looking southward they saw Taygetus rise shoulder above shoulder into the blue, offering a dozen vantage points. But Father Zervas was a cautious man.

"It seems clear enough, Mitsos," he said; "but Taygetus is a big place. This will I do for greater safety. You go straight south, you say, and will be at Kalamata two evenings from now, and on the third night you will sleep at some village on the pass crossing Taygetus over to Sparta. On that night directly after sundown I will kindle a beacon here, and keep it kindled for two hours, and in that time you will be able to choose a well-seen place for the blaze on Taygetus. Look, it is even as I said, the mists gather again; but the winds of God have favored us, and our work is done."

Even as he spoke a long tongue of mist shot up from the valley below, and came licking up the hill like the spent water of a wave on a level beach, and Mitsos ran down quickly in order to find his pony in case it had strayed even thirty or forty yards, before the clouds swallowed them up again. But he found it where he had left it, browsing contentedly on the spicy tufts of thyme and sweet mountain grass, and for a couple of minutes more, before the earth and sky were blotted out, he stared amazedly at the tall gray ruins which stood there crowning the silence and strength of the hills, still unknown to all but a few travellers and to the shepherds that fed their flocks in summer on the hill-tops—a memorial of the life and death of the worship of beauty, and the god of sunlight and health and imperishable youth.

He waited there till the priest joined him, and was surprised to see him cross himself as he passed by the door into the temple, and asked why he did so.

"It is a story of a devil," he said, "which folks tell about here. Whether I believe it or no, I know not, and so I am careful. We will make haste down this valley, for it is not good to be here after night."

The mists had risen again over the whole hill-side, but not thickly, and as they turned to go Mitsos looking back saw a strange shaft of light streaming directly out of the ruined door of the temple—the effect, no doubt, of the sun, which was near its setting, striking through some thin layer of cloud.

"Look," he said to the priest, "one might almost think the temple was lit from within."

Father Zervas looked round, and when he saw it dropped lamentably off his horse and onto his knees on the ground, and began muttering prayers, crossing himself the while.

114

Mitsos looked at him in surprise, and saw that his face was deadly pale, and a strangling anguish gripped at the muscles of his throat. The light cast through the temple door meantime had been choked by the gathering mists, and when Father Zervas looked up from his prayers it was gone.

"Quick, quick!" he cried to Mitsos; "it is not good to be here," and mounting on his pony he fairly clattered down the hill-side, and did not draw bridle till they had reached the main road from Andritsaena.

Mitsos followed, half amused, but conscious of a lurking fear in his mind, a fear bred by the memory of the winter evenings of his childhood when he used to hear strange stories of shapes larger than human, which had been seen floating like leaves in the wind round the old temples on the Acropolis, and cries that came from the hills of Ægina, where stood the house of the god, but no human habitation, at the sound of which the villagers in the hamlets below would bolt their doors and crouch fearfully round the fire, "making the house good," as they said, by the reiterated sign of the cross. Then as he grew older his familiarity with morning and evening and night in lonely places had caused these stories to be half forgotten, or remembered only as he remembered the other terrors and pains of childhood—the general distrust of the dark, and the storms that came swooping down from the gaunt hills above Nauplia. But now when he saw the flying skirts of Father Zervas waving dimly from the mist in front, and heard the hurried clatter of his pony's feet, he followed at a good speed, and in some confusion of mind. Zervas had stopped on reaching the high-road, and here Mitsos caught him up.

"Ah, ah!" he gasped, "but it is a sore trial the Lord has sent me, for I am no braver than a hare when it comes to dealings with that which is no human thing. It is even as Demetri said, for the evil one is there, the one whom he saw under the form of a young man, very fair to look upon, but evil altogether, a son of the devil."

And he wiped a dew of horror from his brow.

Mitsos must have felt disposed to laugh had not the man's terror been so real.

"But what did you see, father?" he asked. "For me I saw naught but a light shining through the door."

"That was it, that was it," said Zervas, "and I—I have promised Germanos to see to the beacon business, and on that hill shall I have to watch while perhaps the young man, evil and fair, watches for me below. I cannot pass this way, for my heart is cold water at the thought. I shall have to climb up from the other valley, so that I pass not the place; and then, perhaps, with the holy cross on my breast and the image of the Crucified in my hand, I shall go unhurt."

"But what was it Demetri saw?" asked Mitsos.

"It was this way," said Father Zervas, who was growing a little more collected as they attained a greater distance from the temple. "One evening, a spring evening, as it might be to-day, Demetri, of our village, whom I know, was driving his sheep down from the hill above the temple, where the beacon will be; and, being later than he knew, the sun had set

115

ere he came down to where the temple stands; therefore, as he could not herd the sheep in the dark down the glen, he bethought himself to encamp there, for the night was warm and he had food enough with him and wine for two men. Inside, the temple is of two rooms, and into the hindermost of these he penned the sheep, and in the other he lit a sparkle of fire and sat himself down to eat his supper. And having finished his supper he lay down to sleep, but no wink of sleep came near him, and feeling restless, he sat up and smoked awhile. But his unrest gained on him, twitching at his limbs and bidding him go; so out he fared on the hill-side to see if he could find sleep there—or, at any rate, get air—for it seemed to him that the temple had grown unseasonably warm, and that it was filled with some sweet and subtle perfume. Outside it was cooler, and so, laying himself in a hollow of the hill opposite the temple gate, he nestled down among the grasses and again tried to sleep.

"But it seemed to him that from below there came dim songs such as men sing on feast-days, and looking down to see whence such voices came, he saw, even as you saw and I, a strong great light shining out of the temple door, and next moment came a clattering and pattering of feet, and out through the door rushed his sheep, which must have leaped the barrier of boughs he had put up, and ran, scattering, dumb, and frightened, in all directions. He got up and hurried down to stop any that were left, for as for herding those that were gone he might as well have tried to herd the moonbeams, for the night was dark but for the space illuminated by that great light that shone out from the temple. So down he ran, but at the temple door he stopped, for in the centre of the great chamber stood one whom it dazzled his eyes to look upon. Fair was he and young, and lithe as a deer on the mountains, and from his face there shone a beauty and a glory which belong not to mortal man; and the lines of his body were soft with the graciousness of youth, but firm with the strength of a man. Over one shoulder was slung a quiver of gold, and his left hand held a golden bow; golden sandals were on his feet, and on his head a wreath of wild laurel. For the rest, he was as naked as the night of full moon in May, and as glorious. Two fingers of the hand which held the bow were rested on the head of one of Demetri's rams, the father of the flock, and the beast stood there quiet and not afraid. No other light was there in the temple, but all the splendor which turned the place to a summer noonday sprang from him. Only in front of the youth still smouldered the fire by which Demetri had eaten his supper, and that seemed in the blaze that filled the temple to have burned low and dim, like a candle in the sunlight, and a little blue smoke from it came towards him, full of some wonderful sweet perfume. The sheep, frightened, had collected again round him, and in that light he could see to right and left score upon score of their white heads and twitching ears; they stood close to him and huddled, yet all looked at that immortal thing within the temple. And as he stood there, stricken to stone, marvelling at the beauty of the youth, and forgetting in his wonder to be afraid, the god—yet no god was he, but only evil," said Zervas, hastily, again crossing himself—"raised his eyes to him and said:

116

"'Thou that makest a sheep-pen of my sanctuary, art thou not afraid to do this thing?

"But he spoke, so said Demetri, not harshly, and in the lustre of his eyes there was something so matchless and beyond compare that he knelt down and said:

"'Forgive me, Lord, for I knew not that it was thine.'

"Then said the other:

"'For penalty and yet for thine honor this ram is mine,' and he struck the beast lightly on the head, at which it sank down and moved no more. Then said the god again:

"'It is long since I have looked on your race; not so fair are they now as they were in the olden days'—and in truth Demetri is an ugly loon—'but this shalt thou learn of me, how joy is better than self-sacrifice, and beauty than wisdom or the fear of God. Look at me only, the proof is here.'

"And at this he held out his hand to him, but Demetri was suddenly smitten by the knowledge that this beautiful youth was more evil than the beasts of the field, and in wild despair he bethought himself of his only safety, and made in the air, though feebly, for his heart was nigh surrendered, the sign of the cross. With that a shuddering blackness came over his spirit and his eyes, and when he came to himself he was lying on the dew-drenched pavement of the temple, and close to him the ram, dead, but with no violent mark upon him; and looking in at the temple door, but coming not in, the rest of the flock, of which none was missing; and morning was red in the east. That is ten years ago, but Demetri will scarce speak of it even to-day, and I had half thought before that it was an idle tale; but when I saw the light shining out through the temple door an hour ago, it was freshly borne to me that it was true, albeit one of the dark things of the world at which we cannot even guess. Yet, as Christ protected Demetri, He will surely protect me when I go on the beacon work, for it is His work; but lest I tempt God, I will climb up that hill on the other side and keep my eyes away from the temple, and plant the holy cross between me and it."

Mitsos knew not what to make of all this. The fact that Demetri had, in Zervas's phrase, wine for two men with him might have explained the significance of what he had seen; but, being a Greek, his mind was fruitful soil for all things ghostly and superstitious.

"It is very strange," he said; "yet, father, you will not go back from the work?"

"I will do it faithfully," said Zervas, "for thus I shall be in the hands of the Lord."

CHAPTER VI

THREE LITTLE MEN FALL OFF THEIR HORSES

It was the middle of March when Mitsos again found himself climbing the steep hill-side into Panitza. Night had fallen two hours before; clear and keen was the sky, and keen the vigor of the mountain air. The crescent moon, early setting, had slipped behind the snowy spearhead of Taygetus, but the heaven was all aglow with stars burning frostily. His work had all been done quickly and well, and after he had seen the beacon at Bassae, three nights before, shine like a glowworm to the north, and then shoot out a little tongue of flame and lick a low-lying star, he had travelled night and day, only giving himself a minimum of sleep, and walking as much as he rode to spare the pony, that seemed, as they came into Panitza with Mitsos only resting a hand on its neck, to be the more weary of the two. He went up the village street to Petrobey's house, but found the door into the court-yard closed, and only Osman at first answered his knocking by furious barking.

"Osman, oh, Osman," called Mitsos, "be quiet, boy, and let them hear within."

Osman recognized his voice and whined impatiently while Mitsos knocked again. At last he heard the house door open, and Petrobey's voice calling out:

"Who is there?"

"It is I, cousin," shouted the boy; "it is Mitsos."

Petrobey ran across the court-yard, and the next moment Osman tumbled out to welcome Mitsos of the clan, and he led the pony in.

"Ah, it is good to see you, little Mitsos," said Petrobey. "You have come very quick; we did not expect you till to-morrow."

"Yes, I have come quick," said Mitsos; "and, oh, cousin, do not talk to me before I have eaten, for I am hungrier than the hares in winter, and the pony is weaker than I for weariness."

"Give him me," said Petrobey, "and go inside; you will find supper ready, and Nicholas is here."

"Nay, it is not fitting that you should look to the pony," said Mitsos.

"Little Mitsos, get you in," said Petrobey; "there are woodcocks for supper and a haunch of roe-deer, but Nicholas and I have eaten all the eels"; and he led the pony off, for he had heard from Nicholas of Mitsos' oath to Yanni, and how, though for a reason Nicholas did not understand, Mitsos had been very loath to leave Nauplia, but had gone at once; and with that fine instinct, so unreasonable and yet so beautiful, to wait on those a man admires, he wished to do this little service for the boy. Nicholas and he had talked the matter over, and Petrobey said it was clear that Mitsos was in love, and Nicholas was inclined to agree, though as to the engager of his affections they could risk no guess.

Mitsos ate a prodigious supper, and Nicholas having given him a handful of tobacco for his pipe, he declared himself capable of talking, and put forth to them a full account of his journey, and in turn asked what news.

"Much news," said Petrobey, "a little bad and a great deal good. The bad comes first, and it is this: Nicholas is afraid that it will soon be known at Tripoli that he is here, and that will be an unseasonable thing. Four days ago he met two Turkish soldiers, and he thinks they recognized him. They were going to Tripoli, and it will not suit me at all if they send again to ask me to find him, for we have other work to do, and already the clan is moving up into the mountains so as to be ready for the work, and to send twenty men again after Nicholas is what I will not do."

"That is but a small thing, cousin," said Nicholas; "but it is the thought of Yanni in Tripoli which sits heavy on me. At present, of course, he is perfectly safe, but supposing a message comes that you and I are ordered to be at Tripoli in three days."

Petrobey laughed.

"Mehemet Salik dare not," he said; "absolutely he dare not. How fat little Yanni will be when he comes out. Turks eat five times a day. They have no cause to suspect me, and if the worst comes to the worst, he can but send out men to search for you."

Mitsos yawned.

"Yet I wish Yanni were here," he said, "for I love Yanni, and I have sworn to him the oath of the clan. But I am sleepier than the wintering dormouse. When do you suppose I may go for him, cousin?"

"In a week or less, I hope, and in the interval there is the fire-ship work for you to learn. Of that to-morrow, so get you to bed, little Mitsos."

Mitsos got up with eyes full of sleep and stretched himself.

"A bed with sheets," he said; "oh, but I thank the Mother of God for beds."

"Also for woodcock and roe-deer," remarked Petrobey. "Good-night, little one."

The next two days Mitsos spent in learning the working of the fire-ship. Every morning before daybreak Nicholas used to leave the village and lie hidden in the pine-woods on the hills above, returning with Mitsos at nightfall. But on the second evening, as they got near the house, they saw a Turkish soldier in the road, himself on horseback and holding two other horses. Nicholas stepped quickly out of the moonlight into the shadow, and beckoned to Mitsos to do the same.

"This means trouble," he said; "I knew it, I knew it. Go you in, Mitsos, and I will wait in the alder clump by the mill, going out of the village, for there will be news for you to bring me."

And he stole along in the shadow of the wall until he was out of sight.

Mitsos waited till he was gone, and then walked unconcernedly forward, whistling the while. At the gate the soldier stopped him.

"Yassak," he said, which means "There is no passing."

Mitsos stared and stood silent a moment, running over in his mind his small vocabulary of Turkish abuse.

"Ugh! cross-legged one, where is your hat?" he said, rudely and cheerfully. "But why should I not see my cousin?"

"There is no passing," said the Turk, and with that he drew out his pistol.

Mitsos hesitated a moment. He was quite willing to rush in and take his chance of the bullet going wide, for he held the Turks in light esteem as marksmen since the adventure with Yanni; but he doubted the wisdom of the scheme, for there were, as the horses showed, at least two more inside. So he turned on his heel.

"I shall go back home, then," he said. "Shall I find more little men there saying I may not see my father? Go home, too, my little man, if you are as wise as you are little, and eat sweets with the women of your master's harem, and wash your dirty face."

The man answered nothing, for he knew well that to fire a shot in a village of the Mavromichales was to put his own head into a nest of hornets that could sting sore. He and the others had entered the village very quietly after dark so as not to provoke any attention, and had been fortunate enough to get to Petrobey's house without being noticed. Mitsos went along quietly enough till he was out of sight, and then ran as he had never run before to the alder clump where he would find Nicholas.

"Quick, quick!" he whispered; "tell me what to do. There are Turkish soldiers at Petrobey's, and they will not let me in. Oh, uncle, this bodes no good for Yanni! What shall I do?"

"Ah, it is even so!" said Nicholas. "Sit you, Mitsos, and let us think."

For five minutes or so they sat quite silent. At last Nicholas spoke.

"I make no doubt what has happened," he said, "and it is all bad. These men have come to Petrobey from Mehemet Salik, and it means his arrest. They have him in the hollow of their hand, for if he goes not there is Yanni in Tripoli, and go he must. What is before us is this: Yanni must be got out of Tripoli at once, and Petrobey must escape on his way there. How shall we do it? Oh, little Mitsos, think as you thought before, and ask the blessed saints to speak to you and me."

Nicholas crushed his hands to his temples.

"And that is not all," he added. "The clan must be warned at once what has happened, and it is useless for them to attempt the rescue of Petros before Yanni is out of Tripoli, for so his life will be forfeit. And I, too, I must—ah, I shall give myself up to those Turks!"

"But why, Uncle Nicholas?" asked Mitsos, fairly puzzled.

"Because it is easier for two men to escape than one, and also because, if they get away from the village with me and Petrobey without alarm given to the clan, they will make less haste to Tripoli, for if I am with them they will not fear that I should get to Yanni first. Oh, Mitsos, this is a good thought of mine! but the clan must keep very quiet, and let the little men think they do not know what is happening."

"Then I am off for Yanni?" asked Mitsos.

"On the instant. Where is your horse?"

"At Petrobey's."

"Then go round to the house of some cousin; go to Demetri and get a horse, and off with you. There is no time to lose. Stay, you do not know where you and Yanni are to go from Tripoli. You must escape by night and go straight over the hills to the edge of the upper Arcadian plain, where stands Megalopolis; there strike southward over on to Taygetus and find your way to the hill above Lada, on the top of the pass, where you watched for the beacon from Bassae. We shall be there. I shall go round the village and see that the whole clan know what has happened and where they will join us on Taygetus; then I shall give myself up. And now, little Mitsos, God speed; remember that we love you, and be very careful and very quiet. Yanni's life depends on you."

So Mitsos stole off in the darkness to go to Demetri's house, and Nicholas went back to the village to warn the clan. In an hour's time messengers had started to the villages round saying what had happened, and giving the clan to know where they were to go when the few preparations which remained with regard to the storing of the powder were completed, and also definitely saying that the outbreak would begin, as soon as possible, by the siege of Kalamata. Then Nicholas went to Petrobey's house and found the soldier still in the road opposite with the horses.

"There is no passing," he said.

"You do not know to whom you are speaking," said Nicholas, haughtily. "I am Nicholas Vidalis, of whom you may have heard."

The answer was what he anticipated, and he found himself covered by the soldier's pistol, while the latter shouted to those inside: "Here is Nicholas Vidalis!" Then, addressing Nicholas, he said, "Move, and I shoot."

Nicholas stood quite still, for he had no wish either to move or to be shot, while another soldier ran out from the house.

"I suppose you have authority for this," he said, "or there will be a settling between us."

"The authority of Mehemet Salik," said the second soldier, "the Governor of Tripoli, to arrest you and Petros Mavromichales and bring you to Tripoli."

They had been speaking in Turkish, and Nicholas, with intention, asked the next question in Greek.

"For what am I arrested?"

"I do not know Greek," said the soldier.

"God be praised for that!" thought Nicholas, and he repeated his question in Turkish.

"For seditious designs against the sovereign power of the Sultan and his deputy in Tripoli, Mehemet Salik."

Nicholas laughed.

"That sounds serious. Shall I go inside, gentlemen? I am your prisoner, and I deliver up my arms," and he handed the soldier his pistol and knife and stepped in. "I should advise you," he added, "to come in, too, for if some of this hot-headed clan see a Turk standing there he will not stand there long entire. Come in, friend, for though I am maliciously accused that is no fault of yours, and I would not see your blood nor the blood of my clan shed."

The soldier followed his advice and led the horses inside, barring the gate behind him.

Petrobey had heard Nicholas's voice, and a great wave of relief came over him. He had been sitting there quite silent, guarded by two soldiers, in a dumb agony of fear, not for himself, but for Yanni. That he himself could escape somehow or other on the way to Tripoli he did not doubt, but his escape meant death to Yanni if still in the town, as the letter from Mehemet said; while if he delivered himself up at Tripoli, the moment the war of independence began, death to both of them. His only consolation had been that Nicholas, at least, was safe. He would have been back an hour before, unless in some way the alarm had been given him, and his appearance now, coming in peacefully and calmly, must mean that he knew what had happened, and had some wise thought within him. Mitsos—and at the thought of Mitsos he looked up suddenly at Nicholas, in the sudden hope that Mitsos had started for Tripoli—and as he caught Nicholas's eye the latter nodded and smiled, and Petrobey felt certain that Nicholas had answered the question he had silently asked him.

Nicholas sat down cheerfully and continued to speak in Turkish:

"This is some strange mistake," he said, "but I shall not be sorry to pay my respects to his Excellency in Tripoli, a duty which I have hitherto neglected."

One of the soldiers smiled.

"And his Excellency will not be sorry to see you. He sent for you, if you remember, last autumn, and your cousin wrote him a letter saying that his bastard kinsman should be sought for and sent when found."

This was a little disconcerting, but Nicholas waved his hand lightly.

"A private quarrel merely between myself and my cousin," he said, "which has long ago been made up. Eh, cousin?" Then, in Greek, "They don't talk Greek, God be thanked!"

Petrobey nodded assent.

"We set off to-morrow, Nicholas," he said, "and that very early in the morning. To-night we have guests with us, and it is time for supper. Please seat yourselves, gentlemen. Poor fare, I am afraid, but we did not know that we should be honored by your presence to-night."

Petrobey clapped his hands, and the servant brought the supper. He was a big, strong lad of Yanni's age, the son of a small farm-holding tenant on Petrobey's land, who had been left an orphan while still quite a young boy. Petrobey had brought him up in his own house, as half servant and half companion to Yanni, exacting little service, but receiving complete devotion.

"Put on supper," he said, in Greek, "and keep your ears well open."

The boy brought in the food, and they all sat down together. The meal had only been prepared for three, but as Mitsos was to have been one of the three, and the Turks were small eaters, there seemed to be plenty of food. All three soldiers, from living among the Greeks, had relaxed their religious abstinence from wine, where the wine was good, and the meal went on merrily enough, Nicholas, in particular, talking and laughing with them, and speaking Turkish with wonderful fluency and accuracy. Under pretext of Petrobey's not speaking Turkish at all easily, it was soon arranged between him and Nicholas that he should speak in Greek and

Nicholas act as interpreter, translating into Turkish the remarks he made to his guests, and his guests' conversation into Greek; and so it came about that long before the meal was over Petrobey was fully acquainted with Mitsos' departure for Tripoli and also Nicholas's idea for the next day, and they discussed at some length, without arousing the least suspicion, their own manner of escape.

This, Nicholas suggested, should be made as soon as possible on the journey; if it could be managed, at the first halt, for Mitsos would have had twelve hours' start, and should have had time to get Yanni safely out. The advantage of doing this early would be that they would still be travelling in the country of the clan, who would, were it necessary, turn out to cover their retreat; and Nicholas suggested that they should have recourse to a very simple expedient, which he had tried with success once before. The lad Constantine would come with them, he proposed, carrying food for the mid-day meal, as it was six hours to the next village; Nicholas, Petrobey, and the boy would be quite unarmed; and the Turks, secure in the knowledge that Yanni was still hostage, would not, he thought, attempt to bind them. That, however, he would ascertain. During their meal, which should be ample and full of wine, the boy should be instructed to cut the girths of the Turks' horses, and get away home as fast as might be. Then after a decent interval they should think about going on, and Petrobey and he, mounting as quick as they could, should ride cheerfully off at full speed across country towards Taygetus. "The soldiers," added Nicholas, with admirable gravity, "will attempt to do the same, and I wish little Mitsos was here to see them, for it does me good to see Mitsos laugh."

All this was conveyed in short sentences, interpolated with Petrobey's supposed replies to the Turks; and Petrobey, who had taken care that Constantine should be in the room while it was going on, said to him, carelessly, holding out his glass:

"If you completely understand, Constantine, fill my glass with water, and then go; if not, give wine to Nicholas."

Constantine took the water-jug in his hand, filled Petrobey's glass, and left the room.

Incidentally, Nicholas, while speaking in Turkish, had begged the soldiers that they might start very early, for there would be big trouble, he thought, among the clan, if they saw their chief riding off guarded by Turks. His desire, he explained, was to get to Tripoli as soon as possible, for, as they knew, Petrobey's only son was held hostage there by Mehemet Salik, and he feared that if there was a disturbance among the Mavromichales, or if—which God forbid!—the clan were so foolish as to fire upon them, Petrobey might be held responsible, and it would go hardly with the son. To this they assented, saying also that, provided their two prisoners would come unarmed, the hostage in Tripoli should be considered security enough, and they should go like gentlemen upon a journey.

Though it was not very early next morning when they started, the village, following Nicholas's directions of the night before, showed no sign of life. But a closer observer might have noticed stealthy faces at the windows hastily and suddenly withdrawn, for the clan, who would have laid their money on Nicholas and Petrobey if all the Ottoman forces were out against them, and who had a keen sense of humor, regarded the affair as a practical joke of the most magnificent order, for Nicholas had told them the night before what the method of escape was to be. So the procession, with one soldier in front, Nicholas and Petrobey in the centre, guarded on the outside by the other two, with Constantine behind driving a pony laden with food and wine for their mid-day meal, went unmolested, though watched by an appreciative audience, out of the village and down the steep hill into the plain. Nicholas relieved the tedium of the way with the most racy and delightful stories, and then all went on in the utmost harmony.

Some three hours later they were come to a large and pleasant-smelling pine-wood, and about half-way through this, where another bridle-path joined the one they were in, leading up towards the farther hill-villages of Taygetus, they chanced upon a clear way-side stream, and here Petrobey proposed they should halt for their dinner. Abundance of juicy grass grew round the water some thirty yards farther down, and tethering the horses there so that they could not stray, for they would be just out of sight of the place where their masters ate, Petrobey told Constantine to get ready the food. However, the sun shone rather warm on this spot, and at the suggestion of one of the soldiers they moved a little higher up into the shade of the trees. Constantine waited assiduously on the guests until all had eaten their fill, and then, bringing more wine from a cold basin in the stream, where he had put it to regain its coolness, he retired a little distance off to eat of the remains of the dinner, execute his orders, and steal homeward.

The others drank and smoked and chatted for some quarter of an hour more, till Nicholas, observing that the sun had already passed its meridian, suggested that, as they had a long day before them, if they were, as he trusted, to reach Tripoli the next night, it would be wise to start. The soldiers assented, but drowsily, for they had again drunk somewhat freely at their prisoners' expense, and they all moved off to where they had left their horses and accoutrements. Nicholas could not suppress a chuckle of amusement when he saw that Constantine had taken the precaution of loosening the flint from the hammers of their guns, and then saying suddenly to Petrobey, "Now!" the two ran forward, unpicketed their horses, and swinging into the saddle, spurred them through the belt of trees which separated them from the pathway towards Taygetus. They heard an exclamation of dismay and surprise from the soldiers, and the feeble click of a loose flint against the steel, and the next moment they were off full gallop up the steep hill-road.

Then followed a scene which would have made the mouths of the clan to be full of laughter, for the first soldier vaulted with some agility into the saddle and started gallantly off in pursuit, closely followed by the second, who had done the same. The first went bravely for about six yards, the second for rather less, and then they rolled off right and left, clutching wildly at their horses' manes, the one into the stream, the other into a fine furze bush. The third, a bulky man, was rather more fortunate, for, being

124

incapable of jumping into the saddle, he put his foot nimbly into the stirrup, only to find his horse standing beside him barebacked and with an expression of innocent surprise, and himself with the curious feeling experienced when we are fain to walk up a step and find there is no step to walk up.

The next half-hour went wearily and hotly for them. By sacrificing one girth they patched up the other two, and one went up the pathway towards Taygetus in pursuit, while the other rode on to Tripoli. The two most agile, as being the lighter weights, took these tasks upon themselves, while the heavier one, who could not ride bareback without pain to his person, walked sorrowfully on, a heavy saddle in one hand, his horse's bridle in the other, a three-hours' tramp to the next village, where he hoped to have his dilapidations repaired.

The adventures of the first who rode after the escaped prisoners were short. Half an hour's ride brought him to the outskirts of a village which was all humming like a hive of bees, and the humorous Mavromichales, who inhabited it in some number, and who were excellent marksmen, sent a few bullets whistling close round him—one went a little to the right, another slightly to the left, a third sang sweetly over his head, and a fourth raised a little puff of dust at his feet. It occurred to him that they might perhaps be able to aim straighter if they wished, for there was a devilish precision about the closeness of the shots that made his heart turn cold, and with one more glance, sufficient however to show him Nicholas and Petrobey bowing politely in the midst of their clan, he turned tail, and just galloped back along the road he had come.

CHAPTER VII

MITSOS DISARRANGES A HOUSE-ROOF

From Panitza to Grythium it was reckoned two days of twelve hours, or three of eight, but Mitsos, who set off about ten at night, got there within thirty hours of the time he started, thus arriving well before daybreak on the second morning; and at sundown that day, looking over the valley of Sparta from the hills leading up to the pass into the plain of Tripoli, he timed himself to be there two hours before sunrise, thus allowing plenty of time for Yanni and himself to get out of the town before the folk were awake. But for the present, as the moon was up, he pushed forward along the road, reserving his halt for the two dark hours after midnight. He had eaten but little that day, and his eyelids felt like the eyes of dolls, laden with weights that would drag them down; but knowing that if he slept he would gravely risk an over-sleeping, he paced up and down by

125

the edge of the field where he had tethered Demetri's pony, eating a crust of bread, which he washed down with some rather sour wine he had got at Gythium. Now and then he would pause for a moment, but he felt physically incapable of keeping awake except by moving, and fearing to fall down and sleep if he stopped, he began tramping up and down without cessation. Luckily he had a pouch of tobacco and his pipe and tinder-box, and he smoked continuously.

But it was better to be moving than waiting, and when he judged that his pony—of which, like all wise men, he was more careful than of himself—had had sufficient rest, he set out again. He had wrapped his capote close round him, for the night was cold, and he was just beginning to feel that if he hoped to keep awake, he had better get down and trot by the pony's side, when the beast stumbled on a heap of stones, and in trying to recover itself stumbled again, and pitched forward right onto its knees, throwing Mitsos off.

Mitsos was unhurt and picked himself up quickly, but the poor brute was cut to the bone, and stood trembling with pain and terror as Mitsos examined it. For one moment the boy broke down.

"Oh, Holy Virgin!" he cried. "But what shall I do?" But the next moment he steadied himself, and paused to think. It was still four hours before daybreak, but by that time he and Yanni would have to be out of the town, and Tripoli was still a two-hours' ride distant. To get there in time with the pony was hopelessly out of the question, and to get there on his own legs seemed out of the question too, for he was as weary as a young man need ever hope to feel. But if there was a choice it lay there. Meanwhile, what to do with the beast? To leave it there, all cut, bleeding, and in pain, through the night, only to die on those bare hills, was a cruel thing, and Mitsos decided quickly. He led it very gently off the road among the trees, and with a strange feeling of tenderness, for that it had carried him gallantly, and done all it could do for him and Yanni, and had met death in the doing, kissed the white star on its down-dropped head. Then drawing his pistol, he put it to its ear, and, turning his eyes away, fired. The poor beast dropped like a log, and Mitsos, with a sob in his throat, looked not behind, but went back through the trees, and throwing away his coat, which only encumbered him, set his teeth and went jog-trotting to Tripoli.

How the next hours passed he scarcely knew. He felt so utterly tired and beaten that he was hardly conscious of himself, his very weariness probably dulled his powers of sensation, and all he knew was that as he pushed on with limbs dropping from fatigue, eyes aching for very weariness, and a hammering of the pulse in his temples, the trees by the road-side seemed to pass, of their own movement, by him like ghosts. Now and then he tripped over the uneven, stony road, and it scarce seemed worth while to make any effort to recover himself; and more than once he felt and knew, but only dimly, that his trousers were torn on the stones, and his knees were cut and bleeding. He thought of the pony which had fallen and cut itself, and felt vaguely envious of its fate.

Lower down the pass where the hills began to melt into the plain it grew warmer, and in a half dream of exhaustion for a moment he thought

126

that a treeless hollow of the hills was the bay of Nauplia, lying cool and dark beneath the night. Nauplia, the bay, the white wall—it seemed that that time belonged to a boy called Mitsos, but not himself; a boy who had been happier than the kings of the earth, whereas he was a foot-sore, utterly beaten piece of consciousness, that would plod along the white ribbon of road forever.

Then suddenly as he thought the sky lightened and grew gray with dawn, and the next moment the day had broken with the swiftness of the South, and when the sun lifted itself above the hills to the east, it showed him Tripoli all shining in the dawn, still about a mile off.

Mitsos stopped dead. He was too late. During the day it would be impossible for him to get into the governor's house, and during the day, some time before the blessed night fell again, the soldiers from Panitza would be there; Petrobey would have escaped, trusting to his getting to Tripoli first; and Yanni would be.... Who was Yanni? Oh, a boy he had travelled with once; they had had a fine time, and he believed he had promised to come and get him out of Tripoli....

Then suddenly with a sob he beat his hands together.

"Oh, Yanni, Yanni!" he cried; "little Yanni!"

There had been a white frost during the night, and the fields were all stiff and glistening. He had just enough sense to strike off the road and lie down under the shade of a tree, sheltered from the sun and untouched by the frost, and there rolled over on his side, and next moment was sleeping deep and dreamlessly like a child tired with play. There he lay without moving, one arm shielding his face from the light, and when he woke it was past mid-day, the blessed gift of sleep had restored him body and mind, the trouble in his brain had run down like the tainted water of a spate, leaving it clear and lucent, and the strength had come back to his limbs.

He sat there some quarter of an hour longer, thinking intently. He had no self-reproach to interpose itself between him and his quest; the accident had been purely out of his own control, and he had done what would have seemed to himself impossible if he had not done it. Then he took stock of the position; and the position was that the soldiers might be expected at any time after four that afternoon; and as it would not be dark till six, there was nothing to do but go on to Tripoli and wait, watching the road from Sparta. If they came before dark he determined to make an attempt to get in, desperate though it might be, for when once they had given their report to Mehemet Salik, there would be no more Yanni.

So he went on and ate at a Greek khan within the town, and then strolled back to the square and examined the house again. Once the door opened, and he went quickly down a side street for fear the porter, who had seen him before, might recognize him; then he took another look at the wall by which he hoped to get access to the house. Under the influence of food and sleep the spirit of his courage had revived, and about two o'clock he went back again down the street leading into the Sparta road, and sitting down a little distance from it, kept his eyes fixed on the point where it vanished round the first hill-side. Three o'clock passed, four and five, and thin white clouds in the west began to be tinged with rose, and

Mitsos' heart tapped quicker; in another hour it would be dark, and time for his attempt. He sat on there till nearly six, and the darkness began to fall in layers over the sky, and the colors to fade out of things; then giving one last look up the road, he turned and went into the town again.

When he arrived at the square the little oil-lamps at the corners were already lit, and the figures of men seemed like shadows. He turned down the street where the low wall stood, but found to his annoyance that only a few paces down was a café, which had been empty during the day, but was now beginning to fill with guests—for the most part Turkish soldiers; and he was obliged to wait. But these had apparently only come in for a glass of mastic before dinner, and in a quarter of an hour there were only left there the café-keeper, who seemed to be dozing over his glass, and an old Greek countryman in fustanella dress. Mitsos, who had stationed himself some hundred yards off, drew a deep breath, and stole noiselessly back in the shadow of the wall.

By standing on a heap of rubbish which lay there he could get his fingers on the top of the wall, and slipping off his shoes, so that his toes might more easily make use of the crevices between the stones, he worked himself slowly up, and in a moment was crouching on the top. Then came the easier but the more dangerous task, for as he crept along the roof of the house where Yanni was his figure would be silhouetted against the sky; but the roof was not more than four feet above the top of the lower garden wall, and bending over it he raised himself up and wriggled snake-wise along the edge. Yanni's room, in front of which stood the pillar by which he meant to climb down into the balcony, was the second room from the end, and, judging the distance as well as he could, he glided along for about nine feet, and then began to make his way slowly down the roof. He had calculated the distance well, and when he was about half-way down, the tiled roof, which was but lightly built over laths, and was not constructed to bear the weight of superincumbent giants, suddenly creaked beneath him, and next moment gave way, and with a crash fit to wake the dead he was precipitated with a shower of tiles right into Yanni's room, and within a few feet of where Yanni was sitting, with his arms tied behind him.

Mitsos did not think whether he was hurt or not, but picked himself up and showed himself to Yanni. Yanni gave one wild gasp of astonishment.

"Oh, dear Mitsos," he said, "you have not come too soon. Quick, cut this rope!"

He whipped out his knife, and had hardly cut the rope when they heard a key grate in the lock, and Mitsos, taking one step to behind the door, sprang out like a wild-cat on Yanni's keeper—who lived next door, and had not unnaturally come in to see what had happened—and threw him to the ground, while Yanni without a second's hesitation bound a thick scarf round his mouth by way of a gag.

"Now the rope," said Mitsos, and they tied his arms to his sides and his legs together, and looked at each other a moment.

"There is the porter!" said Yanni; "he will be here. Shut the door, Mitsos, and lock it inside."

Next they moved the bedstead and all the furniture they could against the door, and barred the windows, and Yanni gave an additional twist to the scarf that bound the Turk's mouth.

"There is not much time," said Mitsos; and pulling the table out of the heap of furniture they had piled at the door, he climbed onto it, and with one vigorous effort brought down all the tiles which were lying loosely between the hole his entrance had made and the outside wall. From the table he could easily spring up onto the top of the wall, and lying along it reached down two great hands to Yanni. Yanni grasped them, and with much kicking and struggling, not having Mitsos' inches, he got himself on the top.

Mitsos turned to him with a suppressed bubble of laughter.

"Eh, Yanni," he whispered, "but it was truth you said when you told me you would grow very fat. Come quickly. Ah, but there's the porter at the door—one outside and one inside, and we two on the roof."

The descent was easily accomplished; by good luck the street was empty; and waiting a moment for Mitsos to put on his shoes again, the two ran as hard as they could down it, away from the square, keeping in the shadow of the walls. From the end of it a cross street led out to the western gate of the town, and drawing near cautiously they saw it had been already shut, and a sentry was standing by it.

Once again Yanni's wit, wedded to Mitsos' strength, was to stand them in good stead.

"Mitsos," he whispered, "he will open the gate for you, for it has been market-day. Go, then, down the road, and I will follow in the shadow of the wall. Then, when he opens the gate to you, hold him very fast, and I will take the key from him and run through. And oh, cousin—but we must be quick."

Mitsos did not quite understand the object of taking the key, but, walking straight on, he asked to be let out.

"From the market?" asked the sentry.

"Surely, and going home to Thana," said Mitsos, naming a village near.

The man took out the key, unbarred and unbolted the door, and the moment the lock was turned Mitsos grasped him tightly round the arms from behind. The sentry was but a little man, and his struggles in Mitsos' grasp were of the faintest; and when Mitsos, with a brilliant smile, whispered, "You scream, I kill!" enforcing his fragmentary Turkish with a precautionary nudge of the elbow, he was as silent as the grave. In the mean time Yanni had passed them, and taking the key from the lock fitted it into the outside of the gate and said, hurriedly, to Mitsos:

"Quick, cousin! throw him away!"

Mitsos, still smiling kindly, lifted the Turk off his feet, and, with a mighty swing, threw him, as Yanni suggested, onto the road, where he fell, pitiably, in a heap, and, once free from Mitsos, called, in a lamentable voice, for Mohammed the Prophet. Next moment Yanni had shut the gate, locked it, and thrown the key away into the bushes that lined the road.

The two looked at each other for a moment, and then Mitsos broke into a roar of good, wholesome laughter, as unlike as possible to the exhibition to which he had treated Yanni after the affair of the powder-mill. Yanni joined in, and for a few seconds they stood there shaking and helpless. Mitsos recovered himself first.

"Oh, Yanni!" he cried, "but I could laugh till morning were there not other things to do! Come away; there will be no sleep for us this night. No, we keep to the road at present and go westward. Come, we will talk afterwards."

For two hours they jogged on as fast as Yanni could, for a month of living in the confinement of a house and garden "has made a hole," as he said, "in my bellows; and as for the fat of me, why, Mitsos, it's a thing of shame." But there was no wind in him for more than the running, and it was in silence they climbed the steep road into the mountains between Tripoli and the plain of Megalopolis. These were cut in half by a small valley lying between the two rows of hills, with a sharp descent into it from each side, going down into which Yanni recovered his wind a little. On the edge of the valley, as Mitsos knew, stood a small khan, the keeper of which was his father's friend, and as a light still shone in the window he and Yanni entered to rest awhile and get provisions for the morning. Anastasis was glad to see him, and asked him what he was doing there and at that time; and Mitsos, knowing his man, told him in a few words the story of the escape, and begged him, if there was pursuit from Tripoli, to say that they had just passed, going to Megalopolis. "For you see," put in Yanni, observing that their host's wits were not of the quickest, "we are not going to Megalopolis, and it will be a fine gain of time to us if they seek us there."

After an interval this appeared to Anastasis to be a most admirable joke, and for five minutes more, as he was cutting them bread and meat, he kept bursting out into a chuckle of delight, and turned to Mitsos, saying, "Then they'll find you not at Megalopolis. Eh, who would have thought it?"

But Mitsos hurried Yanni off again. They had not probably more than half an hour's start, "though it will take them not a little time to clear a way into your room," said Mitsos; and though, through the steepness of the ascent, a horse could go no quicker than a man, there was no time to waste, and they struck off the road a little southward, straight in the direction of Taygetus. All night they went, sometimes walking, but more often running, and when morning dawned they found themselves on the lower foot-hills of Taygetus, but still a day's journey from their rendezvous. But Yanni declared he could go no farther for the present. His eyes were full of sleep; his stomach was dust within him, and his legs were one ache. So Mitsos, after a five-minutes' climb to the top of a neighboring ridge, came back with the tidings that he could not discern man, beast, or village, and decreed that they should lie here all day and not start again till near sunset.

Then said Yanni: "It will be a long talk we shall have before sunset; but, Mitsos, if the day of judgment was breaking not one word could I say for myself till I have slept. Ah, but it is good to be with you again!"

And he turned over and was asleep at once.

Mitsos was not long in following his example, but he woke first, and, seeing by the sun that it was not much after mid-day, got up quietly, so as not to disturb Yanni, and went in search of water. This he found some quarter of a mile below and returned to Yanni, who had just awoke. They took their food down to the spring and ate there, and then, at Mitsos' suggestion, went back again to their first camping place, "for where there is a spring," he said, "there may be folk, and we want folk but little."

"And now," said Yanni, as they settled themselves again, "begin at the beginning, Mitsos, and tell me all."

"I went straight to Nauplia the first night," he said, "and arrived there very late—after midnight; then, next day, I went off."

"Next day?" asked Yanni. "Is that all you care about Suleima? Oh, tell me, how is Suleima?"

Mitsos frowned.

"Oh, never mind Suleima," he said. "She is my affair. Well, next day—"

But Yanni interrupted him.

"Did you not see Suleima?" he asked.

"No."

"Why did you not wait that night and see her?"

"Uncle Nicholas had other work for me to do."

Yanni looked at Mitsos a moment and then laid his hand on his shoulder.

"Mitsos, dear Mitsos!" he said. "Oh, I am so sorry! It was not that, you know, that made you go; it was the oath of the clan you swore to me. Mitsos, don't hate me for it. Surely there is no one like you."

Mitsos looked up, smiling.

"Nonsense, Yanni! Is a promise and an oath a thing to make and break? Besides, it seems to me it is pretty lucky I came when I did. What do you suppose I should be thinking now if I had got back to Panitza and found it was too late, for, in truth, I was not much too soon? What if I had come to Tripoli, as it were, to-night, instead of last night?"

"I will tell you afterwards what you would have found," said Yanni, suddenly looking angry. "Go on, little Mitsos."

Mitsos grinned.

"Little, who is little? I have a cousin smaller than I. Well, for my story."

And Mitsos told him of his journey, of his expedition to Patras and the monastery, and of the coming of the soldiers to Panitza.

"And for the rest," he concluded, "we shall have to ask Uncle Nicholas and your father. There are not many things in the world of which I am certain, Yanni, but one is that we shall find them safe and sound on Taygetus."

Yanni pulled up a handful of sweet-smelling thyme and buried his face in it for a moment.

"Ah, but it is good to be on the hills again, Mitsos," he said, "and to be with you. I shall not forget the Mother of God. My story is very short; I am glad it has not been longer."

"Tell me," said Mitsos.

"Well, for a week, or perhaps a fortnight, I ate and slept, and one day

131

was like another. I saw Mehemet Salik not more than once or twice, and he used always to ask me if I was comfortable and had all that I wished for. It is true that I wished for the hills and for you, but they were things which he would not have given me, so I always said I wanted nothing. Then for another week or so he would come and see me oftener, and asked me about my father and the clan, and whether Nicholas had been seen there again. And I, you may be sure, always told him that the clan were good men and quiet livers, who worked hard in the fields, and thanked God every day that their masters, the Turks, were kind and just to them. That, it seems, was a mistake, for he smiled—these Turks know not how to laugh, Mitsos, not with an open mouth—and said it was very interesting to hear that from one of the clan themselves. And about Nicholas, I said I had seen him when I was little."

"You were never otherwise," remarked Mitsos.

"Oh, cousin," said Yanni, "but your mother bore a silly loon. Am I not to go on with my story, then?"

"Go on, big Yanni," said Mitsos.

"And so it went till but five or six days ago. And then on one morning," said Yanni, suddenly flushing with anger, "he came in looking white and cunning, with an evil face. The Turk who was my guardian followed him—he is a good man, Mitsos, save that he comes of the accursed race—and Mehemet said to me, 'So the clan are good men and quiet, and they thank their God that they have such kind masters. And you, Yanni, who are of the clan, you think they do wisely?'

"I don't think I answered him, for it seemed to me he wished for no answer. And at that his anger suddenly flared up, and he said, 'Answer me, you dog, or I will have your hide flayed off you.' And I noticed it as curious, Mitsos, that his face grew white as he got angry, whereas when a proper man is angry his face is as a sunset. But he did not give me time to answer, for he went on, 'You are dogs, though you are handsome dogs, you Greeks. But it is necessary to tie dogs up sometimes. Thank God you have such a kind master, Yanni, and let your hands be tied behind you quietly.'

"'Why should you do this?' I asked.

"'Be wise,' he said; 'I do not threaten twice.'

"So as there was none to help me, I let it be done."

Mitsos gave a great gulp.

"Oh, Yanni, by a cross-legged Turk!" he said.

"What was I to do? Would it have helped me to fight, and afterwards to be beaten? But Mehemet, I saw, was more at his ease when it was done, and drew his chair a little closer.

"'We shall soon teach you to be quiet and obedient like the rest of your clan,' he said. 'And now for what I came to say. You will soon see Nicholas again, for I have sent for him and for your father. If they come, well and good; I do not really care whether they come or not—for barking dogs hurt nobody. However, they have been barking too loud. And if they do not come, my little Yanni, we shall have to think what to do with you. I have not decided yet'—and the devil came closer to me, Mitsos, and looked at me as a man looks at the fowls and sheep in the market. 'Perhaps there will be a rope for that big brown neck of yours; and yet I do not know, for

132

you are a handsome boy, and I should like to see you about the house, perhaps to hand the rose-water after dinner. Let us see, we would dress you in a blue waistcoat with silver braid, and a red kaftan, I think, and red leggings, with yellow shoes; but I think we would give you no knife or pistol in your belt, for I fancy you have a temper of your own. It is a pity that a handsome boy like you should be so fierce. Perhaps we might even arrange that you were fitted to attend on the women-folk. In any case you will be mine—you will belong to your good, kind masters.'"

Yanni's voice had risen, and he spoke quickly, with a red-hot anger vibrating and growing.

"He said it to me!" he cried, rising to his feet. "To me—free-born of the clan, who have never had any dealings with the accursed race, except to spit at them as they went by! And I—I sat there and said nothing, but for this reason, Mitsos, that I remembered the oath of the clan you had sworn, and I believed, as I believe that the holy Mother of God hears me, that you would come, be it soon or late, and that he should eat his words with a sauce of death to them—the black curse of her who mocked at Christ upon him!"

"Steady, Yanni!" said Mitsos, looking up at his blazing eyes. "Sit down and tell the rest."

"What, Mitsos," cried Yanni, "are you a block of stone or a log, you who are of blood with us?"

"You know I am not. But Mehemet Salik is not on this hill-side. Tell me the rest. If he was here he should never more return to the bestialities of his daily life."

Yanni sat down again.

"Even so. Then day after day he would come in all white and cursing as before, and say, 'The time is drawing near, my little Yanni. They will be here to-morrow or the next day,' as it might be. And yesterday morning he said, 'They will be here to-night.' And I—for I never doubted you, Mitsos—I thought to myself, 'Then I shall not be here to-night'; and as for them, I knew that they would never sit in the house of a Turk. And—and that is all, I think."

There was a short silence, and Yanni stretched out his hand to Mitsos:

"So to you, dearest of all," he said, "I owe my life—once at the mill, and now, once again, life and honor and freedom. Yet is the debt no burden to me, because I love you. But still I would it were the other way. I have no skill of speech, Mitsos, but I know certainly that gladly would I give my eye or my right hand for you, and this is no figure of talk only."

Mitsos took the hand held out to him and shut it between his, looking at Yanni with a serious mouth, but a smile in his dark eyes.

"God send me tears for water and salt for bread," he said, again quoting the oath of the clan, "if I fail you in your need, or love not those who love you and hate not those who hate you."

The sun was already declining to the western hills, and presently after they went down to the spring to eat and drink before they began the tramp through the night. Neither of them had been over this ground

133

before, but it was likely that they would soon come into some path leading from the Arcadian plain to one or other of the villages near the Langarda pass; in any case, even though there were a night's plunging through the heather undergrowth before them, it could scarcely be more than a twelve-hours' journey. Thus, starting at six, they would be at the place by dawn; and, after stowing the remains of their provisions in their pockets, they began the ascent.

Upward they went out of the day into the sunset, and through the sunset into moonrise, and from moonrise into the declining of the moon. The air, warm below, soon grew colder, and their breath, as they walked, hung frostily in the still night. Now and then a whiff of some sweet-smelling shrub streamed across them, or again a roosting pigeon, with a bold noise of its uprising, started still sleepy from its perch in among the whispers of the fir, or a hawk, more cautious, slid into the air. To Yanni, born on the mountain and bred in the open, the spell of the sounds and scents that wander along the hill-side at night was unutterably sweet, and sweet the comradeship of the incomparable cousin. In Mitsos, too, the feeling towards the friend he had saved from death, and worse than death, was father to a very tender affection, for it was a gentle heart that beat so boldly at the hint of danger, and the sweetness of self-sacrifice made him most content. The child within him spoke to his spirit of Suleima, but the boy found his wants fulfilled in the comradeship of Yanni, and made answer with talk of brave adventures done in part and more to do.

About midnight they halted, and already they could see the heights no long distance above them, dappled with snow, and Mitsos, observing this, knew that they had come as high as they had need to go, for the beacon-ground, he remembered, was itself just below the line where the fresh snow lay. They had, an hour before, struck a sort of sheep-track which led in the right direction, but they found that here it went still upward, and leaving it to climb by itself, they struck off to the right, after eating the remains of their food, to follow the contour of the mountain through tracts of pines and open places, and across the scolding streams that rattled down from the snows above, and round deep-cut ravines that broadened out into the larger valleys. By degrees the stars paled at the approach of day, and the dark velvet-blue of the Southern night brightened to dove-color; a few birds awoke in the bushes with sleepy, half-tuned twitterings, and then the sun, great and bold, looked up over the rim of the mountain.

"Look, it is day," said Yanni. "Are we nearly there?"

"Yes," said Mitsos, "there is the beacon-hill. And who is that?"

Swiftly down the hill-side towards them came a great man, leaping and running like a boy.

"Oh, quick, down with you," said Mitsos. "I think there is but one man who can go like that; but it is best. Ah, I thought so; show him we can run, too."

And in two minutes Nicholas, with a face as welcome as morning, was with them.

134

CHAPTER VIII

THE MESSAGE OF FIRE

The Greek camp which was being formed here, nestled airily on the unfrequented side of Taygetus, was square, half of it lying on each side of a rattling stream (loud at this time from the melting snows) which flowed down a steep ravine into the plain of Kalamata. It lay about five hundred yards below the site of the beacon, a conspicuous and stony plateau on the top of an isolated hill, separated on all sides by steep, narrow gullies from the main mass of the mountain. It was Nicholas who had chosen the spot, and chosen wisely, for while the camp itself lay concealed and sheltered from the northern winds, the top of the hill just above it, from which a man could run down in two minutes to headquarters, was an eyry for observation. On the north it commanded the Arcadian plain, the corner of which Mitsos and Yanni had just crossed; on the west, the whole valley of Messenia, with its capital, Kalamata, lay unfurled like a map; and directly under it to the south wound the Langarda pass over Taygetus from Messenia to Sparta.

The camp was walled with a robust barrier of brushwood and peopled with small huts, built on a framework of poles, between which were interwoven branches of fir and heather, and roofed with reeds or furze. In the centre, just on the right of the stream, stood the hut shared by Petrobey and Nicholas, built in exactly the same manner as the others, and only distinguished by a blue-and-white flag which floated over it, bearing prophetically the cross of Greece risen above the crescent of Turkey. Towards the top of the enclosure had stood a belt of pines, most of which had been felled for building purposes, one here and there only having been left to give support to a structure of much more solid and weather-proof workmanship. It was divided inside into two chambers, in one of which were stored powder and ammunition; in the other the rifles and swords. Additional protection was given to the powder-magazine by a coat of felt which was nailed on above the boards of its roof.

The camp was all alive and humming like a hive of bees when the three arrived, for a train of mules from the district round which Yanni and Mitsos had made their first journey had just come in, bringing the secret grindings of the mills from Kalyvia and Tsimova. This was the first consignment of powder which had arrived, and Petrobey was superintending its stowage in the magazine. Elsewhere the thin blue smoke of wood fires, over which men were cooking their coffee for breakfast, rose up straight into the air, and the flicking and flashing of axes in the morning sun showed others still at work on pine-felling. During the last two nights many parties of the clan and the patriots from the villages round had been arriving with their arms and provisions, and a herd of sheep and goats were browsing on the scrub-clad sides of the ravine below the camp. Already there were not fewer than two hundred men there, and before

135

three days Petrobey hoped that the whole depot, consisting of eight hundred men with arms and ammunition, would be assembled. Farther along the sides of the mountain there were three similar camps, and thus the total number of men who would march down from Taygetus onto Kalamata would be a tale of over three thousand. These were all drawn from Laconia, Argolis, and the south of Arcadia, and the number would be raised to close on five thousand by additions from the populous Messenian plain. The patriots in the north of Greece would, at the beacon-signal, rise simultaneously in Achaia as soon as the camps all contained their complement of men.

In the camp discipline and organization were thoroughly ordered and carried out. A body of the younger and more active were stationed on the top of the hill with instructions to report at once any movement they might observe in the country round, and to stop vi et armis any Turk who was seen going up the pass from Messenia into Sparta, for fear of news being taken to Tripoli of the assembling of the patriots. This danger, however, was inconsiderable. All the camps were nestled away from view in hollows of the unvisited mountain-sides, and the only circumstance of suspicion was that within a few days many Greeks had left their villages with laden mules, and with their flocks. Even this was not unusual at the spring-time of the year, for it was common, when April opened up the hills, to drive the flocks higher up to the juicier mountain pasture, where the shepherds would spend weeks at a time cutting down pines and burning them for charcoal. But this flight of Petrobey and Nicholas and the escape of Yanni might easily have become a signal of warning to the Turks, and until all was ready it was most important that no communication of alarm should pass from Kalamata to Tripoli. For the last few weeks the fortification of Tripoli had been undergoing repair, and it was evidently expected that if a rising took place the first attack would be directed there; or at any rate the Turks thought it was safer to have some fortress in a fairly central position, where the families of their countrymen scattered about the country could take refuge from local disturbances.

All the cattle, all the arms, the mules and horses brought to the camp, were put under the disposal of Petrobey. As he was the head of the clan of Mavromichales, of whom the camp was chiefly composed, Nicholas had felt it better that he should have absolute supremacy in all matters, and, as he had said to Priketes, all that he asked for himself was the right to serve. Petrobey was loath to take advantage of his generosity, and only did so on condition that Nicholas would promise to give him advice and counsel on all points, dissent from him freely and promptly where his judgment did not coincide with his own, and at the wish of his men be willing himself to take over the sole command. Meantime, would he take in charge the outposts and messenger corps of the camp, on which devolved the duty of watching the roads and of carrying news from one camp to another?

Nicholas's company had been relieved at the watch on the beacon-station when the two boys arrived, and the three went together to Petrobey. He was busy with the unlading of the powder-carrying mules

136

when they came up, but as they drew near he saw them and ran towards them.

"Now the Blessed Virgin be praised," he cried, "that you have come! We expected you earlier. How was it you did not come before? Ah, Yanni, but your father has wearied for you! Is it a long bill we have with Mehemet? Oh, admirable little Mitsos, the Holy Father reward you for bringing him safe. We will breakfast together when I have finished this job. Get you to my tent with Nicholas."

The unlading of the powder was an operation in which, so Petrobey thought, no caution would be superfluous. It arrived in big mule panniers, covered over with charcoal or some country produce, and the panniers were taken off and carried singly by men barefoot into the magazine. Here others were stationed, whose duty it was to take off the stuff under which the powder was concealed and empty it into small skin bottles, which could be carried by a man, and held more than the ordinary powder-flasks. There were eight hundred of these, one for each man in the camp, and when they were full the remainder were to be stored in light wooden boxes of handier shapes than the panniers for transport on the ammunition mules.

All day fresh bands of men in eights and tens from the Maina country arrived in camp, and news was passed from the other stations along the mountain-side that they, too, were filling rapidly. Among others fifty men had joined the patriots from Nauplia and the plain of Argos, one of whom was Father Andréa, an incarnated vengeance more than priest, and another was Mitsos' father. Mitsos himself, however, was to remain in the camp of the Mavromichales, acting as aide-de-camp to Nicholas, but otherwise the disposition of the men was strictly geographical, since Petrobey's experience told him that men who have known each other fight best side by side. Each camp was organized on the pattern of the Mavromichales, and the captains of each had voluntarily put themselves under the supreme command of Petrobey, for the dissensions which subsequently broke out in the army had not yet appeared. Moreover, the Hetairist Club, since the flight of Prince Alexander Ypsilanti, had given express orders that the direction of affairs in the south was to be in the hands of some local chieftain, suggesting for that office either Petrobey or Nicholas.

A week passed, and the camps were all nearly full, and Petrobey waited impatiently for the completion of his preparations. Partly by extreme caution, and partly by good luck, there had as yet been no collision with the Turks, and apparently no uneasiness felt in Kalamata. A report had come in a couple of days before that two Turkish ships of war had been ordered there for the defence of the town, and to carry off the Turkish inhabitants in case of an outbreak; but, though the bay was carefully watched by those on the beacon-point, no sign of them had been seen. But about mid-day on the 2d of April a scout from the beacon came into the camp, saying that a small band of Turks, twelve in number, under arms, and followed by a train of baggage-mules, were coming up the pass from Kalamata. Petrobey's answer was short and decisive: "Stop them!" and some twenty men were sent out to reinforce the outpost at the beacon.

From the camp nothing could be seen of the road, but a dozen more men were told off to hold themselves in readiness. Then after a long pause, in which each man's eyes sought the eyes of his fellow in a fever of expectation, shots were heard, and in half an hour's time the message came back to Petrobey and Nicholas, who were at dinner, that they had been stopped.

Then Petrobey rose, and his gray eye was fire.

"At last, at last!" he cried. "Oh, Nicholas, the vintage is ripe!"

He waited no longer. Yanni, who was his aide-de-camp, was despatched at top speed to the next station, with orders that an hour before sunset the army was to start on its march to Kalamata, and all the afternoon the stir of going was shrill. The clan were half wild with excitement and eagerness; but all were absolutely in control, and went about their duties methodically and in perfect order, and the work of lading and marshalling the ammunition and baggage-mules was finished by four o'clock. Meanwhile another party had carried up to the top of the hill the fuel for the beacon, which Petrobey had arranged was to be the signal, not only across to the hill above Bassae, but to the patriots collected lower down in the villages of the Messenian plain. Mitsos, who was charged with the lighting of it, was to let loose the tongue of fire which should shout the word all over Greece as soon as dark fell, and then follow straight down the hill-side after the main body. The whole disposition of the force round Kalamata, and the routes by which, converging as they went, they were to march there, had been already arranged, and by five o'clock the clan set out, spreading themselves in open order over the hill-side, the mules alone following the road of the pass, so as to prevent any one leaving the town by other mountain-paths over Taygetus.

As soon as the clan had started, Mitsos, left to himself, ate his supper, and sat down to wait till the darkness of the birthnight of Greece should fall. It had been a hot, sultry day, with a heavy air, and he had packed up and sent on with the mules a heavy woollen cloak, which Nicholas had given him to replace the one he had left behind in his race to Tripoli, and was dressed only in his linen trousers, shirt, and open Albanian jacket. The still air hung like a blanket on the mountain-side, but he saw that clouds had gathered on the top of Taygetus and were moving down westward in the direction of the camp. But they remained as yet high, and though before sunset they had stretched right over from the mountain-top behind to the peak of Ithome in the west, a gray floor of mottled marble, flushed here and there, where they were thinner, with the reflected fire of an angry sunset, the northern heaven was still clear, and his beacon-point close above him stood out black and sharp-cut. Long before dark fell he had already been up to the beacon, in order to arrange the brushwood and firing most handily; the lighter and drier wood he put on the windward side, so that such breeze as there was might drive the flames inward against the larger bushes, which would take the flame less easily. He also tore a quantity of dry moss from the sides of a couple of plane-trees, which grew to the leeward of the hill, and made a core of this within the brushwood, adding a train, in the manner of a fuse, leading

138

outward to where he would apply the light. He had just finished this to his satisfaction, and was about to return to the camp to fetch up the burning lumps of charcoal which he had fed during the afternoon, and which in this wind that had sprung up would soon kindle the moss into flame, when a few large raindrops fell splashing on the ground, and he hurriedly covered the dry, tinder-like furze with thick branches of pine, in order to keep it protected; then for a few moments the rain ceased again, but Mitsos, looking up, saw that the clouds had grown black and swollen with an imminent downpour, and that the storm might break any minute. His next thought was for the burning charcoal below, and he ran quickly down the hill-side in order to carry it under cover of the ammunition magazine; but before he had gone fifty yards the storm broke in a sheet of hissing rain, driven a little aslant in the wind—but for heaviness a shower of lead. However, in hopes of saving the charcoal, he ran on, and raking about in the embers of his fire, already turning to a black slush under the volleying rain, he found a lump of charcoal not yet extinguished. Then sheltering it in his cap, he nursed it tenderly, and carried it into the ammunition magazine. There he sat for half an hour, and from it managed to kindle a few more lumps, while the noise of the rain continued as of musketry on the resounding roof. Then looking out he saw that night had come, heavy and lowering.

The position was sufficiently critical. The beacon fuel would be soaked, and the dry kindling in the centre, he thought, would be insufficient to start a blaze. Then he remembered a flask of spirits which Petrobey had told him to keep with him in case of emergency, and he ran across to fetch it from his hut. The clouds had lifted a little, though the downpour was still heavy; but, looking up, he still saw the outline of the beacon-hill a shade blacker than the sky, showing that it was clear, at any rate, of mists. He groped about the walls of the hut for some little time before finding the flask, and just as he put his hand on it the wind fell dead, the rain stopped as when a tap is turned back, and in the stillness he heard the sound of the footstep of some man unfamiliarly stumbling up the stony hill-side just below. At that he stopped, and then creeping cautiously to the entrance of the hut, peered out. He could see nothing; but the step still advanced, drawing nearer.

Who could it be? It was hardly possible, though still just possible, that this man was some Greek of the clan—yet such would surely have shouted to him—coming from Petrobey with a message, or it might be some benighted peasant; yet, again, for fear it might be a Turk he must needs go carefully, and with redoubled caution he crept out of the hut, still keeping in the shadow, and looked round the corner. Whether it was the rustle of his moving in the dead silence, or the faint shimmering of his white trousers in the darkness, that betrayed him, was only a thing for conjecture, but the next moment, from some fifty yards in front, he saw the flash of a gun, and a bullet sang viciously by him, cracking in half one of the upright posts which bound the sides of the hut together. Mitsos stood up, as he knew he was seen, and called out, cocking his pistol, yet seeing no one, "Speak, or I fire," and in answer he heard the sound of another charge being rammed home. At that he bolted back round the corner of the tent and waited. The steps advanced closer; clearly the man, whoever he was, finding that he did not fire, concluded that he had no arms—the truth, however, being that Mitsos, having seen nothing but the flash of the gun, thought it more prudent to wait until he had a more localized target. But presently the steps paused, and after a moment he heard them retreating with doubled quickness up the hill towards the pass. Then a solution flashed upon him—this could be no patriot, nor would a wandering peasant have fired at him; it could only be some Turk who had seen the Greek army advancing, had somehow eluded them, and was going hotfoot to Sparta with the news. He must be stopped at all costs, and next moment Mitsos was stretched in pursuit up the hill after him, keeping as much as possible in the cover of the trees. Clearly the man had missed his way in the darkness, and had come unexpectedly upon the Greek camp, and seeing some one there had fired.

In three minutes or so Mitsos' long legs had gained considerably on him, and he now saw him, though duskily, with his gun on his shoulder still making up the hill. Another minute saw them within about fifty yards of each other; but Mitsos had the advantage of position, for while he was running between scattered trees the other was in the open. He apparently recognized this, and changed his course towards the belt of wood; but then suddenly, seeing Mitsos so near, he halted and fired, and Mitsos felt the bullet just graze his arm. On that he ran forward, while the man still stayed reloading his piece, and sent a pistol bullet at him. The shot went wide, and Mitsos with a grunt of rage ran desperately on to close with him. But the other, while he was still some yards distant, finished loading, and his gun was already on the way to his shoulder, when Mitsos, partly in mere animal fury at the imminence of death, but in part with reasonable aim, took hold of his heavy pistol by the barrel and flung it with all his force in the Turk's face. He reeled for a moment, and, the blood, like the red of morning, streaming over his face in a torrent that blinded him, Mitsos was on him and had closed with him. When it came to mere physical strength the odds were vastly in his favor, and in a moment, in the blind gust of the fury of fighting, he wrested the man's gun from him and, without thinking of firing, had banged him over the head with the butt end. He fell with a sound of breaking, and Mitsos, still drunk and beside himself with the lust of slaughter, laughed loud and hit him again with his full force as he lay on the ground. There was a crack, and a spurt of something warm and thick came out in a jet against his trousers and over his hand. He paused only one moment to make sure that this was a Turk he had killed, and then without giving him another thought, or waiting to brush the clotted mess off his clothes, he ran down again to set about the beacon.

The wound on his arm was but slight, though it bled profusely and smarted like a burn, and only stopping to tear off a piece from his shirt-sleeve, which he bound tightly round it, tying the knot with his teeth and his right hand, he again put the charcoal, which was burning well, into his cap, and with the flask of brandy set off for the top of the hill. The rain had come on again, hissing down in torrents, and Mitsos, knowing that the fear of failure strode faster every moment, tore the cover of boughs off from the

140

core of moss and furze, but found to his dismay it was quite damp and would not light. It was necessary to get a flame somehow; the spirits and the moss would do the rest if once he could get that; and to get a flame, he must have something dry, though it were but a twig. There was no time to waste; already a big raindrop had made an ominous black spot on the middle of the glowing charcoal, and meantime everything was getting rapidly wetter. In a moment of hopelessness he clutched at his hair despairingly; the thing seemed an impossibility.

Then suddenly an idea struck him, and, tearing off his jacket, he removed his shirt, which had been kept quite dry, and kneeling down with his back bare to the cold, scourging rain put the two lumps of charcoal in the folds of it and blew on them. For a couple of seconds the linen smouldered only, but then—and no Angel Gabriel would have been a gladder sight to him—a little tongue of flame shot up. Mitsos took the brandy bottle, and with the utmost care shook out a few drops onto the edge of the flame. These it licked up, burning brighter, and soon the whole of the back of the shirt took the fire. He crammed it under the thick core of moss and brushwood, and feeding them plentifully with brandy coaxed the flame into the driest part of the stuff. Now and then a little spark would go running like some fiery insect through the fibres, leaving a gray path of ash behind, only to perish when it reached the damper stuff, and once even the flame seemed to die down altogether; but meantime it had penetrated into the centre of the pile, and suddenly a yellow blade of smoky fire leaped out and licked the dripping branches of fir outside. These only fumed and cracked, and Mitsos pulled them off, for they were but choking the flames; and, running down to the edge of the wood, he tore up great handfuls of undergrowth, which had been partially protected from the rain by the trees, and threw them on. Then the fire began to take hold in earnest, and through the thick volumes of stinging smoke, which were streaming away westward, shot lurid gleams of flame. Now and then with a great crash and puff of vapor some thicker branch of timber would split and break, throwing out a cloud of ignited fragments, or again there would rise up a hissing and simmering of damp leaves, like the sound of a great stewing over a hot fire. The place where he had first lit the beacon was all consumed, and only a heap of white frothy ash, every now and then flushing red again with half-consumed particles as some breeze fanned it, remained, and from the fir branches which Mitsos had taken off ten minutes ago, but now replaced, as every moment the hold of the fire grew steadier, there were bursting little fan-shaped bouquets of flame.

Meantime, with the skin of his chest down to the band of his trousers reddened and scorched by the heat, his back cold and dripping, and lashed with the heavy whisp of rain which had so belabored him in those first few moments of struggle between fire and water, his hair tangled and steaming with heat and shower, his eyes blackened and burned with the firing, Mitsos worked like a man struggling for life; now pushing a half-burned branch back into the fire; now lifting a new bundle of fuel (as much as he could carry in both arms), which pricked and scratched the scorched and bleeding skin of his chest; now glancing northward to see whether Bassae had answered him. With the savage frenzy of his haste, the excitement of the deed, and the fury and madness of the blood he had shed dancing in his black eyes, he looked more like some ancient Greek spirit of the mountains than the lover of Suleima and the boy who was so tender for Yanni.

In ten minutes more the rain had stopped, but Mitsos still labored on until the heat of the beacon was so great that he could scarcely approach to throw on the fresh fuel. The flames leaped higher and higher, and the wind dropping a shower of red-hot pieces of half-burned leaves and bark was continually carried upward, peopling the night with fiery sparks and falling round him in blackened particles, or floating away a feathery white ash like motes in a sunbeam. And as he stood there, grimy and panting, scorched and chilled, throwing new bundles of fuel onto the furnace, and seeing them smoke and fizz and then break out flaring, the glory and the splendor of the deeds he was helping in burst in upon him with one blinding flash that banished other memories, and for the moment even Suleima was but the shadow of a shadow. The beacon he had kindled seemed to illuminate the depths of his soul, and he saw by its light the cruelty and accursed lusts of the hated race and the greatness of the freedom that was coming. Then, blackened and burned and sodden and drenched, he sat down for a few moments to the north of the beacon to get his breath and scoured the night. Was that a star burning so low on the horizon? Surely it was too red for a star, and on such a night what stars could pierce the clouds? Besides, was not that a mountain which stood up dimly behind it? Then presently after it grew and glowed; it was no star, but the fiery mouth of message shouting north and south. Bessae had answered.

There was still a little spirits left, and between his wetting and his scorching Mitsos felt that he would be none the worse for it, and he left his jacket to dry by the beacon while he went back to where the body of the Turkish soldier lay to look for his pistol, which he had till then forgotten. He searched about for some little while without finding it, for it had fallen in a tangle of undergrowth; and taking it and the man's gun, which might come in useful, he turned to go. Then for the first time a sudden feeling of compassion came over him, and he broke off an armful of branches from the trees round, and threw them over the body in order to cover it from the marauding feeders of the mountain; and then crossing himself, as the Greeks do in the presence of the dead, he turned away; and going once more up to the beacon to fetch his jacket, which had grown dry and almost singed in that fierce heat, he ran off down the hill to join the clan.

They had gone but slowly, for they did not wish to reach Kalamata till an hour before daybreak, and had, when Mitsos came up, halted at the bottom of the range where the foot-hills begin to rise towards Taygetus. He was challenged by one of the sentries, and for reply shouted his own name to them; and finding Demetri was his challenger, stopped to tell him of the success of the beacon and the answer flared back from Bassae, and then went on to seek for Nicholas or Petrobey to report his return.

Petrobey was sitting by a camp-fire when he came up, talking earnestly to Nicholas and Father Andréa, who had come in from the Nauplia contingent, and only smiled at Mitsos as he entered.

142

"That is the order, father," he was saying; "we want to take the place at all costs, but the less it costs us the better. I should prefer if it capitulated, and not waste lives which we can ill spare over it. All the Turks inside the walls will be our prisoners, and them—"

"Yes?"

"Perhaps the moon will devour them," said Petrobey. "I shall make no conditions about surrender. Good-night, father. And now, little Mitsos; the beacon, we know, got lit. How in the name of the Virgin did you manage to do it?"

Mitsos unbuttoned his jacket and showed the sore and reddened skin beneath.

"There is much in a shirt," he said, laughing, and told his story.

When he had finished Petrobey looked at Nicholas with wonder and something like awe in his eye.

"Surely the blessing of the Holy Saints is on the lad," he said, in a low voice.

PART III

THE TREADING OF THE GRAPES

CHAPTER I

TE DEUM LAUDAMUS

During the night the wind swept the floor of heaven clean of clouds, and an hour of clear starlight and setting moon preceded dawn. Before starting, after an hour's halt about midnight, Petrobey called together the captains of the other three camps and gave them their final instructions. Three companies, those from Maina, Argolis, and Laconia, were to besiege the citadel, while the company from Arcadia was to join the two from Messenia, which would meet them on the plain, and invest the harbor, destroy all the shipping except three or four light-built boats which were to be kept in readiness for other purposes, and watch for the coming of the two Turkish ships-of-war. The Messenians, with a loyal and patriotic spirit, had asked Petrobey to name them a captain for the three companies which would be employed on this work, instead of pressing a local candidate; and in order to prevent jealousy or dissent among them, he nominated one Niketas, of Sparta, who was well known to most of the men, popular, and had seen service on an English ship, where he had worked for two years abroad, for a price had been placed on his head by the Turks for supposed brigandage. He had returned to his country a month ago from the Ionian Isles, and had hastened to put himself in the service of the patriots.

The citadel of Kalamata stood on rising ground about a mile from the harbor, but it was small, and a large, unfortified suburb, chiefly employed in commerce and the silk industry, had spread out southward from its base, making a continuous street between harbor and citadel. The latter was defended by a complete circuit of wall, and on three sides out of the four the rocks on the edge of which the walls stood were precipitous for some thirty feet. Under the western of these, and directly below the wall, ran a torrent-bed, bringing down the streams from the mountains to the north—dry in summer, but now flowing full and turbid with the melting of the winter snows on the heights. On this side the town was impregnable to the Greeks, who at present had no field-pieces or arms of any kind larger than the ordinary muskets then in use, and similarly it would have been waste of time and lives to attack it either on the north or east. On the north, however, was a picket-gate in the wall, communicating with a steep flight of steps cut in the rock. Petrobey's plan, therefore, was to take possession at once of the lower undefended town and blockade the citadel from that side, for thus with a body of men to guard the northern picket, the east and west sides being impassable both from within and without, the blockade would be complete. Meantime the three companies, consisting of Messenians and Arcadians, would cut off the harbor from the town, leaving the Mainats, Argives, and Laconians to deal with the citadel itself.

When day broke the secrecy of their advance was favored by a thick mist, which rose some ten feet high from the plain, and under cover of this, manoeuvring in some fields about a mile eastward from the town, the army split in two, and one half marched straight down to the shore of the bay, and from there, turning along the coast, ranged itself along the harbor shore and on the breakwater, made of large rough blocks of stone, which sheltered the harbor from southerly winds, and the other three, leaving the citadel on their right hand, went straight for the lower town. Half an hour afterwards the heat of the sun began to disperse the morning mists, and as they got to the outskirts of the town the vast vapor was rolled away, and the sentries on the citadel looking out southward saw three companies of soldiers not half a mile off. The alarm was given at once and spread through the lower town like fire. From all the houses rushed out men, women, and children, some still half clad or just awakened from their morning sleep, mothers with babies in their arms, and old men almost as helpless, who ran this way and that in the first panic terror, but gradually settled down into two steady streams—the one up to the citadel to find refuge there, the other to the harbor to seek means of flight. But the army came on in silence, making its way slowly up the narrow streets towards the citadel, without being attacked by the terrified and unarmed inhabitants, and in its turn neither striking a blow nor firing a shot. Two companies only had entered the town, the third remaining on the outskirts to the east, acting like a "stop" in cover-shooting, to drive the inhabitants back again, lest any should convey the alarm to Tripoli.

From the west of the town a bridge led over the torrent, and here Petrobey stationed some hundred men to prevent any one leaving the town across the river; but before long, wishing to concentrate all his forces in the town, Yanni was sent to the party picketed there with orders to destroy the bridge. This was made of wood, but preparations were in hand for replacing it with one of iron, and several girders were lying about on the bank for the approaching work. With one of these as a lever, and twenty men to work it, it was an affair of ten minutes only to prize up some half-dozen planks of the wooden structure, and after that to saw in half a couple of the timber poles on which it rested. The bridge thus weakened drooped towards the water, and soon was caught by the swift stream below. Then, as some monstrous fish plucks at a swimmer's limbs, it twitched and fretted against the remaining portion, and soon with a rush and swirl of timbers and planks it tore away a gap of some twenty feet across, sufficient to stop any would-be fugitives.

Here and there in their passage up the town a house was shut and barred against them, but for the most part the inhabitants streamed out like ants when their hill is disturbed. Once only was resistance offered, when from the upper window of a house a Turk fired upon the soldiers, killing one man; and Petrobey, heading a charge himself, burst in the door, and a couple of shots were heard from inside. Then, without a word, he and the three others who had gone in with him took their places again, and the column moved forward up the street.

The square of the lower town stood just at the base of the rising ground leading up to the citadel, and on its north side was built a row of big silk-mills, all of which had been deserted by their owners on the first alarm, and in these the Maina division took up its quarters. As soon as they and the Argives had made their passage through the town, driving the inhabitants up into the citadel, or down to the harbor, where they were taken by the Messenian division, Petrobey sent to the Laconian corps, who had been acting as a "stop" on the east to prevent the people escaping into the country, and brought them up on the right to complete the line which they had drawn along the south front of the citadel. The Argive corps, meantime, had been divided into two, one-half of which blockaded the picket-gate on the north, while the other was drawn up on the left of the Mainats, between them and the river. This done, the blockade of the citadel was complete; on the west the besieged were hemmed in by their own impregnable rock, below which ran the current; on the south and southeast by the Greek army; on the east again by the precipitous crags; and on the north their escape through the picket-gate was impracticable, owing to the detachment of Argives guarding it.

Three courses were open to them: to make a sortie as soon as the expected Turkish ships would appear and regain communication with the sea; or, by engaging and defeating the Greeks, establish connection with Tripoli; or to support the siege until help came. In the utter confusion and panic caused by the sudden appearance of the Greeks the inhabitants had simply fled like a quail-flock, and the citadel was crammed with a crowd of unarmed civilians. Each thought only for himself and his own personal protection. Mixed in this crowd of fugitives had been hundreds of Greek residents—some of whom, possessed merely by the wild force of panic and without waiting to think what this army was, had rushed blindly with the others into the citadel; but the larger number had joined their countrymen—men, women, and children together—imploring protection with horrible tales of outrage and cruelty on their lips. All those who were fit for active service and willing Petrobey enlisted, and employed them in making a more careful search through the town for any Turks who might remain in hiding. These were not to be killed or ill-treated, but merely kept as prisoners. But the wild vengeance of those who had so long been slaves burst all bounds when they saw their masters in their power, and all who were found were secretly put to death.

The weakness of the citadel lay in its bad water supply. There was only one well in the place, and that was not nearly sufficient for the wants of the crowds who had taken refuge within it. But about mid-day Demetri, the mayor of Nauplia, who was in charge of the division on the north, observed buckets being let down from the top of the citadel wall into the river and drawn up again full. The rocks here overhung a little, and, taking with him some ten men, they dashed right under the walls and to the corner abutting on the river. At that moment two more buckets appeared

146

close in front of them, and he and another, taking hold of them, quietly undid the knots which tied them to the rope. The grim humor of this amused him, and in half an hour there was a row of some twenty buckets, which they had untied or cut. The besieged then attempted to get water farther down, but the rocks there being not so precipitous and sloping outward, the buckets stuck on some projection of rock before reaching the water.

Meantime a column of smoke, rising from the harbor, showed that the Messenians were at their work. One corps had deployed along the shore and took in hand the work of burning all the shipping, while the other was employed in making prisoners of the fugitives from the lower town, who hoped to escape by sea. A few of these, striking eastward across the plain, tried to get into the mountains, and were shot, but the majority, finding themselves between two divisions of the army, cut off from the citadel by Petrobey's division and from the sea by the Messenians, and also being unarmed, surrendered to Niketas, who, knowing no Turkish, but being proud of his English, merely said "All-a-right" to their entreaties and prayers, and had them incontinently stowed away in batches in the harbor buildings. The Arcadians, meantime, had ranged themselves along the breakwater, where they kept watch for the Turkish ships, and, having no work to hand, spent the morning in smoking and singing.

About two in the afternoon word was brought to the captain of the troops within the citadel—one Ali Aga—that two Turkish ships had been seen in the offing approaching Kalamata. A steady south breeze was blowing, and a couple of hours would see their arrival. Ali had watched, in white, contemptuous anger that morning, the destruction of the shipping by the Greeks. The ammunition within the walls was very scanty, and the water supply for this irruption of fugitives was wholly inadequate. Indeed, unless news of their straits was already on the road to Tripoli—and this he could scarce hope, so swift and complete had been the beleaguer—unless a relief expedition was even now imminently starting, he saw that the only chance of saving the town lay in concerted action with the approaching ships, and thus making an attack on the Greek lines from both sides—the citadel and the sea. Thus he determined to wait until the ships came up and engaged the detachment of Greeks on the shore.

The wind still holding, in half an hour the Arcadian contingent on the breakwater could see even from the beach the hulls of the approaching ships, beyond all doubt Turkish men-of-war. The breakwater along which the Greeks were ranged was still only half completed, and masses of rough masonry lay piled and tumbled on the seaward end. Niketas rubbed his hands gleefully as he made the dispositions for their welcome, and exclaimed many times "This is very all-a-right"; then, relapsing into Greek, he gave his orders, and mingled with them a chuckling homily.

"The Turk made the breakwater," he said, "but God and the holy saints, having the Greeks in mind, were the designers. Hide yourselves ever so thickly among these beautiful great stones, like anchovies in a barrel, and when the ship turns into the harbor we will all talk loud to it together. The water is very deep here; they will sail close to our anchovy barrel, and they will see none of us till they turn the corner, for the breakwater which God planned hides us from the sea."

He called up one division of Messenians to join the Arcadian corps, leaving the other to guard the beach, and the sixteen hundred men ranged themselves among the blocks of masonry along the inside of the breakwater, so that until the ships turned the corner not one could be seen, but once round they would be exposed to a broadside of muskets at close range from marksmen concealed by the stones. Niketas himself—for the foremost ship was now not more than a few hundred yards out—crawled with infinite precaution to the end of the breakwater, and smilingly watched its unsuspicious approach. It carried, he saw, many heavy guns; but that was a small matter.

The wind was now light, and the ship was nearly opposite the end of the breakwater when she began to take in sail, and a moment afterwards her helm was put hard aport, and she slowly swung round, crumpling the smooth water beneath her bow, and came straight alongside the wall at a distance of not more than fifty yards. Niketas had told the men to fire exactly when the ship came opposite them. She would pass slowly down the line, and would be raked fore and aft again and again as she went along.

Sixteen hundred men were crowded like swarming bees among the lumps of tumbled stone. As many muskets waited hungrily. Overhead, above the shelter of the breakwater, hummed the breeze; the little wavelets tapped on the edge of the masonry; the stage was ready.

Tall and beautiful she came slowly on till her whole length appeared opposite the ambush. Her decks and rigging were alive with the sailors, who were swarming over the masts and furling sail, or stood ready to drop the anchor on the word of command. On the bridge stood the captain with two other officers, and, marshalled in rows on the aft deck, about two hundred soldiers, carrying arms. Simultaneously through the ambushed Greeks the same thought ran, "The soldiers first," and as the great ship glided steadily past the end of the breakwater the fire of a hundred men broke out, and they went down like ninepins. The ship moved on, and, like the echo of the first volley, a second swept the decks, and close on the second a third. The captain fell and two officers with him, and a panic seized the crew. They ran hither and thither, some seeking refuge below, some jumping overboard, some standing where they were, wide-eyed and terror-stricken. A few of the soldiers only retained their presence of mind, and with perfect calmness, as if they were practising at some sham-fight, brought a gun into position and proceeded to load it. But again and again they were mowed down by the deadly short-range fire of the Greeks, while others took up the ramrods and charge from their clinched hands, only to deliver it up from their death-grip to others. But still the great ship went on, running the gauntlet of the whole ambush, while every moment its decks grew more populous with a ghastly crew of death. The well-directed and low fire of the Greeks had left the half-furled sails untouched, and the wind still blew steadily. But in a few moments more there were none left to take the helm, and, swinging round to the wind, she changed her course

148

and went straight for the low, sandy beach on the other side of the harbor. There, fifty yards off the shore, she grounded heavily, with a slight list to starboard, striking a sand-bank on the port side; and there, all the afternoon, she stood, white and stately, with sails bulging with the wind, but moving not, like some painted or phantom ship with wings that feel not wind nor any gale.

Not till then did Niketas, nor indeed any of his ambushed party, give a thought to the other ship, but when the first ship with its crew of dead turned in the wind and sailed ashore he looked round the corner for the other. It was still some quarter of a mile away, but there seemed to be some commotion on deck, and he was uncertain for a moment whether they were preparing to bring their big gun into play. But he was not left long in doubt, for in a couple of minutes more the ship swung round and beat out to sea again. This disgraceful piece of cowardice raised from the Greeks a howl, partly of derision and partly of rage at being balked of their prey, and a few discharged their muskets at the fleeing enemy until Niketas stopped them, telling them not to waste good powder on runaway dogs. On the first ship the body of soldiers had literally been destroyed, and of two hundred not more than thirty remained. But these, with a courageous despair, after the first few minutes of wild confusion were over, had sheltered themselves at different points behind the bulwarks and furniture of the ship, and were returning the fire coolly, while others began preparing the big gun for action. But these were an easy mark for the Greeks, for they were unprotected, and after five or six more men had been shot down they abandoned the attempt and confined themselves to their muskets. They were, however, fighting with cruel odds against them, for the men on whom they were firing were sheltered by the blocks of masonry on the pier, and hardly more could be seen than a bristling row of gun-barrels. Hardly any of those who had flung themselves into the sea lived to reach the shore, for they also were shot down as they swam, and all over the bay were stains of crimson blood and clothes which they had flung off into the water. One man, indeed, landed two hundred yards away, but even as he stood there wringing the water out of his clothes, which would clog his running, he was shot dead, and fell back into the water again.

Meantime, from the citadel Ali Aga had watched the destruction of one ship and the flight of the other. At the moment when the first had entered the harbor he had opened fire on the Mainat corps; but they, obeying Petrobey's direction, merely sheltered behind the mills, and did not even take the trouble to return it. Encouraged by this, and seeing heavy fighting going on below, Ali was just preparing to make a dash for the harbor with some half of the troops, in order to establish communication, when the firing on the shore suddenly slackened, and he saw one ship sail off without firing a shot, while the other drifted with half-furled sails across the bay, and then grounded. At that he resolved again to wait, for he had no intention of going to the rescue of those who should have rescued him, and indeed, without co-operation from the ship, the attempt would have been madness.

At dusk the firing below ceased altogether, for a boat had put off from the ship bearing the white flag of surrender, and all those who were left on board were removed, their arms taken from them, and they were put into custody. Niketas, who boarded the ship, felt a sudden unwilling admiration for the man who had gone on fighting against such fearful odds. The deck presented a fearful sight—it was a shambles, nothing less. The list of the ship as she struck had drained the blood in oily, half-congealed streams through the scuppers, and it was dripping sullenly into the sea. The small-arms and powder the Greeks transferred in boats to the land, where they were added to the stock, and they made several unsuccessful attempts to get out one or two of the larger guns, which might prove useful if Kalamata refused to capitulate. But all their efforts, in the absence of fit tackling and lifting apparatus, were useless, and after emptying the ship of all that could be of service to them, including a sum of five hundred Turkish pounds, which was found in the captain's cabin, they set light to it for fear it should be got off by its sister ship and so return into the enemy's fleet. All night long the hull blazed, and about midnight it was a pillar of fire, for the sails caught and the flames went roaring upward, mast high. And thus ended the first day of the siege.

All next day the blockade continued without incident, and no attempt was made on the part of the Turks to deliver an attack, nor on that of the besiegers to force their way into the citadel. The pass from Arcadia and that over Taygetus, across either of which any relief expedition from Tripoli must march, were carefully watched, and before such appeared Petrobey declined to make an attack, which must be expensive to the Greek army, when simply waiting would do their work for them; while Ali on his side would sooner capitulate, if the worst came to the worst, than with his fifteen hundred men, ill-supplied with ammunition, engage these six regiments of wolves; for such an engagement, as he knew, would only end in his utter defeat, and the massacre in all probability of all the Turks in the town.

Early on the third morning it was clear that help was not coming from Tripoli, or, at any rate, that it would come too late. The water supply had entirely given out and famine as well was beginning to make itself felt. For two days and nights the citadel had been packed like a crate of figs with defenceless and civilian humanity, more than half of whom had to lie out under the cold of the spring night exposed to the dews and the sun, some of them barely half clad, just as they had been awakened from their sleep when they had fled panic-stricken to the citadel. Below in the Greek army the utmost content and harmony still reigned. The men were well quartered and had all the supplies of the town in their hands, and a considerable amount of booty had been taken, half of which was divided between the men and half reserved by Petrobey for a war fund.

The first bugle had sounded half an hour, and they were preparing their breakfast when a white flag was hoisted on the corner tower, the gate opened, and Ali Aga, alone and unattended, except for a page who carried his chibouk, walked down into the camp. Some Greeks, who had lived under him and had felt his cruel and outrageous rule, saw him coming and surrounded him, spitting at him and reviling him; but here the devilish coolness of the man came to the front, a matter for admiration, and turning round on them he cursed at them so fiercely, calling them dogs and sons of dogs, that they fell back. By the side of the road was sitting a blind Greek, begging. Ali, with splendid unconcern, paused, threw open his red cloak trimmed with the fur of the yellow fox, which he had wrapped closely about him against the chill of the morning, and taking his pistol and string of amber beads out of his belt, felt in the corners of it for some small coins, which he gave the man and passed deliberately on, adjusting his fez with one hand. Once again before he reached Petrobey's quarters he paused, this time to take off one of his red shoes and shake a pebble out of it. Had he blanched or wavered for a moment his life would have been forfeit a dozen times before he reached Petrobey's quarters, but he treated the howling crowd as a man treats snarling curs, and he silently commanded one of the loudest-mouthed to show him the way to their commander.

Petrobey had seen Ali coming, and was sitting outside the house where he had taken up his quarters, and when the Turk appeared he arose and saluted him, telling a servant to bring a pipe for him; but Ali did not return the salute, and merely indicated with one hand that he had brought his own pipe with him, an insult of the most potent nature. To him the Greeks were "all of one bake," and he looked at Petrobey and spoke as if he were speaking to one of his own slaves.

"I find it necessary for me to capitulate," he said, in excellent Greek, "and I am here to settle the conditions."

Petrobey flushed angrily. He was not a meek man, and had no stomach for insults; so he sat down again, leaving Ali standing, and crossed one leg over the other.

"I make no conditions," he said, "except this one: I will order no general massacre; at the same time, it would be safer for all of you not to assume insolent and overbearing airs."

Ali raised his eyebrows, and before speaking again sat down and beckoned to the page who carried his pipe.

"You will not give us a safe conduct to Tripoli, for instance?"

"No."

"You will not allow us to retain our arms?"

Petrobey laughed.

"Such is not my intention. All I will do"—and his anger suddenly flared up at the perfectly unassumed insolence of the man—"all I will do is to forbid my men to shoot you down in cold blood. You will be wise to consider that, for we may not care to grant such terms, no, nor yet be able to enforce obedience to them if we did, on the day when Tripoli is crushed like a beetle below our heel."

Ali shrugged his shoulders and took his chibouk from the hands of the page who carried it.

"Oblige me with a piece of charcoal," he said to one of the Greeks who stood by, and he lit his pipe slowly and deliberately before replying.

"Your terms are preposterous," he said; "I do not, however, say that I will not accept them, but I wish for five hours more for consideration."

"Five hours more for relief from Tripoli, in my poor judgment," remarked Petrobey. "I am afraid that will not be convenient to me. I require 'yes' or 'no'; neither more nor less."

Ali inhaled two long breaths of smoke.

"If I will give neither 'yes' nor 'no,' what then?"

"This. You shall go back in safety, and then when you are starved out, or when we take the place, I will not grant any terms. And we have a long score against you. Your rule has not been popular among my countrymen; those who have lived here under you are full of very pretty tales."

"I suppose the dogs are. I accept your terms."

Petrobey rose.

"Consider yourself my prisoner," he said, not even looking at him. "Take charge of him, Christos, and Yorgi, and order all three corps out, Yanni."

"Another piece of charcoal, one of you," said Ali. "This tobacco is a little damp."

In half an hour's time all the Turkish soldiers and civilians were defiled out of the citadel unarmed between the lines of the Greeks. They were instantly divided up among the different corps, and from that moment became the property of the soldiers as much as the Greek slaves in the last years had been the property of their Turkish masters. Many who had friends were ransomed, many became domestic slaves, and many, in the Greek phrase, "the moon devoured." The flag of Greece was hoisted on the towers, and the work which Mitsos had cried aloud in fire from Taygetus to Bassae had begun.

And on that day which saw the dawning of the freedom of Greece it seemed to these enthusiastic hearts, who for years had cherished and fed the smouldering spark which now ran bursting into flame, that earth and sea and sky joined in the glory and triumph. From its throne in the infinite blue the sun shone to their eyes with a magnificence greater than natural; to the south the sea sparkled and laughed innumerably, and the meadows round the fallen town that day were suddenly smitten scarlet with the blowing of the wind-flowers. And when the work of distributing the prisoners was over, all the army went down to the edge of the torrent-bed, and gave thanks, with singing mouths and hearts that sang, to the Giver of Victory. There, half a mile above the citadel, in a church of which the sun was the light, and the soft, cool north wind the incense that wafted thanksgiving to heaven, stood the first Greek army of free men that had known the unspeakable thrill of victory since the Roman yoke had bound them a score of hundred years ago. Some were old men, withered and gray, and ground down in long slavery to a cruel and bestial master, and destined not to see the full moon of their freedom; in some, like the seed on stony ground, a steadfast heart had no deep root, and in the times of war and desolation, which were still to come, they were to fall away, tiring of the glorious quest; some were still young boys, to whom the event was no more than a mere toy; but for the time, at any rate, all were one heart, beating full in the morning of a long-delayed resurrection. Standing on a mound in the centre were four-and-twenty priests, in the front of whom was Father Andréa, tall, and eyed like a mountain hawk, with a heart full of glory and red vengeance. And, when lifting up the mightiest voice in Greece, he gave out the first words of that hymn which has risen a thousand times to the clash of victorious arms, the voice of a great multitude answered him, and the sound was as the sound of many waters. All the ardor and hot blood of the Greeks leaped like a blush to the surface, and on all sides, mixed with the noise of the singing, rose one great sob of a thankful people born again. Petrobey, with Nicholas on one side and Mitsos and Yanni on the other, hardly knew that the tears were streaming down his tanned and weather-beaten cheeks, and to the others, as to him, memory and expectation were merged and sunk in the present ineffable moment. There was no before or after; they were there, men of a free people, and conscious only of the one thing—that the first blow had been struck, and struck home and true, that they thanked God for the power He had given them to use.

And when it was over Petrobey turned to Nicholas, and smiling at him through his tears:

"Old friend," he said.

And Nicholas echoed his words, echoed that which was too deep for words, and—

"Old friend," he replied.

CHAPTER II

TWO SILVER CANDLESTICKS

For two days longer the army remained at Kalamata in an ecstasy of success. Petrobey posted several companies of men on the lower hills of Taygetus and at the top of the plain, from which a pass led into Arcadia, in ambush for any relieving force from Tripoli, should such be sent. Flushed with victory as they were, nothing seemed impossible, and the spirit of the men was to march straight on that stronghold of the Turkish power. But Petrobey was wiser; he knew that this affair at Kalamata had been no real test of the army's capacity; they had stood with folded arms, and the prey had dropped at their feet. To attack a strongly fortified place, competently held, was to adventure far more seriously. At present he had neither men nor arms enough, and the only sane course was to wait, embarking, it might be, on enterprises of the smaller sort, till with the news of their exploit the rising became more general. In the mean time he remained at Kalamata in order to get tidings from the north of the Morea as to the sequel of the beacon there, and, if expedient, to unite his troops with the contingent from Patras and Megaspelaion. As commander-in-chief of the first army in the field, he issued a proclamation, declaring that the Greeks were determined to throw off the yoke of the Turk, and asking for the aid of Christians in giving liberty to those who were enslaved to the worshippers of an alien god.

The primates and principal clergy of the Morea, it will be remembered, had been summoned to Tripoli for the meeting at the end of March, and the scheme that the wisdom of Mitsos had hatched, to give them an excuse for their disobedience, had met with entire success. Germanos, who both spoke and wrote Turkish, forged a letter, purporting to come from a friendly Mussulman at Tripoli, warning him to beware, for Mehemet Salik, thinking that a rising of the Greeks was imminent, had determined to put one or two of the principal men to death in order to terrorize the people, and with the same stone to deprive them of their leaders. With this in his pocket, he set out and travelled quietly to Kalavryta, where he found other of the principal clergy assembled at the house of Zaimes, the primate of the place. Germanos arrived there in the evening, and before going to bed gave the forged letter to Lambros, his servant, telling him to start early next morning, ride in the direction of Tripoli, then turn back and meet the party at their mid-day halt. He was then to give the letter to his master, saying that he had received it from a Turk on the road, who hearing that he was Germanos's servant, told him, as he valued his life and the life of his master, not to spare spur till he had given it him, and on no account to hint a word of the matter to any one.

Lambros, who had the southern palate for anything smacking of drama and mystery, obeyed in letter and spirit, and at mid-day, while the primates were halting, he spurred a jaded, foam-streaked horse up the road, flung himself quickly off, and gave the forged communication to his master. Germanos glanced through it with well-feigned dismay and exclamations of astonished horror, and at once read it aloud to the assembled primates, who were struck with consternation. Some suggested one thing and some another, but every one looked to Germanos for an authoritative word.

"This will we do, my brothers," he said, "if it seems good to you: I will send this letter to my admirable friend—or so I still think—Mehemet Salik, and ask for a promise of safety, a matter of form merely. Yet we may not disregard what my other admirable friend has said, for if, as God forbid, it is true, where would our flock be without their shepherds? But if it is false, Mehemet will at once send us a promise of safety. Meantime, we must act as if the truth of this letter were possible, and I suggest that we all disperse, and for our greater safety each surround himself with some small guard. And before the answer comes back, it may be"—he looked round and saw only the faces of patriots—"it may be that there will be other business on hand"—and his face was a beacon.

It is probable that more than one of the primates guessed that the letter was a forgery, but they were only too glad to be supplied with a specious excuse for delaying their journey, and followed Germanos's advice.

Then followed those ten days of feverish inaction, while on Taygetus

Petrobey collected the forces which were to be the doom of Kalamata. Evening by evening patient men climbed to the hills where the beacon fuel was stacked, questioning the horizon for the signal, and morning by morning returned to the expectant band of patriots in their villages, saying "Not yet, not yet," until one night the signs of fire shouted from south to north of the land, telling them that the Vintage was ripe for harvest. At Kalavryta, where the first blow in the north was struck, they found the Turks even less ready than at Kalamata, and little expecting the soldiers of God in their companies from the monastery; and on the 3d of April the town surrendered on receiving, as at Kalamata, a promise that there should be no massacre. The place was one of little importance among the Turkish towns, but of the first importance to the revolutionists, lying as it did in the centre of the richest valley in Greece, and in close proximity to Megaspelaion, and it became the centre of operations in the north. Also, it was valuable inasmuch as several very wealthy Turks lived there, and the money that thus fell into the hands of the Greeks was food for the sinews of war.

As soon as this reached Kalamata, Petrobey determined to move. The wholesale success of the patriots in the north showed that they were in no need of immediate help, and to have two different armies in the field, one driving the Turks southward, the other northward into Tripoli, the central fortress of Ottoman supremacy, was ideal to his wishes. But more than ever now soberness and strength were needed; the men hearing of the taking of Kalavryta were wild to unite with the northern army and march straight on Tripoli. But Petrobey, backed by Nicholas, was as firm as Taygetus; such a course could only end in disaster, for they were yet as ignorant as children of the elements of war, and it would be an inconceivable rashness now to venture on that which would be final disaster or the freedom of the Morea. They must learn the alphabet of their new trade; what better school could there be than their camp on the slopes of Taygetus, the lower hill-sides of which were covered with Turkish villages, and where they would not, from the nature of the ground, be exposed to the attacks of cavalry? So, after making great breaches in the walls of the citadel of Kalamata, and filling up the well, so that never again could it be used as a stronghold, they marched back across the blossomed plain and up to the hill camp below the beacon with the glory of success upon them.

Three nights later Yanni and Mitsos were sitting after supper in the open air by a camp-fire. Yanni, still rather soft from his month's fattening at Tripoli—"And, oh, Yanni," said Mitsos, "but it is a stinging affair to have fattened a little pig like you, and never have the eating of it"—was suffering from a blister on his heel, and Mitsos prescribed spirits on the raw or pure indifference.

"If you had been cooped and fattened as I, little Mitsos," said Yanni, in an infernally superior manner, "how much running do you think you could lay leg to? As it is, if you continue to eat as you eat, what a belly-man will Mitsos be at thirty!"

Mitsos pinched Yanni over the ribs.

"Poor Mehemet!" he said, "all that for nothing. I have a fine cousin who is only just twenty, and if you said he was fat, man, you wouldn't give a person any proper notion of him."

"My blister is worse than it was yesterday," said Yanni, pulling off his shoe.

"There was a show at Nauplia last year," continued Mitsos, lying lengthily back and looking at the stars, "and a fat woman in it. When she walked she wobbled like a jelly-fish. Just about as fat as a cousin of mine."

"Oh!"

"She wasn't married, the man said, and was to be had for the asking. I hate fat women almost as much as I hate fat men."

Nicholas had strolled out of his hut, and was standing behind the boys as they talked.

"Now look at Uncle Nicholas, Yanni," said Mitsos, still unconscious of his presence, "he will be some twelve good inches taller than you, and forty years older; but I doubt if you could tie his trousers-strings."

Nicholas laughed.

"I can do it myself, little Mitsos," he said. "Come in, you two; there is work forward."

Yanni sprang up and stepped into his shoe, forgetting the blister.

"A journey," he said, "for Mitsos and me? Oh, Mitsos, it is good."

"Yanni cannot walk," said Mitsos; "he has a blister, and must needs be carried like a scented woman."

"A blister?" asked Nicholas. "Don't think about it."

"So said I," answered Mitsos, "but he has no thought for aught else in God's world."

"Well, come in," answered Nicholas, "and hear what you will hear."

The business was soon explained. The ship which had been seen at Kalamata had gone back to Nauplia, so it was reported, and was to transport thence to Athens several wealthy Turkish families who were fearful for their safety. From Athens it would come back, bringing arms and ammunition, to Nauplia. The time for the fire-ship had come.

"And Nicholas says, little Mitsos," continued Petrobey, "that you know the bay of Nauplia like your own hand, and can take your boat about it as a man carries food to his mouth."

Mitsos flushed with pleasure.

"And in truth I am no stranger to it," he said. "When do I start?"

"To-morrow morning. The ship arrived there three days ago, but will wait another five days. The business is to be done when she is well out to sea, so that there is no time for her to get back. You will want some one with you. Whom would you like?"

Mitsos looked at Yanni.

"Whom but the fat little cousin?" he said.

"The little cousin doesn't mind," said Yanni, with his eyes dancing, and gave Mitsos a great poke in the ribs.

"Ugh, Turkish pig," quoth Mitsos, "we will settle that account together."

"Be quiet, lads," said Petrobey, "and listen to me"; and he gave them the details of their mission.

156

"Big butchers we shall be," said the blood-thirsty Mitsos when Petrobey had finished. "Eh, but the fishes will give thanks for us."

Yanni and he tumbled out of the hut again, sparring at each other for sheer delight at a new adventure, and sat talking over the fire, smoking the best tobacco from Turkish shops at Kalamata, till Nicholas, coming out late to go the round of the sentries, packed them off to bed.

All the apparatus they would require, and also the caique to serve as the fire-ship, were at Nauplia; and they started off next morning unencumbered with baggage, with only one horse, which the "scented woman" was to ride if his blister should tease him. A detachment of the clan who were not on duty, as well as Nicholas and Mitsos' father, saw them to the top of the pass, which they were to follow till they got onto the main road at Sparta, and then go across country, giving Tripoli a very wide berth, and taking a boat across the bay of Nauplia so as to avoid Argos. At Nauplia they were to put up at Mitsos' house, but keep very quiet, and remain there as little time as might be. The caique would be lying at anchor opposite; Lelas, the café-keeper, had charge of it.

The journey was made without alarm or danger. On the evening of the first day they found themselves at the bottom of the Langarda pass, with the great fertile plain of Sparta spread out before them, now green, now gray, as the wind ruffled the groves of olive-trees. A mile beyond the bottom of the pass their way lay close under the walls of the little Turkish town of Mistra, and this they passed by quickly, in case the news of the taking of Kalamata had come and the soldiers were on the lookout for wandering Greeks. But as they skirted along a foot-path below the town Yanni looked back.

"It's very odd," he said, "but we have passed nobody going home; and look, there are no lights in any of the houses."

"That is queer," said Mitsos; "no, there is not a single light. We'll wait a bit, Yanni."

They sat down off the path in the growing dusk, but not a sign came from the town; no lights appeared in the windows, it seemed perfectly deserted, and by degrees their curiosity made a convert of their caution.

"We will go very quietly and have a look at the gate," said Yanni. "It will be pleasanter sleeping in a house than in the fields, for it will be cold before morning up here."

"That comes of living in a fine house in Tripoli," remarked Mitsos. "Come on, then."

The two went very cautiously back to the road which led up to the gate and found it standing wide open.

"That ought to be shut at dark," says Mitsos; "we will go a little farther."

Still there was no living thing to be seen, no glimmer shone from any house, and soon Mitsos stopped.

"Oh, Yanni, I see," he said. "They must have had news of the Kalamata thing, and all have fled. There's not a soul left in the place. Come on, we'll just go to the top of the street."

They left the horse for the time in the outer court of a mosque which

157

stood near the gate, and advanced cautiously up the steep, cobbled road. Everywhere the same silence and signs of panic-stricken flight prevailed. Here a silk-covered sofa blocked the doorway of a house; farther on they came upon a couple of embroidered Turkish dresses; a big illuminated Koran lay with leaves flapping in the evening wind on a door-step, and outside the old Byzantine church at the top of the street, which had been turned into a mosque by the Turks, stood two immense silver candlesticks, four feet high, and each holding some twenty tapers. Yanni looked thoughtfully at these for a minute.

"It is in my mind," he said, "that I will eat my dinner by the light of fine silver candlesticks. Pick up the other, cousin; I can't carry both. Holy Virgin, how heavy they are!"

"Where are we to take them?" asked Mitsos.

"To a nice house, where we will have supper," says Yanni. "I saw such a one as I came up. There was a barrel of wine outside it, and my stomach cries for plenty of good wine. Oh, here's a woman's dress. Eh, what a smart woman this must have been!"

The house which Yanni had noticed was a two-storied café, standing a little back from the street. The upper rooms were reached by an outside staircase from the garden, and as they went up to it a cat, the only live thing they had seen, looked at them a moment with mournful eyes, and then, deciding that they were to be trusted, put up an arched, confiding back against Mitsos' leg, and made a poker of her tail. Below, the house was of three rooms, the outer of which, looking over the plain, was full of the signs of flight. A long Turkish narghilé, with an amber mouth-piece, was overturned on the floor, and on one of the little coffee tables stood another pipe half filled with unsmoked tobacco, while the silk pouch from which it was supplied lay unrolled beside it, and on a shelf were four or five long-stemmed chibouks. A long divan, smothered in cushions, ran round three sides of the room, and the cat, in the belief that her friends were coming back, jumped lightly into her accustomed place and looked at the boys, blinking and purring contentedly. The second room was full of cans of coffee and tobacco, and on a table in the centre stood a dish with two chickens, one wholly plucked, the other but half denuded, and by it an earthenware bowl of water, in which were cool, green lettuces. The third room was a stable for horses; a manger full of fresh hay ran down one side, and in the opposite corner were an oven and a heap of charcoal. The fire had gone out and was only a heap of white, feathery ash, while on the extinguished embers still stood two little brass coffee jugs, their contents half boiled away. Yanni smiled serenely when they had finished their examination.

"You will sup with me to-night, cousin?" he asked, pompously. "Oh, Mitsos, but this is a soft thing we have hit upon."

Mitsos walked back into the outer room, where he closed the wooden shutters and lit all the candles.

"Nice little candlesticks," he said, approvingly. "How I wish the owner of the house could see us. Wouldn't he howl!"

Up-stairs there were two rooms—one with two beds in it, the other

158

with one. The beds were still unmade, just as they had been slept in, and Mitsos pulled off the sheets disdainfully, for he would not lie where a Turk had been. Then, while Yanni kindled the fire to boil the chickens, he rummaged in the store-room.

"A pot of little anchovies, Yanni," he remarked; "they will come first to give us an appetite. Thus I shall have two appetites, for I have one already. By the Virgin! there is tobacco too, all ready in the pipes. We shall pass a very pleasant evening, I hope. Oh, there's the horse still waiting at the gate. I will go and fetch him; and be quick with the supper, pig."

Yanni laughed.

"Really the Turk is a very convenient man," he said. "I like wars. We can take provisions from here which will last to Nauplia. There will be no skulking about villages after dark to buy bread and wine without being noticed."

Yanni put the chicken to boil, and while Mitsos fetched the horse, having nothing more to do, he amused himself by trying on the dress of the Turkish woman which they had found in the street. The big black bernous concealed the deficiencies of the skirt, which only came to his knees, and he had finished adjusting the veil, and had sat down chastely on a corner of the settee, when he heard Mitsos come up the street and call to him from the stable. So he got up and went on tiptoe out of the house and round to the other door, and Mitsos looking up saw a Turkish woman peeping in, who screamed in shrill falsetto when she saw him. For one moment he thought that somehow or other this was Suleima, but the next moment he had rushed after Yanni and hauled him in.

"Is not my supper ready, woman?" he cried, "and why do you not attend to your master?"

They ate their dinner in the best of spirits, for that the hated and despised Turk, whose destruction was their mission, should board and lodge them so handsomely seemed one of the best jokes. Mitsos every now and then broke into a huge grin as he made fearful inroads upon the food and wine, and Yanni kept ejaculating: "Very good chicken of the Turk. The best wine of the Turk; give me some lettuce of the Turk. I wish we could take the candlesticks, Mitsos; but perhaps two peasant boys with heavy silver sticks four feet high slung on their mules might attract attention."

The moon had risen soon after sunset, and after dinner they sat smoking in the garden, which was planted with pomegranates and peach-trees, and fringed by a row of cypresses, which looked black in the moonlight. All was perfectly still but for the sleepy prattle of the stream below. Now and then a nightingale gave out a throatful of song, or some spray of asphodel, ripe to the core, cracked and scattered its seed round it. The cat prowled about the garden, now creeping through the shadow of the trees, or flattening herself out on the ground, and now making springs at some imaginary prey in the moonlight, and when they went up-stairs she preceded them, and, jumping onto Mitsos' bed, lay purring like a tea-kettle.

CHAPTER III

THE ADVENTURE OF THE FIRE-SHIP

They started again early the next morning, having loaded the pony with provisions, for Yanni preferred to suffer from his blister than from hunger, and struck in a southeasterly direction across the plain, leaving Sparta with its red roofs and olive-groves on the left, over low hills of red earth, covered in this spring-time with cistus in full flower, tall white heather, and myrtle in the freshness of its fragrant leaf. About two hours' going brought them to the Eurotas, flowing clear and bright over its shining pebble-bed, on which the sunlight drew a diaper of light and shade, sliding on from pool to shallow, and shallow to rapid, and ford to ford. Here Mitsos, who in his inland life pined for the amphibious existence of Nauplia, came upon a deep pool, and in a moment was stripped and swimming. From there another two hours led them across the plain to the foot of the hills, where they halted and ate their midday meal, looking across the green plain to where Taygetus, rising in gray shoulder over shoulder, met the sky in a spear-head of snow.

So for two more days they went on, sleeping sometimes during the middle of the day under the shade of aromatic pines, or behind some bluff of earth in a dry torrent-bed, and as they got nearer to Tripoli and Argos, marching through the cool, still night over shoulders and outstretched limbs of mountain range, or down through silent valleys all aflush with spring, and spending the daylight hours in some sheltered nook or cave, each keeping alternate watches while the other slept. Thus came they down to Myloi, where they were to get the boat which should take them across the bay, early one morning while it was still dark. So once again in the sweetness of sunrise Mitsos saw the blue mirror of the bay spread out smooth and clear at his feet, and the first rays of morning sparkling on the town at the other side, turning the damp roofs to sheets of gold, and on a white house at the head of the bay, where his heart was.

They were home by nine o'clock, and from there they could see plainly the great Turkish ship, as large as a church, lying close to the quay, showing that they were in time. The attack, as Petrobey had told Mitsos, must, of course, be at night, and through the café-keeper Lelas they learned that she would sail the same evening at midnight, or thereabouts. This was quite to their convenience, for had she sailed during the day they would have had to follow her till the fall of night gave cover to their approach, thus, perhaps, attracting suspicion, and certainly finding themselves many miles from home out at sea when their work was done. Lelas, the café-keeper, to whom they were referred, showed them the caique which Nicholas had told him to keep for Mitsos, and the boy, saying that he would go out a little way at once to see how it sailed, got into it, leaving Yanni on the shore. The latter winked at Mitsos as he got in, and remarking "I am sorry I cannot go with you," for he knew precisely where

160

Mitsos was going, though his chance of seeing Suleima by day was absolutely nil, went back to Constantine's house and waited patiently for his return.

Lelas, who was an arrant gossip-monger, had the news of the town: the Turks were flying in all directions, some to Tripoli, some to Constantinople, some to Athens, such was their consternation at the taking of Kalamata. Many of those about Nauplia were going on board the warship, which was bound for the Piræus, and to return with arms. "And tell me," he said, "what is Mitsos going to do with the caique? I am sure it is some plot against the Turk."

But Yanni, seeing Nicholas had not thought fit to tell him, denied any knowledge of the purpose of the boat.

Meantime Mitsos had put out, and was sailing straight to the white wall. The wind was blowing lightly from the east, and he ran straight before it. The boat, slimly built and carrying more sail than his, was certainly a faster goer than his own before the wind, and he suspected would sail closer to it. Certainly it took the air like a bird, and, though the breeze was but light, was a very sea-gull for moving. That, no doubt, was why Nicholas, whose knowledge of boats was as of one who had never set foot on dry land, had chosen it, and Mitsos glanced towards the big ship moored off the quay at Nauplia, and mentally gave it fifteen minutes' start in an hour's run. "And, oh, I love a blaze!" thought he.

Twenty minutes' scudding brought him nearly up to the wall; there he took in the sail and drifted. There was no one on the terrace; that was unusual on a fine morning, when there were often two or three of the servants about, or a woman from the harem. How quiet it looked! Yet, though he did not see Suleima, it was something to know she was near, sitting, it might be, at the back of the garden, or in-doors; perhaps Zuleika had the toothache and she was unapproachable; perhaps the two were talking together; perhaps they were talking of him, wondering when he would come again....

In the farther of the two walls running back from the sea was a small door, and Mitsos' boat had drifted till this appeared in view, and looking up from his revery he saw that it was open. This was even more unusual; never had he seen it open before, and he sat for a moment or two frowning, wondering at it. Then suddenly the smile was struck dead on his face; a possibility too horrible for thought, suggested by those open doors at Mistra, had dawned on him, and regardless of imprudence he took up an oar, put the boat to land, and tying it up went straight to the open door. The garden was empty, the house-door was open, and, more convincing than all, a hare ran across the path and hid itself in the tangle of a flower-bed.

Then with a flash the horrible possibility became a certainty to his mind. The house was empty and deserted; Abdul and the household had fled; a ship was now at Nauplia to carry away the fugitives; that ship he was going to destroy, consigning all on it to a death among flames from which there was no escape. Abdul was surely there, and with Abdul and his household....

Mitsos stood there a long minute with wide, unseeing eyes; for a

161

moment the horror of his position drowned his consciousness as a blow stuns the brain. Then as his reason came back to him he realized that he could not, that he was physically unable, to carry out his orders. The fire-ship should not start—no, it must start, for there was Yanni with him, who knew about it, and he cursed himself for having taken Yanni. But so be it; it should start, but something should go wrong—he would forget to take kindling for it, or, setting light to it, it should only drift by the other and not harm her. For it was no question of choice; he could not do this thing.

Thus thought poor Mitsos as he sailed home again. It seemed to him that nothing in the world mattered except Suleima, and by the bitter irony of fate the man in the world whom he most loved and respected had told him to destroy with all on board the ship in which Suleima was. On the one hand stood Nicholas, his father, Petrobey, Yanni, and the whole clan of those dear, warm-hearted cousins who had treated him as a brother, yet half divine; on the other, Suleima, and Suleima was more to him than them all; Suleima was part of himself, dearer than his hand or his eye, and besides—besides....

Yanni was having dinner when he entered the house, but there was that in Mitsos' face which made him spring up.

"Mitsos," he said, "little Mitsos, what is the matter?"

Mitsos looked at him a moment in silence, but that craving of the human spirit for sympathy in trouble, whether the sympathy is given by man or beast, overpowered him. Though in his own mind he had settled that he could not destroy this ship, the trouble of his struggle was sore upon him.

"Yanni," he whispered, "there will be no fire-ship. Abdul has gone, has fled with all the household, with Suleima among them. Where has he fled but onto the ship we are to destroy? I cannot do it."

Yanni sank down again in his chair.

"Oh, Mitsos," he said, "poor Mitsos! God forgive us all."

Mitsos glanced at him, frowning.

"'Poor Mitsos!'" he cried; "why do you say 'poor Mitsos'? Do you think I am going to do this?"

"You are not going to do it?"

"No!" shouted Mitsos. "It is not I who choose. There is no choice. I cannot!"

"But the clan, the oath to obey—"

"There are bigger things than clans or oaths. To hell with my oath, to hell with the clan," cried Mitsos.

Yanni sat silent, and Mitsos suddenly flared up again.

"How dare you sit there," he cried, "and let your silence blame me? You, whom I rescued from the house of Mehemet; who but for me would have been rotting in the ground, or worse than that; you, whom I saved when a cross-legged Turk had you down on the ground—"

"Mitsos!" said Yanni, looking at him without fear or anger, but stung intolerably.

For a moment or two Mitsos sat still, but then the blessed relief of tears came.

162

"What have I said to you, Yanni?" he sobbed. "O God, forgive me, for I know not what I said; yet—yet how can I do this? Oh, of course you are right, and I—I—Yanni, is it not hard? What was it I said to you? Something devilish, I know. Don't give me up, Yanni; there is none—there will soon be none who loves me as you do."

Yanni's great black eyes grew soft with tears, and he put his arm round Mitsos' neck as his head lay on the table.

"Oh, Mitsos! poor little Mitsos!" he said again. "What is to be done? If only Nicholas or my father knew; and yet you could not and cannot tell them. Perhaps she is not on the ship, you know."

"Perhaps, perhaps—oh, perhaps she is!" cried Mitsos.

The two sat there in silence for a time, stricken almost out of consciousness by this appalling thing. At last Mitsos raised his head.

"There is nothing more to be said," he muttered. "I have no idea what I shall do. Either to do the thing or not to do it is impossible, and yet by to-morrow it will be done or left undone. But, Yanni, just tell me you forgive me for what I said just now and make indulgence, for this is a hard, weary day for me."

Yanni smiled.

"Forgiveness is no word from me to you, dear Mitsos," he said. "There is nothing you could do or say to me for which you need ask that."

Mitsos looked up at him with dumb, dry eyes and a quivering mouth.

"Forget it, too, Yanni, and tell me it will make no change between us, for, in truth, I do not know what I said."

"There, there," said Yanni, soothingly. "The thing is not, it never has been."

The hours went on slowly and silently. Mitsos said nothing, but lay in the veranda like some suffering animal that has crept away to die alone of a mortal wound, and Yanni was wise enough to leave him quite to himself, for his struggle was one that had to be wrestled out alone without help or sympathy from others. But gradually and very slowly the mist of irresolution passed away from Mitsos' brain, and he felt that he would decide one way or the other. Meantime the sun had sunk to its setting, and Yanni prepared food and took some with wine out to Mitsos.

"Eat, drink," he said. "You have not eaten since morning."

"I am not hungry," said Mitsos, listlessly.

For answer Yanni took up the glass of wine and held it to him.

"Drink it quickly, Mitsos; you are faint for something," he said, "and then I will take it and fill it again."

Mitsos obeyed like a sick child, and Yanni took the glass and brought it back full. This time he waited a moment, and then said:

"You must make up your mind, Mitsos. If you settle to do nothing, tell me, and I must think for myself."

Mitsos nodded.

"I will come in in half an hour and tell you," he said. "That will be time enough. Please leave me alone again, Yanni; it is better so."

Yanni went back into the house. His warm-hearted nature, and his intense love for Mitsos, made him suffer to the complement of his capacity of suffering. He would willingly have changed places with Mitsos had it been possible, for he felt he could not suffer more, but so the other would suffer less. Oh, poor Mitsos, whose strength and habit of laughter availed him nothing!

It was less than half an hour later when Mitsos came in. His face was drawn and white, and he felt deadly tired. He did not look at Yanni, but merely stood in the doorway, his eyes cast down.

"Come, Yanni," he said, "it is time we should start. Where are the cans of turpentine and the wood?"

"In the boat; I put them there."

Mitsos looked up at him sharply.

"So you meant to do it yourself if I did not?"

"I meant to try."

Men walk firmly to the scaffold when they are to die for a good cause, and martyrs have seen their wives and children tortured or burned before their eyes and wavered not, and it was this courage of absolute conviction which nerved the poor lad now. With his whole heart he believed in the right of this exterminating war against the Turk; he had put himself unreservedly at the service of its leaders, and there was an order laid on him. He had made of himself a part of a machine, and should a jarring axle speak to the driver and say it would go no farther, or bid him stop the whole gear? Thus it was that, with a firm step and with no tenderness, but only despair and conviction clutching at a cold heart, he walked down with Yanni to the beach, and, having looked over all the apparatus and seen that nothing was wanting, pushed off, and, helping him to set the sail, took his place at the helm.

The enterprise they were embarked upon was dangerous. The caique in which they sat was piled with inflammable materials and a cargo of brushwood, and carried four large cans of turpentine, with which they would presently soak the sails. They were to run up to the Turkish ship, tie their boat up to it, or entangle it in the rigging, set fire to it, and jump into the small boat they towed behind them and row off. The flames would spread like lightning over the boat, giving them hardly a second to escape, and they might easily be seen and shot at while they were lighting her before they could row off; and this element of danger, perhaps, was a help to poor Mitsos.

The night at least was favorable to their adventure, being thickly clouded and with a fine fresh breeze, thus enabling them to come up quickly, and also under cover of darkness. Otherwise the moon, which was nearly full, would have doubled their peril. The wind was from the east of north, so that the ship would probably run straight before it for a mile or so before turning south out of the gulf, and the time to attack her would be just when she turned, for she would then be far enough from the shore to render her destruction inevitable, and the moment of slack speed as she put about would enable them to run into her the more easily. At present they would approach within about a quarter of a mile, and lie there waiting for her to put out.

There was still plenty of time, and when Mitsos let the boat run before the wind instead of going straight to Nauplia, Yanni had no need to ask him why, for he knew where he was going, and kept his eyes away, for he could not bear to see Mitsos' agony. For a little while the hardness and conviction had left him, and the hour of his agony was on him again. And as they neared the white wall, which glimmered faintly under the cloudy night, he thought his heart would break within him. They passed it quickly under the ever-freshening breeze, and Mitsos looked at it as a man looks on the dead form of his dearest, the house which she had inhabited in life. To him Suleima was dead, a memory only insufferably sweet, ineffably bitter, and when the wall faded again into the blackness he felt as if he had buried her whom he had loved and murdered. Then putting about, they ran past the island and saw the lights of Nauplia grow nearer and larger.

In the foreground was the tall, black hull of the Turkish ship outlined with lights. The deck was brilliantly lit, and they could hear sounds of talking and laughing coming from it. The sailors were evidently preparing to put to sea, for now and then little figures of men like small insects would move up the lines of rigging, adjusting rope or block with busy antennæ, and loud voices seemed to be shouting orders. Then a bell rang on board, and a rope-end splashed into the water and was pulled on deck.

They had drifted a little out to sea, and Mitsos tacked back again to within three hundred yards of the ship, and finding shallow water, cast anchor. Two long hours went by, but neither spoke; only the freshening wind whistled in the rigging, the clouds promised a stormy night, and on board the Turkish ship they made ready to go to sea. A row of open port-holes showed a necklace of light, each light waking a column of reflection from the waters of the bay. Then a lantern was hoisted up onto the foremast, and another run out in the bows. Presently after came the grating sound of the anchor being pulled home, and a small sail was set, sufficient in this wind to take her slowly out of the harbor. Now a light in the town was hidden behind her bows, and another sprang up from behind the stern; she moved along the quay stately and slow, and, clear of the buoy at the end, she put up another sail.

Mitsos watched her intently, and then, without a word, he pulled up the anchor and ran up the sail, and silently they went in pursuit. But their light boat went too fast with its sail full spread, and when they had approached again to within two or three hundred yards he took in a couple of reefs, which equalized their speed, or, if anything, allowed the other to gain on them a little. And so they followed in the wake of the great condemned ship out past the harbor lights, round the end of the peninsula beyond the town, and into the black, foam-flecked gulf outside. The lights grew small and far away, the land faded to a dark shadow, which brooded on the horizon, and the two crafts, one with its immense cargo of human creatures, the other with a couple of beardless Greek lads—but with how strange a burden of anguish and destruction!—were shut off from all sound and sight except the threats of rising waves.

Then Mitsos rose, and pointing to the cans of turpentine:

165

"Empty one on the brushwood in the bows," he said to Yanni, "and give me another."

He climbed up the mast, and, resting the tin on the yard, took out the cork and let the contents dribble down over the sail. When the can was empty he came quickly down again and flushed the whole deck with another tinful, while Yanni poured the fourth onto the remainder of the fuel.

Then, in a hard, dry voice:

"Let out the sail," he said, "and climb into the boat behind, but give me the lantern first."

Yanni handed him the dark lantern first, which they had lit before starting, and, pulling the boat in under the stern of the caique, jumped on board. Under the full-spread sail they drew rapidly near the doomed ship, and when they were within a hundred yards they heard its rudder splash and stir like some great fish under water, and the speed slackened as she turned south. Mitsos, who had never felt cooler or more collected in his life, went straight on, so as to strike her sideways below the huge, overhanging stern. He calculated to perfection the speed they were going and the distance, and just as Yanni became aware of a great black thing with a panel of light in it overhead, he heard a crash, and broken glass fell over him. The mast of the caique had gone right through one of the windows in the stern. Their boat gave a great lurch, and Mitsos sprang off into the small boat astern, still with the lantern in his hand.

"Quick, quick!" he said, "that I cannot do."

Yanni jumped up, and, crouching beneath the stern of the caique, thrust the lantern open into a heap of brushwood impregnated with turpentine. It caught and flared up in a moment, and while from the Turkish ship came sudden confused sounds and runnings to and fro, the flame leaped along the caique from stern to bow, ran like a flash of lightning up the sail, and was driven by the wind with a roar right into the broken panel. Next moment Mitsos, having cast loose their smaller boat, pushed off backward into the darkness, and both the boys, seizing their oars, rowed for life. But the blaze between them and the ship had made it impossible for those on board to see them, and after five minutes or so Yanni, blown and streaming with perspiration, saw Mitsos drop his oar and sink down to the bottom of the boat and lie there as if dead.

Round three-quarters of the horizon was dense darkness, inhabited only by the rushing wind, but in front a column of fire rose up, crowned with clouds of smoke. The flames leaped up over the stern of the ship, the steersman fled for his life farther forward, and left to itself the ship swung round into the wind, dragging its destroyer behind it, the flames from which, driven straight before it, licked greedily round the timbers of its victim. In a few moments the tar in the seams began to melt and run, breaking into flame like burning sealing-wax, and the planks of the upper decks were parted a fraction of an inch as it oozed out. Then the timbers themselves began to fizzle and crack, giving each moment new crevices and footholds for the fire, and the window where the mast of the caique had penetrated showed red burning lips, like a horrible square mouth. Volumes of smoke began to pour forward between the decks, driving those who were throwing unavailing water onto the flames to the upper deck, to make another hopeless attempt from there. The women and children ran forward with shrill screams, and could be seen standing like a flock of frightened sheep huddled together. Then a boat was let down, but before it touched the water a tongue of flame sprang out from one of the big, square port-holes below it, driving upward so fiercely that those who were holding the ropes let go and it fell splashing into the sea. Soon with a crash the aft part of the deck, all charred and no longer able to support its own weight, fell in a huge shower of embers and half-burned or blazing pieces of timber, and again the flames leaped higher and moved forward along the ship. The iron davits supporting the boat corresponding to that which had fallen into the sea, still stood firm, and the boat itself hung unburned for some ten minutes, till the fire reaching up caught it, and set it blazing, hanging there, apart and separate from the greater conflagration like a huge burning signal of distress. Soon, however, the side of the ship which held the davits fell in, and the boat dropped blazing into the water. The fire had now reached to the main-mast, and in a moment caught the sail. Then after a few seconds, in which the smoke redoubled itself, the great sheet of canvas caught and flared up in a pillar of flame. Great burned pieces fell off and strewed the deck; other lighter fragments were borne away like birds in the wind and fled seaward, flapping and blazing. Then, with another crash, a second portion of the deck fell in, and, mingled with the noise the shrill chorus of despair from the women, rose higher and higher. Some jumped overboard and found their death in what might have been their safety; others ran up and down the deck, which grew ever hotter and more blistered, and now scribbled over by lines of burning pitch; some seized up water-cans and buckets, and tried even then to stop the flames; and more than one man ran to where the flames were fiercest, preferring to die at once. Then without warning came the end. A frightful explosion tore the air; the ship parted in the middle, for the flame had reached the powder-magazine, and in smoke and steam and human cries she went down, and a minute afterwards there was silence but for the wind and blackness.

The explosion roused Mitsos and he looked up.

"What was that?" he said to Yanni.

"It is all over," replied Yanni. "She exploded and went down."

"All over, thank God!" and he sank down again.

Yanni bent to the oars, for it was hard work against the wind, and in an hour or so he saw the lights on the quay not more than a quarter of a mile off. It was still crowded with people who had been watching the fire, and he kept out in the darkness until he had passed it, and then came in closer to the shore, so as to be shielded a little from the wind by the land, and rowed steadily on till he came to the landing-place opposite Mitsos' house. Then he touched the other on the shoulder.

"Get up, dear Mitsos," he said, "we are here."

Mitsos raised himself and followed Yanni across the road to the house. They went in, locking the door behind them, and Mitsos, still silent, lay down on the window-seat, staring out dry-eyed into the darkness. But in a few moments a knock came, and Yanni went to the door to see who it was.

"It is I, Lelas," said a voice.

Yanni unwillingly undid the door, and the fat, urbane café-keeper came in, smiling.

"Eh, but you two have lost a fine sight," he said. "A Turkish ship blazing down to the water's-edge, and then bang she went; and there'll not be a soul to tell the tale."

Mitsos, in his window-seat, shuddered and half sat up.

"I wish there had been more on board," continued Lelas. "Why, I'd have given a week's wage if that old Abdul and his poultry-yard of women had been there."

Next moment he was aware of two great hands half throttling him.

"Abdul who? Which Abdul?" said Mitsos, his face close to Lelas, and hissing out the words. "Speak, you damned pig of the pit."

"Abdul—this Abdul here—let go—Abdul Achmet, of course. He and his went to Tripoli yesterday. May you burn in hell for throttling me, you young devil."

But Mitsos heard nothing after "Abdul Achmet." He dropped his hold on Lelas and stood looking across at Yanni a minute, while new life ran in spate through his veins. Then he flung his arm round the neck of the astonished Lelas and kissed him on the cheek.

"Oh, fat man, but I love you for what you have said," he cried. "Yanni, Yanni, we will make the fat man drunk with wine, for he has made me drunk with joy. Oh, oh—"

And he flung out of the room with a great shout.

Lelas felt his neck tenderly.

"Is Mitsos quite mad, or only a little mad?" he asked, severely.

"Quite mad, I think," said Yanni. "Oh, little Mitsos—wait a minute."

He found him outside, but the dry-eyed anguish was turned to a joy which brimmed his eyes. Yanni thrust his arm through his and they stood there a moment in silence, and had no need of speech; nor indeed were there words in which they could frame their joy of heart.

CHAPTER IV

THE TRAINING OF THE TROOPS

Into the Greek camp on Taygetus there came flocking day by day fresh bands of recruits from all the country-side, and in the mouths of all were fresh tales of the rise of the Greeks. The taking of Kalamata had been spark to tinder, and in a hundred villages the patriots had risen, attacking and slaughtering those of the hated race who lived among them, burning their dwellings, and capturing women and children. In other cases, though rarely, the Turks had been prepared, and the tale was of slaughter and pillage among the Greeks; but for the most part the oppressors had slumbered on in their soft, indolent life till the red hand of vengeance had gripped them. Inglorious though these deeds were, they were inevitable, for slaves who break their bonds are not apt to deal judicially, and vengeance—that rough justice—was in this case very just. Then when the slaughter was done the bands would march to join one of the two centres at Kalavryta or on Taygetus; but for the most part the latter, for Petrobey was still commander-in-chief, and to his army belonged the prestige of the siege and capture of Kalamata.

But soon the numbers became unmanageable, and he and Nicholas at length resolved to strike a second blow. Messenia, in which the only stronghold of the Sultan had been Kalamata, no longer gave opportunity for anything but guerilla warfare, but in Arcadia there were several fortified places which would have to be reduced, or at any rate rendered powerless to send help to Tripoli before the latter place was attacked. Chief among these was Karitaena, standing on a precipitous hill above the gorge of the Alpheus, a fortified town, almost exclusively Turkish, and it was against this place that Petrobey suggested the second attack should be made. It was, indeed, high time that the unorganized rabble who were pouring in should have something to do and also learn the elements of war. So his proposal to Nicholas was that he should organize some kind of regiment out of these, taking with him as leaven some of the better-drilled men who had been at Kalamata, besiege and take the place, if possible, and if not, give the men a notion of what a forced march meant, and some idea of military discipline. Meantime Petrobey would move his quarters into the hills between the upper Arcadian plain and Tripoli, so that in case of disaster Nicholas could get quickly back into connection with the rest of the army, and, at the same time, from there the southern troops could watch that fortress. He would, however, quarter a small body of men in the pass between Arcadia and Messenia, and have another depot in the present camp, so that if the Turks attempted to land troops at Kalamata they would find the passes from Messenia both blocked.

Nicholas fell in with the scheme, and two days afterwards set out with perhaps the least efficient army that has ever taken the field. But he had deliberately chosen his troops from the most ill-prepared and untrimmed of the recruits, for somehow or other all this raw material had to be put into shape before it was possible that it should render a creditable or useful account of itself in any serious operations. But they were all hardy, out-of-door folk, accustomed to sleep on the hills and eat the roughest food with health and cheerfulness, and it was just these who would most speedily prove a drag and a demoralization if left idle in camp.

So on the third morning they set out, at an open and scattered double, where the mountain-side was steep, among the budding bushes and tilted rocks, taking the short-cut down to the plain, where it might be possible to give them some semblance of formation. The baggage and commissariat mules had preceded them by a few hours, and were to wait for them when they got down to marching ground.

Two days' march, or rather tramp, brought them to Megalopolis, a sparkle in the centre of the green Arcadian plain. They found the town in the hands of the insurgent Greeks, a body of whom, consisting of about two hundred men, enrolled themselves under Nicholas. Here, too, they heard the same tale of slaughter and pillage of the Turk; but already the selfish evil which was to do such harm to the Greek cause generally—namely, the personal greed for plunder—had crept in, and the insurgents were wrangling over the distribution of the booty. But Nicholas, with a fine indignation which shamed them into obedience, though amid murmurs of suppressed grumbling, was hot with reproach. Was it for a few piastres, he said, that they were up in arms? Was the liberty of the nation to be weighed against a cask of wine or a Turkish slave? And taking the whole matter into his own hands, he reserved half the booty captured for the expenses of the war, and half he divided as fairly as might be among the claimants.

From Megalopolis Karitaena was only a four hours' march, and he was anxious to force the pace so as to reach it early next morning, before rumor of their approach should have gone abroad. The Megalopolis men were as untrained as his own, but they knew the country better, and he organized out of them a corps of skirmishers, who should go in advance and intercept any fugitives who might carry the news of the march into Karitaena. The only chance of taking it was if he could find it unprepared, like Kalamata, creep up to it at night, and either make a night assault or draw beleaguering lines round it before he could be attacked.

Like Kalamata, the town was pregnable only from one side, but on this the road ran steeply up to the gate parallel with the citadel wall, thus exposing the attacking party to a broadside fire if the besieged were prepared. They were, in fact, more than prepared; they were wishfully expectant, and Nicholas fell into a very neatly baited trap.

The skirmishing party had started a little before sunset, while the others were to set out soon after, so as to reach the town by midnight or before, if possible make a night attack, or if not, take up their places, so that when morning dawned the citadel might find itself beleaguered. But the skirmishers, exceeding Nicholas's instructions, had gone too far and were seen from Karitaena, and all that night the Turks made preparations for a long-headed manoeuvre on the morrow. However, Nicholas arrived about midnight, and finding everything quiet, and hearing nothing from the skirmishing party which could lead him to think that Karitaena was prepared, reconnoitred the ground, and decided not to attack it by night, for the gate was strong and well fortified, and without artillery of some kind would not quickly be forced; and he returned to the men and gave orders for the disposition of the troops. Those who were most trustworthy, consisting of the greater part of the Argive corps, were posted along the road and to guard the bridge over the Alpheus, which led to Megalopolis and Tripoli; the less trained soldiers he posted on the north and south, where there was little likelihood of attack. He himself remained with the

170

rawer troops, where his presence was more likely to be needed than with the Argives, on whom he thought he could rely.

Morning came chilly and clear, and Nicholas, on foot, early went forward a little to see if there was yet any sign of movement in the citadel, and, advancing to where he could see the gate, he observed that it was open and that a couple of Turks driving mules were coming leisurely down the path. This was an unexpected opportunity; surely they could storm the place out of hand and have done with it; and going back to the men, he ordered an immediate advance. The Argive troops were to form the vanguard, then the skirmishers from Megalopolis, and in the rear the mixed and untried men, which he led himself; in a quarter of an hour all was ready, and, the Argive corps leading the way, they advanced at a double up the steep path.

Then, when they were streaming up under the walls, the Turks showed that they, too, had a word to say to these summary arrangements. A storm of musketry fire opened on the besiegers from the length of the wall, and, like troops unaccustomed to fire, they did the very worst thing possible, and stopped to return it, instead of advancing. This was hopeless, for their assailants were completely sheltered behind the fortifications and the Greek fire did no more than innocuously chip off pieces of mortar and stone from the walls; and, after losing several minutes and many lives, they pressed on again gallantly enough towards the gate, which still stood open. This brought the second part of the army with Nicholas under fire, but they were now moving rapidly forward, and he still hoped that they would be able to get in. But the fire had a demoralizing effect on these raw recruits, who had seen nothing of warfare but the pillaging of defenceless farm-houses, and as they were shot down one after another they, too, wavered. Once the first three ranks stopped and would have turned to run, but Nicholas, with a voice of cheerful encouragement—"This way, boys, this way!" he shouted. "We shall soon be past this little shower, and then comes our turn."

His voice, the sight of him running on as a man runs to a wine-shop under a pelting of rain, and the words which in the Greek contained a somewhat coarse but popular joke, had the right effect, and they doubled on again to close up the gap between them and the vanguard. Those few minutes had been deadly expensive, yet it was a marvel to see how these men, untried and raw as they were, but fed with hate, faced all the horror of a well-directed fire, the grunt and gasp of death, the involuntary cry of overwhelming physical pain, the writhing body under foot, or, hardly less horrible, the sudden and complete striking out of life; and Nicholas, looking back on the thinned ranks, the terror-struck faces, but the determined advance, thought gleefully, "These are brave men—and this is what they need."

By this time the Argives had very nearly reached the gate, but then the defenders played their second card. Quite suddenly from inside dashed out a band of cavalry, some five hundred in number, who rode full speed down on them. The Argives stopped, and, attempting to make the best of a hopeless job, the front ranks opened fire and a few Turks fell. But the

171

charge came on, the two met with a crash, and the inevitable happened. The ranks of foot broke, and the men poured down off the road onto the steep slope below like water spilled. Resistance was not possible, and the cavalry came on hewing their way through the congested mass of men, and in the mean time the firing from the walls went on steadily. Nicholas seeing what had happened knew that to face this spelled annihilation, and with a fine wisdom, though the words were bitter in his mouth, did the best he could.

"Save yourselves," he cried; "run."

And they turned and fled down the road again, the Turkish cavalry in their rear, hewing, hacking, and discharging their pistols. The rout was complete, each man ran as fast as he could go, while the cavalry, like a swarm of stinging wasps, flew hither and thither, opening out as they reached the plain, and chasing the men as they fled single or in batches of five or six.

Luckily for them wooded hills came down close to the plain here, and they struck for them desperately across the narrow strip of level land, for there the cavalry could not easily follow them, or only man to man. Nicholas, running down the slope from the road, tripped in a bush—as it turned out luckily for him, for a sabre at that moment swung over the place where his head should have been; and the Turk, not waiting to attack him singly when there were many little knots of men among whom he could pick and choose, rode on leaving him; and Nicholas, who had sprained his ankle slightly as he fell, plunged into the brushwood where it was thickest, to find refuge and concealment. His rifle he had thrown away, for it impeded his flight, and he found himself some distance behind the others, who were going in the right direction towards Valtetzi, where Petrobey had told them the camp would be. But though the rout had been complete and utter, and Nicholas was far from disguising the fact from himself, his heart was filled with a secret exultation at the way the troops had behaved for those two or three moments which try the courage of any man when he is being fired at and cannot return the fire. To be shot at when a man may shoot in return, and aim is matched with aim, is known to be strangely exhilarating, but to be shot at and not to shoot is cold stuff for the courage. They had been through the baptism of fire under the most trying circumstances, and with the exception of that one moment of wavering had stood their ground till they were told to stand no longer.

He crept painfully up the hill-side all alone, but the pursuit had passed, and the cavalry, he could see, were returning across the plain to the town, knowing it was useless to follow farther. That fatal road up to the gate was strewn with corpses, almost all Greek, with only a handful of Turks and horses. Other horses, however, were careering riderless about the plain; and Nicholas, limping from his sprain, thought how much more convenient it would be to go riding to Valtetzi than to drag along his swollen foot. A quarter of a mile away he could see two or three of the men trying to capture one of these, but they only succeeded in frightening it, and it bolted up towards the hill where Nicholas was, and a couple of minutes later he saw it burst through the first belt of trees and halt on a piece of open ground below him. There it stopped, and in a minute or so began cropping at the short-growing grass. Its bridle, he could see, was over its head, trailing on the ground.

Now Nicholas was an Odysseus of resource, and having lived in the open air all his days not witlessly, he knew the manners of many beasts, and could imitate certain of their calls to each other so that even they were deceived; and, furthermore, his foot was one burning ache; and, not wishing to walk more than he could help, he preferred that this horse should come to him rather than that he should go to the horse. It was about a hundred yards from him, but a long way below, and it was grazing quietly. So Nicholas, to make it a little alert, and also to assist in bringing it nearer him, took up a pebble, and with extreme precision lobbed it over the horse, so that it fell on the far side of him. The animal, startled by the noise, stopped grazing, and started off at a trot in the direction away from where the pebble had seemed to come and directly towards Nicholas. After a few yards, however, it stopped again, and Nicholas whinnied gently. At that it looked up again and sniffed the air, but before it had continued its grazing he whinnied once more, and then lay flat down on his back. In a moment the horse answered and Nicholas called to it a third time, and heard from below that it had left the open and was pushing towards him through the trees. Once again he called, and the answer came nearer, and in a few moments the horse appeared ambling quickly up the steep incline. For a moment it did not see Nicholas, for he lay flat on the ground, half covered by the bush; but when it did, seeing he lay quite still, it came close up to him and sniffed round him. Then quietly reaching out a hand, he caught the bridle as it trailed on the ground.

This was satisfactory, for, besides getting a mount, he had acquired a pistol which was stuck into its case on the holster, and getting up, he pushed the horse forward through the trees. Half an hour's ride brought him into a bridle-path, running loftily along the mountain-side, and he halted here to take his bearings. Straight in front of him, and not an hour's ride distant, stood the huddled roofs of a village, which he took to be Serrica, but at present he could only see a few of the outlying houses. But at the thought that this was Serrica his heart thrilled within him, for it was the village from which his wife had come. A wonderful return was this for him; already the work of avenging her death had begun, and soon, please God! should a Turk be slain for every hair of her head. Ah, the cursed race who had brought dishonor to her, and to him a wound that could never be healed! Helen, too—little Helen—who ran towards him, crying "Father, father!" Yes, by God, her father heard her voice still, and her cry should not be lifted up in vain!

In half an hour more he stopped to reconnoitre, turning off the path among the heather. His heart pulled him thither, yet for that very reason he would be cautious, and not risk the ultimate completeness of his vengeance. From the slope above he watched for ten minutes more, and, seeing no movement or sign of life in the village, concluded that here, too, the Greeks had risen, and, after driving out the Turks, had gone either to Petrobey or to Kalavryta. And as he looked he saw that a dozen houses at one spot were roofless, showing by their charred beams pointing up to the sky that they had been burned. At the end stood the church dedicated to the Mother of God; and, oh, the bitterness of that! It was there he had been married; from that door he had walked away with the dearest and fairest of women, the happiest man in Greece.

Nicholas hesitated no longer; it was still an hour before noon, and he did not care to travel during the day. He would go down once more to the place, he would see it all again, and let its memories scourge him into an even keener anguish, a keener lust for vengeance, and, putting his horse to an amble down the crumbling hill-side, in ten minutes more he stood in the straggling village street. There was the house—her house—just in front of him, and he went there first. The door was standing open, and inside he found, as Mitsos had found at Mistra, the signs of a sudden departure. His brother-in-law then, to whom the house belonged, must have gone to Petrobey, or Kalavryta, probably the latter, and the thought was wine to him. Husband and brother, a double vengeance, and his should be the work of three men!

He had not eaten that day, but he soon found bread, meat, and wine, and, after stabling his horse and eating, he went out again to the church. Every step seemed a tearing open of the wound, yet with every step his heart was fed with fierce joy. Ah, no, Helen should not call in vain!

The church door was open and he entered. It had not altered at all in those twenty years since he had seen it last. Over the altar hung a rude early painting, showing the Mother of God, and nestling in her arms the wondrous Child. In front the remote kings did obeisance, behind stood the ox and the ass in the stall. And casting himself down there, in an agony bitter sweet, he prayed with fervor and faith to the Mother of the Divine Child. All the hopes and the desires of years were concentrated into that moment, and he offered them up humbly, yet at his best, to the Lord and the Handmaid of the Lord. Then, in the excitement of his ecstasy, as he gazed on that rude picture with streaming eyes, it seemed to him that a sign of acceptance, visible and immediate, was given him. A light as steadfast, but milder than the sun, grew and glowed round the two figures, the rough craft of the artist was glorified, and on the face, so human yet divine, there came the soft and sudden graciousness of life; it was touched with a pitiful sympathy for him, and the eyes smiled acceptance of his offering. Bowed down by so wonderful a pity, he hid his face in his hands, faith struck fear from his heart, and in that moment he felt that he had not prayed alone, that his wife had knelt by him, and that it was her prayers mingled with his that had brought for him that signal favor of the Thrice Holy Maid on his work.

That night, as soon as the sun went down and the ways grew dark, he went on his journey with a soul refreshed and strengthened; he felt that the vow he had made over the dead body of his wife had been attested and approved by Christ and the Mother of Christ, and from that hour to the end of his life never for a day did that gracious vision, like bread from heaven, fail to sustain and strengthen him. And all through the clear spring night the hosts of heaven that rose and wheeled above him were

174

ministering spirits, and the wind that passed cool and bracing over the hill-sides the incense which carried his prayer upward. He, to whom vengeance belonged, had chosen him as His humble but willing agent. His sword was the sword of the Lord.

He crossed the first range of hills by midnight, and then struck the road which led by the khan where Mitsos and Yanni had stopped on their way from Tripoli. It was now within two hours of daybreak, but seeing a light in the windows, he drew rein to inquire whether Anastasis had seen aught of the other fugitives. Looking in cautiously through the windows, he saw that the floor was covered with Greeks, who lay sleeping, while Anastasis, good fellow, was serving others with hot coffee and bread.

Nicholas tied up his horse and went in. As he entered several of the men in a group round the fire turned and looked to see who it was, instinctively clutching at their knives. Then one got hastily up, and his head was among the roof-beams.

"Uncle Nicholas!" he cried, "is it you?"

"Who else should it be, little Mitsos? And what do you here?"

"Petrobey sent me down this morning to see if anything could be seen or heard of you, and when you did not come, and we heard from the others what had happened, we were afraid, or almost afraid—"

"I am not so easily got rid of," said Nicholas. "Anastasis, I shall not forget that you were good to the fugitives. Yes, I will have some coffee."

Most of the men sleeping on the floor had awoke at the noise and were sitting up. Nicholas took a chair and began sipping his coffee.

"Little Mitsos," he said, aloud, "I do not know what the others may have told you has happened, but I will tell you what I saw. I saw a body of men, who knew nothing of war, stand steady under a heavy fire because they were told to stand. I saw them go on under it when there was room to move, but not one did I see do aught else until I had to set the example, and told them to run."

Mitsos grew rather red in the face.

"The cavalry charged on them, and from behind the fortifications came a hail of bullets. And I never desire," he said, striking the table a great thump, "nor would it be possible, to command braver men."

Mitsos held out his hand to the man nearest him.

"Christos, shake hands or knock me down," he said. "I eat my words as one eats figs in autumn—one gulp."

"What have you been saying, little Mitsos?" asked Nicholas.

"I said they were cowards to run away. Oh, but I am very sorry! They are bad words I am eating."

"Well, let there be no mistake, Mitsos," said Nicholas; "down they go!"

Christos, a huge, broad-shouldered country Greek, looked up at Mitsos, grinning.

"There is no malice," he said. "I called you a liar."

"So you did, and there were nearly hard blows. Oh, we should have made a fine fight of it, for we are neither little people. But there will be no fighting now, unless you are wishful, for I will deny no one anything, now

Uncle Nicholas has come. Why, are you lame, uncle? How did you get here?"

"I rode a fine Turkish horse," remarked Nicholas; "may I never ride a finer!"

Mitsos' frank and unreserved apologies had quite restored the amiability of those present, who, when Nicholas had entered, were growling and indignant, for Mitsos had made himself quite peculiarly offensive. But, though he could not clearly see how bravery was compatible with running away, Nicholas must be taken on trust.

Nicholas had fallen in with the last batch of fugitives. Since noon they had been streaming up the hills. Only a few apparently were wounded, and these had been sent on on mules to the camp. Those who had been wounded severely, it was feared, must all have fallen into the hands of the Turks, for there had been no possibility of escape, except by flight. Altogether Nicholas reckoned they had lost three hundred men, and but for his own promptness in seeing the utter hopelessness of trying to stop the cavalry charge, they would have lost five times that number. Having satisfied himself on these points, he turned to Mitsos again.

"How about the ship?" he said; "and when did you get back?"

"Two days after you left Taygetus," said Mitsos; and then, with a great grin, "the ship is not."

"Tell me about it, and I, too, afterwards have something to tell."

Mitsos' story, which was, of course, news to all present, was received with shouts of approval, though he left out that part of it which raised the exploit to a heroism, and Nicholas smiled at him when he had finished.

"It was well done," he said, "and I think, little Mitsos, that I, too, have friends who will, perhaps, aid me, as they have aided you"; and he told them the story of his strange vision.

"And by this I know," he concluded, "that our work is a work which God has blessed, and, come what may, not for an hour will I shrink from it or flinch till it is finished, or till my time comes. Look, the east is already lightening! Get up, my lads, for we must push on to the camp."

In a quarter of an hour they were off, the men marching in good order as long as they kept the road, but falling out when they had to climb the rough hill-side. An hour's walking brought them to the top of the hills, and on a detached spur standing alone and commanding the valley they could see the lines of the fortifications which Petrobey was erecting. He himself, seeing them coming while still far off, rode out to meet them, and Nicholas spurred his horse forward.

"Praise the Virgin that you have come, Nicholas," he said, "for by this I know that there was no disgrace."

"You are right. Had there been disgrace I should not be here. But there was nothing but bravery among the men, and the disgrace, if so you think it is, is on my head." And he told him what had happened.

"They are brave men," said Petrobey, "and yet I think you are the braver for giving that order."

"I should have been a foolish loon if I had not," said Nicholas, laughing.

176

CHAPTER V

THE HORNETS' NEST AT VALTETZI

Since his arrival at Valtetzi three days before, Petrobey had hardly rested night or day. The ground he had occupied and was fortifying with feverish haste was the top of a large spur of hill, going steeply down into the valley, and commanding a good view of it. Its advantages were obvious, for the cavalry, which at present they were particularly incompetent to meet, could not possibly attack them on such a perch, and also it would be difficult for the Turks to get up any of their big guns, of which there were several in Tripoli, to make an assault. They knew that in that town there were at least ten six-pounders, and certainly fifteen more nine-pounders, though since they had occupied the place, and found that the Turk had made no efforts whatever to bring artillery to bear on them, Petrobey suspected, and as it turned out rightly, that they were not all serviceable. Furthermore, occupying Valtetzi, they cut off Tripoli from Kalamata, whither before long, in all probability, the Turks would send a relief expedition by sea. However, by this occupation of Valtetzi there would be two passes to capture before they could send help to Tripoli, and, as he said, "they will be strong men if they take this."

Tripoli itself lay about eight miles to the northeast, and at present the whole body of Greeks was occupied in fortifying the post they had taken. A village, largely Turkish, had stood on the spot, and the demolition of the houses went on from daybreak to nightfall to make material for building up a defensive wall. The soldiers, meantime, as their barracks were converted into fortifications, substituted for them huts made of poles woven in with osiers and brushwood, similar to those they used on Taygetus. The walls, it must be confessed, presented a curiously unworkmanlike aspect—here and there a course of regular square stones would be interrupted by a couple of Byzantine columns from the mosque, or the capital of a Venetian pillar in which a strange human-faced lion looked out from a nest of conventional acanthus leaves. Farther on in the same row would come a packet of roof tiles plastered together with mud, and a plane-tree standing in the line of the wall was pressed into the service, and supplied the place of a big stone for eight upright courses. Above that it had been sawn off, and the next section of the trunk being straight made a wooden coping for five yards of wall. Here a chimney-pot filled with earth and stones took its place among solider materials; here a hearthstone placed on end, with two inches of iron support for the stewing-pot, staring foolishly out into vacancy. Then came a section where the builders had drawn from a richer quarry, and a fine slab of porphyry and two rosso antico pillars formed an exclusive coterie in the midst of rough blocks of limestone. But though heterogeneous and uncouth, the walls were stout and high, and, as Petrobey said, their business was not to build a pretty harem to please the women.

Inside, a hardy sufficiency was the note. The soldiers' huts, though small, would stand a good deal of rough weather; they were built squarely in rows, camp-wise, and the floors were shingled with gravel from a quarry close by. Two houses only had been kept, in one of which were stored the arms, in the other the ammunition, Petrobey and Nicholas, as before, occupying huts exactly like those tenanted by the common soldiers. The mules and herds of sheep and goats were driven out every morning under an armed escort to pasture on the hills near, and penned to the south of the camp for the night. Food was plentiful, and the men seemed well content, for the booty already taken was very considerable.

In ten days more, before the end of April, the walls were complete, and Petrobey, following out the plan he had formed from the first, sent out daily and nightly skirmishing expeditions, who made unlooked-for raids on the villages scattered on the plain about Tripoli, the inhabitants of which, feeling secure in their neighborhood to the fortress, had not yet sought refuge within its walls. Men, women, and children alike were slain, the valuables seized, the flocks and herds driven up to the camp, and the villages burned. In such operations, inglorious and bloody it is to be feared, but a necessary part of the programme of extermination, which the Greeks believed, not without cause, to be their only chance of freedom, their losses were almost to be numbered on the fingers; once or twice some house defended by a few men inside resisted the attack and fired upon them, in which case the assailants did not scruple to set light to the place; and in ten days more only heaps of smoking ruins remained of the little white villages, which had been dotted among the vineyards like flocks of feeding sheep.

Petrobey also established another small camp on the hills to the east of Tripoli, to guard the road between it and the plain of Argos and Nauplia. They had already intercepted and had a small skirmish with troops coming to that place from Nauplia. The loss on the Greek side was about one hundred; on that of the Turks nearly double, for when it came to hand-to-hand fighting the slow and short-legged Turk was no match for the fresh vigor of the mountain-folk. On this occasion they had lain in ambush on both sides of the road, and opened fire simultaneously at the regiment as it passed. The Turks had with them a contingent of cavalry, but on the rocky and wooded ground they were perfectly useless; and their infantry, leaving the road, had driven the Greeks from their ground, though in the first attack they had lost severely. But this readiness to retreat when necessary, and not waste either powder or lives profitlessly, was in accordance with the policy which Nicholas had indicated, and had been the first to put in practice at Karitaena; and it was exactly this harassing, guerilla warfare, in which cavalry could not be brought into play, in which attack was unexpected and flight was immediate upon any sign of a regular engagement, which made the Turks feel they were fighting with shadows. Though their number at the beginning of the war exceeded those of the Greeks, yet each engagement of the kind lessened them in a far greater proportion than their enemies, who seemed, on the other hand, to be mustering fresh troops every day. Had Petrobey at this period consented to give battle in the plains it is probable that his army would have been wiped out if they had fought to a close, and it says much for his wisdom that he persisted in a policy which was tedious and distasteful to him personally. But the Greeks were acquiring every day fresh experience and knowledge, while the strength of the Turks, which lay in their admirable cavalry and their guns, was lying useless.

In the north, however, affairs had not sped so prosperously. Germanos, who was practically commander-in-chief of the army at Kalavryta—less wise than his colleague at Valtetzi—had risked an attack on the citadel at Patras and suffered a severe defeat. As at Karitaena, a cavalry charge ought to have made him follow Nicholas's example, but he stuck with misplaced bravery to his attempt, until a second body of cavalry took him in the rear and cut off his retreat. With desperate courage his men cut their way through the latter, but a remnant only came through; his loss was enormous compared to that sustained by the Turks, and nothing was gained by it, for the citadel of Patras still remained in the hands of the enemy.

News of this disaster was brought to Valtetzi about the 5th of May, with the information that Turkish soldiers, consisting of eight hundred cavalry and fifteen hundred infantry, had set out eastward along the Gulf of Corinth, under the command of an able Turkish officer, Achmet Bey. Five days afterwards it was reported that they had reached Argos, and next day, while a skirmishing party engaged the Greeks on the hills opposite, the rest of the force passed quietly down the road and reached Tripoli the same evening. It was a splendid achievement boldly and successfully carried out, and Petrobey from that hour held himself in readiness to repel any attack that might be made.

Achmet Bey found Tripoli in a poorer state than the Greeks knew, for their incessant ravages on the plain, their destruction of crops and capture of flocks and herds, as well as the great influx of population, had even now begun to make themselves felt within the walls, for the town and the plain in which it stood were cut off from all assistance, and the plain lay barren and desolate. He saw at once that it was necessary to establish connection with Messenia, for the plain of Argos was occupied by bands of insurgent Greeks, and he had himself scarcely won his way through. Though its port, Nauplia, was still in the hands of the Turks, it also was isolated from connection with the main-land by the insurgents of the plain; and the newly created Greek fleet from the islands of Hydra and Spetzas kept it in a state of semi-blockade by sea, and all provisions were got in with difficulty and consumed in the town. But Achmet Bey, not knowing that Petrobey had established posts on the passes over Taygetus from Kalamata and into Arcadia, thought that a successful attack on Valtetzi would enable them to open regular communication with Messenia, and so with the sea.

It was early on the morning of the 24th of May that the attack was made. At dawn the sentries on the walls of Valtetzi saw a troop of cavalry issue from the southern gate of Tripoli, followed by long columns of infantry, and in a quarter of an hour the camp was humming like swarming bees. Petrobey had established a system of signals with the post on the other side of the valley, but he made no sign to them, for it seemed possible that Achmet, hoping to draw them into the plain, would try to seize the pass they held, which communicated with Argos.

It was a clear blue morning after a cold night, and the troops, defiling from the gate, looked at that distance like lines of bright-mailed insects. First, came the infantry marching in eight separate columns, each containing some five hundred men; next, a long line of baggage-mules, followed by horses pulling two guns; and last, the cavalry on black Syrian horses very gayly caparisoned. Nicholas had an excellent telescope, which he had been given by the captain of an English ship in return for some service, and he and Petrobey watched them until the gates closed again behind.

Petrobey shut up the glass with a happy little sigh.

"That will do very nicely," he said to Nicholas. "They will want to entice us and our post on the other side into the plain; but I think we will both of us just stay at home. I don't want to meet those gay cavalry just now, nor yet those two bright guns. We will have breakfast, dear cousin."

The bugle sounded for rations, and Petrobey told the men to eat well, "for," said he, "there will be no dinner to-day, I am thinking, but"—and his eye sparkled as he pointed to the enemy—"there will, perhaps, be a little supper."

The men grinned, and soon the light-blue smoke went up from a hundred fires where they were making their coffee. Two or three sentries only remained on the walls, who were told to report to Petrobey when the column left the road on which it was marching and turned off either westward towards Valtetzi or eastward towards the post on the opposite hills. He and Nicholas had hardly sat down to breakfast, however, when an orderly ran in saying that the post on the other side of the valley was signalling. Petrobey finished an egg beaten up with sugar and milk before replying.

"I am not of the signalling corps, my friend," he said; "let the message be read and brought to me. Some more coffee, Nicholas; it strikes me as particularly good this morning."

The message from the signalling body came back in a minute or two. They were merely asking for orders.

"Stop where you are," dictated Petrobey, "and watch to see if Turkish reinforcements are coming from Argos. If so, signal here at once. If the troops which have come out of Tripoli turn and attack you, run away, drawing them after you if possible. There will be fighting for us. Pray for your comrades."

"And now, dear cousin," he said to Nicholas, when they had finished breakfast, "we will talk, if you please."

An hour afterwards an orderly came in to say that the troops had left the road and were making straight towards Valtetzi, and Petrobey got up.

"Every one to his post on the walls," he said, "but let no one fire till the word is given. Yanni, take the order to all the captains of the companies."

The wall was pierced in all its length with narrow slits for firing, and in half an hour each of these was occupied by four men, two of whom could fire at the same time, while the two behind were employed in reloading their muskets. Outside, the walls were some nine feet high, built on ground which sloped rapidly away in some places at roof angle for two hundred feet, while inside it rose to within five feet of the top of the wall. There a man standing up could see over, and Petrobey took up his place over the gate, where he could watch the troops.

He observed that the infantry had separated into two parties, one of which had left the road and was marching away from them towards the post on the other side of the valley, while the other and larger half was advancing towards them. The cavalry followed the latter, but halted when the hills began to rise more steeply out of the plain. The smaller portion of the infantry was evidently going to try to draw the Greeks from the far post down into the plain, while the cavalry who stayed at the bottom of the pass below Valtetzi would hinder help being sent from there. This Petrobey noticed with a pleasant smile. The others knew exactly what to do, and meantime the force which would assault Valtetzi would be weakened by more than a quarter of its men. Most of it, however, consisted of Albanian mercenaries who were largely in Turkish pay, and who, as he well knew, earned their pay, for they were men of the hills and the open air, who could use a sword and were masters of their limbs.

Each hundred men in the Greek camp—that is to say, twenty-five of these groups of four—were under the orders of a captain, who in turn was under the direction of Petrobey, and in all about two thousand men lined the walls. Of the remainder, fifty were employed in distributing ammunition, and were in readiness to bring fresh supplies to the defenders; a hundred more were ready to take the place of any who might be killed at their posts; and the rest, some eight hundred men, were standing under arms on the small parade-ground in the centre of the camp, under command of Nicholas. They would not, however, according to the scheme he and Petrobey had devised, be required just yet, and he told them to pile arms and fall out, but not to leave the ground so that they could not be recalled in a moment if wanted. Mitsos was in attendance on Nicholas, and Yanni stood by Petrobey ready to take his orders to any part of the camp.

An hour elapsed before the Albanian infantry appeared above the ridge some five hundred yards off, and still in the Greek camp there was perfect silence. Then, opening out, they advanced at a double, intending evidently to try to storm the place. But they had clearly not known how completely it had been fortified, and while they were still about four hundred yards off they halted at a word of command and sheltered among the big bowlders that strewed the hill-side. Still, in the Greek camp there was no sound or movement, only Yanni ran across to Nicholas with the order "Be ready," and he called his men up and they stood in line with their arms. Then a word was shouted by the commander of the advancing troop, and Petrobey saw the Albanians all massing behind a small spur of hill about a quarter of a mile away, where they were hidden from sight.

181

There was a long pause; each individual man in the camp knew that the enemy was close, that in a few minutes the shot would be singing, but in the mean time they could not see any one. Two miles away on the plain stood the glittering mailed insects, the Turkish cavalry; and six miles off, a mere black speck, was the troop which had gone across to the east. The suspense was almost unbearable; every nerve was stretched to its highest tension, and every man exhibited his nervous discomfort in his own peculiar way. Christos, who was stationed at one of the loop-holes straight towards the enemy, merely turned cold and damp and wiped the sweat off his forehead with a flabby hand, expectorating rapidly; Yanni, on the other hand, at his post by Petrobey, had a mouth as dry as sirocco, got very red in the face, and swore gently and atrociously to himself; a young recruit from Megalopolis suddenly threw back his head and laughed, and the sergeant of his company vented his own tension by cuffing him over the ears, and yet the boy laughed on; Mitsos, standing by Nicholas, whistled the "Song of the Vine-diggers" between his teeth; Father Andréa, who had begged to be allowed to serve in some way, and was a loader for the two men next Petrobey, chanted over and over again gently below his breath the first verse of the "Te Deum," last sung at Kalamata; Nicholas stood still, his hawk eyes blazing; but most were quite silent, shifting uneasily at their posts, standing now on one leg, now on the other. Petrobey, perhaps alone, for he had to think for them all, was quite calm, and his mind fully occupied. The spur behind which the Albanians were massed was almost opposite the gate over which he stood. The chances were that they would try to storm it, perhaps try to storm both the gates together, the other of which was diagonally opposite to him.

At last round the shoulder of the hill poured the troops in two divisions, still four hundred yards distant. When the rear had come into the open, the first were about two hundred and seventy yards off, and Petrobey, glancing hastily at their numbers and disposition, spoke to Yanni without turning his head.

"They will make a double attack here and on the other gate," he said. "Run like hell there, and direct the fire yourself; you know the order."

Yanni rushed across the camp, and just as he got up to the other gate he heard a volley of musketry from Petrobey's side. The Albanians had separated into two columns, one of which, skirting round the camp out of musket-range, soon appeared opposite the second gate, at a distance of about two hundred and fifty yards. He waited till he saw the whites of their eyes, and then "Fire!" he cried.

They were moving in open file at first, but they closed as they got nearer, and a solid column of men advanced at a rapid double up the hundred yards incline. The first volley took them when the foremost were about sixty yards off, but it was rather wild, and the men for the most part shot over their heads. Two more volleys were delivered with greater precision before they got up to the gate, but they still pressed on. A party of men had halted on the hill behind, about a hundred and twenty yards off, and were returning the fire, but without effect, for the defenders were protected by the wall, and the bullets either struck that or whistled over the top.

Meantime the Greeks in the centre of the walls between the two gates were still unemployed, but before ten seconds were passed Petrobey saw that they would be wanted, and he sent a sergeant flying across to marshal them, the first rows kneeling, the others standing, opposite the gate on which he stood, which he saw was on the point of yielding to the assault. Nicholas, meantime, had drawn up his men by the gate opposite, and was prepared, in case it was forced, to receive them in the same manner.

Before five minutes had elapsed since the first appearance of the Albanians round the hill, Petrobey's gate burst in with a crash, but the assailants were met by a torrent of bullets from those in reserve inside, which fairly drove them off their feet, and next moment the gate was clear again. Then Nicholas knew his time had come. He divided his men into two parts, and, charging out at the wrecked gate, led them at a double's double, half to the right, half to the left, round the camp, and close under the walls, so that the Greeks' fire went over their heads, and they fell on both flanks of the Albanians who were attacking the opposite gate. At that moment, Yanni, seeing what was happening, stopped the fire from inside the walls, and at an order from Petrobey caused the gate to be opened, and a company of those who had been manning the walls hurled themselves onto the assailants. This triple attack was irresistible, and in a couple of minutes more the phalanx of Albanians was in full rout, and the hill-sides were covered with groups of men in individual combat. The party they had left on the hill, being no longer able to fire into the mêlée, rushed down to join in the scrimmage, and Petrobey, leaving only a small number of men inside, sufficient to defend both gates, called out all the rest and headed in person the charge on the first attacking party.

Up and down the stony hill-sides chased, and were chased, the Greeks. Now and then a party of Albanians would try to form in some sort of order to make a combined assault on the broken-down gate, and as often they were scattered again by knots of men who rushed wildly upon them from all sides. In point of numbers, the Albanians had had the advantage at the first attack, but that short-range fire from the walls had been of a decimating nature, and now the Greeks had the superiority.

Mitsos, who had gone out with Nicholas, found himself almost swept off his feet by the rush of his own countrymen from the gate, and for a few moments he was carried along helpless, neither striking nor being able to strike, but with a curious red happiness in his heart, singing the "Song of the Vine-diggers," though he knew not he was singing it. Then suddenly at his elbow appeared a glaring, fierce face, as crimson as sunset, and he found himself jammed shoulder to shoulder with Yanni, who was swearing as hard as he could lay tongue to it, not that he was angry, but because the madness of fighting was on him, and it happened to take him that way.

"Don't shout, you big pig," called he to Mitsos; "why, in the name of all the devils in the pit, don't you get out of my way?"

"Fat old Yanni!" shouted Mitsos. "Come on, little cousin.

"'Dig we deep among the vines.'

Eh, but there are fine grapes for the gathering!"

"Go to hell!" screamed Yanni. "Hullo, Mitsos, this is better."

They had squeezed themselves out into a backwater of the congested stream of men, and in full front stood a great hairy Albanian with his sword just raised to strike. But Mitsos, flying at him like a wild-cat, threw in the man's face the hand which grasped his short, dagger-like sword as you would throw a stone; the uplifted sword swung over his back harmlessly, while the blade of his own dagger made a great red rent in the man's face, and he fell back.

"Your mother won't know you now," sang out Mitsos, burying his knife in his throat. "'Dig we deep'—that's deep enough, Yanni—'the summer's here.'"

There was little work for muskets, for no man had time or room to load, and Yanni went on his blasphemous way swinging his by the barrel, and dealing blows right and left with the butt, and in a few minutes he and Mitsos found themselves out of the crowd alone but for a dead Greek lying there, on a little hillock some fifty yards from the gate, while the fight flickered up and down on each side of them.

"Eh, but there's little breath left in this carcass," panted Yanni. "Why, Mitsos, your head's all covered with blood; there's a slice out of your forehead."

Mitsos' black curls, in fact, were dripping from a cut on his head, and what with the blood and the dust and the sweat, he was in a fine mess; but he himself had not known he was touched. Yanni bound it up for him with a strip of his shirt, and the two ran down again into the fight. There the tide was strongly setting in favor of the Greeks; but the Albanians were beginning to form again on a spur of rock, and stragglers from below kept joining them. Petrobey, thinking that this was preparatory to another attack on the gate, as an additional defence drew off some hundred men from the Mainats—who had stuck together, and were the only company who preserved even the semblance of order—when he saw that there was no such intention on the enemy's part, for the body suddenly wheeled and disappeared over the brow of the hill in the direction of the plain, followed by those who were fighting in other parts of the field. For the time they had had enough of this nest of hornets.

They retreated in good order, pursued by skirmishing parties from the Greeks, who followed them with derision, and bullets; but Petrobey's orders had been that they should not advance beyond the broken ground and expose themselves to an attack by the cavalry, and in half an hour more they had all come back to camp.

The skirmish had lasted about three hours; but Petrobey knew that the fighting was not over yet. The cavalry had been moved from the plain onto one of the lower foothills to which the routed Albanians retreated, while the detachment which had started as if to attack the Greek post on the hills to the east had evidently been recalled, for it had passed the road along which the troops had first come, and was now marching straight across the narrow strip of plain which separated it from the range on which

184

Valtetzi stood; an hour afterwards it had joined the cavalry below, and half an eye could see that another assault was being planned. The long train of baggage mules was left on the plain, but between them and the Greeks was the whole body of Albanian and Turkish troops, which, so it had seemed, and not incautiously, to Achmet Bey, was protection enough. Soon it was seen that the troops were in motion again, and the whole body of infantry and cavalry together moved up the slope towards the camp. They were marching up one side of a long ravine which was cut in the mountain from top to bottom, and they had posted scouts along the two ridges to guard against any attack which might be contemplated from their flank. Half a mile farther up, however, the cavalry halted, for the ground was getting too steep and bowlder-sown to permit a farther advance; but in case of sudden retreat they could prevent pursuit being carried farther.

Petrobey saw what was coming, but he hesitated. His mouth watered after the baggage train below, but he feared to weaken the defence of the camp by sending men for that purpose. Nicholas, however, was clear. Guns and ammunition and baggage were fine things in their way, but not worth measurable risk; every hand was needed at Valtetzi, and, besides, any movement from the Greek camp, even if they sent the men round by a circuitous route down the next ravine, would be observed by the scouts; an opportunity, however, might come later.

For three hours more desultory and skirmishing attacks were made by the Albanians on the camp; four times they advanced a column right up to one or other gate, and as many times it was driven back—twice by a sortie from the inside, twice by the heavy firing from the walls; and at last, as the sun began to decline towards the west, they were called back, and retreated hurriedly towards the cavalry. Then Nicholas saw the opportunity; the scouts had been withdrawn from the ridges, for they no longer expected an attack from the flank, and he with a hundred Mainats set off down a parallel ravine hotfoot to the plain, while the rest of the men, under Petrobey's orders, followed the enemy at a distance, keeping their attention fixed on them in expectation of another attack. Achmet Bey at last thought that the Greeks had fallen into the trap he had baited so many times, and hoped to draw them down into the plain, where he would turn and crush them with his cavalry.

They were already approaching the last hill which bordered on the level ground when Petrobey, who kept his eye on the plain, saw Nicholas and his band wheel round the baggage animals, shooting down their drivers, and force them up the ravine down which they had come. On the moment he gave the order to fire, and the Greeks poured a volley into the rear of the infantry. The Turks were fairly caught. If Achmet sent the cavalry on to rescue the baggage, the Greeks, whose numbers were now far superior to the infantry, would in all probability annihilate them; if, on the other hand, he kept the cavalry to support the infantry, the baggage would be lost. He chose the lesser evil, and as the ground was now becoming smoother and more level, he directed the cavalry to charge on the Greeks, and Petrobey fairly laughed aloud.

"Run away, run away," he cried; "let not two men remain together."

The cavalry charged, but there was simply nothing to charge. Up the hill-sides in all directions fled the Greeks, choosing the stoniest and steepest places, and dispersing as they ran as a ball of quicksilver breaks and is spread to all parts of the compass.

Again the retreat of the Turks began, and once more the Greeks gathered and engaged their attention. In the growing dusk no attack could be made, for the horses were already beginning to stumble and pick their way carefully to avoid falling, while the Greeks still hung on their rear and flanks like a swarm of stinging insects. When the hills began to sink into the plain Petrobey, too, sounded the retreat, and the men, though tired and hungry, went singing up the hill-side. At first some sang the "Song of the Vine-diggers," others the "Fountain Mavromati," others the "Swallow Song," but by degrees the "Song of the Klepht" gained volume, and by the time they entered the camp again the men were all singing it, and it rang true to the deed they had wrought. And thus they sang:

"Mother, to the Turk
I will not be a slave,
That will I not endure.
Let me take my gun,
Let me be a Klepht,
Dwelling with the beasts
On the hills and rocks;
Snow shall be my coverlet,
Stones shall be my bed.
Weep not, mother; mother, mine,
Pray that many Turks
Bite the dust through me."

CHAPTER VI

THE ENTRY OF GERMANOS

Petrobey was not slow to follow up his advantage. By them in their mountain nests the Ottoman force now in Tripoli was evidently not to be feared in the offensive, nor could it dislodge the Greeks from the positions they had taken up upon the high and hilly ground. On the other hand, the Greeks were not capable of meeting cavalry, and they must at present keep to the hills, and not attempt to blockade the town closely, for in so doing they would have to leave their heights for the plain in which the fortress stood, and expose themselves to the horse. But with the ever-increasing numbers that were e flocking to the Greek standard, the camp at Valtetzi

186

was rapidly getting insufficient in accommodation, and at the same time any additional position on the hills would be another link in the iron chain which was being forged round the town; and now, when it was unlikely that the Turks would risk a further engagement at once, was the moment for advancing another step.

Exactly to the west of Tripoli, and within rifle-shot of its walls, stood three steep spurs of hill, known as Trikorpha. The same stir of primeval forces which threw up the crag on which Valtetzi stood, must have cast them up bubbling and basaltic through some volcanic vent-hole, long after the great range behind was fixed. They were like the ragged peaks of slag cast out by a gaseous coal consuming in the fire, and, standing some four hundred feet above the plain, were yet most conveniently near the town. Nearly at the top gushed out a riotous cold stream from the dark lips of the rocks, fringed with shivering maidenhair and dripping moss, and behind on the mountain was good pasturage for flocks. Lower down, where the stream-bed widened, burst a luxuriant patch of oleanders and stiff cushions of cistus and spina sacra; but the heights themselves, save for the water-course, were barren. The three peaks were joined to each other by a sharp rocky ridge, but all were isolated from the mountains on one side and the plain on the other.

Petrobey set about securing this position without delay, though, in truth, the Turks were in no temper to prevent him, and the work sped apace. The place was nigh impregnable, and the walls, of rough blocks of stone gathered from the peaks, were made as much with a view to clearing the ground for the soldiers' huts as to providing the place with a defensible wall. From here, too, by night they could push their devastating raids right under the walls of Tripoli itself, for it was but a stone-cast to the foot of their eyry; and early in June the larger part of the men encamped at Valtetzi took up their quarters in this new nest, swarming there as in spring the overfull hive sends out its colonists. The Argive corps remained in the old nest, under the command of Demetri, who the year before had been mayor of Nauplia, while in the new position the Mainats, under Petrobey, occupied the northernmost of the three peaks; Nicholas, with a regiment chiefly of Arcadian troops, the southernmost; and in the centre a smaller body from the parts about Sparta, under the command of a local chieftain, whom they had followed, one Poniropoulos, a man as crooked in mind and morality as a warped vine-stem, but who, as he was chosen leader by his contingent, was of necessity in command.

Meantime from every part of the country was coming in news no longer of butchery of unarmed Turks in defenceless farm-houses, but of regular sieges of Turkish towns, sometimes successful, sometimes still protracted and of uncertain issue. Several of the Greek islands, notably Psara, Spetzas, and Hydra, had risen, and had already sent out that which was so sorely needed—a fleet to watch the coasts and destroy Turkish ships—thus preventing them from bringing men, provisions, or ammunition into the Peloponnesus. Already during May had this fleet performed some notable exploits, chief among which was the destruction of a Turkish frigate bringing arms and men from a port in Asia Minor. She

187

was caught just outside Nauplia, and, after a desperate resistance, boarded and taken. Only two days later two Hydriot brigs overtook a vessel sailing from Constantinople to Egypt with rich presents on board from the Sultan Mahmud to Mehemet Ali, a cargo which caused shame and dishonor to the captors. All on board were ruthlessly murdered, the persons of women were searched for treasure, which they might have concealed about them, and the sailors, disregarding the convention under which they sailed, whereby one-half of the prize taken was appropriated to the conduct of the war, seized on the whole and divided it up, and, fired by the lust of wealth so easily gotten, became privateers rather than fellow-workers in a war for liberty. Returning to Hydra, they found embroilments of all sorts going on between the primates and the captains of their fleet, and throwing in their lot with the former, they cemented the alliance with a sufficient share of their booty and prepared for sea again, each man thinking for naught but his own coffers. Yet there were tales of exploits and great heroisms also, and notable among them the deeds of the Capsina, a girl of Hydra, and head of the clan of Capsas, who sailed her own ship, working havoc among the Turks. There was something strangely inspiriting in the tale, for it seemed she took nothing for herself, but gave all her prizes to the war fund; also, she was more beautiful than morning, and dazzled the eyes of men.

On the second cruise three ships from Spetzas crossed straight over to the Peloponnesus to assist in the blockade of Monemvasia, which was besieged on the land side by a freshly enrolled body of men from the southern peninsula, chiefly from Sparta and the outlying portions of Argos. The town was known to be very wealthy, and the commander of the Greeks, finding that until communication by sea was intercepted it was impossible to starve the town out, while his own force was inadequate to storm it, had invited the co-operation of the fleet, stipulating that a third of the spoil taken should go to the soldiers, one-third to the fleet, and one-third to the national treasury. But scarcely had the ships arrived when quarrels began to break out between the fleet and the army; a spirit of mutual mistrust and suspicion was abroad; and the soldiers, on one hand, accused the fleet of making a private contract with the besieged, to the effect that their lives would be spared and themselves conveyed to Asia Minor in ships on the surrender of their property; while the sailors brought a counter-accusation that there was a plot on foot among the infantry to attempt to storm the town and carry off the booty before they could claim their share. Every one looked after his own interest, and the only matter that was quite disregarded was the interest of the nation. But to the soldiers more intolerable than all was the conduct of three primates from Spetzas, who took upon themselves the airs and dignities which the Greeks had been accustomed to see worn by Turkish officials; and though to a great extent this war was a religious war, yet the peasants had no mind to see the places their masters had occupied tenanted anew by any one.

This example of the island primates was to a certain extent followed by their brethren on the main-land. There had sprung into existence, in the last month or so, two great powers in Greece, the army and the church, still in that time the mistress of men's souls; and the primates, who before the Turkish supremacy had been temporal as well as spiritual princes, wished to see themselves reinstated in the positions they had held. Many of them too, such as Germanos, at Patras, had worked with a true and simple purpose for the liberation of their country; and now that the people were beginning to reap the fruits of their labors, they looked to receive their due, and their demands, on the whole, were just. But never were demands made at so unseasonable an opportunity, for while the military leaders shrugged their shoulders, saying "This is our work as yet," they obtained but a divided allegiance, for the people were devoted to their church. The result was a most unhappy distrust and suspicion between the two parties. The primates openly said that the object of the military leaders was their own aggrandizement to the detriment of other interests, the military leaders that their reverend friends were interfering in concerns outside of their province. Even greater complications ensued when the primates themselves, as in the case of Germanos, were men who fought with earthly weapons, and he, taking strongly the side of the church as against the army, was the cause of much seditious feeling.

The personal ascendency of Petrobey and Nicholas was a large mitigation of these evils in the army at Tripoli, but both felt that their position was unsettled, depending only on popular favor, and matters came to a crisis when Germanos himself came to the camp from Patras with an armed following. To do the man justice, it was jealousy for the church, not the personal greed of power, which inspired him; as a prince of that body and a vicar of Christ, he had invested himself with the insignia of his position. But it was the royalty of his Master and not His humility which he would fain represent, and if he had remembered the entry of One into His chosen city, meek and sitting upon an ass and a colt, the foal of an ass, his heart would have been better turned to the spirit of the King of kings.

Not as such entered Germanos into the camp. Before him went a body of armed men, followed by six acolytes swinging censers, then the cross-bearer, holding high his glittering silver symbol wrought but lately, on which Germanos had lavished the greater part of the booty which had been his at the taking of Kalavryta, and then borne in a chair on the shoulders of four monks the archbishop himself. His head was bare, for in his hands he carried the gold vessels of the sacrament, those which the Emperor Palæologus had given to the monastery at Megaspelaion, and over his shoulders flowed his thick, black hair, just touched with gray. His cope, another priceless treasure from his own sacristy, was fastened round in front of his neck with a gold clasp, set with one huge, ancient emerald. It covered him from shoulder almost to foot, all shimmering white of woven silk, with a border wrought with crimson and gold pomegranates, and thinly below showed the white line of the alb and the ends of his embroidered stole. Of his other vestments, seven in all, the girdle was a rope of gold thread, the knee-piece hanging below it was embroidered with the three Levitical colors, the cuffs were of lace from Kalabaka, and the chasuble was of cambric, close fitting and sleeved according to the use of

Metropolitans. Behind came another priest carrying the office of the church, bound in crimson leather with gold clasps, and the remainder of his armed guard followed—in all, three hundred men.

It was an act of inconceivable folly, but a folly of a certain magnificent sort, for in Germanos's mind the only thought had been the glory of the church. He had travelled five days from Kalavryta, and so far he had been received by the posts of the Greek army with reverence and respect. But his reception here, he knew, was the touchstone of the success of his party, for the scornful Mainats looked askance on clergy, and left them to do their praying alone. But he had come, so he believed, to demand the vassalage of the people to the King of kings, and that duty, so he thought, admitted neither delay nor compromise.

Yanni, who was lounging on the wall with Mitsos in the afternoon sun, preparatory to starting on a night raid down in the plains, saw him coming and whistled ominously.

"There will be mischief," he said, softly, to Mitsos. "Germanos is a good man and true, but these little primates are not all like him."

"I wish they would leave us alone," grumbled Mitsos; "that little monkey-faced Charalambes is doing a peck of harm. He tells the men that all the fighting is for the glory of God. I dare say it is, but there are blows to be struck, and a paper man would strike as well as he. Oh, Yanni, but Germanos has got all his fine clothes on. Would I had been born an archbishop!"

The procession was now passing close under them, and, looking closer, Yanni saw what Germanos carried, and got down and stood uncovered, crossing himself. Mitsos saw too and followed his example, but frowning the while. It struck him somehow that this was not fair play.

Petrobey received the archbishop with the greatest respect, and had erected for him another hut next his own. An order went round the camp that every man was to attend mass, which would be celebrated at daybreak the following day; but after supper that night Petrobey, Nicholas, and the archbishop talked long together. Mitsos, to his great delight, was put in command of some twenty young Mainats, who were to prowl about and do damage, along with other parties, and Germanos, who looked on the boy with peculiar favor, gave him his blessing before he set out.

"You were ever a man who could deal with men," he said to Nicholas, as the boy went out, "and you have trained the finest lad in Greece. But we have other things to talk of, and let us shake hands first, for I know not whether what I have to say will find favor with you. For we are friends, are we not?"

Nicholas smiled.

"Old friends, surely," he said. "May we long be so!"

"That is well," said Germanos, seating himself; "but first I have to tell you news which I hope may bind us even closer together, though with a tie of horror and amazement. Our patriarch, Gregorios, whom I think you knew, Nicholas, was executed at Constantinople on Easter Day, by order of the Sultan!"

Nicholas and Petrobey sprang from their seats.

"Gregorios!" they exclaimed in whispered horror.

"Executed, dying the most shameful death, hanged at the gate of the Patriarchate. Ah, but the vengeance of God is swift and sure, and the blood of another martyr cries from the ground. Oh, let this bind us together; hanged, the death of a dog; he, the holiest of men."

Germanos bowed his head and there was silence for a moment.

"That was not enough," he continued, his voice trembling with a passionate emotion. "For three days he hung there, and the street dogs leaped up to bite at the body. Then it was given to the Jews, and I would sooner have seen it devoured by the dogs than cast into the hands of those beasts; and they dragged it through the streets and threw it into the sea. But pious men watched it and took it to Odessa, where it was given burial such as befits the body of one of the saints of God. And though dead, he works, for on the ship that took it there was a woman stricken with paralysis, and they brought her to touch the body, and she went away whole."

Nicholas was sitting with his face in his hands, but at this he looked up.

"Glory to God!" he cried, "for in heaven His martyr now pleads for us."

Petrobey crossed himself.

"Glory to God!" he repeated. "But tell us more, father; what was the cause of this?"

"He died for us," said Germanos; "for the liberty of the Greeks. As you know, he was in the secrets of the patriots, and one of the agents of the club which supplied funds for the war was found to have letters from the patriarch, which showed his complicity. Immediately after the execution the election for a new patriarch took place, and Eugenios, of Pisidia, was chosen, and his election ratified by Gregorios's murderer."

Nicholas struck the table with his fist.

"I give no allegiance there," said he. "Is the church a toy in that devil's hands, and shall we bow to his puppets?"

Germanos looked up quickly.

"I wanted to know your opinion on that," he said, "and you, Petrobey, go with your cousin? But in the mean time we have no head."

"But at the death of a patriarch," asked Nicholas, "what is the usual course?"

Germanos hesitated.

"You will see," he said, "why I paused, for it is in the canon of the church that till the next patriarch is appointed the supremacy of the church is in the hands of the senior archbishop."

Nicholas rose.

"There is none so fit as yourself," he said, "and here and now I give you my allegiance, and I promise to obey you in all matters within your jurisdiction, and for the glory of God."

Germanos gave them his blessing, and both kissed his hand; and when they had seated themselves again he bent forward, and began to speak with greater earnestness.

191

"And that, in part, is why I am here," he said, "to accept in the name of the church the allegiance of the Greek army. We must not forget among these night attacks and skirmishes and sieges that for which we work—the liberty of Greece, it is true, but the purpose of her liberty—to let a free people serve the God of their fathers, and pull under no infidel yoke to the lash of unbelievers. Believe me, my friends, how deeply unworthy I feel of the high office which has thus come upon my shoulders, but help me to bear it, though in that the flesh is weak I would in weakness shrink from it. But much lies in your power and active help, for I know what deep influence both of you, and deservedly, have with these men. Yet since to every man is his part appointed by God Himself, I would not recoil from the task and heavy responsibility which are on me as head of this people, who are fighting for their liberty; and though I am not jealous for myself, as some would maliciously count me, I am very jealous for Him with whose authority I, all unworthy, have been invested."

Germanos paused for a moment, his eyes fixed on the ground, and Nicholas, looking across at Petrobey, half began to speak, but the other by an almost imperceptible gesture silenced him. But Germanos paused only for a moment and went on, speaking a little quicker, but weighing his words.

"For who is the general we all fight under, but One? Who is the giver of victory, but He alone? And I—I speak in a sort of proud humility—I am the head of His bride, the church, and the shepherd of His flock, this people. Do not misunderstand me, for I speak not for myself, but for Him. Already dangers, not those from our enemies the Turks, but from friends more deadly than they, compass us about on all sides, and are with us when we sit down to eat and take our rest, and if we are not careful they will poison all we do. Already at Kalavryta, whence I am come—already, as I hear, at Monemvasia; but not, as I hope and trust, here—are there greedy and wicked men, who, raised to power for which they have no fitness, having no self-control, and being therefore incapable of controlling others, save in the way of inflaming their lusts by example like beasts of the fields, already have many such, finding themselves in command of some small local following, led their men on by hopes of gain and promises of reward. They are becoming no better than brigands, despoiling the defenceless, and each man pocketing his gains."

Petrobey here looked up.

"Pardon me," he said, "though such conduct has taken place on certain ships, I think that there has been none among the soldiers. Half the booty taken is put aside for the purpose of the war; half, as is right, is shared among those who acquire it."

Germanos looked at him keenly, and went on with growing eloquence.

"You have hit the very point," he said, "towards which I have been making. Half, as you say, is put away for the purposes of the war, and though I think that is too large a proportion, still the question is only one of degree, and we will pass it over. Half again, as you say, is shared among those who acquire it. There is the blot, the defect of the whole system.

192

What are we fighting for? For wealth or for liberty? Surely for liberty and the glory of God! To fight in such a cause, and to fall in such a cause, is surely an exceeding reward. But what of the glory of God? Is it not to Him that this, no niggardly tithe, but half the goods we possess, should be given? Is it not He who has given us the strength to fight, and the will before which even now the Turk is crumpling as a ship crumples the waves? And for this shall we give Him nothing? Shall every peasant possess his hoard taken from the Turk, and the church of God go begging? Have we not given our lives to His service, without hope of reward indeed, but very jealous for His honor? And how shall we serve Him as we ought, when our churches stand half ruined to the winds of heaven, and our monks, to support themselves, must needs hoe in the fields and vineyards, and bring but a tired frame to the blessed service of the church? Is it not there this should be bestowed—on the church, on the priests and the primates, on the heads and princes of the church, to be used by them for the glory of their Master? Some of us, I know, would wish to endow a king to rule over a free people, in royal obedience, for so they phrase it, to a people's will. Is it not enough to have for our king, our Master, our tender Friend, the King of kings? This only is the kingdom whose citizenship I covet, for it is beyond price, and it is but a dubious love for Him that is ours, if we give Him, as we fondly tell ourselves, our hearts, and withhold from Him our gold and silver. Not in such manner worshipped the kings of the East. Long was their journey, and yet we who fight are not more footsore than they; but did they come empty-handed to worship? Gold and frankincense and myrrh they gave, their costliest and their best. Heart worship let us give, and lip worship too, and let our hands be open in giving; it is in giving that we show, poorly indeed, but in the best and only way, the sincerity of our hearts. Ah, it is no pale spiritual kingdom only that God requires, but the pledge of it in a glorious liberality, the fruits of His bounty given to Him again. Let there be a splendor in our service to Him, riches, wealth, all that is beautiful, poured out freely; it is our duty to give—yes, and our privilege."

Petrobey and Nicholas both listened in dead silence, for they respected the man, and they revered his office. Of the honesty and integrity of his words, too, neither felt any question; but when in the history of warfare had ears ever heard so impractical a piece of rhetoric? Did Germanos really suppose that these soldiers of theirs were risking life, possessions, all that they had, for the sake of the heads of the church? Already the primates had done infinite harm by their pretentious meddling, giving themselves the airs of deposed monarchs, for whom it was a privilege to fight, and encouraging seditious talk among the men by hinting openly that the military leaders were in league with the Turks, making conventions with them by which their lives should be spared on the sacrifice of their property. Germanos himself, as they knew, was a man of far different nature; this scheme of his, by which half the booty should be placed unreservedly in the hands of the heads of the church, to be used for the glory of God, was as sunshine is to midnight compared to the vile slanderings of his inferiors. But how would the army receive it? Was

Petrobey, as commander-in-chief, or Germanos, as head of this people of God, to go to them, saying, "You have risked your lives, and it is your privilege to have done so for the glory of God; risk them to-morrow and the next day and the next day, and when the war is over, and unless you lie on the battlefield, you creep back to your dismantled homes, account it a privilege that you have been permitted to give to the primates and priests the fruits of your toil"?

Yet, though Germanos was accounted a man of integrity both by Petrobey and Nicholas, how could there but be a background to the picture he had drawn? He was a man to whom power and the exercise of power had become a habit, and the habit almost a passion. Though this scheme, by which the church would be restored to its old splendor and magnificence, the glory of those days when from Constantinople came the emperor humbly and suppliantly with great gifts, had for its object the glory of God, yet inasmuch as he was a man of dominant nature he could not be unaware nor disregardful of what it would mean to him personally. What a position! The chances were ten to one that he would be chosen to fill the places of the martyred patriarch, instead of the Bishop Eugenios, well known to the Greeks as a middle-minded man, who strove to keep well with both Ottoman and Greek. For, in truth, this was no time for diplomatic attitudes; each man must take one side or the other, and now to consent to take from the hands of the Sultan the insignia of his victim was to declare one's self no patriot. Greece would certainly repudiate the appointment and choose a supreme head for itself, and among all the primates and bishops there was none who was so powerful with his own class, and so popular among the people, as Germanos. As every one knew, he had thrown himself heart and soul into the revolution; he had raised the northern army, he had headed the attempt on the citadel of Patras in person. The chosen head of a new and splendid church, rising glorious in the dawn of liberty, sanctified by suffering, proved by its steadfastness to endure, a church for which blood had been shed, and, as he had said, no pale spiritual kingdom only, but a power on earth as in heaven! It was not in the nature of the man to be able to shut his eyes to that; it could not but be that so splendid a possibility should be without weight to him. His next words showed it.

"Is it not a thing to make the heart beat fast?" he went on. "I would not take the pontiff's chair in Rome in exchange for such a position. A new church, or rather, the old grown gloriously young again, a spiritual kingdom throned in the hearts of men, yet with the allegiance not only of their souls, but of their bodies and their earthly blessings. And I," he said, rising, "I, the unworthy, the erring, yet called by a call that I may not disobey."

But Nicholas, frowning deeply, interrupted him.

"I ask your pardon, father," he said, "but is it well to talk of that? Surely in this great idea which you have put before us there is nothing personal. It is the kingdom of God of which we speak."

Germanos paused a moment.

"You are right," he said; "you have but reminded me of my own words; it is in His name and none other that I speak."

194

"There is another point of view, father," continued Nicholas, "which, with your permission, I will put before you. I speak, I hope, as it is fitting I should speak to you; and yet, in mere justice to the position my cousin and I hold, we must tell you that there are other interests to be considered. For days past there has been division among us, here not so widely as at other places, but division there is—and that, too, at a time when anything of the kind is most disastrous. There are in the camp priests and primates who have been saying to the men, but not with your nobleness of aim, that which you have indicated to us. This war, they tell them, is a war of religion; they are the champions and ordained ministers of religion, and it is to them the soldiers' obedience is due. What did they get for their pains? A shrug of the shoulders, insolence, perhaps the question, 'Are we fighting or are you?' And they answer, 'For whom are you fighting? For your captains and leaders, let us tell you; it is they who will reap the fruits of your toil; it is they who will get the booty for which you have spent your blood and left your homes.' Now, before God, father, that is a satanic slander; but if this talk continues, who can tell but that it may become in part true? For as the army increases we have to appoint fresh captains, and often it happens that some band of men come in with their appointed leader, whom we have to accept. These are not all such men as my cousin and I should naturally appoint; and what we fear is this; and our fears, I am sorry to say, are justified by what is taking place at Monemvasia. These captains talk to each other, saying, 'The primates are trying to get the whole spoils of the war for themselves. Two can play at that game. If this war is for the enrichment of the leaders, let it be for the enrichment of the leaders who have done the work.' And some of this talk, too, has reached the men, with this result: some believe what the primates say, and already distrust their captains; some distrust the primates, and say that it is not they who are doing the work, and why should they look for wages? But the most part of those who have heard this seditious talk distrust both, and are each man for himself. And all this is the fault of the primates. This is no place for them; for those of them, at least, who have taken no part in the war. It is the work of soldiers we are doing, not the work of priests. The danger is a real one; as you say, it is a danger from those who sit at meat with us, and more deadly and more intimate than that we experience from our enemies. There was none of it before the primates came among us. I have said."

Nicholas spoke with rising anger; the thought of these mean, petty squabbles poisoned the hopes which had ruled his life for so long. Were they all to be wrecked in port on the very eve of their fulfilment? Strong as the Greek position now was, inevitable though the fall of Tripoli appeared, yet he knew that an army demoralized is no army at all. Was the honey to turn to bitterness? Was that fair day that seemed now dawning to come in cloud and trouble?

Germanos had listened with growing resentment, and he burst out in answer:

"You are wrong, Nicholas; believe me, you are wrong! It is the primates who have to put up with insult. This army of yours is a band of

195

wanton children, long chid and beaten, breaking out from school. It knows neither reverence nor respect, where respect is due."

"Ah, pardon me again," said Nicholas; "the first duty of the soldier is obedience to those who are put over him as captains and commanders. To them he has never yet failed in respect nor in obedience."

"These soldiers are men, I take it," said Germanos, "and the first duty of man is to obey those who are over him in the Lord."

"But, father, father!" cried Nicholas, pained himself, but unwilling to give pain, "is this a time, now when we are in the middle of the operations of the war, to talk of that? Of course you are right; that every Christian man believes. But our hands are full, we have this siege before us, and it is injudicious of these primates to stir up such talk now. Oh, I am no hand at speaking; but you see, do you not, what I mean? It is the Lord's work, surely, but the means by which it is accomplished is swords in unity, men bound together by one aim."

"And that aim the glory of God," said Germanos.

Nicholas made a hopeless gesture of dissent and shook his head, and Petrobey, who had hitherto taken no part in the discussion, broke in:

"Surely we can do better than wrangle together like boys," he said. "It is no light matter we have in hand. But let us talk practically. What Nicholas says is true. Father, there is mischievous talk going on, and there was none till the primates came. What do you propose to do? Will you help us to stop it? Will you speak to the men? Will you tell them that, though you are a primate yourself, yet you believe in the integrity of the military commanders, and that though our soldiers' duty as men exacts obedience to the rulers of the church, yet their duty as soldiers exacts obedience to their commanders, and trust in them?"

The question was cleverly chosen. To refuse to do as Petrobey asked would, without an explanation, be wholly unreasonable; to comply would be tantamount to telling the soldiers to disregard the primates. Germanos hesitated a moment.

"I do not wish to put myself outside my province," said Germanos, "and I am here only as the head of the church, and not as a military leader. To interfere with the ordering of the army is not my business."

"Then how much less," said Nicholas, eagerly, "is it the business of your inferiors to do so? Will you, then, tell them to follow your own most wise example?"

Germanos was silent, but his brain was busy, and yet he had no reply ready.

"See," said Nicholas, "a little while ago you asked us to help you, but now we ask you to help us, for the danger is no less to your party than to ours. Speak to the primates if you will, or speak to the captains; they will perhaps listen to you."

"At any rate, I asked not your help against my own subordinates," said Germanos, in a sudden flash of anger; "if you want help against your own men, I can only say—" and with that he stopped short, for an insult was on his lips.

Petrobey sat down again with a little sigh, but Nicholas answered Germanos according to his own manner.

196

"Then if you are so good as to think that our own affairs are out of hand," he said, with angry sarcasm, "it will be time to think of helping you when we have put them in order. Let me quote your own words: 'I am not jealous for myself, but I am very jealous for the honor of the army, and I have myself a pledge of the favor of God on my undertaking.'"

Germanos held up his hand pacifically.

"We shall gain nothing by quarrelling," he said, "and I am in the wrong, for I was the first to speak in anger. What is this pledge of which you speak?"

Nicholas told him of the vision at Serrica, and when he had finished it was gently that he answered.

"Surely the Mother of God looks with favor on you, Nicholas!" said the archbishop; "and for her sake, if not for our own, let us see if we cannot put an end to these unhappy divisions of which you tell me. You lay the whole blame on my order; are you sure that you are not hasty?"

"There was at least no seditious talk before the primates came," said Nicholas.

"I, then, have a proposal to make," said Petrobey, "and it is this: The men are divided; some side with the primates, some with us. The two parties are bitterly opposed. If a supreme council was appointed, consisting of primates and commanders, might not the division be healed?"

Nicholas shook his head.

"I do not wish to make difficulties," he said, "but the case is this: The siege of Tripoli is the work of the army. What have the primates to do with it? I might as well demand a seat in the synod of the church."

Germanos's eyes brightened. He realized the impossibility of pushing his first demand just now, and this, at any rate, would be a step gained. For the rest, he trusted in his own ability to soon get in his hands the chief share of the work of the supreme council, which Petrobey had suggested, and with the most diplomatic change of front, he proceeded to conciliate Nicholas.

"My dear Nicholas," he said, "I wish with all my heart you had a place in the synod of the church. As a priest you would have soon earned one; but you selected another vocation, in which I need give no testimony to your merits. But consider, dear Nicholas, this is a national movement, and the church is a great national institution, and has always had a voice, often the supreme voice, in the direction of national affairs. You must not think we want to interfere in military matters; you will not find Charalambes, for instance, or, for that matter, me, wishing to lead a sortie or direct the fire. In England, as you know, there are two great legislative houses—one composed of the lords of the land, without initiative, but with the power of check; the other, the elected body—the voice of the people. You generals are the elected body, on you the initiative depends; but we primates correspond to the titular power. And where can you find so splendid and august a government as that? See, I come to meet you half-way; it is not the time now to talk of the supremacy of the church, meet me half-way, and allow that in national concerns we should not be without a voice. There are two powers in this new Greece; if they are in accord, the danger we have spoken of melts like a summer mist."

Nicholas looked across at Petrobey.

"You would have me follow?" he asked. "Well, I consent."

Germanos was careful not to betray too much elation at the success of this scheme, and he soon spoke of other things. Prince Demetrius Ypsilanti, whom the Hetairia, or Club of Patriots in north Greece, had chosen to take the place of his treacherous and inefficient brother, was shortly to come to the Peloponnesus. Hitherto the proceedings of the club had been very secret and their funds intrusted to a few agents, such as Nicholas and Germanos; but the rapid success of the war, and its still more brilliant promise—for in north Greece as well it had spread like fire—had rendered all further concealment unnecessary, and they came forward now as the authors of the liberty of Greece, a credit which was, through their admirable agents, due them, and they were exercising their undoubted right in giving the command to whomever they would. Germanos also assured Petrobey and Nicholas that they were both in the highest favor with the club, and that Prince Demetrius was most amicably and warmly inclined to them. He might also tell them that the prince had no intention of interfering in the conduct of the war, which he was content to leave in more experienced hands; but he was coming as the head of the Hetairia, which had organized and financed the outbreak of the war, and he was sure, so thought Germanos, to approve of the step they had decided on, to appoint a national senate, and no doubt he would take his place at the head of the assembly.

CHAPTER VII

THE RULE OF THE SENATE

From this conversation among the three sprang into being the Peloponnesian Senate, than which no more futile apparatus has ever been devised to guide the affairs of a nation. From the first harmony was impossible between the two parties, and the only result it achieved worth mentioning was that it diverted the time and energies of the military leaders from the work to which every muscle should have been strained— the fall of Tripoli. So far from reconciling the divisions among the soldiers, it merely encouraged partisanship, for it was known that the senate could not agree on any point worth the deliberation. Petrobey was more than once tempted to resign his seat, but to do that was only to throw the wavering balance of power firmly into the hands of the primates, while between Nicholas and Germanos there ripened, as bitter as a Dead-Sea apple, an enmity only to be reconciled at a death-bed, for Germanos, so Nicholas considered, and did not scruple to say, had deceived both him and his colleague. He had professed the highest, most altruistic aims; what guided his conduct was the most selfish and personal policy. This, it is to be feared, was partly true, though not entirely, for Germanos had been sincere when he opened to the two his scheme for the glory of the church; but finding supremacy, like the fruit of Tantalus, still dangling beyond, but seemingly only just beyond, his reach, and stung intolerably at his failure, the personal motive crept in, and before long usurped the place of the other.

Nicholas had hoped great things from the arrival of the prince; but they, too, were doomed to be disappointed. He was given an enthusiastic welcome by the army, the majority of whom were sickened with this atmosphere of intrigue, and Petrobey instantly took his place as his subordinate; but the prince gave him to understand that it was his wish that the conduct of the siege should continue in the same hands. Germanos, too, welcomed him cordially, with a due recognition of his position, for he hoped to win him over to the side of the church. For the time it seemed that some solution of their difficulties was imminent, and in the hands of a stronger man, no doubt, such universally recognized authority would have found a means of reconciliation.

But Prince Demetrius was terribly unfitted for the responsibility. His principles were honorable, but by nature he was weak and undecided. He inclined first to one party, then to another, with no diplomatic yielding, which will give an inch to gain a yard, but with the pitiful futility of one who has no knowledge of men, no habit of command, and no certainty of himself. To the soldiers this weakness manifested itself openly, and unhappily not erroneously, in his personal appearance. He was under middle height; his manner, always stiff and awkward, was sometimes insolent, sometimes timid—an unfortunate demeanor, for he was neither the one nor the other, but only excessively self-conscious and shy. His face was thin and pinched, and his hair, although he was only thirty-two, was already gray and scanty, giving him a look of premature old age. Being short-sighted, he blinked and peered, as Mitsos said, like a noonday owl, and his voice was querulous and high-pitched. Yet he was of an upright mind, indifferent to danger, and free from the besetting sin of his race, avarice. All these outward defects corresponded but too well with the inadequacy of his nature; a strong man with not so honorable a heart as he had might easily have filled his post better, and the uprightness of his character, at a crisis where uprightness was the quality wanted, could not make itself felt, but which to the army and the council was but the bubbling that came from a man half drowned, when what was wanted was a firm voice and a loud and no drowning cry. Moreover, he was morbidly sensitive about his own dignity and position, and there was something comically tragical to see that puny frame with bent shoulders presiding over a company of strong men, and hear that little screechy voice prating of "My wish" and "My command." On one side of him sat Germanos, courtier-like and full of deference, plying him with his titles, as the nurse gives suck to a baby, while the prince, drinking like a child, would be well pleased, and pipe, "What you say is very true. It is my wish that the church should be fully recognized. Yes, quite so, my dear archbishop; but I think our friend, the gallant commander of this army, of which I, as the commander-in-chief, as the viceroy by the wish of the Hetairia—yes, exactly—has something to say on the subject."

Then Petrobey would lay before the prince the urgent need of doing one thing before all others. Tripoli must be taken; surely the claims of the two parties could be settled afterwards. That was the work most important to them. For three weeks now since the beginning of June had they waited at Trikorpha, and the provisions of the array were already beginning to be exhausted. The herds were being thinned, the lower pasture was drying up in the summer heat. Must not steps be taken here at once? And Prince Demetrius would answer something in this manner:

"What you say is very true, my dear Petrobey, and I quite agree with you that there is no time to be lost. Would you not form a committee and deliberate what is to be done, and then submit your results to me to receive my sanction? You spoke, I remember, about the formation of some cavalry corps; a very wise plan I thought it, and I meant to have some talk with you about it. But really the days have slipped by so. Yes, we must, indeed, be up and doing, and my orderly has just informed me, gentlemen, that dinner is ready; and I shall be pleased to see you, my dear archbishop, and you, commander, at my table. Dinner will be served immediately, and our deliberations, gentlemen, in which I think we may say we have made some solid progress, will be adjourned till to-morrow at the usual hour."

Nicholas saw that there was no help here, and he set himself to thwart Germanos with all his power. He considered that the presence of the primates in the camp rendered the army powerless, for it was eaten up with intrigue, slander, and incessant accusation, provoking counter-accusation. At the meetings of the senate he opposed Germanos on every point, whether or no his suggestions were honorable or expedient, and allying himself with any one who would join him in upholding the army against the church, ranged himself side by side with crooked and unscrupulous men like Poniropoulos and Anagnostes, mere brigands and adventurers, who, without any motive but their own greed, had got together a band of peasants, and were in command of a mere disorderly rabble; men who in his soberer moments he knew were as detestable as, in his furious anger against Germanos, he thought the primate to be. Every day the meetings of the senate grew more and more disorderly, and gradually Prince Demetrius saw that he was no more than a cypher in the eyes of these men. Of personal ambition Nicholas had none; honestly and with his whole heart he cared for nothing but the success of the revolution and the extermination of the Turk, and he used his great power and influence for the defeat of the intriguing primates, being convinced that till the question between the two parties was settled nothing could be done. At any rate, he was free from all stings of conscience; his conduct might be unwise, but he acted from impeccable motives, and there was enough truth in his allegations against Germanos to give them a sting that was wellnigh unforgivable.

200

It was already more than half-way through June, and still the army remained inactive. Petrobey had so far succeeded in rousing the prince as to permit him to make arrangements for regular supplies being sent to the camp; but there was still no talk of an assault on Tripoli, or indeed any preparations for ensuring its success. The senate had met as usual that morning, and the meeting had degenerated into a fierce brawl between Anagnostes and Nicholas on the one side, and Germanos and Charalambes on the other. It was in vain that the prince tried to restore order; they listened to him no more than to a buzzing fly, when at length Germanos, bitten to the quick by some intolerable taunt of Nicholas's, rose from the table, saying he would take no further part in the deliberations of the senate.

"There must be an end," he said, "to this. How long ago is it, Nicholas, since you swore allegiance to me?"

"Allegiance in all things in your jurisdiction," replied Nicholas, "and to the glory of God, not to the glory of Germanos."

The heat of his anger did not excuse the words, and the moment afterwards every better feeling within him would have had them unsaid, but Anagnostes, sitting at his elbow, applauded vehemently.

"Silence, you there," said Germanos, in a white anger. "You will hear my voice no more here; but let me tell you, you are not rid of me. We will see what the people say to such treatment as that I have been subjected to."

"Go to the people," shouted Nicholas; "see how the Mainats receive you!"

"The Mainats?" said Germanos; "the Mainats, whom I hold a degree only above the Turks?"

"My dear archbishop—my dear archbishop," piped the prince.

"But there are true and loyal men in Greece besides those hounds," continued Germanos, not even hearing the prince speak.

"Archbishop," said the prince again, with a certain dignity, "I command you, I order you, to be silent."

Germanos turned round on him, still mad with rage.

"You order, you command?" he said, with infinite scorn, and broke into a sudden, unnatural laugh.

Prince Demetrius flushed, and on all the senate fell a dead hush. For once the man showed the dignity of birth and breeding, and standing up, he faced the angry prelate. His nervous, weak manner had left him; he rose to the occasion.

"You will please to take your seat, archbishop," he said. "I have a few words to say."

Germanos looked round and saw on all sides eager, attentive faces bent, not on him, but on the prince. His anger still burned like fire within him, and he paused not to consider.

"I prefer to leave the room," he said. "I take no further part in these proceedings."

"You choose to disregard my request," said the prince, and with that his voice rose sudden and screaming and fierce; "I will therefore order—Sit down!" he cried.

Germanos's anger went out as suddenly as lightning at night is followed by darkness, and he realized what he had done. The prince's favor he had forfeited hopelessly, and though the prince was nothing, he had forgotten in the man's insignificance the power he represented. Henceforth he would have to fight without the expectancy of help from there; and feeling his schemes already threatening to totter and fall about his head, in sheer blank bewilderment he sat down.

The prince stood silent a moment and then spoke.

"I feel," he said, "that all the good I hoped to do, and all the efforts I wished to make for the great cause, are not to be fulfilled. With the exception of the commander of this army, the senate generally have chosen to disregard my presence here. From Petrobey, however, I have always had courtesy and respect. The party of the church, in particular, has chosen to adopt an insolent demeanor towards me, the like of which I accept from no man. You have seen, gentlemen, the example their head has given them. I regret the decision which I have long thought was possible, but which has been forced upon me. Gentlemen, I leave the camp to-day. The meeting is adjourned."

Then turning to Petrobey, and bowing to the rest:

"Come with me," he said; "we will leave this assembly together," and taking his arm, he left the room.

Half an hour later he quitted the camp with a small guard, leaving the rest of his retinue to follow as quickly as they could get ready. But the news of his departure and the reason for it spread like wildfire through Trikorpha, and the men, who still regarded him, partly because of the marked favor he showed to Petrobey, partly from the prestige of the revolutionary Hetairia which he represented, as their champion, were wildly indignant with the primates. A riot nearly ensued, and had not Petrobey and other commanders, notably Nicholas himself, had them guarded in a place of safety, it is not improbable that some would have been murdered. Germanos, however, who, whatever his faults were, was perfectly fearless, refused all protection, and when one of the Mainats passing near him, spit at him, the archbishop dealt the man a blow which knocked him off his feet, and passed on without hurry or discomposure, though he was in the middle of the clan. But the Mainats, who were without a particle of reverence for him, but had a deep respect for personal pluck, appreciated the act fully and made no attempt to stop him, though a minute before it was very doubtful whether he would have reached his quarters alive.

All day the feeling in the camp against the primates rose higher and higher, for, from the soldiers' point of view, the prince was their protector not only against them, but their own commanders, who, as the primates had told them, rousing suspicion if not belief in their minds, were employed in making private arrangements with the Turks, promising them their lives in exchange for their property. No one, it is true, had breathed a suspicion about either Petrobey or Nicholas, for they stood beyond any shadow of scandal, and for the time the ugly thoughts the primates had suggested were cast aside in the fierce indignation excited by the immediate cause of the withdrawal of the prince, for which the primates alone were to be thanked. A knot of angry men assembled outside the building where primates and muskets were stored, demanding that they should be given up to be dealt with as they deserved; and, indeed, such a fate was not unmerited, and it would have saved a world of trouble to Petrobey. For they were responsible for all this doubt and division; they were traitors in the camp, and in time of war a traitor is worse than a regiment of foes. Next day there was no abatement of popular feeling, and in the afternoon the whole body of commanders and captains went to Petrobey, after exacting a promise from their men of quietude in their absence, asking that the prince might be petitioned to return, for his absence could but end in one thing, the death of all the primates, either with the authority of the commanders, or, in default of that, by mutiny.

Petrobey readily consented to go in person, for things were at an absolute impasse, and without the prince's co-operation and presence he was really afraid that the worst might happen, and in the name of the entire army, and with the earnest appeals of the primates, he waited upon him at Leondari, a revolted town not far from Megalopolis. The prince at first hesitated, or seemed to hesitate, but privately he was very much gratified at what seemed so universal a mark of confidence; for on thinking his action over, it had appeared to him that he must cut but a sorry figure if he returned to the Hetairia, saying that the army disregarded his authority and met his commands with insolence, while if he came back, his withdrawal assumed the aspect of a most successful piece of diplomacy. Accordingly, at the end of the week he returned amid the welcoming acclamations of the army, and was pleased to accept—having insisted on the same—the apology of Germanos, which was bitter herbs to that proud man, but to Nicholas as sweet as honey in the mouth.

Throughout July, but waning with the moon, continued the reign of that incompetent, but honest man, Prince Demetrius. His indecision amounted to a disease of the mind; he seemed morally incapable of acting, or, through his pretentious viceregal claims, of letting others act for him; a creature afflicted with acute paralysis of will. Inside Tripoli there was still no famine of food or water, and though Achmet Bey saw that escape was impossible, for the weakness of the troops inside would have rendered an attempt to cut through the occupations on the hills quite hopeless, yet he was in no mind to surrender when no attempts were made to induce him to do so. There were provisions in the camp which would last three months more, for the harvest had been got in before the occupation of Valtetzi; the ravages of the Greeks had destroyed only the villages and the winter crops, and Mehemet Salik remarked one morning that one seemed safer in Tripoli than anywhere else.

And the hot month throbbed by, while to the Greeks every day's close saw another day lost.

CHAPTER VIII

THE SONG FROM TRIPOLI

Early in August news came to the camp that the Turks in Monemvasia had made a proposal for a capitulation, for it will be remembered that a small fleet of vessels from Spetzas was blockading it by sea, in addition to a regiment from south Greece by land, and these tidings gave Prince Demetrius a most ill-conceived idea. The terms of the capitulation were discussed at a meeting of the senate, and caused a very considerable difference of opinion, Nicholas and Petrobey advising that the Turks should be given a passage over to Smyrna, or some Asia Minor port, on condition that they surrendered their arms, refunded the expenses of the siege—for the soldiers had been serving without pay—and further, gave an indemnity of ten thousand Turkish pounds, which should be divided among the fleet, the army, and the national treasury. Germanos and his party opposed this. Monemvasia was notably one of the wealthiest towns in the Peloponnesus, and he proposed that the besieged should only be given their lives on the surrender of all their property. Prince Demetrius went to the other extreme. The Hetairia would charge itself with the arrears of the soldiers' pay, since it was for that very purpose its funds had been raised; to the soldiers was due their pay and nothing more, and if easy terms were granted to Monemvasia, the Turks in Tripoli would be more disposed to capitulate. The discussion degenerated into wrangling, but in the middle of it Prince Demetrius suddenly commanded silence. Since the affair with Germanos, he had secured the formalities of obedience, and he was listened to in silence.

"I shall go to Monemvasia in person," he said, "to receive and to accept the capitulation of the town as commander-in-chief of the army, and viceroy, appointed by the supreme council of the Hetairia. The troops there, so I hear, are out of hand, and the Mainat corps under their commander, Petrobey, will accompany me. We will continue to discuss the terms of the capitulation, and observe a little more decorum."

But the senate had experienced his deficiency in power of command too long, and his words were like the words coming from the mouth of a mask, when every one knew how insignificant a figure stood behind it. The autocratic tone was ludicrous, and in this particular case peculiarly out of place. Petrobey, who, when it was possible, supported the prince, now found himself obliged to oppose him, and, with a courtesy he found it hard to assume, spoke in answer:

"Your highness will remember," he said, "that the siege has been going on for three months, and has been entirely the work of the people. The Hetairia has not helped them in any way. It is surely, then, their right to demand their own terms, and the surrender must be made to the captains of the blockading forces, or to whomever they appoint, and to no other."

The prince flushed angrily.

"Do I understand, then, that I am not the commander-in-chief of the whole army?"

"Your highness is commander-in-chief over all the army which has been organized or supplied by the Hetairists or their agents. The force that blockades Monemvasia was raised by private enterprise before your appointment by the Hetairia, and during your stay in the Morea you have not either taken the command there or assisted that force. The commander of the land force there is a member of this senate, and no doubt he will obey its resolves."

"Sooner than that of the viceroy?"

"The viceroy also is a member of this senate," said Petrobey, with some adroitness.

The prince was silent a moment.

"The senate will, therefore, vote as to whether Monemvasia is to be occupied in the name of the senate or in my name," he said, shortly.

For once there was unanimity between the two parties, and it was decided that Monemvasia was to be occupied in the name of the senate. The discussions about the terms of the capitulation were then renewed, but as it was felt that the commander of the blockading force had more voice in the matter than any one else, Germanos, with the amiable desire of perhaps thwarting Nicholas, whose proposal had been more moderate than his own, suggested that this point should be settled between the commander and the prince upon the arrival there of the latter, for it was absurd that commanders of a force which was besieging Tripoli should have a voice in the matter. Nicholas, knowing that Petrobey would be there too, and that he had more influence with the prince than any one, acquiesced with a smile, saying that Germanos's sage reflection applied equally to primates who were not in command of anything.

So for a time the centre of the war, like some slow-moving stream, shifted to Monemvasia, and during the whole of August half the army lay idle on the hills round Tripoli; and with the departure of the prince the tales of scandalous slander were again taken up by the primates, the result of which was to appear later. Germanos, though he must have known what was going on, held aloof, and did not mix up in the affairs of the camp; though, to his shame be it said, he appeared to make no effort to check the outrageous intrigues.

To Nicholas, however, the month was full of work, and he at once put in hand arrangements for the regular supplies of the camp, and was occupied with drilling the men; under his wise yet severe rule the unorganized troops began slowly to take shape, and his example shamed many of the other idle and irresponsible captains into following his lead, though, having little knowledge of military matters themselves, it must be concluded that their men were not able to advance to a high degree of efficiency. Meantime, among the men themselves the utter inability of the prince either to check abuses or to enforce discipline had become apparent, and from the time of his departure for Monemvasia his power may be said to have ceased altogether. And when the news of what had taken place at that town came to hand, from being nothing he became ridiculous.

The nightly raids ceased, for all the cultivated land round Tripoli was already devastated, and neither in the town nor in the camp was any particular vigilance observed. The Turks knew it was hopeless to attack Trikorpha; till the return of Petrobey the Greeks had no thought of attempting to storm the town; and Mitsos, brooding inwardly one night on the rough wall where he and Yanni used often to sit, had an idea which arose from this inaction.

For several weeks after the adventure of the fire-ship his anxieties about Suleima had been stilled, for that escape seemed to him so heaven-sent that with childlike faith he had no manner of doubt but that the saints watched over her, and though at times his heart went a-mourning for her absence, yet he trusted an unreasoning conviction that at the time appointed he would see her again. The strong probability that she was in this beleaguered town did not at first weigh on him at all. Some day, when provisions ran short, it would capitulate, and there would be a repetition of the scene at Kalamata; or they would storm it, and there would be fighting inside. But the women would all be in the houses, and even if the houses were attacked she would remember what he had told her, and cry out to them in Greek, saying she was of their blood, and all would be well. But when the excitement of the skirmish at Valtetzi, now nearly two months ago, and the move to Trikorpha, with all the delightful night-raiding, was over, and was succeeded by an inaction sickened by the odious intrigues of the primates, he began to weary sore for her, and then to be filled with panic fears as unfounded as his first security. Safety in a siege, there was no such thing! A chance bullet, an angry Greek, and a repetition of that infernal butchery of women and children on board the ship bound for Egypt. What was more horribly possible? A burning house, a falling wall, and then a mass of pulped bodies.

On this particular night his fears grew like the monstrous visions of some hag-ridden nightmare. A hundred terrible scenes loomed enormous before him, and in each Suleima, with white, imploring face, was struck out of life, now by a bullet, now by a sword. Below, in the part of the town nearest him, where five or six big houses were built on the wall, there gleamed rows of lights from narrow-barred windows, and from each Suleima's face looked out from a room burning within, while she shook the iron bars with impotent hands as the flames flickered and rose behind her.

The thing became intolerable; he rose and walked about, but found no rest. Thirty yards away the soldiers' huts began, and he could hear sounds of singing from the big shanty-built café a little farther on. The sentry had just been on his rounds, and Mitsos exchanged a word or two with him as he passed, and he would be back again in half an hour. The wall inside was only six feet high, outside perhaps ten or twelve, but with plenty of handhold for an agile lad, and the next moment, without thinking where or why he went, he had clambered up and dropped down on the other side.

Did he not know where he was going? Ah, but his heart told him.

206

Somewhere in that fiery-eyed town, into which entrance was impossible, was she for whom he was made, she with the eyes of night and the history of his soul written on the curves of her lips. And inasmuch as she was there, the rekindled fever of his love drew him thither, neither willing nor unwilling, but steel to the magnet, a moth to the star. He had taken off his shoes in order to get a better grip in the crevices of the wall, and went down barefooted over the basalt rocks all ashine with dew. The moon had strayed westward beyond the zenith, casting his shadow a little in front of him, and round his head as he walked moved an opaline halo. Then he crossed the mountain stream and stood in it for a moment, for the coldness of the moon and the eternal youth of night had entered into its waters, making them vigorous and bracing. A little wind drawing down its course was full of the scent of water and green things, and streamed out to renovate the hot air of the plain. Then on again through a little belt of vineyard, still close to the camp and not destroyed, where the stream talked less noisily in the soft earth, with a whiff of summer from the ripening bunches, and the scuttle of some disturbed hare come down to feed on the leaves. Then he crossed the stream again, which lay in an elbow southward, and, pushing through a clump of oleanders which rose above his head, came out into the plain. The earth was warm under foot after the cold rocks, and he ran plunging across it, till, getting within a stone's-throw of the wall, he crept more slowly, and finally lay down in the shadow of a felled olive-tree, and looked to see if there was aught stirring.

The battlemented line of the wall opposite to him stood up clear-cut between the moon and the lights of the town, twenty feet above him, and ran on southward into vague shadow, untenanted. Fifty yards to the left it was interrupted, or rather crowned, by half a dozen big houses, built flush with the wall, pierced by several rows of rather narrow windows, the lower of which were barred, the upper, from their height, needing no such defence. As he crept up alongside of these he heard the subdued murmur of women's voices from within the first house—the home, perhaps, of some Turkish captain and his harem; and the sound of women's voices made mirth to him, and he listened for a while, smiling to himself. From the next house came more such music, and once a woman walked to the window and stood looking out for a minute, or perhaps two, unveiled and playing with the tassel of the blind-cord, till from within some one called her by a purring Turkish name, and she turned into the house again.

He crept slowly on to the end of the line of houses, where the battlemented wall began again, and feeling closer to Suleima in the sound of women's voices, came back and lay down again in the shadow of a tall toothed rock. It was something to be alone, away from the jarring camp, and to be nearer to her. His portentous nightmare beset him no longer, and his anxieties again were charmed to sleep. One by one the lights went out in the windows opposite, and the houses became blackness; the shadow of the rock moved a little forward in the setting moon, and he shifted to be in the shade again. Another half-hour went by, and the mountain ridge hid the moon.

Presently afterwards a man appeared on the top of the wall to the right. Mitsos, perhaps, would not have noticed him but that he waved some white linen thing up and down once or twice, and then waited again, and after a time uttered some impatient exclamation. Mitsos watched him, puzzled to know what this should mean, when suddenly a possible solution dawned upon him, and he crept up, still in the shadow, to below where the Turk was standing, and whistled softly.

Then a voice from above said:

"You are late. Here is the paper signed," and a white thing fluttered down. This done, the Turk turned, and, without waiting for a reply, went southward down the wall.

The paper, whatever it was, was in Mitsos' possession, and putting it in his pocket, for it was too dark to read it, he crept back to his old place to wait a few minutes more there before going back to the camp. Lights showed only in one house now, and before long they, too, were quenched, and the black mass of flat roofs rose against the sky silent and asleep. Then suddenly and softly from out that blackness, like a bird flying in the desert, came the sound of a voice singing, and at those notes Mitsos thought his heart would have burst. For it sang:

"Dig we deep among the vines,
Give the sweet spring showers a home,
Else the fairest sun that shines"—

It stopped as suddenly, dying like a sigh, and looking up he saw framed in one of the dark windows the upper part of a girl's figure dressed in white. And without a pause the boy's voice answered:

"Lends no lustre to our wines,
Sends no sparkle to the foam."

The prattle of the stream above alone whispered in the stillness. Then a voice softly asked:

"Mitsos?"

"I am here; and oh, dearest one, is it you?"

A little tinkle of laughter rippled from above, ending in a sudden, quick-drawn breath.

"At last I see you again," she said, softly, "but I don't see you at all. Mitsos, little Mitsos, is it well with you?"

Mitsos crept silently out of the shadow and stretched out his arms to her. "It is well in all but the great thing—that we are not together. But that will be soon, dearest; oh, please God! it will be soon."

Suleima leaned forward from the window.

"You must not wait here, nor must I; I am at a passage window, and though the house is dark, one never knows. So go, beloved, beloved, beloved, and I shall not be waiting long, shall I? And, Mitsos, there will soon be ... soon, maybe, I shall come to you with a gift."

"A gift?" said Mitsos; he then understood, and "Ah! dearest of all," he whispered.

"Yes, even so," said Suleima; "but, oh, Mitsos, I pray that you may soon be able to take me away, that soon this horrible town will fall."

"Before long it must be," said he; "and when the end comes run to meet the enemy as your deliverer, crying 'I am of your blood.' Oh, my heart, forget not that!"

Suleima turned quickly, hearing some sound within, and whispering "Good-night," was gone again, leaving Mitsos alone.

Heaven had opened; and walking on air, he went back to the camp, and waiting below the wall till the sentry had gone by, he climbed in again where he had got out. For the most part the men were gone to bed, but he passed a few on his way back to the little hut he shared with Yanni and two Mainats, all of whom had gone with Petrobey, and, undressing quickly, lay down on his bed to feast alone on this great happiness. With the irrepressible hopefulness of youth his fears had vanished before the sight of the one—they had never been, and he set himself to tell over, like a rosary of hallowed beads, the moments of the night. Not till then did he recollect the mysterious paper which he had received, and then, getting hastily up, he struck a light on his tinder-box, and lit a small, oil-fed wick. The illumination was dim and flickering, but the handwriting was large and clear, and by holding it close to the light he could easily read it. It was very short, and written in Greek:

"Abdul Achmet promises to pay to Constantinos Poniropoulos the sum of two hundred Turkish pounds, on condition that he and his harem are, on the termination of the siege of Tripoli, insured security from outrage or massacre. For the transport and expenses of travelling to a place of safety for each person ten pounds in addition will be paid.

"(Signed) ABDUL ACHMET,
"Ex-Governor of the City of Argos."

Mitsos read it through once without taking in the meaning, far less the whole bearing, of it, and then putting it back in his pocket blew out his light, and lay with wide-open eyes staring at the darkness, while the full meaning of the words slowly dawned on him.

First came hot indignation. A Greek captain at the head of five hundred men was privately trafficking with the besieged for his private gains. But close on the heels of his anger came fierce, overwhelming temptation. Abdul Achmet was the owner of Suleima, and to Mitsos this paper meant not only safe conduct to Abdul, but to her. Had it been in his power he would have doubled the bribe to the further side of possibility to secure that, and thrown his own soul into the bargain. Suleima safe, no more fear for her, nor any chance blow upsetting a too sanguine security! And because he loved her with a true and honest heart all thought of himself was absent; he would have paid the demand of angels, men, and devils to secure her from hurt or death, even though—and he ground his teeth at the thought—security meant only to go on living in the harem of Abdul. All the nightmares of the day before the expedition of the fire-ship

209

he lived through again, feeling at first that there was no question of choice before him, that somehow or other he must let this note go to Poniropoulos. For this was the more insidious temptation, as it could be managed so that no one, or at the worst the man for whom it was intended, should know his share in it. Yet here again was the choice between two impossibilities; but slowly as before, aching and bruised in spirit, he struggled back to choose the honorable.

But thus a new difficulty stood in his way. It was his clear duty to let Nicholas know of this clandestine traffic, and in so doing Mitsos would have to tell him of his own absence by night from the camp without leave. Nicholas would ask the reason, and probably be very angry with him, though as he had not been detected, but confessed it himself, the offence would find mitigation. But how came he to be waiting under the walls of Tripoli?

Mitsos thought this over for some little time before he arrived at the best and most obvious solution, namely, to tell Nicholas everything. The taking of Tripoli could not be far off, and he knew that when that came near he would, for her greater safety, let others know the prize the town held for him, and a week or two sooner or later did not make much difference. So, not wishing to delay and risk a hot resolution, he put on his clothes again to go to Nicholas's quarters. He had just got outside his hut when he heard the voice of the sentry challenging some one without the camp, and "but for the grace of God," thought he, "there goes Mitsos."

"Who goes?" called the sentry again. "Speak, or I fire."

Mitsos did not hear the reply, but the sentry stood still, while a man clambered over the wall and spoke a few words to him. Standing in the shadow of his doorway not thirty yards off, Mitsos could see who both of them were, and recognized Poniropoulos and the burly Christos.

"Fifty pounds to say nothing of this," he heard Poniropoulos say.

There was a short silence, and Mitsos longed to hear the offer refused. But the greed of the country Greek was too strong.

"Fifty pounds?" answered Christos; "when do you pay me?"

"On the day Tripoli falls."

Again there was a pause, and Mitsos suddenly made up his mind to interfere, and he strode out of the shadow to where the two were standing. They stood asunder a few paces as he came up and took Christos by the arm.

"For the love of God say 'No,' Christos," he said. "Ask him first what his business was outside."

Poniropoulos came a step nearer.

"You young cub," he said, below his breath, "what business is it of yours?"

Christos looked from one to the other.

"He has promised me fifty pounds," he said.

"O fool!" said Mitsos, "there will be a fight between you and me that will cost you the best part of a hundred in blood and bruises, if you don't listen to me. Besides, I don't want to get you into trouble."

Poniropoulos looked thunder at the boy, but inwardly he was disquieted.

"Go to your kennel, you cub," he said, "or I report you to-morrow morning for insubordination."

Mitsos gave a short laugh.

"Very good," he said, "that shall be to-morrow, and it is yet to-night. Look you, Christos, there will be trouble if you do not listen to me. That is all."

He turned back to his hut in order to give Poniropoulos time to be off and leave the coast clear, for he wished to get to Nicholas without making a disturbance in the camp, and, shutting the door, waited for five minutes till he heard Poniropoulos walk off one way and Christos continue his rounds. Then going out again he went straight to Nicholas's quarters and knocked at the door.

Nicholas was asleep, but awakened at once at the sound, and called out to know who was there.

"It is I, Mitsos," said the boy, "and I want to see you at once, Uncle Nicholas."

"Wait a minute, then," and from within came the sounds of the striking of a flint.

"I can't light this," said Nicholas; "come in, though."

Mitsos entered, feeling glad there was no light, for it made his story easier to tell.

"There is a powder-box where you can sit, little Mitsos," said Nicholas, "or sit on the end of the bed. Now, what brings you here?"

Mitsos felt in his pocket and found the paper.

"This, which I am holding out to you," he said. "On it is written that Poniropoulos, for the sum of two hundred pounds, will insure safety to Abdul Achmet and his house when Tripoli falls."

There was a moment's silence.

"The black devil!" said Nicholas. Then suddenly, "How came you by this, Mitsos?"

"That is what I am going to tell you."

Mitsos found it rather hard to begin, and after a moment Nicholas spoke again—kindly, but gravely.

"I am listening, Mitsos," he said. "Hush! there is some one coming. Keep quite quiet."

Immediately after a knock came to the door, and Nicholas let it be repeated before he answered.

"Who is it?" he asked.

"Christos Choremis," said the voice, "the sentry for the last two hours."

"Well?"

"Half an hour ago, sir, the Captain Poniropoulos climbed in over the camp wall. I thought best to tell you at once."

"Did he explain where he had been?"

"No, sir."

"Open the door, Christos," said Nicholas. "There is one question more. Did he offer you money not to say anything about it?"

Christos shifted from one foot to the other.

211

"No, sir," he said, at length.

"You did quite right to tell me," said Nicholas. "You can go."

"Now, Mitsos," said Nicholas, when the footsteps died away, "you can begin and tell me how you got this."

Then Mitsos, with many pauses, told him all that had taken place between him and Suleima from the time he had first heard the voice out of the darkness down to this night, when again it had come to him, lying outside the walls of Tripoli, and Nicholas heard him in absolute silence.

"And, oh, uncle, if it be possible," cried Mitsos, "let her be safe when the end of the time comes. For there is no one like her, and it has been hard for me."

Nicholas heard it in wonder and amazement, but he had one more question to ask.

"But when you blew up the Turkish ship, Mitsos," he said, "did it not occur to you that she might be on board?"

"I thought she certainly was there," said Mitsos, "and it was not till it was all over I heard she was not."

Nicholas reached out in the darkness and took Mitsos' smooth hand in his. "God forgive us all!" he said; "and can you forgive us, little Mitsos?"

The pain and relief of telling all the story to a man whom he trusted and loved had been too much for the boy, and he choked in trying to find his voice.

"There, there!" said Nicholas, soothingly; "but what is the matter with the young wolf? He has had good news to-night, has he not? and has he not seen the one he loves? There is no cause for this, little Mitsos. But this will I do: by the oath of the clan I swear to you that nothing shall stay me—not fever, nor wounds, nor booty, nor glory, only honor alone—from doing what in me lies to save her from all peril. Will that do, little one?"

Mitsos pressed his hand, but could not speak.

"But this you must promise," went on Nicholas, "that never again will you go out of the camp by night without leave. It leads with other men to ugly things, and to-morrow there will be one man the less in the army. The treacherous villain! But to-morrow he leaves the camp with disgrace and hissing, for he has made true the false slander of the primates, and brought shame on us all. And now go to bed, Mitsos. The service you have done in discovering this atones for your fault. Poor little cub, but it has been a hard time for you."

Next day Poniropoulos was publicly expelled from the camp, and afterwards Mitsos sought out Christos and in private told him that he was a better fellow than he had supposed, and that the lie he had told Nicholas to screen the captain found favor in his eyes. Christos was reasonably surprised that Mitsos knew of the falsehood, and relieved to find he was not disposed to quarrel with it, and the two went off and put away a quart or two of resined wine, for which Mitsos paid.

The news that Monemvasia had surrendered, and the details of its surrender, were bitter and sweet and tragic and absurd. Prince Demetrius, it appeared, defying the senate, in a fit of impotent rage against their perfectly proper opposition to his wishes, had insisted on signing the treaty of capitulation with his own name as viceroy of the country, effendi or lord of the country, and what not, and the Turks, opening the gates in order to go down to the ships and take their promised departure, found themselves met by a crowd of angry Mainats, who considered that the treaty as signed by the prince and not by the senate was null and void. A riot took place, and several Turks were killed on the point of embarking; but the better part of the Greek officers, seeing that the capitulation had been signed, and that whoever was to blame the Turks were not, soon stopped it, and let the embarkation proceed, but not before five men had been killed and several houses sacked. Monemvasia had surrendered—so much was good; but all the rest was bad. The fleet and the army distrusted each other, and the soldiers distrusted their commanders, who, thanks to the primates, were represented to them as having made private treaties with the wealthier Turks, and there was a fine quarrel as to who should set up the Greek standard on the fallen town. In one thing only was there unanimity, and that was in the feeling towards the prince. He had shown himself weak and indecisive before, and that had been forgiven him; he had shown himself dilatory and incapable, and the commander under him bore the blame; but now he showed himself, though with characteristic futility, evading and tampering with the recorded vote of the senate, in which he had acquiesced at the last meeting in Tripoli. The futility of his act was comic; his motive was warped and crooked. In a word, in that moment all the rags of authority which he had brought from the Hetairia were torn from him, and for all practical purposes his connection with the revolution may be said to have been over.

Without doubt the capitulation was hopelessly mismanaged, and the Turks got off without paying a penny towards the expenses of the siege. If the same terms were given to every fortified place in the Morea, the national treasury and the funds of the Hetairia would be certainly drained dry before half the country was evacuated; and though morally nothing can excuse the scenes of horror which were about to take place, yet palliation may be found in those two things—that without plunder gained from the Turk the war was impossible, and that the nation was a nation of slaves, long ground down by cruelty of all kinds, now in the first hour of its freedom. The despised but long dominant race was underfoot, and they stamped it down.

The Mainat corps was still at Monemvasia, where Petrobey was raising fresh recruits for the siege of Tripoli, and the prince occupying his leisure time, of which he had twenty-four hours every day, in trying to festoon the walls of the town with red tape, when news came of the fall of Navarin, a port on the west coast. Ypsilanti had sent there a civilian from his suite to represent the shadow of nothingness and the senate, one of the worst type of men, who, under the guise of patriotism, had got together a large band of freebooters, to plunder and seize all that he could lay hands on. Before the capitulation, which granted the besieged their lives and safe transport to Egypt or Tunis, had been concluded, many of the Turks had, under stress of hunger, escaped from the town, and thrown themselves on the mercy of the Greeks, with whom they had lived on friendly terms. But the town itself refused to capitulate till starvation compelled. Already for four days nothing could be bought, for a couple of sparrows or a half-starved cat represented a few hours' life, whereas a bushel of gold represented—a bushel of gold. One man the day before the surrender was found with a secret supply of food, on which he had subsisted for some days, the remains of which were seized from him by two starving savages and devoured before his eyes, after which they pelted him with all the money they had about them, telling him he was well paid. Perhaps some strange premonition of their fate induced the gaunt garrison to hold out; perhaps tales had reached them of what had been the fate of those who had thrown themselves on the mercy of the besieging army; and it was not till August 19th, just a fortnight after Monemvasia was taken, that the capitulation was signed.

For that day an eternal blot of infamy is black against the Greeks. Hardly had the garrison evacuated, giving up their arms, when the representative of the Peloponnesian senate thrust into the fire the treaty of capitulation, so that all evidence against him might be destroyed, and himself gave the signal for the massacre to begin. A pretext was easily found, and a blow given to a Greek by a Turk for insisting on searching the person of one of his wives for treasure concealed about her was enough, and in an hour no Mussulman was left alive. Women were stripped of their clothing, and rushing into the sea to hide their shame were shot from the shore; babies were snatched out of their mothers' arms and flung in their faces; others, remembering the fate of the patriarch, hanged men and women from the lintels of their own doors; others, it is said, were tortured before some one of their persecutors, more humane than his fellows, despatched them. Here, in mockery of the Turkish atrocities, a man was offered the choice between Christianity and death, and when he chose the former, was "baptized with steel" or crucified; a dozen or more were burned alive in a house where they had run for refuge. In an hour the infamous work was finished, and then arose quarrelling over the booty. Knives and rifles were brought in to settle the disputes, while in the mean time two Spetziot ships quietly went off with the greater part of the spoils.

Thus ended a day, the disgrace of which will only be forgotten when the glory of men like Nicholas has faded too. Dark and horrible in part as were the deeds which were to follow, no cruelty so cold-blooded and preconcerted stains the other pages of the war. Cruelties there were, and many black and shameful deeds, but deeds wrought in hot blood and in the drunkenness of revenge; and happily the massacre of Navarin is unapproached and unparalleled.

CHAPTER IX

PRIVATE NICHOLAS VIDALIS

Before September was a week old the Mainat corps, with Petrobey and the prince, were back at Tripoli. The course events had taken at Monemvasia had inclined the latter again to the side of the primates, for he interpreted the attitude and action of the army with regard to the capitulation of the place as an insult levelled at him. Germanos was not long in perceiving this; but being acute enough to see that the prince's authority was just now naught but a paper sceptre, he reasoned that his friendship was equally valueless, unless he could manage to rescue for him a few rags of the authority of which he had, by his own folly, denuded himself. In any case the support of the primates was a prop to the prince, and as the power of the primates varied in inverse ratio to that of the military commanders, Germanos set to work again to discredit them with the troops. There it was that the strength of the revolution was beginning to lie—not in the prince, who could not command others, nor in the senate, which was unable to command itself, but in the people and the soldiers, who now for more than four months had waited for the fall of the city, still obedient to many utterly incompetent captains, and still steadfast in their watchings on the hills. And Germanos's subtle brain, spinning threads out of itself like a spider, was busy to catch the army, while in the end the army, like some great blundering bee, burst unheeding through his palace of silk, and left him angrily hungry and in ruins.

The tales of slander went on, and another captain was detected in his infamous traffic with the besieged. It was certain also that provisions were being sold to the men within the walls, for one night a Turk was captured outside, and to save his life, confessed that the besieged were supplied at starvation rates with bread and fresh meat. Upon this second detection Petrobey gave notice that if another case occurred the offender would be shot, and the night sentries were doubled. But whether the treason was more wide-spread than they feared and the sentries were bribed, or whether the traitors were cunning enough to elude them, never came to light; but more evidence was found that the traffic still went on, and one day, at a meeting of the senate, Germanos rose and denounced the whole body of officers.

"The siege still drags on," he said, "and where are the preparations to bring it to a conclusion? In the name of patriotism, I ask, Where? To whose advantage is it that all these men are kept here from their homes and their work, when the grapes are already growing ripe for the gathering, and there is none to gather them, but only the birds? Is it the men who prefer to stop here in these kennels, roasted under the mid-day sun, and doing tedious hours of drill? Is it to the advantage of the primates that we remain here, while our churches stand empty and the tithes are remitted? Is it the most noble Prince Demetrius who detains the army on this inhospitable mountain? The reason is not far to seek. Who was it who was found trafficking with Abdul Achmet for the safety of the Turk and his harem, if not one of these captains? Who was it but another of his class who, last week only, was detected in the same treasonable business? Who is it now who is selling, as you all very well know, provisions to the besieged at rates which make a man soon rich? To whose advantage is it that we linger here, while within the town the Turk lives at ease and knows no lack, being sure no attack will be made, and only waiting till these infamous men are satisfied? The siege of Tripoli is this called? There has never been any such thing. This is the market-place of Tripoli—a busy, profitable market; and the men who bring their country produce for sale are none other than the captains of the army. In particular, there is one among them who might have brought the siege to an end six weeks before, had he wished. While the most noble prince—whose eyes I feel it my duty to open on this point—was, and is, with us, the captains have the excuse that his authority is over them, that without his consent they can do nothing. Very sedulous, no doubt, are their efforts to obtain his consent. Yet there is a speciousness about such an excuse, and we will leave it. But during the whole month of August Prince Demetrius was not with us, and Nicholas Vidalis was supreme here. I ask him, therefore, before you all, why, if he is an honest man, he did not attempt to take the town?"

Several times during this speech an angry murmur went up from the military section of the senate, but Nicholas more than once rose to his feet and quieted them with an uplifted hand. He himself listened attentively with a smile on his face, and when Germanos alluded to his honesty he laughed aloud. For ever since Mitsos had told him the story of his own part in the war, unsuspected by all, and only divulged when necessity drove—of his silent, boyish heroism, his uncalculating elimination of self—Nicholas had been privy to a secret shame at his own deeds, or rather his own words. To withstand the primates in so far as they injured the cause was well; but was it seemly to brawl, to throw ineffectual words about, to waste, as he called it, "good anger on an unprofitable thing"? What fruit had his angry gibes and sneers borne? Were the primates wagging their unamiable tongues less zealously? Were they not even speaking bitter truth when they said that nefarious traffic was going on between the captains of the army and the besieged? If the evil was to be checked, it must be checked another way, and not by sprinkling the scandal-mongers with insults. For a long time he had contemplated taking a certain step, and now that opportunity offered itself so fitly he took it with as light a heart as that which a tired man bears homeward. At the same time the openness of the accusation prompted an equal openness. Germanos should be answered once for all with his own frankness, and then for the highest trump card to take the honor-laden trick.

So Nicholas, still smiling courteously, asked permission from the prince, and in dead silence made his reply, speaking very quietly.

"We have open dealings at length from the archbishop," he said, "and though I have dealt very openly with him from the first, yet never before has he favored me thus. He has told us that no preparations are

216

being made for bringing the siege to a conclusion. That, with the permission of all present, I declare to be a deliberate lie. Ah, I must ask you to sit down," he said to Germanos, as the latter rose angrily to his feet. "You have had a fair hearing, and I claim and shall receive the same. A lie," he continued, "because I can tell him it is untrue; a deliberate lie, because there is no need for me to tell him. He was here throughout the month of August—a month to which he again alluded later—and he knows that during that month I was a tired and busy man, for I was drilling successive companies of men all day, and if he knew anything of military matters he would be well aware that it was my pleasure to see them improve considerably, so that now the greater part of them are efficient soldiers. He has told us that it is not to the advantage of the soldiers to remain here, and that was in a sense true, though not wholly; for if it is to the advantage of these men that Greece becomes a free country—and it is their duty to help in securing its freedom—it is to their advantage that they remain here, for here they can acquire that knowledge which will enable them to fight successfully. He went on to tell us that it was not to the advantage of the primates to remain here. Then why, in the name of God, do they do so? for it is not to the advantage of the soldiers that they cause divisions and dissensions among us. Let them go home and gather in the tithes their hearts desire. No one, not even I, will try to stop them. Yet they do not go, and we must suppose it is for some one's advantage that they stop. Can it be that some of them have an idea of getting possession of even a considerable part of the booty we shall take? Can it be that one of them— yes, no other than the archbishop—came here in the name of his Master and asked certain men—no other than Petrobey and myself—for half the spoils which would be taken, giving half to the national treasury, and to the men—the soldiers who had fought and bled for it—the rest? Those spoils were to be devoted to the glory of God, and who but His priests, the primates and bishops, were to be trustees? And on that chance of getting, not half the spoils, but still enough to make it worth while to wait, we shall find the reason of their stopping here."

Nicholas looked across at Germanos, who sat white and shaking with anger, and for a moment his passion flamed up.

"Sit there and hate me!" he cried, "for that will not harm me! If your motives were honest, why should I not tell them? and, if not, there is more cause for them to be known."

Germanos suddenly started up.

"It is an infamous slander!" he exclaimed; but Petrobey, without moving from his seat, turned to the prince, speaking loud enough to be heard by all.

"What my cousin has said is perfectly true," he remarked. "I was present myself."

"Please to sit down, archbishop," said the prince. "Nicholas Vidalis is speaking to us."

"This man has told us," continued Nicholas, "that an infamous traffic is going on between the Turks and the captains of this army. We all know, unhappily, that there is some truth in that. Two months ago, when this assertion was as yet false, he was saying the same thing, and he and others busied themselves in spreading reports that it was so. Was that the part of an honorable man—to spread those infamous lies about us, to slander and defame us to our troops? Is not the motive as clear as the noonday? By sowing discord and dissension and mistrust in our ranks he hoped to see his grand scheme realized, to have the army flocking to him, pouring in gold and treasure for the glory of God into the hands of his trustees. No great success has attended these efforts, and when Prince Demetrius left the camp I do not know that the primates found themselves very popular men. Finally, an attack has been made on me personally. You have been told that at any time during the month of August I might have stormed the town if I had wished. That is a black falsehood, though perhaps not deliberate, since the archbishop knows nothing of military affairs. For, in the first place, my hands were full—it was necessary to bring a mere disorderly rabble to military efficiency, and that, to the best of my power, I did; and, in the second place, though I was in command of these troops, I had agreed with my superior in command not to make any attempt while the army was weakened by the withdrawal of the Mainat division, who were at Monemvasia. I appeal to him to know whether this is or is not true."

"It is true," said Petrobey.

"As to my having profited by these delays," continued Nicholas, "you have only my word against the word of another; but if the archbishop has any evidence to bring on that point, I should be glad to hear it. I wait for his reply."

There was a dead silence. Germanos sat voiceless, with his eyes on the floor.

"If he is thinking over the evidence in his mind," said Nicholas, "fitting it together as a witness and an accuser should, let him say so, and I will wait."

Still there was silence, and Germanos, still proud and full of hate, sat there without speech.

"So it is even as I told you," said Nicholas; "and these are malicious and lying words he has spoken against me. I am a man easily provoked, and, to my shame I speak it, one to whom forgiveness is a hard matter; but that, or so I think it, is a thing for which I ask pardon, not of man, but of God. Here, in this assembly, I have been accused of the blackest offences; but the accusation was blacker still, for it was the fruit of malice and falsehood. This is no matter for words of regret from one or of pardon from the other, for there is in my heart no pardon, and in his, I am very sure, no regret. Yet can I rid myself of the need of either? My heart is sick of intrigue and dissension, accusation and slander answering accusation, and I will have no more of them. As I stand in the presence of God I have only one thought, and that is the freedom of my country, and I do not serve it by spending my time throwing words at men whose salt I would not eat. It is not so very long since another said his voice would be heard no more here, yet since then it has not been silent. To-day those words are mine; but, before I go, one word. For the love of God, if any who sit here suspect me of

218

treachery, treason, or any of those things of which I have been accused, as he hopes to be forgiven at the last day, let him stand out and say so."

Once again there was a dead silence, and Nicholas's face brightened, for the silence was sweet to him.

"So be it," he said, at length. "I go hence untouched by slander."

Then unbuckling his sword, he laid it on the table in front of the prince.

"My seat in the senate, sir, I resign," he said; "my commission as an officer I resign also. By birth I am a Mainat, and with your highness's permission I wish to be enrolled among the private soldiers of the corps."

Then turning to Petrobey:

"Old friend," he said, "once more we are together in the clan."

And with a step as light as a boy's, and a heart springing upward like a lark, rid at last of the burden of personal ambition, he left the room and went straight to where the corps were quartered.

Nicholas found Mitsos and Yanni sitting on the wall of the camp near the Mainat quarters, lecturing a small audience on the use and abuse of fire-ships, for another attempt had been made on a vessel of the cruising Turkish squadron, with the result of first half-roasting its navigator and then completely drowning him; but the men seeing an officer approach got up and saluted.

Nicholas, still with a singing heart, told them to be seated, and, lighting a pipe, drew in the smoke in long, contented breaths.

"This is the first tobacco I have enjoyed since we came here," he said, "for tobacco is tasted by the heart. Never again, lads, need you jump up when I come, for I am no longer an officer, but just a private like yourselves."

Mitsos stared aghast.

"Uncle Nicholas, what do you mean?" he gasped, wrinkling his eyebrows. "Is this Germanos's doing?"

"Not so, little Mitsos, for neither Germanos nor another could do that, but only myself. I have resigned my place in the senate, I have resigned my commission, and all that is left of me is plain Nicholas; but a man as happy as a king, instead of a bundle of malice and a bag of bad words which squirted out like new must. Eh, but I am happy, and it is God's own morning."

And he puffed out a great cloud of smoke and laughed out a great mouthful of laughter.

"But what has happened?" cried Mitsos, still feeling that the world was upsidedown.

"This has happened, little one," said Nicholas; "that a foul-tempered man has made up his mind to be foul tempered no more, and as the thing was an impossibility when he had to sit cocked up on a chair opposite the proud primates, why he has been sensible enough to refuse to sit there any longer. And as he was tired of tripping up on his fine tin sword, he has given it back to the fine tin prince. And may that man never do anything which he regrets less. Ah! here come my superior officers. There will be talking to do, but little of it will I lay my tongue to."

219

And he sprang up and saluted Petrobey.

Petrobey came up, quickly followed by two or three of the other officers, among whom was the prince, smiling at Nicholas through his annoyance, as the man stood at attention comely and erect.

"Drop that nonsense, dear cousin," he said, "and come to my tent for a talk. Look, we have all come to fetch you."

Nicholas looked at him radiantly.

"I have had a set of good minutes since I left you," he said. "Say your say, cousin, but little talking will I do."

The prince came forward with a fine, courteous air.

"We have come," he said, "to beg you to reconsider this step. I fancy you will find no more insults awaiting you in the senate."

"Your highness," he said, "I can look back on my life and say I have done one wise thing in it, and that this morning. And if, as you say, there are no insults awaiting me in the senate, that confirms my belief in its wisdom."

"But this is absurd, Nicholas," remonstrated Petrobey, "and all the primates, even Germanos himself, regret what you have done."

Nicholas laughed.

"That is a sweet word to me," he said, "and you know it. But I am no child to be coaxed with sugar."

"But think of us—we want your help. You have more weight with the men than any of us!"

"I shall not fail you," said Nicholas, "and if I do my duty in the ranks as well as I hope, I think I shall be more useful there than anywhere else."

"But your career, now on the point of being crowned," said Petrobey, eagerly. "The prince has promised—"

But Nicholas waved his hand impatiently.

"I have just got rid of my career," he said, "and I feel like a tired horse when a stout rider dismounts and loosens the girth. Do not attempt to saddle me again. Ah, dear cousin," he went on, suddenly with affection and more gravity, "even you know me not at all if you speak like that. Believe me, I care only for one thing in this world, and that is the object for which we have labored together so long. That cause I serve best here, and for these months I have been puffing myself up to think that fine, angry words were of no avail. But I will try them no longer; I am sick of anger, and my belly moves, whether I will or not, when I sit there and have to listen—you know to what. Leave me in peace. It is better so."

He glanced across at Mitsos a moment, who was standing by.

"I wish to speak to you alone, cousin," he said to Petrobey, "but that will wait. Meantime, I thank you for all your friendliness to me, and I decline entirely to listen to you. The thing is finished."

Petrobey saw that, for the present at least, it was no manner of use trying to persuade him, and left him for a time; and Nicholas, remarking that it was time for rations, and that these officers were horribly unpunctual, took Mitsos by the arm and led him off to the canteen, telling him on the way what had happened.

Mitsos was furiously indignant with Germanos, and vowed that the camp should ring with the hissing of his name, but Nicholas stopped him.

"I neither forgive nor forget," he said, "but it is mere waste of time and temper to curse. The harm is done, leave the vermin alone; oh, they have bitten me sorely, I don't deny that, but if we are going scavenging, as I pray God we may, let us begin in our own house. There are purging and washing to be done among the men, I fear, little Mitsos. And from this day, if there is any traffic or dishonorable barter among the corps of the clan, have me out and shoot me, for I make it my business that there shall be none. Now we will go and get our rations. I ordered supplies of fresh beef for the men yesterday; that was a good act to finish up with, and see already I reap the fruits of it."

Nicholas remained perfectly firm, and Petrobey eventually desisted from his attempt to persuade him to take up his commission again, for he might as well have tried to lever the sun out of its orbit. But he still continued to ask Nicholas's advice about the affairs of the army, which the latter could not very well withhold. Among the men, and especially among the Mainats, he underwent a sort of upsidedown apotheosis. Germanos had made villanous accusations; here was a fine answer. As for that proud man himself, he found his position was no longer tenable. So far from being able to profit by Nicholas's action, he discovered, though too late, that he had overreached himself in making so preposterous a statement about his enemy, and the army buzzed away through his fine woven web, leaving it dangling in the wind. He saw that his chance of power was over, and, accepting the inevitable, took his departure for Kalavryta, where he hoped his authority remained intact. But, alas! for the triumphal reception by the united army—alas! too, for his chance of the Patriarchate. His name, which he had prospectively throned in the hearts of myriads, was flotsam on the tide of their righteous anger against him, thrown up on the beach, tossed to and fro once or twice, and then left. His followers, the primates and bishops, less wise than he, still stayed on, hoping against hope that the popular favor would set their way. But the evil he and his had done lived after them; nothing now could undo the distrust and suspicion they had caused, for their first malignant slander had found fulfilment, and the army distrusted its officers, while the officers were not certain of their men. Nicholas had cleared himself, leaping with a shout of triumph free from the web spun round him; others had not the manliness to do the same, to challenge the evidence, for they knew there was evidence.

Nicholas found opportunity to tell Petrobey about Mitsos' love affairs, but a few days afterwards news came to the camp that a landing of the Turks from their western squadron was expected on the Gulf of Corinth, near Vostitza, and the prince, with some acuteness, found in this rumor sufficient reason to make his presence there desirable. Petrobey, wishing to have a speedy and reliable messenger who could communicate with the camp in the event taking place, sent Mitsos off with him, and before the end of the third week in September the prince took his departure in some haste, hoping to regain in fresh fields the loss of prestige he had suffered here and at Monemvasia. The news, if confirmed, was serious, for it meant that the Turkish squadron had evaded the Greek fleet and threatened the Morea from the north, while, if once a landing was effected, the Turks would, without doubt, march straight to the relief of

221

Tripoli just when its need was sorest. The prince left the camp with much state and dignity, but with nothing else, and Mitsos, to whom he had given a place on his staff as aide-de-camp extraordinary to the Viceroy of Greece, with the rank of lieutenant in the Hellenic army, pranced gayly along on a fine-stepping horse, and for the first time fully sympathized with Nicholas's resignation. They travelled by short marches, "like women," as Mitsos described it afterwards, and one night the aide-de-camp extraordinary, having occasion to bring a message to his master, woke him out of his sleep, and saw the commander-in-chief in a night-cap, which left a deep, bilious impression on his barbarian mind wholly out of proportion to so innocuous a discovery.

For a time, at least, in Tripoli there was no more intriguing between the besiegers and the besieged, for Petrobey redoubled his vigilance, and every night sent down a corps of trustworthy men to lie in wait round the town. Meantime he knew a strong band of cavalry and a large force of Albanian mercenaries were within the town, and in the citadel was enough artillery to be formidable; so that while there was a chance of capitulation, provided the rumor of the expected landing of troops on the Gulf of Corinth continued unconfirmed, he was unwilling to make an assault on the town. But it began to be known that the fall of Tripoli was inevitable, and from all over the country the peasants flocked together on the hills waiting for the end and a share in the booty. It was in vain that Petrobey tried to drive them back; as soon as he had cleared one range of hills they swarmed upon another like sparrows in the vines, springing as it seemed from the ground, or as vultures grow in the air before a battle. Some came armed with guns, requesting to be enrolled in the various corps; others with sickles or reaping-hooks, or just with a knife or a stick. Every evening on the hills round shone out the fires of this unorganized rabble, gathering thicker and thicker as the days went on.

Then, on the 24th of September, a refugee from the town was captured and brought to the camp, and being promised his life if he gave intelligence of what was going on inside, told them that famine had begun; that many of the horses of the cavalry corps had been killed for meat, and that unless help came the end was but a matter of hours. Once again Petrobey consulted Nicholas, who advised an assault at once; but the other argued that as long as no news came of the reinforcements from the north the case of the town was hopeless, and as it was for the Greeks to demand terms, they might as well wait for a proposal to come. Nicholas disagreed; there had been treachery before in the camp; there might be treachery now. Let them, at any rate, minimize the disgrace to the nation. Petrobey in part yielded, and consented to do as Nicholas advised if no proposals were made in three days. In the mean time, since there was no longer any fear of the cavalry, they would move down closer onto the plain and directly below the walls. Then, if fire was opened on them from the citadel, they would storm it out of hand; but if not—and he had suspected for a long time that the guns were not all serviceable—they would wait for three days, unless Mitsos came back saying that reinforcements were on the way from the north.

222

CHAPTER X

THE FALL OF TRIPOLI

The order to break up camp was received with shouts of acclamation, and all day long on the 25th the processions of mules passed, like ants on a home run, up and down the steep, narrow path from the plain. The Mainat corps were the first to move, and took up their place opposite the southern wall, and worked there under the sun for a couple of hours or more throwing up some sort of earth embankment; while in the space behind marked out for their lines went up the rows of their barracks, pole by pole, and gradually roofed in with osier and oleander boughs. On the walls of the town lounged Turkish men, and now and then a woman passed, closely veiled, but casting curious glances at the advancing troops not four hundred yards from the gate. The men worked like horses to get their intrenchments and defences up, and by the time each corps had done its work, the huts behind were finished; and, streaming with perspiration, the men were glad to throw themselves down in the shade. As there was no regular corps of sappers and engineers, each regiment had to do its intrenching and defence work for itself, and they worked on late into the night before the transfer of the entire camp was effected. Meantime Petrobey had ordered the posts on the hills to the east to close in, and by noon on the 27th he saw his long-delayed dream realized, for on all sides of the town ran the Greek lines. Still, from inside the beleaguered place came no sign of resistance, attack, or capitulation; but towards sunset a white flag was hoisted on the tower above the south gate, and a few moments afterwards Mehemet Salik, attended by his staff, came out, and were met by Petrobey. Yanni, as aide-de-camp, was in attendance on his father, and he had the pleasure of meeting his old host again.

Mehemet followed Petrobey to his quarters, Yanni looking at him as a cat in the act to spring looks at a bird. He was a short-legged, stout man, appearing tall when he was sitting, but when he stood, heavy and badly proportioned. He had grown a little thinner, or so thought Yanni, and the skin hung bagging below his eyes, though he was still hardly more than thirty. He looked Yanni over from head to foot without speaking, adjusted his green turban, and then, shrugging his shoulders slightly, took a seat and turned to Petrobey.

"I have been sent to ask the terms on which you will grant a capitulation," he said; "please consider and name them."

"I will do so," replied Petrobey, "and let you have them by midnight."

Mehemet glanced at his watch.

"Thank you; we shall expect them then."

He rose from his seat and again looked at Yanni, who was standing by the door. The two presented a very striking contrast—the one pale, flabby, clay-colored, slow-moving; the other, though there were not ten years between them, fresh, brown, and alert. Mehemet continued looking at him for a moment below his drooping eyelids without speaking, and then the corners of his sensual mouth straightened themselves into a smile. He held out his hand to the boy.

"So we meet again, my guest," he said; "your leave-taking was somewhat abrupt. Will you shake hands?"

Yanni bristled like a collie dog, and looked sideways at him without speaking, but kept his hands stiff to his side.

"You vanished unexpectedly, just when I hoped to begin to know you better," continued Mehemet.

But Petrobey interfered sternly.

"You are not here, sir, to confer insults," he said.

Mehemet turned round slowly towards him with a face of sallow death.

"Surely my teeth are drawn, as far as the boy is concerned," he said; "but let me know one thing," he continued, "for I have a heavy wager about it. Did you bribe the porter, or did you get through the roof?"

"Through the roof," said Yanni, as stiff as a poker.

"I have lost. I said you bribed the porter. He shall come out of prison to-night and have poultices, for he was much beaten. Good-evening, gentlemen."

Yanni turned to Petrobey with blazing eyes.

"Cannot I kick him now?" he whispered.

"How can I give you permission?" said Petrobey.

Yanni looked at him a moment and then his lips parted in a smile, and he went out of the tent.

Mehemet was a few yards down the path, going towards the gate of the camp where his staff was waiting, and in three strides Yanni caught up with him.

"Oh, man!" he said, and no more; but next moment Yanni's foot was deep in the folds of his excellency's baggy trousers. His excellency was lifted slightly forward from behind, and picked himself up with a cry of lamentation, for the pain had been exquisite. Yanni was by him with a brilliant smile on his face.

"You insulted me under the flag of truce," he said, kindly, "and under the flag of truce I have answered you. There is quits." And he turned and went back to his father.

Petrobey appeared to be absorbed in writing, and he did not look up, but handed Yanni a paper.

"Go at once to the captains whose names I have written here, Yanni," he said, "and tell them to come immediately to consult about the terms of capitulation. I thought," he added, "that I heard a slight disturbance outside. Can you account for it?"

"It seemed to be the settlement of some private difference, sir," said Yanni. "It is all over."

"Is the difference settled?"

"There is a very sore man," said Yanni.

The conference among the captains lasted only a short time, and in a couple of hours the terms were despatched to Mehemet. The Turks were to give up their arms and were to be allowed, or rather compelled, to leave the Morea. They were further to pay the indemnity of forty million piastres, that being approximately the cost of the war, including the provisions and pay of all the men, from the time of its outbreak. In less than an hour the answer came back. The demand was preposterous, for it was impossible to collect the money, but in return they made a counter-proposition. They would give up the whole of their property within the town, renounce all rights of land, retaining only sufficient means to enable them to reach some port on the Asia Minor coast, but demanding leave to retain their arms in order to secure themselves from massacre on the way to Nauplia. They also insisted on occupying the pass over Mount Parthenius, between the Argive plain and Tripoli, until the women and children had been embarked in safety. This precaution, they added, was due to themselves, for they had no guarantee that without their arms the Greeks would not violate the terms of the capitulation as they had violated them at Navarin.

The Greek chiefs refused to consider the proposal, for if the Turks distrusted them, they at least had no reason to trust the Turks; and if the regiments in the town occupied Parthenius, what was to hinder them from marching on to Nauplia and remaining there? Nauplia still held communication with the sea, and they had not spent six months in reducing Tripoli only at the end to let the besieged go out in peace to another and better-equipped fortress.

Once more affairs were at a deadlock, and at this point Petrobey made an inexcusable mistake. He ought, without doubt, to have stormed the place and have done with it; but when, in a moment of weakness, he put the proposal to the captains, the majority of them were for waiting. The reason was unhappily but too plain. They knew that famine prevailed in the town, they knew, too, that its capitulation was inevitable, but they saw for themselves a rich harvest gained in a few days by secretly supplying the besieged with provisions, and for the next week Germanos's bitter words were terribly true. This was no siege of Tripoli; it was the market of Tripoli.

On the 28th came another proposal from the town, this time not from the Turks, but from the Albanian mercenaries who had formed the attack on the post at Valtetzi in May. They were fifteen hundred strong, and good soldiers, but as mercenaries they had no feelings of obligation or honor to their employers, and did not in the least desire a fierce engagement with the Greeks; and now that all idea of capitulation was over, for neither side would accept the ultimatum of the other, it was clearly to their advantage to get away, if they could, with their lives and their pay. The town would, without doubt, fall by storm, their employers would be massacred, and their best chance was to stand well with the besiegers. They, therefore, offered to go back to Albania, and never again to enlist in the Turkish service, provided they might retire with their arms. The Greeks, on their side, had no quarrel with them; many were related to them by ties of friendship and blood; they had no desire to gain a bloody and hard-won victory if there was a chance of detaching the mainstay of their foes, and they agreed to their terms.

The weather was hot and stifling beyond description, and the Mainats who were on the south felt all day the reflected glare and heat from the walls as from a furnace. In that week of waiting Petrobey lost all the confidence of the clan, for they alone were blameless of this outrageous traffic, that had sprung up again, and they were waiting while Petrobey let it go on. He had asked the advice of men who were without principle or honor, who were filling their pockets at the expense of the honor of others, and though he himself was without stain, yet his weakness at this point was criminal. It seemed that he refused to believe what the army knew, and persisted in judging the whole by the behavior of the clan themselves. Nicholas appealed to him in vain, but Petrobey always asked whether he had himself seen evidence of the scandal, and being in the Mainat corps, he had not. In vain Nicholas pointed out that a week ago they knew that famine was preying on the besieged, yet a week had gone and the famine seemed to have made no impression. How was it possible that the town could hold out unless it was being supplied? And how could a commander know what was going on among the hordes of peasants who flocked to the camp? Now that the evil was so wide-spread and universal, a whole regiment perhaps profited by the traffic; and where was the use of any man informing his captain?—for the captains were the worst of all.

Meantime, inside, Suleima watched at her latticed window and looked for Mitsos. A week ago she had watched the men streaming down from Trikorpha to the plain, and had hardly been able to conceal her joy, while round her the other women wailed and lamented, saying that they would all fall into the hands of the barbarous folk. On the other side, away from the wall, the windows of the harem looked out onto a narrow, top-heavy street, the eaves of the houses nearly meeting across it, and on the top again was a large, flat roof, where they often went to sit in the evening and chatter across the street to the women on the house opposite. By day a ribbon of scorching sunlight moved slowly from one side to the other, and often Suleima would sit at the window which overhung the foot-path, watching and watching, but seeing, perhaps, hardly a couple of passengers in as many hours, for this was only a side street where few came. By leaning out she could just catch a glimpse of a main thoroughfare which led into the square, but only Turks passed up and down. The others looked at her with wonder and pity, thinking her hardly in her right mind to be smiling and happy at such a time, for close before her lay the trial and triumph of her sex, and the Greeks were at the door. The harem generally, and also the chief wife, whose slave she was, knew her condition, but from a feeling partly of pity and affection—for she was a favorite with all—partly from indifference, had not accused her to Abdul. Abdul himself, in the excitement and preoccupation of the siege, had not been in the harem more than twice in as many months, and thus her state had escaped detection.

So she went about with her day-dream and snatches of song, painting in her mind a hundred pictures as to how Mitsos would come. Should she see him stalking up the narrow street, then looking up and smiling at her, bringing the news that the town had capitulated and he had come to claim her? There would be a step on the stair and he would come in, bending to get through the door; and then, oh, the blessedness of talk and tears that would be hers! Or would there come a shout and the sound of riot and confusion, and streaming up the street a fighting crowd? He would be there in the middle of it all, slashing and hewing his way to her. He would look up—that he would always do—and see her at the window, and then get to work again, dealing death to all within reach. Perhaps he would be hurt, not much hurt, but enough to make her lean over him with anxious face and nimble, bandaging hands, and the joy of ministering to him leaping in her heart. It was towards this vision that she most inclined, to Mitsos, fighting and splendid as fresh from the dust and the ecstasy of struggle, coming to her—the mistress and lady of his arm—lover to lover. Or would he come by night silently beneath the stars, as he had come before, or with a whispered song which her heart had taught her ears to know, and take her away while the house slept, out of this horrible town, and to some place like in spirit to the lonely sea-scented beach near Nauplia, into remoteness from all things else? In these half-formulated dreams there was never any hitch or disturbance—doors yielded, men slept, or men fell, and through all like a ray of light came Mitsos, unhindered, irresistible.

But after three or four days her mood changed, and from her eyes looked out the soul of some timid, frightened animal. Why did he not come—by night or in peace or in the shout of war? What meant this sudden increase in their food, for now for more than a week they had lived but on sparing rations? Yet the fresh meat and new bread revolted her; she was hungry, yet she could not eat. The women were kind to her, and Zuleika used to make her soup and force her with firm kindness to drink it; they were always plaguing her, so she thought, not to prowl about so much, to rest more and to eat more, and when she understood why, she obeyed them. For a few nights before she had slept but lightly, and her sleep was peopled with vivid things—now she would be moving in a crowd of flying fiery globes, she one of them; now the dark was full of gray shapes that glided by her windily with a roar of the remote sea, but at the end they would disperse and leave her alone, and out of the darkness came Mitsos, and with that she would dream no more. But waking and the hours of the day changed place with the night, and it seemed that she moved in a nightmare until she slept again.

But when she understood the reason for which they pressed her to rest and eat, she quickly regained the serenity of her health, and during the last two days of waiting, though her fears and anxieties crouched in the shade ready to spring on her again, they lay still, and the claws and teeth spared her.

But one morning—it was the 3d of October—there was suddenly a tumult in the streets, and cries that the Greeks had come in, and Suleima went up to the house-top to see if she could find out where they were entering, prepared to run out into the street to meet them, crying to them as her deliverers, as Mitsos had told her. In the brightness of that sudden hope that the end had come, she felt no longer weary or ill, and she looked out over the town with expectant eyes. But by degrees the tumult died down again, and, bitterly disappointed, she crept back to the room of the harem where the women were sitting to ask what this meant. None knew, but in a little time they heard a renewed noise from the street, and running to look out, they saw a small body of Turkish soldiers advancing, and in the middle a very stout lady riding a horse. Behind her came two servants driving horses with big panniers slung on each side, and the stout lady talked in an animated manner to the soldiers, pointing now to one house and then to another. Then looking up at the window of Abdul Achmet's house, out of which Suleima was leaning, she shouted some shrill question in Turkish, which Suleima did not catch, and the procession turned up into the main street, seeming to halt opposite the door leading into the front court-yard.

In a little while Abdul Achmet, with a eunuch, came in, at whose entrance Suleima drew back behind the other women and wrapped her bernouse round her. He wore a face of woe, and behind they could hear the voice of the stout lady, who found the stairs a little trying. She entered the room with a shining, smiling face, and sat down puffing on a sofa.

"And when I've got my breath again," she said, volubly, as if still in the middle of a sentence, "I'll tell you who I am, and what I am going to do, and what you are going to do. A hot morning it is, and there's no denying it, and though I've seen many pretty faces in my day, sir, I can't remember that I ever set eyes on anything so nice as your little lot. And what may your name be, my dear?" she said, turning to Suleima, who shrank from her without knowing why; "but whatever your name is, it was a fine day for your kind master when he first set eyes on you."

She looked at Suleima more closely, and waiting till Achmet and the eunuch had left the room: "Poor lamb! and so young, too," she said, kindly enough; "and now I've got my breath a bit, I'll tell you my business. I'm a Greek by birth, though you can hear I talk Turkish like the Sultan himself, and as for my name, why, it's Penelope."

Suleima suddenly burst into a helpless fit of laughter at this funny old woman, though she was not funny at all, she thought, but simply a fat, disgusting old hag. Penelope stopped short at this unseemly interruption, and for a moment seemed disposed to resent it; but some womanly feeling came to her aid, and she pulled a great bottle of some strong-smelling stuff out of her pocket and applied it to Suleima's nose as she sat rocking herself backward and forward with peals of laughter.

"She'll faint if she laughs like that," she explained, "and this will pull her together a bit. Get some brandy, one of you, quickly. There, there, my dear," she went on to Suleima, "be quiet now, be quiet, it's all right, and take a spoonful of this, it'll do you good."

Suleima gradually recovered herself through a spasm of coughing and choking, and the brandy brought her round.

"I am sorry for laughing," she said, no longer shrinking from the woman; and speaking low to her, in Greek, "but I am not very well. And, oh, tell me, you look kind; have you seen Mitsos? Where is he? Why does he not come?"

Penelope started in surprise.

"My poor little one," she answered, in Greek, "what does this mean? But wait a minute."

Then, speaking in Turkish again:

"I thought I'd seen her before," she explained aloud, "and she says she comes from Spetzas, which is my home. And what I've come for is this, and I'm here to help all you women. You will give up to me all your money and jewels, my pretties, for the Greek commander, who is a relation of mine"—this was not the case—"wishes neither to hurt nor harm you; but if you are found, any of you, with jewels or money about you, why, it may be the siege of Navarin over again. So now I shall wait here, and each of you will fetch all you have; and to make things sure and certain, I'll just search you as well. This girl," and she pointed to Suleima, "shall come to me first; so get you all gone, and I'll call you in one at a time."

They all dispersed to their rooms to get their trinkets and money, and in a few moments Suleima came back, and the other closed the door quickly behind her.

"You are a Greek, child," she said. "Yes, put your bits of finery in my basket; we have not much time."

She heard Suleima's story with many raisings of the hand and exclamations of wonder, and when she had finished she kissed her, like a true woman, with pity and affection.

"Poor child, poor child!" she soothed her, "I will do the best I can. God knows what will happen when the end comes, for the camp is like a pack of wolves. This Mitsos of yours has some glimmerings of sense, but look at the risk you run if you do as he tells you. Fancy running to meet a lot of wolves, you in your Turkish dress, crying you are a wolf too. Ah, dear me, dear me, and the child and all! But this is my idea: separate yourself at all costs from the other women. If they stay in the house, run; if they run, stay here. Do not be seen with them; unveil your face, as the Greek women do, and if possible avoid a mob of Greeks. If you have to go into the street keep in a side street, where perhaps stragglers only will come. And the Lord be with you, poor child!"

Suleima clung to this woman—usually coarse and greedy, but one who had the springs of true womanliness in her—as to a rock of refuge, and without searching her, but kissing her again affectionately, she waited till the girl's tears had subsided before opening the door and calling in the next woman. In turn they all passed before her and gave up their valuables. There was but little money, for the women spent it for the most part on finery, and poured into Penelope's basket turquoise collars, fine filagree work from the bazaars, bracelets set with pearls or moonstones, and ear-rings of all sorts. The search was hastily done, for she had many houses to visit, and with a curious mixture of humanity and greed she wished to make as rich a harvest as possible—since she received a share of what she got—and at the same time do all she could for these poor caged women. And so for two days, as there were many houses to go to and much to be got, sometimes with difficulty—for some of the women would have preferred to run the risk of having valuables concealed about them—she

229

went on her rounds of greedy mercy, and it was not till the morning of the 5th of October that she went out again to the camp.

During those two days matters outside had gone from bad to worse. Anagnostes had been detected trafficking with the besieged, and when Nicholas laid the proof of his guilt before Petrobey, he buried his face in his hands and said he could do nothing. That hour of weakness, when he had consulted men who he knew would only give him selfish and dishonorable counsel, had broken his authority like a reed. Anagnostes's corps shared his guilt, probably down to the youngest man in his service, and if he punished one he would have to punish hundreds.

"And, oh, Nicholas," said Petrobey, in piteous appeal, "if ever you have loved me, or can still remember that we are of one blood, help me now, by what way you will. I was ever honorable, but I have been as weak as water; your strength and your honor are both unshaken."

This was on the morning of the 5th; and before Nicholas could reply, a shrill, rather breathless, voice bawled to Petrobey from outside, and Penelope demanded admittance. It was not her way to ask twice, and she followed her demand up by putting her red face through the tent-flap, and, entering herself, bade her servants, laden with jewels, also to enter.

Petrobey turned one last look at Nicholas.

"You will help me?" he said.

"I was always ready," said Nicholas, smiling, and he went lightly out of the tent.

Some fine wrangling was going on in the Mainats' quarters when he appeared, and two men appealed to him.

"Is it true that the woman has taken all the spoils to Petrobey's tent?" asked one.

Nicholas dived at the meaning of the question.

"His honor is untouched," he said; "they are there only for safe keeping; I swear it, and will go bail for my life on it."

Then to himself: "The time has come," he thought, "when even he is not spared."

"Look you, lads," he said, aloud, "to-day Tripoli falls. When it has come to this, that you can suspect him, it is time. We make the attempt— we Mainats, who were ever the first at great deeds. Come, summon the men. Yes, I have the authority—more than that, I have promised to help, and there is only one way."

In five minutes the word had gone about, and the corps, some five hundred strong, flocked eagerly to hear Nicholas. He went with the captains into the officers' tent, and, forgetful of his rank among men who had always treated him as the king of men, bade them sit down.

"In ten minutes," he said, "the corps must stand under arms, and a moment's delay after that may spoil everything. I lead the way, and we go at a double's double straight to the Argos tower. At that corner a man can climb the wall, for there are rough, projecting stones. How do I know that? Because I climbed it last night when I was on sentry duty. So much for the vigilance of those moles and bats who are stationed there. With me I shall have a rope, which I shall fasten to the battlements, and then, in God's name, follow like the bridegroom to the bride-chamber. The man behind me carries the Greek flag, which he hands me as soon as I am up. Ah, my friends, grant me that one sweet moment. Yet—no, we will vote for the man who shall do that."

A deep murmur—"You, you, Nicholas, Nicholas"—ran round, and so another moment of happiness, so great that it was content, was given him.

"And now up with you," said Nicholas. "Ah, let us shake hands first. O merciful God, but Thou art very good to me!"

The attempt was so daring, so utterly unexpected, that the Arcadian corps stationed opposite the Argos tower merely stood in amazement, as with a clatter and a rush the Mainats streamed by them and up the wall in front. Agile as a cat, for all his sixty years, Nicholas laid hand and foot on the rough masonry, and the next moment he had dashed down the single sentry on the tower, who was smoking and talking to a woman on the wall. Then fastening the rope to one of the battlements he turned again to perform the crowning act of his adventurous life, and, before two men had swarmed up, the Greek flag waved from the tower.

CHAPTER XI

FATHER AND DAUGHTER

Nicholas waited there for perhaps a minute, while the Mainats swarmed up and formed in lines on the broad-terraced wall. He had mounted to the zenith of his life, the glorious visionary noon of his hopes was his, the work of years crowned, and the foul disgrace of the week of waiting over. When forty men or so had joined him he bade them follow, and, falling on the guards at the gate, forced his way through, and with his own hand drew back the bolts and flung it open. The Arcadian corps opposite had seen the flag wave on the tower and poured in, sweeping the Mainats along with them up the main street of the lower town.

A pack of wolves Penelope had called them—aye, and the wolves were hungry. Six months' waiting in inaction, all trust in their captains gone, and the treacherous marketing of the captains gone likewise! The soldiers knew that for days past promises of protection had flowed in on the besieged, and signed papers promising to pay king's ransoms had come out; but there was little chance now of these ransoms going where they were promised. The soldiers would have a hand in that promised gold, it was their hour now; the captains might flourish their infamous paper bargains; let them, if they could, protect their pashas, and let them collect their rewards from those who spoiled the palaces.

There was such order in the ranks as the water of a river in flood observes when it has broken its banks; among the besieged such resistance as sticks and straws show when the torrent catches them. Close on the heels of the regular troops fighting to gain an entrance came the mob of peasants, the scavengers of the siege, who had come for the pickings. The troops thrust them back till they had themselves got in; some were ground against the walls, some thrown under foot in the narrow gateways and trodden by the heels of the advancing columns. Once inside, each man went where he willed or where the stream of men bore him, most of them making for the large houses stood round the square, where the richest booty was expected. Close above stood the citadel, with empty-mouthed guns pointing this way and that, but silent, and if those months had been roaring with an iron death none would have regarded. Petrobey, who had joined the Mainats, wondered at this; the Turks, he thought, might at least sell their lives as dear as they could, but the reason was not known till three days later, when the citadel fell. All thoughts of discipline or order were out of the question; he was jostled along with the others; he was one among many, and all were equal, and each was a wild animal.

The attack had been utterly unexpected by the besieged, and on the north side of the town provisions were being conveyed over the walls even while at the Argos gate the flag of Greece was flying. The hoarse roar of crowds came to the servants of Mehemet Salik as they were returning to the house with meat and bread. There was no mistaking that sound, and they dropped whatever they had and fled home for refuge, only to find the women of the harem and the other servants streaming out to seek escape. The long-delayed day had come, the stronghold and centre of the Turkish power was in the hands of those who had been slaves so long, and each link of the chains that had held them was broken by another and another Turk stabbed, shot, or trampled to death. The Mainat corps gained the square first and cut into the mob escaping from Mehemet's house, and a lane of blood and bodies marked their march. Mehemet and a few soldiers had barricaded themselves in an upper story and fired a few shots at the men at the rear of the column, who pressed forward unable to get in; but in ten seconds the foremost men had passed up the stairs, broken through the barricaded doors, and were on them. As was their wont, they fought in silence, and for the most part with knives only, and inside the room only the trampling of feet, short gasps, and a sharp cry or two were heard against that long hoarse roar outside. Yanni, who was among the first, forced his way to where Mehemet was standing, still pale and unconcerned, defending himself desperately, and as if introducing himself:

"He who was to serve in your harem!" he cried, and stabbed him to the heart.

Here and there in the streets a group of Turks collected, but the wave of men passed over them, leaving naught but wreckage behind, and others ran up to the citadel gates, where they beat on the door demanding admittance. But before the gates could be opened the Mainats, who had finished their work at Mehemet's, were on them, as they stood close pressed, men and women together, in a living wall. For an hour that piece of shambles-work lasted; they met resistance, for the Turks were not lacking in courage, and when it was over, and the living wall was only a tumbled pile of death, they went back, still silent and stern-featured, but leaving some thirty or forty of their clan behind them, whose death they were going to avenge.

Meantime the Albanian mercenaries, who had concluded a truce with the Greeks, hearing the tumult begin, formed under arms in the immense court-yard of the palace of Elmar Bey, their commander, prepared, if the Greeks attempted to violate their conditions, to charge—and with a fair chance of success—this disorganized rabble, and cut their way through. The mob was swarming outside the iron-barred gate, and some were even attempting to break it in, when Anagnostes, who was among them and saw the danger, struggled up to the gate, and by his immense personal strength pushed away the Greeks who were trying to force it. One man, thinking that there was some vast treasure within, and that Anagnostes had made an agreement by which it should be guarded for him, ran at him with a drawn sword, crying "Treachery!" and the other lifting his pistol calmly shot him dead. For a few moments his life hung on a thread, but he succeeded in making the men nearest him understand that inside were the Albanians, who had made a truce and only desired to leave the town; and forming a certain number of men across the street to stop the mob, secured a clear space for the Albanians to march out. Thence they went straight down the road to the Argos gate, round which lay the poorer quarter of the town, by this time almost entirely deserted by the Greek troops, though the hordes of peasants were swarming into the houses to secure all they could lay hands on, and then out of the town, where they took up their quarters in the deserted camp at Trikorpha, whence they watched the destruction of the city, and from there on the seventh day marched north to the Gulf of Corinth, took ship across the Gulf, and at length reached their mountain homes in safety.

The house of Abdul Achmet, where Suleima lived, was near the western gate of the city, opposite to which were stationed the Argive corps. Though the Greek troops there could not see across the houses to the gate where the flag was flying, they heard the tumult of shouts and firing begin, they saw the sentries on the gate turn and fly, and without waiting for news or instructions they assaulted the gate and tried to force it. But it held firm against their attack, and they had to blow out the staples of the bolts before they could get in. The main street up towards the square lay straight before them, and they poured up it to where they could see the crowds battering at the houses, killing all the Turks, men, women, and children, whom they met flying away. Among the foremost was Father Andréa, a priest of the Prince of Peace no more, but a fury of hatred. In ten minutes his long, two-edged knife was red from point to hilt, and as he dealt death to the masses of refugees one sentence came from his mouth, "The sword of the Lord!" But just at the corner, where the side street ran down to the little door opening from Abdul Achmet's house below the harem window, a Turk whom he had charged attacked him, evading his upraised knife, and knocked him over, only to find death two yards off. Andréa hit his head against the curbstone of the pavement, lay there for a few moments stunned, and came to himself with the world spinning round him. He rose and staggered out of the blinding sunshine into a cool, dark doorway, some yards down the street, to recover himself a little and to stanch the blood which was flowing from his head; but his knife, which had been struck from his hand, he picked up and carried with him.

Meantime Suleima, from the latticed window, had seen the charge of the Argives, and the terrified women, calling on Allah and the Prophet, ran trembling and sobbing about like frightened birds caught in a net. Abdul did not appear; he had probably run from the house, and the servants seemed to have fled too. Some of the women were for following their example and trying to escape to the western gate, which was only two hundred yards off, as soon as the road was more clear; others were for climbing up to the roof, and hiding themselves there; others for shutting themselves into some small chamber in the house, hoping they would not be discovered. At length, amid an infinity of wailing clatter, they agreed on this, and Suleima, obedient to Penelope's instructions, waited among the hindermost, and then turned to slip down-stairs and out. Zuleika saw her and cried to her to come back, then seemed disposed to follow herself, but Suleima heard her not, and glided down the stairs like a ghost. On the first landing she stopped for a moment and took the veil off her face; her black hair streamed down over, her shoulders reaching to her waist, and she tied it up in a great knot behind her head. Then she wrapped her bernouse round her, and waited a moment till she was certain that none were following her. A strange new courage made steel of her muscles; never in her life had she known so warm a bravery, for when she was out in the boat with Mitsos, or returning to the house after one of those excursions, she had trembled with fright lest she should be discovered, and all this last week she had had sudden qualms and shiverings of terror at the thought of the innumerable dangers that lay before her. But now that the time had come she slipped down the stairs as calmly as she went to her bed or her bath; she thought of herself no longer, but of the unborn babe she carried. A moment's faltering, a babbling word where a firm one was wanted, would be death to that which was dearer to her than herself, and she hastened to the doorway, and seeing that the side street seemed deserted, slipped out, strong in the strength that is the offspring of the protective instinct for that which is as intimately dear as self, and dearer in that it is not self, which only women can know. That day saw many bloody and cruel acts, and many cowardly and craven things, and perhaps only one deed of instinctive, unconscious heroism, and that was Suleima's sublime attempt to save the child of him she loved.

As she opened the door, the roar of death and murder rose like the roar of the sea, and yet the dread of loneliness to one bred in a chattering harem was hardly less terrible. Whither should she go on her desperate attempt? Looking up the street to the main road leading to the square, there suddenly came into sight a woman running distractedly with shrill cries towards the western gate, and, even as she passed, a Greek coming up from the opposite direction ran her through the body, and wiping his sword on her dress, passed on. Cold fear rushed like a river round her

234

heart, yet she would not give it admittance. She must be brave; she would be brave. There was no safety within, that was sure; among the rest of the Turkish women how should she be spared? To the south a column of black smoke rose from a quarter already burning; flame and sword were around her. Then for fear she should lose her courage altogether if she delayed, she drew one deep breath and stepped out into the street, terrible to her in its emptiness, more terrible still in the thought that at any moment it might sing and roar with death.

Now it was so that the moment after Suleima stepped out of the doorway Father Andréa, only thirty yards off, got up with a heart that was one red flame of anger. He had wrapped a rough bandage round his bleeding temple, and that blow had stung him to madness, while in his hand, so thought the wild, revengeful man, he held the sword of the Lord, dripping with the blood of the ungodly. Man, woman, and child, they were all one accursèd brood. With this thought whirling in his brain like some mad, dervis thing he looked down the street and saw a Turkish woman walking towards him, and "The sword of the Lord!" he cried again.

The woman fled not, but ran towards him, crying out "Save me; I am of your blood!" And seeing by the long, black robe and hair that streamed over his shoulders that he was a priest, "Save me, father!" she cried again, "I am of your blood!"

"Mother of devils! mother of devils!" muttered Andréa; but then stopped suddenly, with arm uplifted, not ten yards off, for over his wild brain there came the astonished thought that she had spoken Greek. At the sight of that red knife, and at those fierce words, Suleima uttered a little low cry of despair; but in a moment her strength came back to her redoubled, and she flung aside her bernouse, showing the lines of her figure.

"Would you slay me, father?" she cried again, "I who am of your blood? and see, I am with child!"

Father Andréa paused, stricken out of thought for a moment, and wiped his blade against his cassock. "Greek, she is Greek," he said to himself, "yet from the house of the Turk."

Suleima stood as still as a marble statue and as white. The black bernouse had fallen to the ground, and her silk robe flowed loosely round her figure. He moved a step nearer.

"You are Greek," he said to her. "How came you here?"

"I know not," said Suleima. "I was taken by the Turks ten years ago, or it may be twelve. Take me away, father, out of this horrible town."

The two were standing close together in the deserted street. From above came the wails of women, for the Greeks had forced their way through the door in the main street into Abdul Achmet's house, and from the square roared the mob. Andréa looked at her in silence for a moment, his brows knitted into a frown, his brain one mill-race of thought, suggesting a possibility beyond the bounds of possibility. At length he spoke to her again, wondering at himself.

"I will save you, my daughter," he said; and as the words passed his lips his heart throbbed almost to bursting. "Quick! come with me! Ah, wait a moment!"

235

And he thrust her back gently into the doorway out of which she had come, while a mob of his countrymen poured by the opening into the main street.

When they had passed he turned to her again.

"Come with me now," he said, making her take his arm, "and come as quickly as you can. Pray to God without ceasing that we get out safe. I am too bloody to pray."

Once more before they reached the main street they had to hide in the doorway where Father Andréa had sat, and, waiting there, he suddenly turned and took her hands, and with his soul in his eyes looked at her in dumb, agonized appeal. Suleima met his gaze directly and returned the pressure of his hands.

"You will save me, father?" she said again.

"I will save you," he replied; "in the name of God, I will save you! Come again on; the mob has gone by."

They hurried on towards the western gate, he half carrying her, in time to get out before another band of men streamed down from the mountains round. Father Andréa took her to his hut and bade her wait there for him while he went and got a pony, for she was in no state to walk. All thought was drowned in one possibility, and without speaking to her again he placed her very gently on the beast, and, taking the rope-rein in his hand, led it along onto the road to Argos and Nauplia. The camp was absolutely empty, and there were none to stop or question this strange pair, and they plodded across the plain and stopped not, neither spoke, till Tripoli had sunk behind the first range of the low hills which lay spread round Mount Parthenius. There he led the pony off the path and left her in a shady hollow, while he went on to the village of Doliana, half a mile away, to get food and drink for her. Her time, he knew, must be very near at hand, and his one thought was to get her safe to Nauplia.

Only once on that ride had Suleima spoken, and that when they struck the road.

"We are going to Nauplia?" she asked, with a sudden upspringing of hope in her heart.

"To Nauplia, my daughter," said Andréa. "Speak no more till we talk together."

"But father, father," she cried, "tell me one thing. Where is Mitsos? Oh, take me to Mitsos."

"Mitsos, Mitsos?" said Andréa.

"Yes, the tall Mitsos, who lives in that house near the bay."

Father Andréa stopped.

"What do you know of Mitsos?" he said, almost fiercely, and as the girl's tears answered him, he bowed his head in amazed wonder.

As soon as he had left her there and was out of sight he knelt down on the hill-side.

"O God, O merciful and loving One," he cried, in an agony of supplication; "if this be possible, if this be possible, for to Thee all things are possible! Did she not speak to me and call me 'father'? Oh, in Thy infinite compassion let her word be true! Did I not call her daughter while my heart burned within me? O merciful and loving One!"

236

He found Suleima where he had left her, and the food and wine made her strength revive. When she had finished he came and sat by her.

His voice trembled so that at first he could not form the words, but at last, getting it more in control:

"My daughter," he said, "we will rest here a little until the noon heat is past. And—and, for the love of God, answer me a few questions. When was it you were taken to the house of the Turk?"

His anxiety made his voice harsh and fierce, and the girl shrank from him. He saw it, and it cut him to the heart.

"Ah, my poor lamb!" he said, "have pity on me and answer me."

"It was ten years ago," said Suleima, "or perhaps twelve. I do not very well know."

"Can you remember anything about it?"

Suleima shook her head wearily.

"I do not know; I was so young. And I am so tired, father. Let me sleep a little, and when I wake up I will think and tell you all I know. You have been very kind to me."

And she dozed off and slept without moving for near an hour, with Andréa sitting by her. Then she stirred in her sleep, and without opening her eyes shifted her head so that it rested on his knee, and so slept again.

At last she woke, and seeing him above her, sat up.

"Has Mitsos come?" she asked. "Will he come soon? I have slept so well," and she smiled at him like a child for no reason except that she smiled.

"You were asking me—" she said, at length.

"Yes, yes," said Andréa.

"It is so little I remember," she said; "I was so young. But it was near Athens somewhere, and on a journey with my father, that I was carried off to the house of Abdul Achmet."

"Abdul Achmet?" whispered Andréa.

"Yes, Abdul Achmet. He lived in Athens then; he moved to Nauplia afterwards. It was in the summer, too, I remember that, and that I was with my father."

She had sunk down again with her head on his knee, but here she raised herself on her elbow and looked at him.

"He was a priest—yes, he must have been a priest, for he had long black robes and long hair; only his hair was black, not gray, like yours. Ah—"

Then to Andréa the blessed relief of tears came—the great sobs that come from a man's heart—a pain and an exquisite happiness; and lifting her closer to him, he kissed her.

"Theodora," he cried, "little lost one. Ah, ah, merciful and compassionate God. Do you not remember, my little one? Do you not know? Your father—am I not he whom you called 'father' as soon as you saw me? God put that word in your mouth, my darling. God sent me to fetch you; and I who would have murdered you—O blessed Mother of compassion and sorrows—I—Theodora, Theodora—the gift of God."

Thus spoke they together, with many questions and answerings, till Andréa was certain and content.

CHAPTER XII

THE SEARCH FOR SULEIMA

Half an hour after they had gone Nicholas had made his way down to where he was told Abdul Achmet's house stood, mindful of his promise to Mitsos. Two or three of the Argives, who had taken possession of it, and were ransacking the rooms for booty, stood at the door, and told him that the prize was theirs.

"Oh, man," said Nicholas, "I come not for booty; the gold is yours. But there is a Greek woman in the house; it is she whom I seek."

The men still seemed disposed to resent his entry, but they knew him, and, even in the face of all the disgrace the captains had charged, believed him clean-handed.

"Come," said he again, "I take nothing from the house, and when I go out you shall search me if you will. Only take me to where the women are."

The women of the harem had been locked into the room overlooking the narrow street by which Suleima had fled, while the men searched the rest of the house; and Nicholas, hearing that the mayor, Demetri, was of the party, told him what he wanted.

"Of course you can go in; friend," he said. "Here, one of you, take him to the room."

The women were sobbing and wailing together, and one cried out in Turkish as Nicholas entered:

"Kill us if you will, but be quick."

"I touch you not," said Nicholas. "Tell me, is there not a Greek woman among you?"

Zuleika, for it was she who had spoken, stopped crying for amazement.

"She has gone," she said. "Oh, that I had gone with her. She would not stop within, but went down-stairs and out, I suppose. And in a few days, perhaps sooner, will her baby be born. Oh, what are you going to do with us?"

And she caught hold of him by the arm.

Nicholas disengaged her fingers, but gently.

"You are sure she has gone?" he said. Then to the soldiers who were with him: "Will you allow me to search the other rooms; it is only she whom I want?"

"And what should you want with her?" said one of them, gruffly. "All that is in the house is ours."

"Oh, man, do not be a fool," said Nicholas. "The woman is a free Greek, and free she shall be. She was carried off by this Turk years ago. Come, let me go into the other rooms to be sure she is not here, for if she is not I must seek her outside. It is a promise, and a promise to little Mitsos."

The other consented, still reluctantly, and Nicholas looked through

238

the house from roof to cellar, but found her not. And "Ah, poor lad," he thought, "but this will be bitter news, for if she has gone into the streets, God save her!"

It was now one hour past noon, and in the hot, breathless air already the thick sour smell of blood hung about the street. The square was a shambles, neither more nor less, and the dead lay about in heaps. With the peasants from the country had come in hungry, half-wild dogs, and as Nicholas passed the square again, now deserted by the besiegers for the great mass of the town which lay higher up the slope towards the citadel, two or three of these slunk away with red dripping mouths from their horrible banqueting; but one, hungrier or bolder than the others, stood there over the body of a child snarling at him. The sight sickened him, and he shot the animal through the head. Black patches of flies swarmed in hundreds over the congealed pools of blood, and rose with an unclean whir and buzz as he approached. The heat was stifling, and from the tower where he had planted it but four hours ago the flag hung in folds round its staff. The deadly taint of death was in the air, with the foul odors of flesh already putrefying. Nicholas felt suddenly faint and weary, but seeing a stream of water running down one of the gutters in the square all red and turbid, he followed it up and found where it sprang from—a leaden pipe out of a lion's mouth in one of the side streets. He drank deeply of it, and bathed his face and hands there, and feeling refreshed followed on towards where he knew the Mainats would be. Mixed with the dead were not a few Greeks, and as he passed up the street he saw with a sudden pang of horror three or four bodies, apparently lifeless, stir, and from below there came out the hand of a living man, striving to get hold of something by which he could pull himself up. Nicholas turned the bodies off and found a Greek soldier below, whom he carried into the shade, and fetched him water. The man was but slightly wounded in the arm, the gash was already beginning to clot over, and Nicholas, having bound up the place with a strip of his fustanella, left him, for there was much work to be done.

Right and left from the houses in the street came cries and screams, and now and then a woman, with her clothes perhaps half torn off her, would steal out like a cat, and seeing Nicholas, either steal back again or run from him. After each of these, he shouted some sentence in Greek, but got no response. Once a child ran up to him, howling with tears and pain, and showed him a horrible gash in its arm, wantonly inflicted by one of his countrymen, babbling to him in Turkish that it could not find its mother. Then Nicholas, despite his fierce vows to have no pity on man, woman, or child for the wrong that had been done to him and his by that pitiless race, waited ten minutes to bind up the wound, and—for what else could he do— bade the child get out of the town, for its mother was outside. On his way he passed several Greek soldiers, one dragging a woman after him, another with his hands full of a pile of gold and silver, the smaller pieces of which dropped through his fingers as he walked. Nicholas inquired where the Mainats were, and was told he would find a number of them at a big square house on the slope up to the citadel gate, which they had just entered. Fighting seemed to be going on in an upper story, and even as he

239

approached a group of men, Turks and Greeks mixed, appeared on the house-top. Next moment two who were struggling together toppled and fell against the thin railing which lined the roof; it broke under their weight, and both men, still clutching at each other's throats, fell toppling over into the street with a horrid crash and sound of breaking. The Turk was living and moved feebly, but the head of the Mainat was smashed like an egg.

At that moment Yanni appeared at the door of the house, his face flushed, and the fire of fighting hot upon him.

"You here?" he cried to Nicholas. "We thought you must be dead. Oh, how wild Mitsos will be when he finds that he has been out of it!"

"It is of Mitsos, too, I am thinking," said Nicholas. "Oh, Yanni, come and help me; there are butchers enough. Help me to find her."

Yanni stared at him a moment before he understood.

"Suleima," he cried, "God forgive us all! She in this town, and I had forgotten, and the Mavromichales are gone mad! If she is there—oh," and he threw down his knife, and looked stupid-like at his hands which were red and caked with blood and dust.

"Come and search for her, Yanni," said Nicholas again; "she is not in the house of Abdul, and every moment that she is in the streets may be her last."

"She left the house! Are you sure?" asked Yanni. "Where is it? Let us run there."

"I have been already," said Nicholas. "See, Yanni, you go one way and I another, and we will meet here again in an hour. Speak in Greek to every woman you see."

"Yes, yes," said Yanni; "which way shall I go? Oh, Mitsos, poor little Mitsos, and I killed two women myself, for they had knives and tried to stab me."

"Here, go steady, and be sensible," said Nicholas, for the boy seemed half beside himself. "Pick up your knife again; you were going unarmed. Do not stop, even to kill. Walk about, go where you hear a woman cry—God forgive us, but that is a task for a hundred—and speak to all in Greek. And be back here in an hour. Where is Petrobey?"

"In the house," said Yanni, and went off in the direction Nicholas had told him.

On that mad and ghastly day Petrobey was one of the few who had kept his head, and getting together a few sensible men, he had systematically worked his way up the street, stopping only to kill where there were signs of resistance. Open doors and men flying unarmed he left alone; there were plenty to do work like that; but he forced door after door where barricades had been put up, and attacked bodies of soldiers, who still from time to time charged out of some house or other, trying to force their way out to one of the gates. Without him and a few resolute bands of men it is possible that great slaughter would have taken place among the unarmed rabble who had followed the Greeks, and that a considerable body of men would have collected and won their way out of the city, and over the now undefended hills to Argos or Nauplia. He had also ordered up, under an armed escort, a train of provision-laden mules for the

Mainats who were with him, and these supplies had just arrived before Nicholas came up.

"Stay with us and eat, dear cousin," he said to Nicholas, "for men cannot fight fasting. And, oh, Nicholas, but my life and all I have are yours, for you did not fail me when God and man forsook me!"

"Give me something, then, to take with me," said Nicholas, "for I have work before me. That girl of Mitsos' had left the house before I got there, and God knows where she is, alive or dead. I love the lad, and indeed we owe him a debt we can never repay for all he has done, and I should never forgive myself, nor hope for forgiveness, if I did not do what I could to find her."

Petrobey shook his head. "She may have taken refuge in some other house," he said. "If not—"

"Why should she fly from one house to another? If she is alive she is either somewhere in the streets, or it is just possible she has escaped."

Petrobey shook his head again.

"One woman fly in the face of that mob? God be with your kind heart, Nicholas. Poor little Mitsos, poor lad!"

Nicholas tore off a crust of bread, and staying only to swallow a draught of wine, went out again into the blinding glare of the streets. Everywhere it was the same ghastly scene over again: heaps of bodies; gutters with slow, oily streams of blood flowing and congealing; here a Turk wounded and in the last agony of death; there some young country lad shot through the heart, lying with open mouth and glazed eyes, which stared unblinkingly at the sun. Sometimes a woman lay across the path, while a little baby, still living and unhurt, lay beside where she had fallen, and groped with feeble, automatic hands for her breast. By them all without stopping went Nicholas, peering about for any sign of a living woman, but finding none. Very few apparently had been so desperate as to run into the street like Suleima, and though he felt the search wellnigh hopeless he went on. Once he came across a woman lying in the path, not yet dead, and as he bent over her she opened her eyes and spoke to him in Turkish. Nicholas questioned her in Greek, but she did not understand, and he went on again. In a little more than an hour he was back and found Yanni waiting for him, but he too had seen no sign of her they had never seen but sought.

All that afternoon the work went on, and at sunset Petrobey set a strong watch at all the gates, and he with most of the men went to sleep in the camp outside, where the air was less stifling and the poisonous breath from the murdered town came not. But Nicholas, who still hoped against hope, would not leave the place; by night, he thought, if Suleima was in hiding somewhere in the town she might try to steal back to the house, or attempt to escape by one of the gates; and he sat waiting in the doorway of Abdul Achmet's house till he fell asleep from sheer weariness, having seen naught but the dogs paddling about on their horrible errands. He woke early, before it was dawn, shivering and feeling ill; and thinking that his chill came only from exposure to the night air, got up and walked about, waiting for day. As soon as it was light he went out of the south gate to the

241

Mainat camp, and had breakfast with Petrobey, who shook his head sadly over the absence of news.

Some sort of order was restored in the camp that day, and a third part of each of the four regular corps was stationed to blockade the citadel, while the others, in a more orderly manner and under the command of officers, went on with the sack of the town. The rabble who had passed in the day before were driven out of the place, and a watch set at each of the gates; but these measures were only half successful, for many took to hiding in the deserted houses, or, having been ejected, climbed back again at the Argive tower, or at other points of the walls where they could find entrance. Already many of the Greeks were ill with an ill-defined fever, which Petrobey put down to the effects of the foul, pestilence-laden atmosphere, and he employed a number of men to cart the dead out of the city and burn them. But they were not able to keep pace with the massacring which went on all day, and that evening the fever took a more pronounced and violent form in many of the eases, and before the morning of the 7th fifty or more Greeks, chiefly countrymen, who had slept two nights in the streets, were dead.

Just before dawn on the 7th a party of Turks made a sortie from the citadel and broke through the Greek lines. The alarm was given at once by the sentries, but the Turks were already among them before they were able to make any resistance, and after not more than ten minutes' fighting, they had broken their way through, and were doubling down the street towards the Argive gate. The guard there had sprung to arms at the sound of the disturbance above, and they engaged the Turks with somewhat better success, but more than half the original number got through and made straight for the unguarded hills between the plain and Argos.

Nicholas, who had passed a feverish, tossing night, feeling weak and weary, yet unable to sleep, had sprung up at once on the alarm, and was among the first to meet the charge. In the darkness the fighting was wild and random; they fought with shadows, and parrying a sword thrust aimed at his head, though he turned the blow aside, he felt the weapon wound him just below the shoulder, and the edge grate on the bone. Such rough aid as could be given him was at once administered. His arm was tightly bound above the wound to stop the bleeding from the severed artery, and, after the rough but often effective surgery of the day, the severed ends of the artery were cauterized and bound up, and the edges of the wound were brought together. No serious consequences were expected, for the flow of blood was soon checked, but for the present any further search for Suleima was out of the question. But a couple of hours later he grew more feverish and restless, and by ten o'clock on the morning of the 8th he was delirious, down with that swift and terrible fever which during the past night had already claimed many victims.

At mid-day the remainder of the garrison in the citadel surrendered unconditionally from want of water, for the whole supply had come from the lower town, and ten minutes later the Greek flag was flying from the tower. The shouts with which it was hailed roused Nicholas, who had sunk into a heavy sort of stupor, and he found Yanni sitting by his side.

"What is it?" he asked. "Have they found Suleima?"

"It is the citadel which has surrendered," said Yanni; "they have hoisted the flag on the tower."

Nicholas half raised himself. "Then the Morea is free from Corinth to Maina," he said. "O merciful and gracious Virgin! It only remains to find Suleima."

Presently after, he sank back into a stupor again, though every now and then he would stir and mutter something to himself.

"Why does not little Mitsos come?" he said, once; "tell him I want him. I did all I could to find her, but it was no use. Little Mitsos, there will be no more fire-ships ... it was a devilish task to set you ... don't you see the flag is flying; Tripoli has fallen; the Turks and their lusts are over forever; we are free!"

Then suddenly, in the loud strong voice which Yanni knew so well: "The Lord is a man of war!" he cried.

The news had run about the camp that Nicholas was down with the fever, and for the moment all paused when they heard. As every man in the place knew, his was the glory of the deed, and he the chief among those few to whose name honor, and nothing disgraceful, no weak deed or infirm purpose, were written. They had moved him out of the town unto the higher ground of the citadel, and into the top room of the tower on which the flag was flying. A great north wind sprang up that afternoon, and from the room where he lay could be heard the flapping of the flag. Those of the men who had any knowledge of medicine came flocking up to the citadel, begging to be allowed to see him, and suggesting a hundred remedies; and of these Petrobey chose one, who seemed to be sensible, and who it appeared had pulled a man through the worst of the fever, and he gave Nicholas such remedies as they could get.

That afternoon there was a division of the spoils taken, and in the evening, but not before a terrible and bloody deed had been done, three corps went back to their homes, the Mainats alone remaining. The Argives and Mainats, at any rate, had no hand in that devilish work, which must be passed over quickly. All the Turks—men, women, and children—who were found still alive were driven to the ravine behind Trikorpha, and some two thousand in number were all murdered.

It was, indeed, time to leave that pestilence-stricken town. During the day the fever had broken out with redoubled virulence among all those who had quartered themselves in the lower parts of the town, and the angel of death followed the victorious battalions into Arcadia, Argos, and Laconia, striking them right and left, and strewing the road with dying men. The judgment of God for those three ruthless days had come quickly. Mitsos' father, who had escaped unhurt, doing his quiet duty in the ranks of the Argives from the first, saw Petrobey before he left.

"Tell Mitsos to come quickly," he said. "And did you know Father Andréa has not been seen since the first morning?"

Meantime, in the north, it was found that the rumor of the Turkish landing was groundless, and Prince Demetrius was hurrying back to Tripoli. Germanos had joined him; but two days' march off the town, news of its capture was brought to them, on which Mitsos obtained permission to go on ahead to report the prince's coming, and announce that no landing of Turks had taken place. He travelled night and day, for his heart gave him wings, and late on the night of the 8th he reached Tripoli.

The unutterable stench in the streets struck him like death, and turned consciousness to a horrible dread. Shutting his eyes to the ghastly wreckage that strewed the ways, more horrible under the dim, filtering light from the clear-swept sky than even in daylight, he went quickly up to the citadel, where he supposed the troops would be. He was challenged by the sentry at the gate, who, seeing who he was, admitted him at once. He was taken straight to Petrobey's quarters, in the room just below where Nicholas lay.

The boy's voice was raised in eager question, but Petrobey hushed him.

"My poor lad," he said, "you must be brave, for we know you can be brave. We have not found her, and in the room above Nicholas lies dying. He has been asking for you; go to him at once, little Mitsos. I will send your food there."

Mitsos gave one gasping sigh.

"She may yet be here," he said; "where are the women and the prisoners?"

"There are no women and there are no prisoners," said Petrobey.

Mitsos stood silent a moment, looking at the other with bright, dry eyes, and swaying a little as he stood.

"And Uncle Nicholas is dying and has asked for me," he said. "Let me go to him."

CHAPTER XIII

NICHOLAS GOES HOME

The room was lighted by an oil-lamp, turned low and shaded from the sick man. Yanni, who had been watching all night, was lying on the floor, dozing from sheer weariness; but he woke at the sound of Mitsos' entering, and got up.

"Oh, Mitsos, you have come," he whispered, "he has asked for you so often."

"Leave me alone here," said Mitsos, and the two were left together.

Nicholas was lying with eyes only half closed, and Mitsos knelt by the bed.

"Uncle, dear uncle," he said, "I have come."

Nicholas only frowned, and passed his hand wearily over his eyes.

The other bandaged arm was lying outside the thin bed-covering under which he lay.

"I looked everywhere," he muttered, "and I could not find her. Will little Mitsos ever forgive me, I wonder—yet I did all I could. Why does not the dear lad come? Has he forsaken me?... No, it will never do; this traffic brings disgrace on us all. Stop it, Petrobey, stop it, in God's name.... Ah, that is better, up, up, hand over hand, quick, give me the flag. Where is the flag, O devils of the pit? but give it me. Ah, you are no better than the Turks.... Yes, I will pay you well to give it me, if that is what you want. A million piastres? I will give you two millions.... Ah, up with it."

The muttering sank down again into silence, and the eyelids drooped wearily. Mitsos, kneeling there, felt that the life was leaving him. Suleima dead, Nicholas dying, there was but little left of the Mitsos he knew. Dry-eyed he knelt there in the blank, black despair of a hopeless anguish. If only it was he who was lying there! There was nothing to live for; everything was gone in this moment of victory, when his heart should have been larklike, soaring with song.

Petrobey brought him in food and wine.

"Drink, little Mitsos," he said; "it is very good wine."

But Mitsos would not even look at it.

"Leave me alone," was all he said; "I will call you if he wants you. Oh, go, man," he repeated, in a shrill whisper, and with a sudden burst of childish, impotent anger, which gave Petrobey a more pitiful moment than he had ever known; "may not my heart break in peace?"

It had been past midnight when Mitsos came in, and already the stars were beginning to pale in the east when Nicholas stirred and woke. He saw Mitsos by him, and knew him and smiled to him. He spoke slowly and faintly.

"Ah, little Mitsos," he said, "so you have come at last, but not much too soon. My poor lad, you know I did all I could; Yanni and I looked for her everywhere, but found her not. Oh, little Mitsos, my heart is bleeding for you. Tell me you know I did all I could."

At the sound of that dear voice, obeying again the will and the brain of the man he loved, no longer wandering idly as a thing apart, Mitsos broke down utterly, forgetting all but the dear, dying uncle.

"Oh, you will break my heart if you speak like that," he sobbed. "I know—how can I but know?—that you did all the best and noblest of men could do. Oh, uncle, I cannot do without you. Oh, come back, come back."

Nicholas's hand gently stroked the boy's head as he knelt with his face buried in the bed-covering.

"Why, Mitsos, Mitsos," he said, "what is this? We are behaving as but poor weak folk—I, whom the merciful God is taking, and you, who He wills shall live and go on with the work we have begun. A man's life is but short, but, God knows, mine has been partly very sweet; and out of what was bitter He has given us a wonderful victory. From Corinth to Maina, little one, a free people thanks Him. But that is not all. From Thermopylæ to Corinth must those thanks go up, and it is you, first among all the first, for whom that work is waiting. Promise me, little one, you will not fail. For

245

this was the oath you swore, and already, oh, my dearest lad, you have kept it well."

"I promise, oh, I promise," sobbed Mitsos; "but what am I without you?"

"God is with you, little Mitsos," said Nicholas, "and He will be with you, as He has been with you till now. Tell me, is Ypsilanti coming back here?"

"He is on his way, and Germanos with him."

Nicholas frowned and raised his voice a little.

"I will not die with a lie on my lips," he said. "He is a bad man; I forgive him not, and see that you do not trust him."

"Oh, uncle," said Mitsos; "what does it matter now? Think of him not at all, then. This is no time for little things."

Nicholas lay silent a moment, still stroking Mitsos' hair.

"After all, what does it matter?" he said. "The man has failed; that is enough. He shall not poison these few minutes. Oh yes, I forgive him, little one. I do really; tell him so when he comes. If he were here I would take his hand. But"—and a faint smile came round his mouth—"do not trust him too far, all the same."

His face was growing very white and tired in the pale gray morning before the dawn, and Mitsos, at his request, gave him water and put out the lamp.

"There is but little more to say," he whispered, "and it is a selfish thing; yet, as you love me, I think you will hear it gladly. Little Mitsos, I am happier than the kings of the earth. I am dying, but dying in the shout of victory. Oh, I am happy on this morning. But, poor lad, whom I love so, it is hard—"

His face flushed suddenly.

"Victory! freedom!" he said, raising his voice again with tremulous excitement; "that is the singing bird in my heart, that and you and the clan, and Catharine and the little one. Ah! merciful God, but I am a happy man. Where is Petrobey? Call him in, him and the dear clan. Kiss me first and for the last time, and then bring them all in, as many as can stand in the room."

Mitsos hurried out to fetch them, and found Petrobey's room full of men waiting for news from the sick bed, watching faithfully through the night, and he beckoned them silently up. The sun had just risen, and the first ray clean and bright fell full on the bed where the dying man lay. By an effort he raised himself on his elbow, and looked at them with bright, shining eyes as they trooped in. At that sudden movement his wound broke out afresh, and a great gush of blood poured down.

Then suddenly he sprang to his feet.

"Shout, shout," he cried, "for the freedom of Greece! Ah, Catharine, I am coming; I am coming very quickly."

On the word a great shout arose from the men crowded into the room, and in the glory of that triumphant cry, standing there in the dawn of the newly-risen day, he fell forward, and his strong soul went forth free from the death that had no terror for him.

They took his body up to the Turkish mosque which crowned the citadel, and at the east erected a tall, rough, wooden cross, and there he lay all day, and the clan came and looked their last on the man they had loved. The hawklike, eager eyes were closed, the eager nostrils were still, and the dignity of death gave the face a wonderful sweet seriousness, and a tranquillity which it had seldom worn in life. The prince and Germanos arrived before noon, knowing only that Tripoli was taken, and Petrobey, to whom Mitsos had told what Nicholas had said, found words which were a humbling and an awe to that proud man, and together the two went to where he lay. Then said Germanos:

"I never did him honor, God forgive me, in life; but you will let me do him honor, now?"

The funeral was fixed for sunset, and he was to be buried just outside the mosque on the highest ground of the citadel. The first part of the service would be in the mosque, the remainder at the grave, and Mitsos, returning just before sunset from his finished and hopeless quest, went straight there. All day, first in the town and then in that valley of death behind Trikorpha, he had sought among the heaps of the dead, longing rather to know and see the worst, to look once more on her face, than to carry about with him this load of torturing uncertainty. He prayed that he might find her undisfigured, that her face might be quiet and calm like Nicholas's, for he felt that it would be a thing of consolation to know she had died quickly. One thought only sustained him through those terrible hours, and that the remembrance of the words Nicholas had spoken. He had bargained to sacrifice himself and all that he held dear for that which was already won, and in the very flush and presence of victory he would not give way to the desolation and despair which beset him. All day beneath a burning and malignant sun he moved among the heaps of the slain, turning over body after body, only to find more beneath. The kites and preying hawks chid shrilly over his head, but he heeded not and worked on, and a little before sunset only had he finished, and sat down on the hill-side for a moment to eat, for he remembered that he had not eaten that day, and he felt suddenly faint with hunger. Then rising he went back to the town and up to the mosque.

The sun was just setting, and before they left the mosque it was already twilight; but the men had a number of pitch torches, and the procession went out to the grave, headed by thirty Mainats, who carried these, and stood round the newly dug grave, while the body, with its face uncovered, according to the Greek use, and dressed in soldier's clothes, was placed in the coffin and lowered. At the head of the grave stood Germanos, and at the foot Petrobey with Mitsos. Many of the clan who stood round were weeping unrestrainedly and without shame; but Mitsos was perfectly quiet and calm. Only once when the first spadefuls of earth rattled on the rough coffin lid did he move, and ran forward a step to the edge of the grave with one sob so piteous and broken that Petrobey clinched his teeth to prevent himself, too, sobbing aloud. But after that he was quite quiet again, and Germanos, who had read the service, stepped forward and gave the address at the grave.

"This day," he said, "is the birthday of a new-born people, and it is so that Nicholas would have you think of it. To all of us has come a great and wonderful victory, and to all has come a terrible loss; but I pray God, clan of the Mavromichales, to none of you such an unavailing regret as is mine. Of myself I would not speak to you, but for this, that before Nicholas died he forgave the cruel wrong I had done him, and it is that forgiveness of his alone which gives me any right to be here. You knew him, he was of the same blood as you, and it is for you all to lament not nor wail, but think only that God in His infinite kindness has let him see the dawn of this day, and then, while the flood of joy burst his heart, has taken him to Himself. To work for a great cause, as Nicholas worked, and as none but he, was a great reward; to see the fruit of his labors and so die, in the very flush of victory, is what comes to but few. By his rank and his work his was among the highest places in all Greece; but how did he die? As a common soldier, serving in the ranks, and by his own choice. And to me that appears—though the cause for it is a bitterness and regret of which I cannot speak—a wonderful and an appropriate thing. Nicholas—the victory of the people."

The darkness had completely fallen while he spoke, and overhead, through the sombre smoke of the torches, the stars peered out of an infinite depth of blue. In front of Germanos rose the mould of freshly raised earth, for they had filled up the grave before he began speaking, and the wooden cross from the mosque had been fetched out and planted on the top of it. Round in dense ranks stood the Mainats, the flickering glare of the torches striking strong light and shadows on their brown faces. But by degrees the torches planted on long stakes round the grave began to burn low; now and then one would shoot up with a sudden flare and die out again, and in a few minutes more they had all burned down, and only smouldering red cores of glowing ash remained. From the darkness Germanos's voice came slow and solemn at first, but as he went on he gained force and vigor.

"The birthday of the people—think of this day thus, and then of him whom you loved—the victory of the people. This is no time for lamentations nor weeping, for how did he take leave of you? Not with a wail, nor with any regret, but with a shout. Think of him, then, as he took farewell; happier, as he said to one of you, than the kings of the earth; mourn if you will for those who mourn, but rejoice with those who rejoice. And he went from us strong and with but one thought, which overmastered all. Thus it is no night nor valley of death he has gone into—or so it appeared not to him—but the dawning of the fresh day. Then, turning his brave eyes forward from dawn to dawn, what eyes should meet his, or what name should be on his lips? You heard it yourselves. And is there any cause for sorrow there? Do we weep and wail when the bridegroom meets the bride, or when after some long journey a faithful man goes home to her he loves? Ours is but a selfish grief if we look at it rightly. Let, then, this thought make you strong, and because you loved him turn from yourselves, who, God knows, have cause enough for grief, and think of him and the shout and rapture of his passing. Out of the day he has passed to the day, out of life into life, a faithful man made perfect. Call to him, then, once more, let him hear the shout which he led; let him hear again, for so we believe, the voices he knew, the shout of the men he loved and loves. The freedom of Greece, and Nicholas—the victory of the people!"

From the darkness the shout was taken up and repeated till it seemed to shake and split the darkness. As from one throat, it burst up thrice repeated, and then together they called Nicholas's name aloud, and went in silence back to their quarters. Mitsos returned with Petrobey, feeling somehow strangely strengthened. All he had been trying to feel all day had been said for him, and all that was brave within him—and of that there was much—rose and caught at it triumphantly, and he clung to it with conviction and courage in his heart.

The Mainats were to leave next morning, but Mitsos dreaded any hour spent in inaction, and he decided to go himself at once and again travel through the night. To stop here was only to talk of Nicholas, or to grow feverish again with the hopeless, impossible hope that Suleima was still somewhere in the town. With a good horse he could reach Nauplia next day soon after dawn, and he longed with the longing of a child in some distant land for the familiar places. Here all that spoke to him of Suleima spoke in words of blood and cruelty, which stabbed and stung him into a sense of maddened rage and regret. There, perhaps, with the thrill of home about him, his anguish would change to something less terrible, and not so discordant to the image his heart held of her. Even now, when so few hours had passed, he seemed to have lived with the sorrow for a lifetime, and realized that it was for a lifetime it would abide with him. The place where he had lost all he loved had a brooding horror over it; he could not think of her as he wished to think; but by the cool bay, the dark headlands, and that beach, with its whispering reeds, surely he would find an aspect of sorrow different to this, instinct with the bitterness of something which had once been infinitely sweet, instead of with the bitterness of horror and hatred. Above all, he dreaded the moment of waking next morning, and though many morrows stretched away before him, each with its cup of remembrance coming with the light at the end of sleep, yet it would be something over to get rid of this one, to have another four-and-twenty hours with his sorrow, which perhaps might help to prepare him for the pangs of that first moment of the waking to consciousness again, and the dead weight of grief which would have to be taken up anew. Then his father was there, and oh, how Mitsos longed for that quiet, protective presence. Here, it is true, were the dear clan; but the clan, though the best of companions, gave not the fellowship he wanted now. He wanted to be alone, and yet to have some one who loved him present with silent sympathy that needed no words. Even the companionship of Yanni, who followed him with the eyes of some dumb creature that knows its master is suffering, yet cannot console him, was irksome. None understood this better than poor Yanni himself; and though he tried to keep away he could not, and followed Mitsos, unable to say a word to him, and yet unable to leave him.

Mitsos rose from where he had been sitting in Petrobey's room and walked across to him.

"I think I shall go home at once," he said. "It will be better that I should be there."

"But not to-night, dear lad," said Petrobey, "and not alone. We are all coming to set you on your way to-morrow."

Poor Mitsos nearly broke down again at this. Somehow, a kindness reached the seat of tears, while his sorrow passed it by.

"No, I will go alone and now," he cried. "Oh, I cannot say what I think. You are all so good to me; but I want to be alone. Say good-bye to them all for me; I should not be able to tell them myself—and good-bye. Before long, I doubt not, we shall meet again; for I promised him always to be ready, and I shall always be ready."

Petrobey kissed the boy.

"Little Mitsos," he said, "we are not men of many words; but you know, you know. God keep you."

Yanni was watching Mitsos with hungry eyes, and he turned from Petrobey and went to him.

"Come out with me, Yanni," said Mitsos, "while I get my horse. Come as far as the gate, if you will."

Mitsos' horse was stabled below, and in silence the two went out together. Then, as they turned to walk down the deserted street to the gate, Mitsos passed one arm through the bridle and put the other round Yanni's neck.

"Yanni," he said, "you do not think me unkind? But it is this way with me: that somehow or other I must get used to these awful things, and I am best alone. We have had merry times together, have we not? and, please God! we shall be together many times yet; and, though I see not how, perhaps merry times will come again. I want to be alone with myself to-night and then alone with my father, for with him it is different. But of all others in the world—why need I tell you?—it is you I would choose to be with. You understand, do you not?"

"Yes, dear Mitsos," said Yanni, rather chokedly, "and if ever you want me, either come, or I will come to you. For, oh, Mitsos, I'm so sorry for you that I don't know what to do or say; and I owe all to you, and yet I can do nothing."

And with that he fairly burst out crying.

They walked on in silence to the Argive gate, and then Mitsos stopped.

"So let us do as Nicholas would have us do," said he, smiling at the other, "and think only of this wonderful birthday of the people, as Germanos said. And now I am going. So good-bye, Yanni, dear Yanni!"

"Oh, Mitsos, let me come!" cried Yanni. "No, no; I did not mean that. Good-bye and God speed!"

And he turned quickly and walked back into the town without another word or look.

CHAPTER XIV

THE HOUSE ON THE ROAD TO NAUPLIA

The horse Mitsos rode had been stabled all day, and coming out fresh into the cool night air kept him busy for a time snuffing uneasily at the wafts of foul air that blew from the town, and shying right and left at shapes that lay on the road-side. Once a dead body was stretched straight across the path, and the brute wheeled round, nearly unseating Mitsos, and tried to bolt back to Tripoli again. But by-and-by, as it got used to the night, and the steadiness of the lad's hand gave it confidence, it went more soberly, and settled down into a gentle trot up the road leading from the plain over the mountain. As they left the town behind the air grew fresher, and soon came pure and cool from the north. The night was clear, but for a few wisps of cloud that drifted southward in wavering lines of delicate pearly gray, so thin that the starlight suffused them and turned them into a luminous haze. The path lay low between bold rocks that climbed up on each side, and to the right, among oleanders, a stream talked idly, as in sleep. Above, the stars burned bright and close, set in the blue velvet of the sky; and to the east the blue was tinged with dove color, showing that the moon was nigh to its rising. From some shepherd's hut on the hills came the sharp bark of a dog, sounding faint yet curiously distinct in the alert air, as in the north sounds come sharp-cut and ringing on a frosty night. As he went higher the dry smell of the summer-scorched vegetation was changed for something fresher, coming from the upland pastures, and while his horse, now requiring no attention, went with straining shoulders and drooped head up from slope to slope, Mitsos knew that he had been right to come alone. Since those nights he had spent with Suleima between sea and sky, the loneliness and quietude of night, and the setting of the secret hours he had spent with her, had always woke in him an undefined, incommunicable thrill, a calling up of those dear ghosts of the past. To be alone at night was nearest to being with her, and often in these last weeks he had stolen out of his hut when the camp was still and night at its midmost to conjure up that same feeling, which the sight of objects associated with some one loved brings with it. Infinitely dear as she had been to him, there lingered round the remembrance of her a something dim, something in common with starlight, and great vague stretches of silent sea, and the pearliness of the sky before the imminent moonrise. It was that complexion of his sorrow he wished to recapture. Tripoli was like dreaming of her through the horrible distortion of a nightmare; this the serener bitterness of a quieter vision. Round his thoughts of Nicholas there hovered a splendid halo; the glory of his life and the triumph of his death made the heart bow down in a kind of thankful wonder, drowning regret. For if he, as Germanos had said, had gone like the bridegroom to the bride, should those who loved him mourn? Strangely mixed had come the boon for which Nicholas, for which Suleima, had died, and at present he was too stunned to be able to picture it, or the price paid, with clearness of focus,

251

for this limited mind within us is soon drowned by shocks like these coming in spate together, and we do not realize them till the first turbid flood has passed.

The moon had risen before he reached the top of the pass, and, following a strange but overwhelming desire, he pushed on quickly, for he longed to look on the bay again by night. Another hour's quick riding brought him to the head of a ravine which ran straight down to the sea, and at the bottom, lying like the clipping from a silver nail, was the farther edge of the bay, ashine with the risen moon; and when Mitsos saw it his heart was all athirst for home. Gradually, as he went down, the lower hills marched like shadows to the right and left, and between moonsetting and sunrise he stood on the edge of the shelving cove again, where he had brought the fish to land one night, and once again all was still but for a whisper in the dry-tongued reeds and the lisp of sand-quenched ripples. But never again would he and one beside him sit there filled through and through with love, and never again would the man he had loved pass by like the shadow of a hawk on one of those swift, secret errands. Yet, as he had hoped, there still lingered round the place a sweetness of sorrow. Horror had come not here, nor any bloodshed, nor crash of war, and none knew the message the spot held for him, its garnered store on which his heart had fed. Then leaving it, still rounded by the infinite night, he passed on by the white house at the head of the bay, whose sea-wall had been to him the gates of love flung open, and just after sunrise he struck the road on the other side of the water, and three hundred yards off were the whistling poplars by the fountain, and his father's house and the garden-gate, and the grave and memory of his boyhood. The risen sun spun mists out of the night dews and webs of sweet smell from the damp earth. It struck a galaxy of stars from the burnished surface of the bay, and from the heart of some bush-bowered bird it drew forth an inimitable song.

So he was come to the gate, where he tied up his horse while he should go inside, yearning to see his father; but as he walked up the path, raising his eyes he saw him already out and working in the vineyard beyond, and he would have passed by and gone to him there when, of a sudden, he stopped, and his heart stopped too.

For the house door was open, and from inside—it seemed at first only his own thoughts made audible—came a voice singing, and it sang:

> "Dig we deep among the vines,
> Give the sweet spring showers a home."

Then came a little feeble cry as from some young thing, and the singing stopped, and a mother's voice, so it seemed, cooed soothing to her baby; and with that Mitsos passed not on to the vineyard, but went in.

Suleima, busied with the child—the "littlest Mitsos," so she told herself—heard not his step till he was in the doorway, but then looked up, thinking it was her father, though earlier than his wont. And with a choking cry, hands outstretched, and a voice from a bursting heart:

"Suleima!" cried Mitsos.

THE END